# THE ARSONIST

Stephanie Oakes

*Dial Books*

DIAL BOOKS
An imprint of Penguin Random House LLC
375 Hudson Street
New York, NY 10014

Library of Congress Cataloging-in-Publication Data

Oakes, Stephanie (Young adult author), author.
The arsonist / by Stephanie Oakes.
Summary: Molly Mavity and Pepper Yusef are dealing with their own personal tragedies
when they are tasked by an anonymous person with solving the decades-old murder of
Ava Dreyman, an East German teenager
whose diary was published after her death.
ISBN 9780803740716 (hardcover)
| 1. Mystery and detective stories. 2. Mothers and daughters—Fiction. |
| 3. Identity—Fiction. | 4. Kuwaiti Americans—Fiction. |
| 5. Epilepsy—Fiction. | 6. People with disabilities—Fiction. |
| 7. Germany (East)—History—20th century—Fiction. |
PZ7.1.O19 Ar 2017    [Fic]—dc23    2016032499

Printed in the United States of America

1 3 5 7 9 10 8 6 4 2

Design by Nancy Leo-Kelly and Cerise Steel
Text set in Dante MT

Excerpt from *Fahrenheit 451* reprinted by permission of
Don Congdon Associates, Inc. © 1953, renewed 1981 by Ray Bradbury

To my family

*It was a pleasure to burn.*

*Fahrenheit 451* by Ray Bradbury

# Molly

Dear Pepper,

Do you have any idea how depressing it is in this room right now? Your dad can't look at you for longer than a couple of minutes before falling into tears. You're not breathing on your own, and I can't see your bandaged head without remembering that you were recently punched in the brain by the bottom of a swimming pool.

They say you might never wake up.

I've spent the afternoon doing exactly what your nurses warned me not to do: looking up stuff on the Internet. You probably know by now that telling me not to do something is a super-effective method for getting me to do that very thing. I wish I'd listened to them. The stats about people who wake up from comas are pretty disheartening.

So I started typing as a distraction. It almost, *almost* feels like I'm talking to you right now.

Maybe, on some level, you're listening.

Being in the hospital reminds me of the moment I crushed my foot. I've been hobbling around all summer with that cast, and the thing sweated and itched like hell, and the whole time you wanted to know how my foot ended up like that.

"Did you lose a fight with a man-eating crocodile?"

"Did you get in an industrial accident?"

"Did you just get mad at someone and kick a wall?"

Well, consider today your lucky day, because I'm finally spilling the secrets. First, though, I'll tell you another thing you wanted to know—how I came by my unfortunate nickname at the Keller School.

Picture me, Molly Mavity, twelve years old. Peak awkward years. My head was an uncombed sprinkler of orange doodles. I wouldn't get braces for another year, but boy could I use them. My face had kind of rebelled, turning splotchy and greasy and pockmarked, which was pretty cruel of the universe to do, in light of everything else. Twelve was not a kind year to me.

My cousin Margaret also attends the Keller School, and I hadn't even been there a week before she'd told every girl there about my father, who was in prison awaiting trial for burning six people to death. You remember it, right, Pepper? The Burning Summer, those months when the town would wake up to the smell of smoke, and the police would find the empty shell of a house stuffed in some corner of the city, burned from the inside out. Those were my father's fires, the fires of the infamous murderer-arsonist of Monterey. The fires that would send him to death row.

My first week at Keller, I discovered a pile of matches in my personal cubby. A group of girls stood nearby, snickering. Not all seventh graders are dungholes of the highest order, but these were. I felt myself boil inside. I wanted to gather the matches, and throw them precisely into their eyeballs so the jelly would run down their faces like I'd seen in an old kung fu movie.

Instead, I picked up two matches, shoved them between my top lip and gum, red heads facing down like bloodied fangs, and turned to the girls. "I vant to suck your blood," I told them.

They exchanged looks of genuine horror, like they were afraid I would actually go full vampire on them. Strangely, I felt that this reaction was the best thing that I'd accomplished in a long time. That was the day that I discovered my greatest weapon: being a complete weirdo.

Every school has one. The weirdo follows no rules. The weirdo is lawless.

Which leads to how I received my nickname: Milk Pee Mavity.

"How does a person get a nickname like that?" you've asked me. "Did you pee into someone's milk? Did you drink milk that was actually pee?"

No, I didn't *drink pee*, Pepper.

It happened like this: I was making my way through the cafeteria line during my first year at Keller. As I reached for a milk carton from one of the crates arranged on the counter, the cafeteria lady said, "Don't take one of those. They're about to expire."

"You're going to throw them out?" I asked.

"That's what you do with expired milk."

I examined one of the cartons. "These don't expire until tomorrow. And anyway, don't you know the sell-by dates are just a suggestion? The companies mark them early so they can trick you into buying more."

The lady sighed. "Wouldn't you rather have a carton of fresh milk?"

"I'd rather not waste fifty perfectly good ones. A cow had to have her udders sucked on by some metal industrial milker for these."

"All right," she said, "if you really want this much milk, it's all yours. But remember the rule." She pointed to a sign above the door. NO FOOD TO BE TAKEN OUT OF THE CAFETERIA.

"Game on," I said.

I lifted the milk crate, walked to my empty table, and proceeded to open carton after carton of milk, draining each in the span of a moment.

In *Matilda*, when the evil headmistress orders Bruce Bogtrotter to eat an entire cake, the other kids cheer Bruce on. That is not what happened to me. When the girls in the cafeteria began to notice the growing pile of emptied milk cartons scattered across my table, there were no cheers. A hush spread. Soon, the only sound was my labored breath and occasional milk burps. In between cartons, I rested my head on the table like an athlete not sure if they can go on.

The cafeteria lady watched me, arms crossed over her chest.

There were only thirty-three cartons, but it didn't matter. After twenty, my stomach felt like an overinflated water balloon.

At last, by some miracle of human anatomy, I arrived at the last carton. I threw it back and swallowed with difficulty, and as I prepared to lift my arms in the air in victory like an Olympian at the finish line, the bell rang and the other girls dispersed to their classes.

I waddled down the hall to English and eased into my chair just after the bell. At first, I felt okay. As the minutes passed, though, a point somewhere inside my middle began to radiate pain. I jammed my knees together, squeezing every muscle in my nether regions until I was shaking. It was ten minutes before the bell when, leaning over my desk, I raised my hand.

"Miss Markowitz, can I go to the bathroom?" I asked.

Miss Markowitz surveyed me from the front of the room. "You were late to class, Molly, if I'm not mistaken. I'll just assume that you planned in a bathroom stop during the passing period."

"But I didn't," I said, my voice strained.

"Well, I'm sorry, but that's your responsibility."

*Well, I'm sorry, but you're a megalomaniac,* I thought. Does it feel good, I wondered, controlling children's bodily functions? What kind of sick world is this where we can't allow human beings to relieve themselves without permission?

What happened next was born purely out of spite. Could I have held it? Maybe. But with every second of my bladder paining, I grew more furious at Miss Markowitz, and factory milk farming, and at my aunt for making me come to this messed-up school, and at both my parents for leaving me, and eventually the fury could not be contained. I clenched every muscle, then relaxed them all at once.

"Molly's peeing!" someone shouted.

Thirty-three milk cartons make a lot of pee, Pepper. The puddle of it crept across linoleum floor of the classroom, and the other students leaped to stand on their seats. Miss Markowitz opened and closed her mouth, at a loss for words.

I wasn't upset by the noises my classmates were making, or embarrassed by the feeling of pee turning cold against my skin. I was *gleeful*. I felt *strong*. I haven't peed publicly since that day, but I've never stopped looking for that feeling. I started calling it *the art of not giving a fuck*. It is my superpower.

From that point onward, I was Milk Pee Mavity and there wasn't much point in trying to make friends anymore. And so I wore the badge of weirdness as my distinguishing characteristic, and started spending a lot of time alone.

Which leads to how I crushed my foot back in February.

It was going on five years without anyone to talk to besides my aunt and my one friend, Marty, both decades older than me. Maybe I thought climbing up tall places would make me seem cool. Like somebody might see me up there and think,

"There goes Molly Mavity. She peed herself in seventh grade but really she's a badass. I bet she's really fun and intelligent, too. Someone you could get a fro-yo with, you know?"

That day, I climbed to the top of the train bridge behind my childhood home on Syracuse Road, the one I lived in before my family split apart like an orange. When missing my mother grew bigger than me, I'd go up there to look at my old house and think of the last time I saw her before she vanished: blond curls pinned to her head with a silk scarf, the cliff of the Château de Nice beneath her, a dead drop of blue behind. My eyes pained at the brightness, but I couldn't budge my eyes away. My mother was magnetic.

When I heard the rattle of the train, I would've almost certainly been fine had I not turned to look at it, kicking my foot out a little. The train wasn't even moving very fast, but the momentum of it collided with my foot with enough force to, in the burst of a second, shatter almost every bone inside.

Seconds later, I was lying in the salty stream below the bridge, my foot exploded apart inside my shoe. The pain was indescribable. It tasted, in the back of my mouth, like lemons. Above, that train kept on trucking. The conductor probably hadn't even seen me. Crying a little, or maybe a lot, I called Marty and said, "Can you come get me? My foot was killed in a train accident," and Marty replied, "Sure thing," because Marty is cool like that.

So there you go, Pepper, two nuggets of information you've

been asking for all summer. That wasn't so hard! I think I'll continue with this truth telling. It gives me something to pass the time with while you decide if you're going to wake up.

In the enclosed record, you will find the answers, those secrets I refused to tell you for the sake of my mysterious pride, and even those moments that you were present for but didn't understand the whole truth of.

You are formally invited to understand everything.

Signed, your inscrutable friend,

Molly P. Mavity

Encl.: the truth (eighty-two pages)

# Pepper

*World History*

Dear Ms. Eldridge,

It has been approximately one week since I first met you in the school cafeteria, and it is only now that I realize that I am owing you a thank-you for your kindness on that day. I was reluctant to talk to you, which I think you'll find is understandable considering the previous meetings I've had with school officials, starting last year when the guidance counselor informed me that I was heading toward not graduating.

"You must be joking," I said suavely. "All my teachers like me."

"Do you know what your grades are?" the counselor asked.

"I'm sure they're not as terrible as you say."

She proceeded to show me my grades, and it was somewhat like the feeling of viewing the earth very high from a plane, except instead of fields and bodies of water, it was rows and rows of Ds and Fs, and some Cs.

But mostly Ds and Fs.

The counselor pursed her lips. "You can't get by in this life with just a smile, Ibrahim."

My forehead wrinkled, both because she called me Ibrahim,

which nobody does, and because this was my personal philosophy which she had just shat upon.

There were more meetings after that, about one per academic term, but the credits were not growing much. "Don't you *care*, Mr. Al-Yusef?"

"Yes, I care," I mumbled, but even as I did, I knew that I did not care in the way she meant. Since I first came to America, I saw the way school pummeled the other students. They were stressed to the maximum. I once saw a kid get sick in class because he was so freaked out about a math test. I heard about a girl whose hair fell out when she took too many AP classes. That's the kind of thing that's supposed to happen when a person eats too much mercury. This was ridiculous.

"It's official," she told me. "You will not graduate. You'll need to repeat next year."

I took the news like a champ. I stood proudly, and made a speedy exit into the hallway, where I immediately crouched down and let out a strangled sound. I had to have known this would happen, right? I knew, but I didn't *know*, you know?

I carried this heavy feeling inside my chest up until the moment of our meeting last week.

I was in French when I got one of those little pink notes they give kids when they have to go to the office to get yelled at by an adult. I shuffled out of class with my seizure pug, Bertrand, huffing at my side. You remember Bertrand, yes? If not, allow me to remind you of his rotundness, his lolling tongue, and the way he seems always to be wheezing in the back of his throat. Halfway down the hall, Bertrand flopped onto the floor and refused to budge. I was left with no choice but to drag him by his harness the rest of the way, his reflective Mylar vest making an audible whiz across the linoleum, and kids in their classrooms craned their necks to see. Bertrand is forever embarrassing me like this.

When I entered the office, I observed you immediately. You seemed so familiar and calming, like one of those ladies who host television programs about baking cakes and arranging furniture.

Ms. Eldridge, you were obviously charmed by me as well. You motioned with your hand for me to walk with you to the empty cafeteria for more privacy.

"Pepper—you like to be called Pepper, right?"

"Yes," I said. Now that I was close to you, I noticed that a large healed gash stretched along your hairline.

"We want to help you graduate. I'm from the school district," you said. "We know you've had some setbacks in life. You have been identified as at-risk for dropping out. Does that sound like the truth?"

I nodded, though within my thoughts I had already dropped out.

"That's a problem for us."

I wasn't understanding you, so I raised my hand.

"Yes?" you asked.

"This might be off-topic, but how did you get that scar on your forehead?"

Your hand flew automatically to smash your bangs over your scar and shook your head in a bemused way. "Pepper, my scar isn't relevant to this conversation. I'm here to see if you'd like to participate in an alternative graduation program. You would need to write a thesis on the subjects that you still need credits in to graduate."

You held out a page with computer printing that said, "Physics, Human Anatomy, American History, Geometry," and a bunch of other subjects. There was even that stupid Personal Safety class that the school requires, which I only flunked because I already knew everything about stranger danger, so I didn't bother showing up for the final.

"How long is it needing to be?" I asked.

"At least three thousand words per subject."

My voice died in my throat. I coughed a dry cough. "I am not, it's not . . ." I coughed again. "My writing is not good," I said at last.

In reality, I enjoy writing, at least the part that involves taking a picture inside the soft squishiness of my brains and using words to pull it into the real world, but in school this is hardly ever asked of me. It is always literary essays and personal essays and persuasive essays and how-to essays and analytical essays and et cetera essays to infinity and beyond. (I have never told anyone this, but I'm not entirely certain that I know what an essay is, though I have written twenty or thirty of them.)

"Can it be poems?" I asked.

You moved your head no. "It must be an academic thesis. You'll have until the end of the summer. Visit some museums, interview people, do what we call 'action research.' Run into the world headlong and *learn*. Show us you're ready to move on to post-secondary life."

I pictured running headlong into the world. It sounded painful. "I don't know," I said. "It sounds like a lot of work."

"You're not going to pass up an opportunity to graduate just because it'd be hard, are you?"

"Um," I said. "Yes, that is just exactly why."

Your head turned. "What do you want to do with your life, Pepper?"

I almost told you the truth, but I stopped myself when I remembered that my dream is impossible and you would likely stomp on it like the guidance counselor did when I told her. I suppose I will tell you now, though, since I think that you might not be like that after all. Here is the truth:

Since I can remember, my most robust and fervent dream is to become the president. Of which country? Of this country, America. I have known since forever that it could not happen. I wasn't born here. Still, that never stopped me from wanting it.

When I first came to Monterey, the teacher at the immersion center gave me a red book, the first American book I ever owned, and it was all about the presidents. I read about their pets and their hobbies and their wives. To see their faces, I started to understand what America looked like. There was something specifically American about George Washington's underturned lip and Woodrow Wilson's tiny glasses, which the book told me were called "pince-nez," which must be French for "tiny glasses." And John F. Kennedy's straight, large teeth, which seemed practically to protrude from his mouth when he smiled. My heart was twelve years old when it really wanted something for the first time. It wanted me to have my picture in this book.

You blinked, waiting for a response.

"I want to fix cars," I said. "Like my dad."

You paused a long, long time.

"There are a lot of kids out there who would love an opportunity like this," you said. "I've looked at your records. You haven't had excessive absences. Your homework completion rate is pretty abysmal, but I don't think you're lazy. You're underserved, and right now you're one of a million kids in America falling through the cracks because no one ever took the time to know exactly why you're struggling. But you're eighteen. You know what that means? You're old enough that no one else is going to save you. You have to save yourself."

You shook my hand, and stood and walked through the swinging cafeteria doors. I stared at them for long minutes, the way they slowly swung until settling into stillness.

You had left the paper with the list of subjects I needed to make up, along with the guidelines for the program and your e-mail address.

I decided there was absolutely no way I would be capable of doing the essays.

I didn't speak of this rendezvous with my friends, who call ourselves The Four Horsemen, after some idea that we are apocalyptic in our sexiness. I might have told Shawn, my best of all friends, but that night we were attending a party on the floor of the Hacienda Street pool. It hadn't yet been filled for the summer because a raccoon had built a nest inside the filtration system and fed all the components to its young.

This wasn't a party in the way that most people think of parties. It was just three of us so far, sitting at a card table, becoming sweaty in the air of new summer, playing our favorite game, Master Quest. Master Quest has the honor of being the only game nerdier than Dungeons and Dragons. There are prop wands. There are wizard hats. You get the picture.

I arrived late because Bertrand insisted on tinkling on every leaf in the neighborhood. Bertrand was gifted to me by people who provide "disabled minority youth" with "life-saving service animals." I'm not aware of the extent of Bertrand's training because he has never given the tiniest of warnings about a seizure. For one thing, I do not have them very much anymore. For another, Bertrand is a gargantuan beige lump, who can hear nothing over the sound of his own breathing.

The game board was already set up and Wallace and Reggie were in position, staging their orcs and adjusting their faux beards. I held Bertrand under my arm as I descended the ladder to the bottom of the pool.

"Hey, Pepper!" Reggie said, scratching his curly hair. "The news is out, my friend."

I stopped in my tracks. Bertrand squirmed like a fat worm under my elbow so I set him on the popcorn-textured pool floor. I thought Reggie was referring to my predicament of not graduating. "What are you talking about?"

"Today? Sixth period? Tell me you heard," Reggie said.

I shook my head.

"Petra Mirkovsky announced that her guy-fast is done."

"What?" I asked. I sat at the game table and pretended to arrange my pieces on the board.

"A bunch of people overheard her telling her photography friends that she's quote 'Recovered from her meditative journey of self-discovery.'" Reg rolled his eyes. "So, you gonna tap that or what?"

I swallowed hard. Petra was a banned topic, just like not graduating, and my mother, and the epilepsy, and my father's fish tanks, and a hundred other things that cramped my laid-back lifestyle to think about.

Wallace finished laying out the pieces. "Don't pretend you're not in love with Petra," he said in his nasal, Spanish-clipped voice. His head was lowered over the game instruction book, face covered in a shiny gray polyester beard. "Grow some hair on your balls or the man society will be forced to confiscate them."

"I don't like her," I insisted. Bertrand had rolled on my own wizard beard and gotten it glued to his back, and suddenly he looked like a mythical ridgeback pug, fitting into the game perfectly.

"Why do you stare at her, then?" Reggie asked. He was the coolest member of our group by dint of being half black and appearing like a basketball player, even though, as he informs everybody who will listen, he objects to basketball on the grounds that it's "too easy." "Why do you *drool* over her?"

"I—I," I stammered. "I happen to admire her dress sense."

"Her *dress sense?*" Wallace sneered.

"Yeah. It reminds me of my mom."

Just remembering this now makes my cheeks inflame, Ms. Eldridge.

"Didn't your mom wear, like, a burka?" Reggie asked.

"A hijab," I corrected. "And that's not what I meant. Petra's . . . classy. You don't see a lot of girls like her."

"Now you *really* need to relinquish your balls," Wallace said.

The giant security lights crackled to life at the same moment that a series of knocks rang out from the chain-link fence above, set to the rhythm of "The Imperial March."

Reggie tipped back in his folding chair to get a better look. "Just come down, Shawn! Don't make us get up."

"Dude, breach of protocol!" came a whisper from above.

"I'll do it," I said. I pulled myself up the metal ladder on the side of the pool and peeked out toward where the sun was setting like a blood orange. "All quiet on the Western front."

Shawn popped up from where he'd been hiding behind a bush, one hand on his Panama hat, his translucent skin flushed. He jumped down into the shallow end and set a paper bag of beer in the middle of the board.

"What did I miss?" Shawn asked, plopping down on a chair.

"Just started," I said. "Reggie's chief warlock killed one of your elf soldiers."

"Dude, you were supposed to be protecting me," Shawn said.

"Don't blame Pepper. He was distracted," Reggie said.

"By his cruuuu-uuush," Wallace teased, pulling the word out.

"More like by his hard-on," Reggie corrected.

I reached over and smacked him on the back of the head. "Shut your beautiful face, Reggie."

Shawn sighed. "You need to just go for it with Petra already. Then when she rejects you, I can go back to talking shit about her."

Shawn hates Petra for no other reason than she and her friends are "cool nerds." According to Shawn, this is against nature.

"What sort of shit would you have to talk about Petra?" I asked.

"Where do I *begin?*" Shawn said, leaning back in his chair. "For one thing, she's pretentious as fuck. Exhibit A, she goes by Patty her whole life, then joins the literary journal and suddenly she's *Petra.*" Shawn did jazz hands.

"I'm not going to criticize someone for changing their name," I said.

"Have you seen her graphic novel?" Shawn continued. "She works on it in studio art. I don't think the main character is *supposed* to be Petra, but it looks just like her. Glasses. Suspenders. Camera."

"Wonder what her superhero name is," Wallace said.

"Captain Uptight McBitcherson," Shawn said. "Buttwad. The third."

I looked around for something to distract them, but saw only Bertrand lying on his back so everyone could see his ample nipples, another thing he does to embarrass me. He knows my beliefs that boy dogs have no business owning nipples.

"Can we just get back to the game?" I said.

We played through several more turns in silence until Shawn killed Reggie's chief warlock, which made him swear and swat at the air, accidentally knocking over his bottle of Corona and covering the game board with fizzy beer, at which point Wallace jumped up, dark curls bouncing, shouting, "Towels! We need towels!"

"OW!" I shouted. "You stepped on my ankle."

"Well, it's an emergency!"

"Whatever . . . Wall*ass*," I grumbled.

Reggie snorted. "Wallass. That's my boy."

"Will you guys shut up!" Shawn hissed, a rigid finger to his lips. "Level one voices behind enemy lines."

We broke into the locker rooms and found some crispy, chlorine-infected towels in a wad, and used them to dry the game board.

"Pepper, my friend, I just need to say one more thing about Petra," Shawn said seriously.

"You really don't," I said.

"Nooo, no, I do!" Shawn slurred, his eyelids heavy. "If you really like her, *like* her, don't freaking pussyfoot around it. 'Never be ashamed of liking something that you like.' Best advice my grandfather ever gave me."

"Your grandfather said that?" I asked, knowing where this was going.

"He did, right before he was mauled to death by that bear. You know, the one from the commercials."

"Smokey the Bear?" I asked.

"That's the one," he said, belching. "'Only you can prevent forest fires.' Last words my grandfather ever heard." Shawn was getting tipsy. When Shawn drinks, he tells lies—big, unsustainable, theatrical lies. He once went an entire night trying to convince us he was the first test-tube baby.

"I thought your grandfather died at the Alamo," I said.

"Pepper, *never* be ashamed of liking something that you like." Shawn burped loudly. "Santa Anna told me that."

We heard a metallic clunk and the beam of a flashlight swept over Shawn's face.

"What the hell?" came a voice from above. Behind the blinding circle of light, we could see the oblong shape of a security guard, the shadow of his nightstick slashing the wall behind us.

Shawn leaped up. "Abort! Abort!" he shouted. "Operation Mountain Lion! Operation Mountain Lion!"

"What's Operation Mountain Lion?" Wallace screeched.

"Pack up your shit and run!"

Reggie tried to stand and got his feet tangled in his folding chair and ate it on the cement floor of the pool.

"My face!" Reggie screamed.

"There goes your modeling career," Wallace snorted.

Reggie swept his legs and toppled the card table, sending the game pieces flying. "There goes your girlfriend." At this, Bertrand started barking his horrible grating bark that makes me want to tear the hair from my head.

Wallace scrambled around placing game pieces in his open palm.

"Wallace, THERE'S NO TIME!" Shawn yelled.

"This is a limited edition!"

"Tell that to the judge!"

"Shawn, calm down and help," I said. "And Reggie, quit crying, you're not even bleeding."

Reggie reluctantly removed his cupped hand from his face. Meanwhile, the security guard stood above us, shaking his head.

"I never thought I'd so regret having the personal philosophy of never leaving a man behind," Shawn said as he scrambled around the concrete, retrieving metal foot soldiers and orcs. Once we'd chucked everything into Wallace's game box, the four of us clambered out of the shallow end and hopped the chain-link fence. The security guard stood on the other side of the pool with his hands on his hips.

"You don't have to run," he called. "It's not like I'm gonna chase you!" But, to us, we had the very wind of the devil at our backs, and we flew down Hacienda Street like real knights, past the insomniac glow of the 7-Eleven, hopping over low fences, our legs whisking across the tops of bushes made plump by humidity. Wallace still wore his wizard's beard and Shawn was struggling to keep his Panama hat on, and we were free, wild nerds in the heat of a summer night, not long before we were all consumed by the idea that it was time for everybody to grow up, and maybe that's what we were running from, really.

# Molly

Hi, Pepper,

I'm sure you're wondering why I decided to write you these letters.

The thought first occurred to me after a nurse sat your dad, Shawn, and me down and explained the "gravity of the situation." All this means is that being in a coma is really bad for your health. She said, when you wake up, you'll most definitely have some memory loss. Almost all coma patients do. Which leads to these letters.

I decided I was going to tell you the truth, Pepper, about what happened this summer, about Ava Dreyman, about my mother.

I've tried talking to you, but I'm not sure you can hear me. Your face is limp, and there's a tube in your mouth that siphons pureed food into your stomach because you can't chew. I asked your nurses to make sure the mush they're giving you is halal, even though you told me once that you don't care. I figure it's best to be on the safe side.

Seeing you like this makes me think about cosmic rightness. It's this idea that everything happens for a reason because the universe wills it. I have a hard time imagining why the universe would want you in this hospital bed, but there've been other things this summer that might've been spelled out in some kind of star pattern. Take us, for instance. We probably never would've met if it hadn't been for Ava Dreyman.

The universe first introduced me to Ava Dreyman in my Women's Studies seminar at Keller, all the way back before summer started. At this point, I hadn't met you yet, but I had met a crap ton of doctors who did their best to assemble the puzzle of my foot over the course of a handful of surgeries.

"This is a complicated break, but it should be healed by June," my doctor told me when I was getting casted up. "Just in time for all the swimming you're bound to do." I didn't correct him, but I wasn't planning on spending my summer at the pool.

This summer, I was sure my mother was going to find me. I was nearly eighteen, and my father was scheduled to die sometime in the near future. It was the ideal moment for her to come back.

A lot happened the year I turned twelve, besides the Milk Pee incident and the problematic issue of my face. The year I turned twelve was the year my mother disappeared.

Everyone else considers it the year my mother killed herself.

I had never heard of Nice before my mother woke me in our house on Syracuse Road, her fingers cold over my lips, and whispered, "We're going very far away now, and we're never coming back." When I asked if my father would join us, and my mother shook her head, I wasn't surprised. I knew, some-how, that the reason we were taking off had something to do with the smoke smell my father never managed to wash away.

Three weeks later, she had disappeared.

I say disappeared because there's no way she'd ever kill her-self. I know this for a million reasons, but chief among them is her last meal: yogurt and madeleines, which are cookies shaped like shells. If she was planning to die, she would've gone out in style, a ten-course feast, champagne, dessert, and kissed the waiter. She was spectacular that way. Yogurt and madeleines made no sense.

Right after it happened, I didn't cry. I don't generally cry over things. Instead, my brain gets hot and rubbery and I feel like I might combust. After my mother disappeared, my brain was so hot, I thought I was going to boil over.

When my father picked me up from the airport in San Francisco, he drove through the orange groves and didn't say a word. When I think of him, it's this picture: a quiet, bearded, red-haired blurriness at my periphery, hands grip-ping the cracked steering wheel, the sky blushing against a horizon of windmilled hills. It was only a month later that he lit an abandoned house on fire, killing six, and the police took him away.

So, yeah, a lot happened the year I turned twelve. I went to live with my auntie Ro after that, who actually isn't my aunt but my dad's cousin. She was extremely concerned that I was about to "go down a dark road" after what happened with my parents, so she enrolled me at the Keller School.

I have been attending the Keller School, the very exclusive, very female day school in Pacific Grove ever since. The Keller School is a special school for special girls. Girls with anxiety disorders and eating disorders, self-esteem problems and drug problems. My specialness lies in being "a child of trauma." That's what they call someone with parents like mine, but in a weird way, it makes it sound like I never had parents at all. It's like, "Over here you have Jenny, child of Susan and Mark, and over here is Alisha, child of Anthony and Greg, and over here is Molly, child of trauma."

In the fall, I'll start my senior year, and everyone else's eyes are already full of college brochures and entrance exams. My eyes are full of my mother's face, which I can't seem to shake out of my head.

Women's Studies was my final class before the summer started. Like many of the classes at Keller, it was mixed age, and I'd been taking it alongside Margaret, who's a year younger than me. We wouldn't be having a final exam. Instead, Dr. Feinstein reserved the final day of the seminar as a "Dinner Party of Powerful Women," wherein every girl in the class was expected to "have meticulously researched an important woman from history and come dressed as that woman, complete with props, mannerisms, accent, as well as being prepared to speak as that woman for the entire night."

"Everyone must participate in order to pass. No exceptions will be made," Dr. Feinstein said, looking straight into my eyes.

You will not be surprised to learn that I loathe costumes. I have never gone trick-or-treating, and the very idea of pretending to be something I'm not makes me ache, deep down in my DNA. When I entered Dr. Feinstein's classroom, my nerves were jangling like a pocket of loose change. The desks had been pushed to the sides of the room, and the girls milled around with small plates of pita chips and hummus, Marie Curie having a forced conversation with Benazir Bhutto. The girl who came as Sylvia Plath had fashioned herself a cardboard oven to hang around her neck, but Dr. Feinstein made her take it off and put it in the trash can. "I expressly told you, no death props."

Dr. Feinstein was dressed as Virginia Woolf in a loose drop-waist shift, her long, silver-shot hair tied back in a lank knot.

"I don't believe we've met," Dr. Feinstein said in a fake English accent, taking in my lack of costume. "I'm Virginia."

I shook her hand. "Mary Magdalene, pleased to meet you."

Dr. Feinstein's face fell a fraction. "How odd. You look exactly like a girl I know named Molly Mavity."

"No, I assure you," I said. "I've got a cross, representing my love for Jesus; I've got this sack of coins here, representing the money I have earned performing the oldest of all professions. And I've got red hair."

Dr. Feinstein shook her head. "Nowhere in the Bible does it say Mary Magdalene had red hair."

"But all the ancient paintings show her—me—with red hair."

"Most scholars think that's simply paint degradation," Dr. Feinstein said. Her smile stiffened. "Before, when I thought you came as Molly Mavity, I was going to commend you."

"Why?"

"Because every year I hope one of my girls will come dressed as herself. It takes some guts to put yourself next to the most important women in history."

"I'm not an important woman."

"Not with that attitude."

Dr. Feinstein sauntered away to listen in on Maya Angelou and Simone de Beauvoir.

"*Guten tag*, bitches!"

Heads snapped toward the doorway where my cousin Margaret stood.

She was wearing a dark wig, stick-straight around her shoulders with a ridge of blunt bangs. Her thin frame was draped in a button-up shirt that she'd tucked into a tweed skirt. To top it off, protruding from the middle of her abdomen was the ivory hilt of a prop knife, surrounded by a circle of fake blood.

I couldn't tell who Margaret was supposed to be dressed as. You can, though, Pepper. You're probably shaking your head right now.

Some girls laughed over the low jazz playing in the background. Dr. Feinstein crossed her arms and looked Margaret over for a long moment.

"Good afternoon," Dr. Feinstein said formally. "I'm Virginia. And you are?"

"Pleased to make your acquaintance. I am Ava Dreyman," Margaret said in a clumsy impression of a heavy German accent. "Or Sally Bailey. It's so hard to keep all my names straight!"

I'd heard of Ava Dreyman, but only in the way you've heard of Grover Cleveland or Millard Fillmore (actually, Pepper, you're probably the only person on Earth who knows real things about Grover Cleveland and Millard Fillmore). I knew that Ava Dreyman was a historical figure from the Cold War, and that she was famous for keeping a diary, Anne Frank–style, and also like Anne Frank for being killed by Germans sometime in her teens.

Dr. Feinstein's forehead wrinkled in a serious way. "What do you call that sticking out of your belly?"

Margaret glanced down to where Dr. Feinstein was pointing and gasped as though she hadn't noticed it before. "Well, I suppose that's the knife that killed me. Drat!"

"Margaret," Dr. Feinstein said, dropping her English accent, "I specifically said no part of the costume should depict your historical figure's death."

"Who is this Margaret you speak of?" Margaret asked, a frantic grin stretching her face. "I know only that I am running for my life from the East Germans. Help me, Virginia!" She grabbed Dr. Feinstein by the forearms and shook her. "Save me!"

"Margaret, cut it out!" I hissed. "You're acting crazy."

The intake of breath from the other girls in the room was audible. I realized, at once, I had said the wrong thing.

"*Me?*" Margaret asked, letting Dr. Feinstein's arms drop. She pointed to my chest. "*Me*, crazy? That's hilarious. What about you, Milk Pee?" Margaret had the fire in her eyes she gets when she's been drinking. It was just like her to come to school plastered.

"That's enough, Margaret," Dr. Feinstein said.

Margaret ignored her. "Yes, what about you, Molly?" she said, pacing toward me. Margaret's finger jabbed me right in the chest, above the neckline of my sweater vest. I stepped backward into a classroom chair, stumbling. With Margaret's back to her, Dr. Feinstein loped to her desk and picked up her phone. I knew without hearing that she was calling the office.

"I'm Mary Magdalene," I said weakly, holding up the cross around my neck.

"You want to know how I died, Molly?" Margaret said. Her breath smelled like peppermint.

"You were stabbed?"

"I was murdered," she said. "And you'd know all about that, wouldn't you? More than any of us."

"Margaret, it's time to stop this," Dr. Feinstein commanded.

"Molly Mavity," Margaret spat. "Your father taught you

everything he knew, didn't he, before you moved in with us? Worst thing that ever happened to me." Inside, I felt myself shrink. "Don't look at me like that—who'd ask for their creepy cousin who pees her pants and talks like a robot to move in because her dad landed himself on death row? It's bad enough you have to go to my *school*. And that first night? Did I ever tell you? I slept with a knife beneath my pillow. I thought you'd murder us all in our sleep."

"Shut up!" I said, but it came out small, barely loud enough to be heard. My hands were beside my head, but no matter how hard I pressed against my ears, Margaret's words snuck in.

"Crazy. Flat-out insane. Lunatic. Nutcase."

"We don't use words like that here, Margaret," Dr. Feinstein scolded.

"Look at her," Margaret said. "A psychopath. Just like her dad."

I didn't hear the rest because I'd already started screaming, the high-pitched shriek of a teakettle. I threw the first thing near me—my prop of fake money in its leather satchel—and reached for the next thing I could find—the cross around my neck—reefing it off until it cut into my skin and finally broke, and sent it sailing across the room toward Margaret, but it only clattered to the floor.

The next moment, the classroom door slammed open and two administrators stood in the doorway. They looked past me, to Margaret.

"Margaret," one of them said, "we need you to come with us."

"I'm not going anywhere," she said. "My name's not Margaret, it's Ava Dreyman."

"Take her to Dr. Lawrence," Dr. Feinstein said. Dr. Lawrence is the school psychologist. Margaret hates him with intensity. He messes with her prescription dosages and leaves damning messages on Auntie Ro's voice mail.

"No!" Margaret shouted, and made a rake of her fingers, lashing at one of the administrators' faces. The other rushed forward and grabbed Margaret by the wrists. She arched her back and screamed while they dragged her from the room, the ivory hilt of the fake knife wavering. It occurred to me that it must've looked a lot like that when Ava Dreyman's body was carted out of a torture chamber in East Berlin.

This was the first real thought I'd ever had about Ava Dreyman. I couldn't know yet that, in just a few weeks, I would become intricately entwined in Ava's mystery. I would sift through secrets not spoken since the night she was killed in that white-tiled basement room.

First, though, there will be a key, and the post-office box it opens.

There will be the diary and the bone-handled knife.

And, Pepper, there will be you.

# Ava

October 23, 1986

I thought my first entry in this diary would center around my birthday party, where I received it wrapped in brown paper, and what it was like to meet Paedar for a birthday coffee yesterday, just like grown-ups. And I'd write lying on my bed in my room in my family's apartment in Friedrichshain, but instead I'm sitting outside on a bench in the windswept park, afraid to go home because that's where my mother is, and I can't look at her right now because she is a murderer.

It was foolish to follow her down into the bowels of the Stasi central office at midnight, but when I woke last night after hearing the apartment door close, I knew she was up to something terrible. I trailed her through the streets, which were quiet, glowing with the distilled green light of streetlamps, the glass of storefronts passing her warped image around like a ghost's. I skirted the edges of buildings with my fingertips. I thought I could stop her.

I must not have known her at all.

Just before the Stasi administration building, she paused to stare up the black, curving sides of it. Many floors up, two rectangles shone with dull yellow light. Some employees working late. My mother adjusted the large black duffel bag strapped across her back and stretched her neck athletically, then ran toward the building. I slipped just behind her through the green-tinted glass entrance she must've bribed some underpaid night worker to leave unlocked.

I followed silently behind, past rows and rows of desks, past silent locked doors the uniform color of milk. The blaze in her eyes was so focused, she didn't notice the pale slap of my shoes behind her at every turn. She found the custodial stairwell that descended dozens of feet beneath the offices to the studied spot she'd selected from blueprints late at night when she thought I'd gone to bed.

I hid behind the huge metal body of a boiler and watched. She tipped her black bag over and let the pounds of grainy, yellow accelerant slough out. From her pocket, she took a lighter.

"Mother," I could have cried.

I could have.

I could.

With a flick, she made a flame. It filled her eye, the one facing me, and stroked her pupil like a small, sharp hand. She dropped the lighter and the accelerant burnished in a slow-moving line, and for a brief moment there was no smoke, only my mother shadowed by a pile of fire, big and mighty as any god.

In a rush, smoke engulfed the basement room and she turned to run. A moment before, her mouth had made a thin, meaningless line, but now she was smiling. A blazing grin that stretched the muscles of her cheeks. I ran up the stairwell as fire jettisoned from the wood-walled basement, eating straight up through chalky ceiling tiles.

I ran into the street, through the glass doors that were already groaning with heat. My mother was gone.

Panting, I watched the building smolder for endless moments, smoke erupting out from it like an enormous chimney. I could still see those two windows on an upper floor, lit with some other kind of light now.

"Halt!"

A man dressed in a gray suit marched toward me with his arm held rigidly out, palm flat.

"What business do you have here?" he demanded.

I pointed numbly at the building. "I was watching the fire."

His hair was a glossed black and his eyes, the shape of tear-drops, bent toward his nose in a way that made his entire face seem too big. I could tell he was Stasi, and high-ranking, too, by how casually he dressed. Only the high-ups are allowed to walk around out of their dress uniforms.

"It's past your curfew, little one."

"I heard the noise. I know I shouldn't be out." I cast my eyes to the pavement, my face folding in my best attempt at inno-cence. "I'm sorry."

"Out this late so near the Wall. Someone could think you were trying to escape."

"That's impossible," I said.

"It's not," he said. "And it's my job to hunt them down."

His blunt-edged fingers brushed a small pin on his lapel, a crest encircling the head of a wolf. A Storm Wolf. The brightest graduates of the Stasi University, the Storm Wolves are trained for one job: to hunt down escapees and dissidents who flee from the German Democratic Republic.

"You've done that?" I asked.

He nodded. "I follow their trail to wherever they're hiding and bring them back. I've been to the white sands of Israel, the Black Sea, Thailand even. They always go looking for water. Always."

"Why, do you suppose?" I asked.

His face was so strangely placid, I thought he must have spent years building that mask. "Ocean," he said. "It's the one thing we haven't got in the GDR. They convince themselves they need it, that once they look at all that water, their problems will be erased. They don't realize that broken people are broken, in the GDR or by the sea."

I put my chin out coyly. "What if I said I was planning an escape?"

He barked a laugh, pointing a finger at me playfully. "You, madam, wouldn't get past the dogs."

"Dogs?"

He nodded. "And if by some slim chance you did make it past them, you'd have to crawl under a field of barbed wire, lit up by spotlights brighter than day. All around, there are snipers high up in the towers."

"So it would be wiser to escape in the daytime," I said.

He squinted, his smile falling away by half. "Why do you ask?"

"It's just that most people would think it's easier at night. I guess they'd be wrong."

"You're right. Unfortunately, the ones that get away slip right under the border guards' noses. Fake papers, simple lies, good acting. Have you any experience in the theater?"

"A little. I played Wendla in *Spring Awakening* at my school."

"You die in that one, don't you?"

"Yes, but offstage," I replied. "I could've done a wonderful death. I was far better than my classmates, and the boy who played Melchior? Horrid."

He stared down at me with a look in his eyes that seemed to be thinking I was the most peculiar thing he'd seen in some time. "What is your name?"

"Ava Dreyman." I realized too late I should've made up a name.

"Ava," he said, suddenly serious. "You shouldn't be in a hurry to volunteer for death in this country. You might just get your wish."

He clapped his hands together efficiently. "Well, little one, it's time to get you home. You live near here, I take it?"

"Oh, don't worry about me," I said. "I can get back safely on my own."

"Your safety is not my concern. It's after curfew. You cannot walk the streets without an official escort. Address?"

"Seven Bötzowstraße," I muttered. "Apartment 2034."

His feet slapped sharply as he strode off in the direction of my building. It was eerie, walking the dark streets with a member of the Stasi. I held my backbone a little straighter, trying to seem older.

"Bit far to hear the flames?" he asked when we reached my street.

"I have impeccable hearing," I said in a way I hoped was nonchalant. "And I'm a very restless sleeper."

He smiled and I knew he accepted what I was saying. I could hardly believe it, but I had the upper hand in this situation. I was dealing with this in a way my mother never would have: subtly, gracefully. Nothing so obvious as lighting a building on fire.

"In the future, resist the impulse to investigate noises from the street, hmm?" he said. "We have men for that."

I nodded.

"I wonder what your parents will say about your little midnight escapade."

"You need not tell my parents!"

He threw his head back and laughed. "Of course I will. They'll be up wondering where you are."

I swallowed hard. My mother would be up all right, but not thinking about me. She'd be buzzing still about the fire, probably smoking cigarette after cigarette, jumping up every other minute to pace and relive individual moments of her triumph, maybe even writing the whole thing up on a contraband typewriter on the kitchen's parquet floor, out in the open and everything.

What if, though, she'd not arrived back yet? What if she'd taken the long way—what if she'd stopped by Georg and Margarita's to rendezvous? What if we knocked on the door of an apartment with a conspicuously absent mother?

The Stasi man and I took the clinking elevator up to the twentieth floor, then walked into the belly of our heavy concrete building. The corridor was dark, lined with yellow wall lamps whose curved glass covers rattled in their holders as we walked. We were far from the expensive apartments with views of the street or courtyard. Ours was interior, windowless. You could hear a crying baby somewhere through the walls.

At number 2034, he knocked on the door sharply, three times.

My mother threw the door open. Her face, which was still high with the remainders of that grin, went slack.

"Madame Dreyman?"

Her eyes slipped from the man to me, and back to the man. "Yes?"

"You look upset. Is something wrong?"

"I open my door at two in the morning and see my child escorted by a man I've never seen before. Of course something's wrong."

She smelled of smoke. Not just cigarettes. A heavier smoke.

"You needn't worry. I am with the Stasi. Your daughter is perfectly safe."

Behind her, the radio was on. The newscaster, who didn't sound quite awake, talked hurriedly about a fire at the GDR Federal Building.

"I take it you've heard about tonight's fire?" the Stasi man asked.

"It's all they're talking about on the radio."

"Do you know anything about this fire? Who started it, perhaps?" he asked, smiling. "You could save me a lot of time."

My mother frowned at him, silent. She wasn't going to play along with his brand of interrogation humor. I wanted to kick her hard in the shin. She could ruin everything, right now. She could get our names on a list. She could get us arrested and never heard from again.

"Did you not notice your daughter was missing?" he asked.

"I thought she was asleep," my mother said.

"You didn't think to check on her?"

"My daughter is fourteen years old. I trust her to get through the night without falling out of bed."

He frowned. "And why were you up so late?"

"I'm a restless sleeper."

"A family trait," the man said. I laughed a little, but he didn't. His eyes were still locked on her indignant face. "Do you have a witness for your whereabouts this evening?"

"My husband is asleep."

"How am I to believe you've been here all evening? That you haven't broken curfew like your daughter?"

"There's nothing I can say, I'm sure, to convince you."

"How long ago did you wake up?"

"About fifteen minutes."

"What did you do?"

"I turned on the radio. I got a glass of water."

He brushed past her, into the apartment. With the back of his fingers, he touched a glass of water on the counter, feeling the temperature. He strolled over the tamped-down carpet, running his fingers over the ancient thready wallpaper, plucking knickknacks from their place on the bureau to examine each one before replacing it.

"What is your occupation?" he asked.

"I repair mimeographs for the state."

"Fine work. And your husband?"

"A writer."

"Oh, writers," he said reluctantly. "Seems there are a thousand subversive journalists for every loyal one."

"My husband is a proud Socialist. He only reports on topics

the GDR has sanctioned. None of his articles has ever been the subject of an inquiry."

The Stasi man tipped his head toward my mother. "That you know of."

I felt the room drain of warmth. My mother's face seemed to become bloodless. "All the subversive journalists are long gone. You've seen to that."

"Have I?" he said in mock surprise. "And where have these subversive writers gone? If you had to guess."

"I don't know things of that sort."

Why was my mother being so resistant? Why did she refuse to play the game?

The man turned to me. "Where do you think those naughty writers have gone to, Ava?"

"Somewhere warm, by the sea."

He chuckled. "You've a wise daughter, Madame Dreyman."

"It's not your place to say anything about my daughter," my mother said, turning to me. "This man didn't do anything untoward, did he, Ava? He didn't touch you, did he? Down there?"

"Mother!" I gasped, my cheeks turning hot. "Don't say such things in public," I said, adding a small laugh to the back of my throat.

"You are speaking about a member of the Stasi," the man said. "I think you shouldn't make such casual accusations. You understand the consequence of defiance."

"Do you understand the consequence of oppression? Do you know what the people will do once they've had enough?"

The man smirked, like he found this conversation amusing. "What people do you speak of?"

"Everyone! You think you've weeded them all out, everyone who would speak out against the state, but you're wrong. Those people still live in this country. They've just grown small and locked inside the bodies of people who will do anything to get along. But someday you will push too far, you Stasi, and those little people inside of us will grow and grow and outnumber you."

"You seem very educated on the matter."

"I'm only observant."

"I'm observant, too," he said. "My job is to observe."

My mother crossed her arms. "Perhaps you're looking at the wrong things."

He let out a small laugh. "I was trained in human observation techniques at the Stasi University by the finest professors in the GDR. But clearly my education pales in comparison to that of a repairwoman who can't afford a street-facing apartment in the cheapest part of the city." He cocked his head to the side, studying her face. "A quick double-blink, indicating you're uncertain. Touching your ear, an attempt to appear relaxed. And that little speech you gave was practiced. You've said it before, many times probably, but I'm guessing I'm the first member of the Stasi you've entertained with it."

My mother swallowed.

He extracted a small notebook from his inner jacket pocket and clicked a pen. "First name?"

"Mirka."

He wrote it down. "And your husband's name?"

"Hans."

"And the little one here is Ava." He closed the notebook. "I am Captain Heinrich Werner. I look forward to learning *much* more about these restless Dreymans. Have a lovely evening. And get yourself to sleep, little one. School in the morning."

We watched him leave, waiting until the clink of the elevator descending had receded before either of us exhaled.

I turned to her, my body flooding with anger. "Mother, why would you antagonize him like that?"

"I did nothing but state my beliefs," she said.

"Don't you realize what's going to happen now? Our names are going on a list. We'll be watched. I might even have lost my spot at a university because of your foolishness. Not to mention your running out in the middle of the night, starting that fire."

"I don't know what you're talking about," she said. She lifted the drinking glass from the kitchen counter and let the water fall into the sink.

"Mother, don't insult me."

"You're a child," she snapped, slamming the glass on the counter. "Thinking you know something and truly knowing are two very different things."

"I know a hell of a lot more than you! You can't insult a Stasi officer to his face. We're all dead because of you. You've killed father. You've killed me."

She held up her hand as if to slap me. "Never say such things!"

"But I'm only taking your approach. Saying whatever I want because I think it's the truth."

"You—you are a *child*," she repeated sternly, as though it might start meaning something the more she said it.

Angry tears sprung to my eyes. "Yes, I'm a child," I said, "because I still have to live with you and pay for your mistakes. That's the definition of a child, isn't it? Well, one day, Mother, I'll be long gone from here and you'll be the only one left paying."

# Pepper

*Astronomy*

Dear Ms. Eldridge,

Hello, and welcome to my second essay. Today, we will tackle astronomy, one of my most hated subjects. For instance, did you know that the universe is a cold and uncaring black hole of nothing? I'm sorry, I'm getting snippy because of something that happened today which ruined my life.

Though I have completed one essay against my better judgment, your reply did not contain the answer to the question I asked regarding how you came by your scar. Under normal circumstances, this wouldn't bother me overly, but your omission forces me to deduce that the story must be a good one. I hope it involves sword fighting.

What your note did say was that my previous submission was a nice personal essay, but I should try to make the next one more factual. Presently I looked some facts up using Wikipedia.

Fact: The sun produces so much energy, every second it releases the equality of 100 billion nuclear bombs. That's a lot.

Fact: If a human was placed on any other planet, they'd

either freeze to death, burn to death, suffocate, or be crushed by the gravitational pull.

Fact: The universe is terrifying.

How are the above facts supposed to make me feel? They're terrible things to teach children, and I think astronomy—nay, all science—should be banned from our schools immediately. For the sake of the youth.

And that's all I have to say about astronomy. I know you said these essays should be several pages long, which is why I'll now transition into another story, about the extremely distressing thing that happened today during school.

Firstly, another fact: I am handsome and suave and generally people like me. But on this day people were smirking—there is no other word for it—and some were even *giggling* at me, and it's all because of Petra Mirkovsky.

This story requires a piece of background information which I vehemently dislike discussing, but I will do it for you, Ms. Eldridge, and for the scientific community as a whole. Allow me to tell you about the day I was born. Truly, it was a grand event, one for the history books.

I came from a country called Kuwait. I was born in Al Ahmadi, which you'd probably only know of because, in Al Ahmadi, you're never more than three inches from oil. In truth, if there's been an oil spill, the ground is springy with it. I remember running out in the oil fields and the earth beneath my feet would budge like a trampoline. I remember peeling up chunks off the ground with my fingertips, easy as scabs.

We lived in a one-room duplex situated beneath the constantly moving shadows of the oil wells. Things were getting bad nearby, and my parents had been warned to leave. My father did not listen. "This is my home," he said. "They will not take me from my home."

On the day I was born, my mother and father could hear the rattle and *BOOM* of dynamite set off inside underground shafts in the distance, and the ground roiled beneath their feet. Plumes of fire erupted across the horizon where the oil wells were being exploded by Saddam Hussein. Soon, my parents heard a patter on the roof, but if they imagined it was rain, that thought died when the windows began to blacken. The oil fell from the black clouds above like rain that is impossible. In moments, the room was completely dark.

"Milk," my mother said. "Ishaq, get me some milk." My mother was hugely pregnant with me and her muscles were creaking like old wood. My father leaped to the kitchen, grateful to be doing something. When he got back with the milk, the room was empty. He opened the door on to the black-painted night and shouted her name. Out in the oil storm, my mother was running toward something, and at that precise moment I decided it was time to enter the world, and it was all over too quickly for my father to do anything.

He spent hours out there, choking on smoke, searching the

new-sprung lakes of oil, sometimes falling into them so in no time he was a slick-black color, and every part of him was crying from the sting. The glass of milk sat on the stoop, becoming slowly brown.

In the darkness, silhouetted against the fires, my father glimpsed a human shape. It might've been my mother, he hoped, until the shape became big and hulking with a disfigured, round head. To my father, eyes drunk on oil, it looked like a monster,  but at the next moment the figure comprehended itself into the body of a soldier—an American one, and in his hands was a baby, its small unclothed body touched by oil even before it had touched another human.

I am sure you can guess that the baby was me.

The soldier showed my father where my mother floated at the edge of an oil pond that had gushed angrily from a spot where the earth was exploded. Nearby, a fire burned, shaking its smoke like flags. She lay on her back, white scarf smudged, droplets of oil coating her open eyeballs. Everything was doused with the color of orange light, soft and pulsing from the fires that glowed across the horizon.

She was still beautiful, he said, and it was true that she even looked peaceful, in her face and in her eyes, but only because she was dead.

The soldier was young, with buzzed ginger hair beneath his sand-colored helmet, and he stayed with my father several hours.

"We're all going to die here," my father said in his grief. "Even the baby. Especially him."

"You're wrong," the soldier said.

"How can you know?" my father demanded. His hands were shaking around the bundle of me.

So the soldier told him about a bay in California, where he was from, where you can stand on a rock and see nothing but ocean, where you can forget that there is any such things as oil and fire. He told this for himself as much as for my father, because the soldier's soul was oil-spotted and ruined by now, too.

The soldier said his name was Winston Mavity, and he'd come to Kuwait because there was nothing left for him in America.

Eventually, when my father and I finally left Kuwait, it was impossible for us not to move to Monterey. I was eleven years old when he told me—we will go to America and live no longer in this place called Arabia, irregardless of the fact that the beaches are nice and the waters produce the biggest pearl oysters one could ever wish for. It was happening to be holiday times and the last glimpse I saw of my home country was the palm trees on the hot stretch of beach, the fronds spilled over with big bright colorful glassed lights the size of limes.

In Monterey, my father searched for Winston Mavity, but he was in no phone book, and even when I became skilled at the Internet, I could not find him. He was dead or did not wish to be found. Sometimes, my father approached red-haired men

and asked if they were called Winston, but every time it led to
nothing, and more often led to an embarrassing or difficult situation, my father being thick-necked and hard-of-English, and
yes, Arab looking, which is a tough thing to be in America.

My father took me to the aquarium many times in the beginning, and it was here that I felt our difference for the first
time, among the pale families with hair like yellow corn, and
even the plastic windows of teal water and fish couldn't distract
me from the feeling of eyes on me, because there was always
someone watching us, but pretending not to. We spent the
most time in a circular room at the back end of the aquarium
where nobody stayed for long because the fish were so ugly and
ordinary. Behind the glass walls were dozens of brown wedge-
shaped bodies. RAINBOW TROUT, a plaque read.

"Your mama," my dad said, "she would love this."

I looked up at him. He was wearing the cowboy hat that was
starting to make me embarrassed in public. Beneath the brim,
his eyes were smiling.

"Dad, I think she would hate this," is what I wanted to tell
him, but I knew this would be unacceptable.

In Al Ahmadi, before I was born, my father had tried his
hand at big-game fishing. When he got off work at the oil
company, he'd rent a boat and catch the biggest swordfish
and marlin anyone had seen. He said it was the most thrilling
thing he'd done. That it was how men should be, wrestling
with something every bit as big as you. Not shoving your

fingers into oil and hoping the land doesn't collapse beneath your feet.

"It's not right," my mother would tell him.

"Nuriyah, I'm a fisherman. Killing fish is what I do."

"The ones you catch are the size of men, so they must have souls the size of men's. You should be helping to save their lives, not ending them."

My father ignored her. He later said it was the worst thing he did in his life.

I looked back at the aquarium trout. Most of them had mashed-in snub noses, their hooked jaws constantly ajar. Above the burbling of the oxygenator, I could hear little thudding noises. I watched one trout swim full force into the glass. He bounced off and swam in the other direction.

"They're trying to get out," I said, my voice rising. "That's why they look like that."

"They're happy in there," was all he said.

The next day, he spent more dollars than we could afford on his first fish tank. Later, when he could buy an old tin boat, he went out on the bay and brought back a mid-size rockfish. With every fishing excursion, he transplanted something new into our aquarium. Once, he brought back a tiny leopard shark. He said it was too much a baby to do any harm to the others, but when I got back from school that afternoon, they were all dead, the rockfish and the yellowtail and the sturgeon. The shark swam on its side in the blood-choked water, gills gasping.

I stood there all afternoon beside an oblivious Bertrand until my dad got home from work, because I was too terrified to do anything but stare. Eventually, the shark rolled fully onto its back and settled that way, its cream-colored belly staring at the ceiling.

"We'll get a bigger tank," was all my dad said when he got home. He started dumping the bloody water onto the lawn, bucket by bucket.

This was the way of things for a while until the Burning Summer, when we'd have to sit in the smoke for days, feel it push deeper and deeper into our skin, until the smell was a part of us.

My dad and I were out fishing in the bay when we heard that they'd finally captured the arsonist. On the horizon, a black smear from his most recent fire hung over the poor part of town where half-built housing complexes stood empty, construction halted when the developers ran out of money. My father fiddled with the dials on a weatherproof radio he purchased at the Goodwill.

"Firefighters have recovered at least six bodies from the scene. Though the houses were never occupied, they have recently been the home of dozens of squatters, most believed to be recent migrants from Mexico. Three of the bodies have been confirmed as children."

"Oh no," my dad said. "Those poor people."

We were pretty far out in the bay now, within sight of Rake

Island. They say the island once housed a mental asylum, and that even now you could find rooms with silver examination tables and cabinets full of straitjackets. I don't know if I believe the stories. From the water, nothing was visible but shaggy cypress trees.

I felt the fishing pole jerk. My line was taut in the water.

"We got something," I said. I leaned backward with the pole, struggling to reel it in. Whatever was on the other end was heavy and fighting. I got up on my knees and pulled back with the pole. Seawater sloshed over the boat's side.

"You want me to take over?" my dad asked.

"No," I grunted. Finally, a gray body the size of a python broke the surface.

"Wolf eel," my dad said, sounding excited. "He's gonna try to slip it."

He crouched by the edge of the boat and the next time the eel broke the surface my dad was there, clamping his hands around its body. The eel shook its thick head side to side. It had gray skin and bulbous eyes and heavy, snapping jaws. I threw the pole to the bottom of the boat and flipped the lid off of an orange bucket half filled with seawater. We threw the eel in, and it landed with a heavy splash.

My dad looked down into the container, panting. "He'll look good in the tank."

"Will he get along with the ray?" I asked. "They'll have to share territory."

"They won't have a choice," he said.

The newscaster on the radio started speaking frantically. "We have it from multiple sources that the arsonist has turned himself in. He is identified as Winston Mavity, a thirty-seven-year-old commercial welder with no prior convictions."

My head swiveled to look in my father's eyes. He was still staring at the eel, flipping its body around in circles in the bucket. I barely heard the newscaster say, "Mavity is a veteran of the Gulf War who lives on the outskirts of Monterey with his young daughter," because I was watching my father's knuckles, gripping the boat's edge, become slowly bloodless.

"It's him," my dad said, and that was all he needed to say.

I put my head between my knees, still breathing hard from before. I licked my lips and my tongue came away salty. Maybe I was crying; I don't know. My mind could only flit between Winston Mavity and the wolf eel, which was so ugly, I didn't want it in my life, but there it would be, every day, because there was no point trying to convince my dad that stealing fish from the wild wasn't ever going to bring my mother back.

All of this is leading to something, Ms. Eldridge, leading straight toward the reason why I've decided never to place my feet inside the walls of Herbert Hoover High School ever again. The reason is Petra Mirkovsky.

In terms of astronomy, Petra is the most stunning creature in the observable universe. Fact. I never had the guts to do anything about it before. But, something shifted in me the night the Horsemen and I ran from the security guard at the pool. I felt, I'm not sure, lighter? I decided I should consider taking my friends' advice. I was going to ask Petra Mirkovsky out.

My math teacher let us out a minute early, and I found Petra at her locker in the junior hall as I walked to lunch. Petra's a year younger than the Horsemen and me. The two of us were pretty much the only kids in the hallway. *Perfect timing,* I thought. *It's meant to be.* (Ms. Eldridge—this is supposed to be foreshadowing. Nothing is perfect. Everything is shit.) Petra was beautiful in a way that shouldn't have been beautiful—a big chunky sweater that hid practically all of her upper body, a pleated skirt with glossy black shoes. She wore thick bangs that covered half her face.

"Hi, Petra," I said.

"Oh, hello, Ibrahim."

"Um." I licked my lips, which had suddenly become very dry. "I bet you're planning on eating at some point in the next week."

She looked me.

"Would you, um, wanna eat some food with me sometime?"

Her eyebrows shot up. "Actually, I've been meaning to ask you something, too. Would it be all right if I interviewed you for the *Complacent Sparrow*?"

I blinked. Petra is the editor of Hoover's literary journal, the *Complacent Sparrow*. In every edition, she does an interview with a member of the student body. Usually it's one of her arty friends who do photography or printmaking and want to move to Portland when they graduate, which was why it was extremely perplexing that she asked *me* to be interviewed.

"Interview me?" I asked. "Why?"

"You're . . . interesting."

"I—I know I am interesting. I just don't know what I would say."

"You can just be yourself."

I shuffled my feet uncomfortably. It was being myself that I was wary of. I'm obviously terribly attractive, yet that doesn't tend to translate well to the page.

"You're different," she continued. "Most people in high school are afraid to be different. But you—it's got to take a lot of bravery being you."

The bell rang for lunch and Petra said she'd meet me after school on Friday in the *Complacent Sparrow* offices, which were in a closet attached to an English teacher's classroom.

"I can't wait, Ibrahim," she said.

All week, I was practically dying with excitement. After school ended on Friday, I threw everything in my locker and fast-walked to the *Complacent Sparrow*'s office. The walls of the tiny room were plastered with past covers of the magazine, mostly abstract or charcoal drawings of birds. Petra was going over something in a notebook, legs crossed. I made a noise with my throat and she looked up.

"Hi, Ibrahim. Come on in."

The office was so small that when I sat down, our legs were

almost touching. She had on pale pink tights, and I could see her knee bones. Petra took out her iPhone and turned on the audio recorder.

"It's all right if I use this for college applications next year, isn't it?" It's long been established that Petra wants to attend NYU and study journalism there. "I already know it'll be a standout piece."

I nodded vehemently. "Of course."

"Thanks, Ibrahim. I'm really grateful you agreed to do this."

The whole thing should have struck me as odd right off the bat, because she asked me different questions than what she usually asks. Normally it's just, "Tell me about your current art projects," and "What band inspires you?" but she asked about my family, and Kuwait, and my friends. She made lots of understanding noises with her mouth and once even touched my knee, which unbolted something in my chest and made it easier to let everything come gushing out.

In the end, she took my picture beside the American flag by the office, and I felt dignified and extremely handsome, like I always imagined looking in my presidential portrait.

"I'll get you some copies when it's printed," she said. "You probably want to give one to your dad and everything."

My foot fell to the ground harder than I expected. I remembered my dad for the first time since the interview started. For those moments with Petra, I'd forgotten I had a father, and I'd forgotten about the Horsemen, and I'd forgotten about Bertrand, even though he was right there by our feet the entire time, huffing the air like Krazy Glue. I grew unsettled.

Fact: The earth spins at a thousand miles an hour.

Fact: This makes me feel like throwing up.

You see, Ms. Eldridge, my mind isn't suited for science, especially not astronomy. Because whenever anything goes wrong, I feel that thousand miles per hour spinning inside my head. I have to clamp my eyes shut, and clamp my lips closed, and clamp the cheeks of my buttocks together just to feel like I'm not going to fling off into space. This is why I failed physics, and chemistry, and biology. It seems like everything I've ever learned is meant to make me afraid.

There are little distribution boxes for the literary journal drilled into the shiny tile hallway walls. Every day, I watched the boxes, waiting to see if my edition would show up.

Today was the day.

I knew immediately that something was horribly wrong. Instead of a minimalist drawing of a sparrow, it was my *face* staring up from the cover. My heart plummeted into my bowel. I did not look dignified. I did not look handsome. I definitely did not look presidential. I looked stupid. My curls of hair needed a trim and my teeth were more crooked than I realized and my mustache, which I had thought was growing in quite nicely and made me appear supremely badass, looked like lines from a fine-tip Sharpie, and the effect was not at all awesome.

Ms. Eldridge, you have seen how I look in person, so you're

probably thinking I'm being hard on myself. I thought so, too. Until people actually started picking up the journal and reading the interview and openly laughing at my private matters.

My fingertips began sweating all over the glossy pages as soon as I started reading.

*I sit down with Ibrahim Al-Yusef on a chill spring day. He enters the office tentatively, and every inch of his gawky frame seems to be trying to take up less space. He wears a collared shirt that I suspect he chose specifically for the occasion, as most know him for his novelty T-shirts and slouched jeans. He holds the nylon leash of his service animal, an obese lapdog named Bernard, behind his back as though its presence could in some way be obscured. Everything about Ibrahim is deliberate: the way he carefully positions his body, the practiced staccato way he delivers his words to conceal a noticeable accent. Most people wouldn't waste the time it would take to understand why Ibrahim is the way he is, but I sense there is a greater story hidden beneath the surface, and it's my duty as a journalist to see through the exterior. After all, as Pulitzer Prize–winner Charles Winifred said, "Journalism is a calling to lever the beautiful truth from even the ugliest, the lowliest of specimens." What is Ibrahim Al-Yusef's veneer attempting to cover? That is the question I enter this interview with.*

**Ibrahim, thank you for joining me.**

You can call me Pepper.

**Ibrahim, how are you today?**

I'm doing good. I mean, doing *well*. Is that the right one? I never know. [laughs nervously] How are you today, Petra?

**I'm well. Part of the work of the *Complacent Sparrow* is breaking down social groups and attempting to find universality in every member of the student body. You're known on campus as not exactly belonging to a social group. Tell me, is that a deliberate choice?**

Uh . . . what do you mean social group? I have friends, if that is what you're asking. I am friends with Shawn Fitzgerald, and Wallace Sanchez, and Reggie Johnson.

**That's what I mean, Ibrahim. All of your friends are also members of identified social groups. Reggie is an athlete, and Shawn is in chess club and Future Chemists, and Wallace is a DECA member. You're none of those things.**

I never—I guess I never thought about that before. I didn't think it was important. I mean, it's not like they're real.

**What do you mean?**

It's not like we'll have that stuff when we grow up. It's just for school. If you like them, that's fine, but if you don't like them, you should be okay with just doing the things you like to do.

**What do you like to do?**

I, um, I don't know [shrugs].

**You don't know what you like to do? What are your hobbies? What do you do when you're not at school?**

Well . . . sleep [laughs]. I like video games. I go fishing with my dad. I don't really like that, though, because he keeps the fishes in a tank at our house and it always smells like seaweed and fish poop [laughs].

**What about your religion? Is it true you're a practicing Muslim?**

I—no.

**I was fairly certain that you were a Muslim.**

I mean, not really. My dad hasn't practiced for years, not since—not since my mom died. He says he stopped seeing the point of it.

**That brings me to another set of questions, Ibrahim. You have a terribly interesting personal history. Can you tell me about how your family came to America?**

Well, I don't talk about that with most people. But I guess you're not most people, Petra [giggles]. I was twelve when we arrived. We had been waiting until we were picked to receive green cards through the American lottery system.

**And where was your mother?**

She—she died the night I was born. In the oil fires.

**Oh, that's awful. Ibrahim, for the sake of readers, I'm going to provide some historical background. The Kuwaiti oil fires occurred during the Persian Gulf War, when the Iraqi military set fire to hundreds of oil wells across Kuwait. Does that sound accurate to you?**

Uh, I guess.

**Can you tell me more about your mother's death?**

I guess I came too early and my mother died and an American soldier saved me. But not my mother. She was too dead already.

**How did she die?**

We think the bleeding that I caused. Or else the oil in her lungs. It was too chaotic to get a real answer, and she had to be buried.

**What was she like?**

I don't know really. She was pretty, my father says. She had beautiful eyes, like you, Petra [giggles].

**How do you feel not having a mother?**

Well, I can't ever be sure. I never had nothing—I mean anything, to compare it to. I guess, all of my life, I wonder what I'm missing, not having a mother.

**If you had to guess, what would you say you're missing?**

It's—maybe it's the thing that most kids have that I don't. Like, the feelings like everything will be okay in the end. Even if they disobey their parents, even if they don't study, even if they skip school one day. But I always assume everything's about to go horribly wrong, and it'll be my fault.

**That must be a lot to carry around. Do you ever get overwhelmed by it?**

Yeah.

**What do you do then?**

Sometimes . . . sometimes if I pinch myself really hard, that works. And also . . . never mind. It is stupid.

**It's all right.**

I close my eyes and imagine being the president. And I'm sitting in the Oval Office, getting my presidential portrait taken, and I look really suave and American like JFK and the expression on my face is like "I got this," and I've even gone into the mall and picked out the kind of suit I'll wear. I'm gonna look sick.

**But you're not American.**

I—I know. I'm not saying it's a dream that will ever come true.

**What do you think that does to you, knowing your dream is something you can never achieve?**

I guess—[pauses] I guess it makes me feel like there's no point to anything that I do.

Currently, I would like to crawl into one of those black holes in the sky where:

    a) There is no light, and

    b) There is no sound, and

    c) There is no such thing as humiliation.

The Horsemen met me in our lunch spot at the back of the auditorium where it's private but for the drama kids on the stage, practicing their Oscar speeches.

"Sorry, man," Wallace said.

"Yeah," Reggie said.

"What a bitch," Shawn said. "She even got Bertrand's name wrong. Journalistic fail."

I shook my head because, even in that raw hour, I had already learned something.

Fact: The truth can hurt you. Even your own truths. If you let people put their dirty fingers on your truth, before you know it, this precious thing that once was only yours is covered with grime.

Stupid Petra. But, most of all, stupid me.

"You can go into hiding for a couple of days," Shawn said. "Call in sick."

"If I do that, I'll probably never come back," I said.

The Horsemen chuckled.

"No, really," I said. "I think I'm maybe not coming back to school."

Ms. Eldridge, they still did not know the truth about my lack of credits to graduate. I had been keeping it from them. But now? Well, there didn't seem to be a reason anymore.

"Can't you do summer school?" Reggie asked after I had explained the situation.

"I can do nothing," I lied, because I didn't feel like telling them about the essays.

"Shit," Reggie said.

"Fuck," Wallace agreed.

"Christ," Shawn whispered.

There wasn't much else to say. They are all going to college next year—they've been accepted to CSUMB, the local college that pretty much everybody at our high school will go to.

"So, you'll just do an extra year at Hoover before college," said Wallace casually, as though it wasn't the most horrible reality one could ponder. "It's not a big deal."

"I'm just gonna drop out."

"*Drop out?*" Shawn asked. I looked away. My friends weren't exactly the intellectual elite at Hoover, but even to them, drop-ping out was impossible.

"So what?" I asked. "It's not like a high school diploma buys you anything anymore."

"It buys you a shit ton more than not having one," Shawn said. "What are you gonna do?"

"Get a job."

"Killing rats or cleaning toilets, maybe," Shawn said.

"There's nothing wrong with jobs like that."

"Says the kid who's wanted to be president since he was twelve."

"Well, that's not gonna happen, is it?" I asked. "Like Petra said, it can *never* happen. And I'm wasting my life and letting everybody down." My throat clenched like a fist.

"So the answer is to give up on life?"

"I won't be—"

"Yes, you will!" Shawn shouted, his cheeks turning pink. "I'll tell you exactly what's going to happen. You're gonna sit on your lazy ass and feel sorry for yourself. You're gonna live at the Cyber Café playing Sheildcraft until you're absorbed into the seat cushion and have to be scraped off with a spatula."

"Shawn, just shut your . . . stupid . . . up . . ." My words were coming out all messed up like they do when I get upset. "You don't have a say," I pronounced finally.

"Well, I'm your best friend. I should have a say," he said, his voice rising. The drama kids were looking over the backs of the velvet seats to see what the commotion was. "I'm not gonna be quiet while you throw your life away. Just tell me you'll think about getting your GED, or *some*thing."

I shook my head and the shaking almost became nodding because it's usually easier to agree with Shawn. But I heard Petra's words repeated in my head like a skipping song: he and Reggie and Wallace are part of something. They are athletes, and future chemists, and whatever the hell DECA is. They are all going to be something someday.

But not me. I'm not anything at all.

# Molly

Hey, Pepper,

You went in for another surgery today, so they didn't let me visit you. I'm trying really hard not to think about your head being cut open and your brain being shown off to everyone in the room. Just . . . don't die, Pepper. Please.

Now, where were we?

It's been a week since the dinner party at Keller, and school is over for the year. It's early evening, and I'm out on the board-walk with Margaret and her friends because my aunt insisted I go.

With one ear, I listen to the ocean crashing on the concrete seawalls, and with the other I listen to the conversation of Margaret and her friends. Margaret has recently dyed her stringy hair pinkish-red. The crown of her head is wrapped in Christmas garland with little gold stars, and her eyelids are smeared with teal glitter, creased from hours of wear.

"We are the girls of summer!" Margaret shouts into the night.

The others giggle. I don't entirely mind tagging along, not

even after all the horrible things Margaret said during the dinner party. I love sensing, by the salt air, the sea just beyond the darkness.

On the boardwalk, it's late enough that almost all of the tourists have gone back to their hotels. The tourist industry is one of Margaret's favorite topics of conversation. She loves watching them crawl over the well-lit parts of town and guessing where they're from.

"Ohio," she mutters about an overweight woman taking a picture beside the statue of John Steinbeck. "Got to be."

"How can you tell?" I ask.

"She's got a, what I call, a BAMF," Margaret explains. "Big-ass muthafucking fanny pack."

The other girls laugh. I just shake my head. Margaret really has no way of telling where someone's from based on how they look, but in her mind, she's always right and her friends never bother to find out for themselves. This is one of the things that makes me wonder if I've been lucky to have so far missed out on friendship with people my own age. Friendship seems to imply forming some kind of nonverbal pact to go along with your friends even if they are absolute idiots.

If I have a best friend, it's Marty. You've never met him, Pepper. My auntie Ro is a psychiatric nurse, and Marty was at one point a patient of hers. Now he lives in a group home and visits my house for socialization and life skills. Marty's been all over the world, seen practically everything, and I like listening to him, even if Margaret makes fun of me for having a sixty-five-year-old best-slash-only friend.

I walk three steps behind Margaret and her entourage, who patrol the night streets with Popsicles melting down the sides of their fists and a pop in their hips that I couldn't replicate in a thousand years, even without the cast that weighs down my right foot. At least I ditched my crutches a couple of weeks ago.

Margaret's friends are other girls from the Keller School—Joyce, Kimber, and Brielle. They are all unbearable for different reasons. Joyce has a fake British accent, Kimber flirts aggressively with all the teachers, and Brielle is dating this irritating kid named Grayson, who has a ratty brown ponytail and a 35 mm camera always slung around his neck.

Margaret finishes her Popsicle, throwing the stick to the ground without reading the joke. There are no tourists around and the girls have grown quiet, looking for something to talk about. Joyce's eyes land on me.

"Hey, Molly," Joyce asks, "have you ever had a boyfriend?"

"No," I tell her, suddenly feeling clammy and strange.

"Why not?"

"I never wanted one."

"What do you *mean*?" Brielle's face has stretched into a scandalized grin, as though she's never heard anything weirder.

"Are you gay or something?" Joyce asks.

"It's okay if you are," Kimber says quickly.

The answer is I don't know, but I'm certain saying that would make them freak out, so I don't say a word. Worst of all is Margaret's expression, like a scientist surveying an experiment.

"I can tell by your body language that you're very uncomfortable," Kimber says, in the tone of someone who's been to a lot of therapy sessions.

My stomach has turned queasy from the looks on the girls' faces, and the neon lights of the nearby bars have grown too bright, so I reach inside my pocket where I keep my key, enclosed in the envelope it came in five years ago. I thumb the hard outline of it against my palm. It doesn't make me feel better, but it gives me something to concentrate on.

"What do you have?" Brielle asks, looking into my hands.

My arm straightens to hold the envelope to my side. "Nothing."

"It's not nothing—it's a letter," Joyce says. "Let us see, Molly."

As I begin to protest, Joyce snatches the envelope from my hands. "No return address," she says. "Who sent it to you?"

I have to bite down on my cheek to stop myself from hitting her and grabbing the envelope back. I pull in several breaths through my nose.

"Do you have a secret admirer we don't know about?" Joyce asks.

The other girls giggle as though that's the most ludicrous thing they've ever heard, all except Margaret. For once, Margaret's face is expressionless. Her red-stained lips turn under.

"Molly thinks her mother sent it to her," Margaret says flatly.

"But your mom's dead," Kimber points out because, in her mind, it's perfectly plausible I might've forgotten.

"Molly doesn't believe that, though," Margaret says. "She thinks that her mom faked her death. Witness protection. And she's been biding her time until it's safe to get back in contact."

The other girls' eyebrows shoot upward.

"I never said witness protection," I mutter, though Margaret's summary isn't otherwise inaccurate. I pull my elbows in and decide Margaret won't ever understand me either. Because I don't need friends, and I don't need boyfriends, and I especially don't need anyone to believe me. I only need to be right about this, because the only thing I believe in anymore is that my mother is alive.

Pepper, I never told you why. I'm telling you now.

In the time it took the French police to confirm the body that washed up on the beach was my mother's, I had been alone in Nice for three days. The social worker assigned to me gave me the afternoon to myself after they officially ruled my mother's death a suicide. My flight home was to depart that night. I walked the pebble beach one last time, watching my sneakers traverse the endless curve of white rocks, then climbed the stairs back up to the promenade and sat on one of the white metal benches, stretching my feet on the railing before me.

"It's the most beautiful thing I have ever seen," a voice from nearby said in accented English.

I turned to look above me. An older woman with a blunt, shaved-looking head stood behind my bench. She wore walking shoes and a Windbreaker, just like the droves of old, too-tan French people who used the promenade to exercise.

"The sea," the woman explained. "I never knew something like this could exist. When you grow up away from it and you see it for the first time, it makes all the sadness in the world disappear."

I turned to look back at the water. "I've lived my entire life beside the ocean. It doesn't make me happy."

The old woman shook her head. "You've grown used to beauty. That's the worst crime you can commit."

I didn't respond. I could think of many worse crimes.

The woman walked away. I tried to watch the sea again, but it barely registered. My mother was dead. What could a bunch of water do for me now?

I stood, stuffing my hands in my pockets, and walked across the street to the hotel room we'd shared. Her suitcase was still open on the unmade bed, silk blouses and skirts spilling out haphazardly. I sagged onto the mattress. My eyes landed on something lying on the nearby desk. I leaped up from the bed.

A single white envelope lay on the dark surface. On the front, printed in square, red letters, was my name. *MOLLY.*

I slid my finger beneath the flap. Inside, I found a postcard. The picture was a colorful drawing of the Château de Nice, the sea stretching beyond it like a million smashed gemstones. I winced; this was the last place I'd seen my mother. It was from here that the police said she had jumped to her death. I turned the card over and read the message.

*I am so sorry, darling. I wish there was a way to explain, but nothing I say will make any difference. The world inside our minds is a wild, complicated place, and some decisions are impossible to explain. You're going to be sad for a while, and then you're going to be angry, but someday you're going to understand, and by that time, I will find you again and you can ask me all the questions you want.*

I read the card again and again. The message was typewritten, but it was obvious in every inky stroke that my mother had written this. I found the envelope and turned it over. Out fell a key. My fingers were shaking around the small piece of metal, the words *Monterey USPS, Box 5255* pressed onto its key tag.

Suddenly, I didn't feel so sad about returning home.

"Look!" Joyce shouts, her fingers rummaging inside my envelope. "There's a key inside. What's it open, Molly?"

I snatch the envelope back from Joyce and shove it inside my shirt, close to my body. "It's to a PO box."

"What's inside it?" Kimber asks.

"A whole lot of nothing," Margaret interjects. "Molly goes there all the time. Never finds a thing. But that doesn't stop her from hoping one day her mother will put something there, and they can be a family again."

"Why all the cloak-and-dagger stuff?" Kimber asks. "She's your *mom*. Why would she pretend she was dead in the first place?"

"She must be afraid of someone," I say. "Someone who wants to hurt her."

"Your dad?" Joyce asks.

"Molly's dad is in prison," Margaret says.

"Maybe someone was after her," I said. "Maybe she witnessed a crime and feared retaliation."

Margaret scoffs. "But you know what's wrong with that, Molly? They found her body. They matched her DNA."

"I never saw the body," I say. "And they said it was really smashed up on the rocks so . . ." Brielle darts a bunched-up look of skepticism over to Joyce. "So, maybe it wasn't really her they found."

"That seems like a pretty big stretch," Joyce says.

"But it's more than that," I say, the pitch of my voice rising. "She was right there and then she was gone. People don't just vanish. I know she didn't kill herself. I know it."

Margaret scoffs. She shakes her head, her face disbelieving. "I don't understand how you can lie to yourself like that," she says.

"You promised Dr. Lawrence you'd try.

"You promised my *mom* you'd try.

"You know what she's sacrificed making room for you.

"Why are you making that noise?

"Your mother is dead.

"Just get *over* yourself, Molly.

"Stop humming, you weirdo!

"YOUR MOTHER IS DEAD!"

I whip around, my arms going rigid, and shove Margaret with the meat of my hand. I aim for her shoulders, but my hand strikes her hard in the throat. I can feel the bands of cartilage bend, and then Margaret is doubled over, making horrible noises like she's gagging.

"Shit, Molly, what's your problem?" Brielle asks.

"You always take things too far," Joyce says.

I hold my arms before me in apology. "I—I didn't mean—"

"Get away from me!" Margaret gasps.

The girls glare at me from where they're leaning over, rubbing Margaret's back. I don't know what else to do.

So I run.

Through the neon-printed streets, I run. My cast is cumbersome but I don't feel any pain, so I run harder, the red sockless Croc on my other foot slapping the pavement, my ear to the ocean, which whispers in its panting voice that there is something wrong with my brain, that I am wired wrong. I've heard that expression forever—"You've got your wires crossed"—and I imagine there really are needle-thin lines of copper running the length of my mind, shoved through the soft pink tissue in the wrong direction, the metal corroded and twisted. I will never be able to reach in there and straighten them out. I don't know how.

My breath comes hard as I sprint through the night door of the Monterey Post Office. The thunk of my cast on the floor echoes through the dimly lit, high-ceilinged post office box rooms that look identical, all lined with little brass doors matching the color of my key. I don't need to scan the numbers on the doors to find mine. I have opened this door a million, million times.

I skid to a halt, eye level with my door, and push the key into the lock. The hinge opens smoothly. I slide a rectangular black box out onto my forearm and lower it onto a polished bench in the center of the room.

I clasp the box's metal lip and push the top up.

Empty.

Just like it has been every time I've checked it for the last five years.

I pick up the box and shake it like I want to break it apart because I do.

And, then, like a dream, a cream-colored rectangle the size of a playing card flutters through the gray light to the floor.

A feeling like electricity shoots all the way to my toes. I lift the little weightless thing away from the floor. There is writing on the back in even typewriter script.

*Dear Molly, I'm sorry I haven't been in contact. It's a funny thing, the whole world thinking you are dead. You almost start to believe it, that you're a ghost and that everyone else is alive. I can't explain why it's impossible to simply tell you what I know, to tell you with my own voice, not a typewriter, but someday you will understand. I hope that day is soon.*

The edges of my eyes pulse with the rhythm of my heart-beat. I know something, with certainty.

It is my mother.

It is my mother.

It is my mother.

I paw the inside for anything more, craning my arm around to feel all the metal sides, and my fingers come in contact with something slick. Shoved along the back wall is a rolled tube of paper. I grasp it and press it flat. A boy's smiling face peers up from the cover. His head is haloed by the American flag and dark curls of hair fall over his forehead. And, most amazingly, encircling him is a thick line of red marker. Beneath his face, someone has written in even print, *He has the answers.*

I touch the glossy cover with fingers that are sweating and nervous.

Do you know what I am thinking the first moment I see you? Do you, Pepper?

I am thinking you are the most amazing thing I have seen in my entire life.

# Ava

October 24, 1986

The moment I arrived home from school, I threw my book bag on the floor and sprinted to the nearest desk lamp, fumbling beneath it with my fingertips. With my thumbs, I wheedled the orange throw pillow, searching for a seam of stapled wire placed there by the Stasi to listen in on my family.

"You're being ridiculous," my mother whispered when she saw me with my hands splayed over the thready wallpaper, feeling for the bevel of a cord. "They couldn't track the arson to us if I held a match beneath their noses."

"You're wrong," I told her. I've seen their faces, the Stasi men. They could smell the smoke in our minds if they got close enough.

"Mother, where are the socks you were wearing this morning?" I asked as I watched her shake out the bag she takes to the local gymnasium where she does calisthenics.

"I don't know," she said, combing through her clothes. "I probably left them in the changing room."

"You can't do things like that!" I shouted. "The dogs! Don't you know they collect dissidents' smells in jars?"

"Where on earth did you hear that?" she asked. "I'm not afraid of those choirboys. Besides, I'm not a dissident."

My mother does things like that, makes our situation seem smaller than it is, somehow convincing herself that she wouldn't be put in front of a firing squad if the Stasi found out everything she's done. Four people died in the fire that night. You'd think she'd feel the weight of that.

"You couldn't look more like a dissident if you tried," I grumbled.

My mother's whole being is arranged out of protest. She wears no makeup, buys the same brand of shoes my father wears, keeps her hair clipped closely to her head. I almost understand. Women here are expected to have long hair and at least try to be beautiful. So she gets backward glances in the street and, from the back, it looks like my father's walking hand in hand with a man because my mother wears pants, too.

But I see things differently. Why wouldn't she want beautiful long hair so she satisfies the expectations of all those who are so disapproving of differences? Not just to fit in, but to make them think she's playing by their rules. Use it to her advantage. And then, when it counts, surprise people. Turn the tables.

My mother never surprises anyone. People look at her and have her all figured out.

I refuse to be like that. They'll never figure me out. The Stasi, my parents, anyone.

- - - - -

October 30, 1986

It's a week since my mother's fire and I've seen Captain Werner every day on my walk home from school. He leans casually against a telephone pole reading a paperback. He sits in the park across the intersection, an apple in his fist. Paedar walked me home today, but I rushed upstairs to tell my mother that Captain Werner was sitting in a car opposite our apartment building.

"Berlin isn't a big place," my mother said. "He might live around here."

"You *can't* believe it's just a coincidence that he's outside our building."

"The Stasi have bigger things to worry about. Now hush. You'll worry your father."

My father is older than my mother by a couple of years, but to any observer, it would seem like twenty. He's quiet and bookish and I love him except that he refuses to acknowledge how wrong and reckless my mother is.

The misery of this day was exacerbated by the fact that my parents forced me to accompany them to visit Aunt Kruger in the afternoon. We had to walk there because we couldn't afford the gasoline for our old-model Trabant. We climbed the stairs of Aunt Kruger's mammoth apartment building, deep into the windowless center where the smell of rotten things never fades. My father opened the door, and I peeked around him to see Aunt Kruger sitting in her darkened living room, rays of lamplight catching on the dense cigarette smoke that hung like a fog.

"It's not too late," Aunt Kruger croaked. "You can leave. It won't hurt my feelings."

"Nonsense," my father said. "We'll just arrange some tea." He and my mother walked into the kitchen, and I was left with no option but to sit beside Aunt Kruger on her moldering couch. She's not my real aunt, but a friend of my father's from their student days.

"Your father needs to stop being so damn considerate," she said. "I've dealt with it since university and it's finally starting to annoy."

"He cares about you," I said. "We all do, Aunt Kruger."

She took a rattling drag on her cigarette. "If you cared about me, you'd find a crate big enough and mail me across the Wall."

"You don't mean that," I said. "Things will get better. The government—"

"What?" she snapped. "They'll forgive me? Governments aren't people. They do not forgive. They bide their time. And that's all they're doing with me."

Aunt Kruger was once a writer, except no GDR publication will print her work and the government won't let her leave, all because of one misstep: She published an article in a Western newspaper about the artistic restrictions of the East.

Between you and me, I think Aunt Kruger is a bit of a dolt for thinking she could get away with that. But, then, all the adults here seem a little too trusting of the Stasi. They hate them, but they don't fear them enough. Maybe that's what growing up is: feeling bigger than all of your fears.

"If you're wise you'll get out," Aunt Kruger said, pointing at me with her cigarette. "They will break each of us down until all that's left of us is a pile of ashes."

I thought of my mother, the fire she set. "Have you heard of Captain Werner?"

"Of course," she said. "Stasi. Storm Wolf, they say. Cruel, by rumors. Why do you ask?"

"I heard he lives in the neighborhood."

Aunt Kruger's eyes narrowed. "You avoid him, girl, if you see him. When someone's slighted him, he's like a dog with a bone until he's ruined them." She paused, turning to me. "Will you read something for me? Out loud?" She reached to the floor and held out a sheaf of typewritten pages. "Something new I wrote. I'd like to hear it in someone else's voice."

I got an image of Aunt Kruger in her apartment all day, smoking and reading her own stories out loud. The idea seemed almost too sad to bear.

I cleared my throat and began reading. The story was about a woman walking through a big, open green field until she happened across the body of a man, slumped in the grass, shot in the head. It seemed as though he was someone the woman knew, but I didn't find out because I heard a noise that made me look up.

Tears were coursing down Aunt Kruger's face. She was

peering somewhere far away. My father stood behind me. "It's probably time to leave," he said.

As we closed the door carefully behind us, I caught a glimpse of Aunt Kruger sitting in her chair, her fingers held loosely over her eyes.

There's really no end to what the Stasi can do, if they want. They've been almost lenient with Aunt Kruger: She's still alive, still in her own apartment. The Stasi can make people disappear. They can pull you from your bed and lock you away for the rest of your life. I've grown up hearing about what they do on patrols, speaking to neighbors and recording everything in their black notebooks. You see them sometimes, holding up yardsticks to measure the angle of TV antennas to tell if people are picking up Western signals, entering homes to shake the place out like a pair of old slacks. In a Stasi's tool kit, they carry a metal comb for digging through plywood furniture, carpet brushes to sweep up particles that are run through machines and converted to proof that somewhere, someone had a dissident thought that fell to the floor, heavy like gunpowder.

November 8, 1986

At night, when she thinks I sleep, my mother assembles typewriters. I've watched her sitting cross-legged on the parquet floor, silhouetted against the pale kitchen lamp, her fingers blackened with ink from the ribbon coiling through her hands. She keeps her supplies and typewriters behind some loose bricks in the wall between the bathroom and the kitchen.

The very last step of any typewriter is the decal. She melts down a red plastic fork in a teapot and pours it into a mold she pounded from a one-mark coin. It was the smell of burning plastic that woke me up the first time I caught her. When I padded down the hallway, she was adhering the loose decal to the paper support, and I could see it was in the shape of a flame. Enemies of the State all over the GDR use my mother's typewriters. She has even used one to write a few editions of her own subversive newsletter, *Der Brandstifter. The Arsonist.*

"Fire is the cleanest way to destroy something," she told me when I was very young. It was around then that she taught me how to start fires that burn quick and hot, fires that can smoke out a room of people, fires that only require the rubbing of something sharp against something wooden. "If you're arrested, don't hesitate. Burn them, choke them, pour the smoke into their lungs. You don't die without taking a few of them with you."

I blinked in fear.

"You might have to defend yourself one day," she said. "Every young woman should know how."

As I grew older, I saw that people like my mother were the ones who suffered the most. The people who never made a fuss got to go on holidays, and buy candy in the West, and were generally allowed to live their lives however they wished.

"Those people are sheep," my mother said.

"Sheep don't get detained," I replied. "Sheep don't get shot."

She looked me hard in the eyes. "We are not like them, Ava," she said. "We have to be ready to fight, and when the enemy gets you, one day, you show them what I taught you. When they lock you in the darkness, become an arsonist. When they put you under house arrest, or defile your name in public, or make you live beneath the rules that will suffocate you, become an arsonist. When they put a pistol in your hand and make you shoot your best friend, and when they throw you in a death camp, when you see everyone around you get sick from the poison they're feeding them, light a fire that will *destroy* them. A fire they won't forget the next time they try to do it to someone else."

November 9, 1986

This morning when I woke, the radio was silent, which was odd as it's Sunday, and there were none of the egg smells and chatty noise my parents generally make. I peeked around the corner, to the kitchen where my parents were huddled.

"Kruger's been detained," my mother said quietly.

"What happened?" my father asked.

"They traced the pamphlet she made last month to her apartment complex. They searched every flat. In her carpet, they found a few rubber letters from her collapsible printing press. No larger than a centimeter but they found them."

"Could they trace her to us?"

"No, it's not possible," she said. "At least, I don't think so."

"You don't sound as certain as you were."

"I'm not certain of anything anymore! First Bergman and Haas, now Kruger. They only have to get Georg and Margarita and we'll be practically the only ones left in Berlin still fighting."

"We could go to Leipzig," my father suggested.

"And that wouldn't draw attention? Only counterrevolutionaries move to Leipzig anymore. We have Ava to think of."

My father mumbled something unintelligible.

"What, Hans?"

"We didn't think of Ava when we burned down that building."

"You're saying *I* didn't think of Ava when I burned down that building. Well, I did, Hans, and I shouldn't have to explain that to you."

"Ava doesn't need a mother who's in prison."

"Better a mother with convictions than one of these passive sheep. She'll understand when she's older."

*No, I won't!* I wanted to shout, and my father seemed to sense that because he turned and saw me standing in the doorway.

"Good morning, darling," he said cheerfully, all the hushed anxiety dropped from his voice.

My mother turned around, startled by my existence. "Why aren't you at school yet?" she snapped.

"It's Sunday."

She shook her head. "I—know that. I want you to go to Georg and Margarita's today."

"I was going to meet Paedar."

"You can see Paedar at school," she said. "You shouldn't be wasting your time with him. God, he looks like a Hitler Youth."

"Mother!"

"Well, it's true. He's too much like your trained puppy, Ava. It's not healthy for either of you, for his heart or your ego."

"You're right, Mother. Heaven forbid I get the impression that I was pretty or worth a damn."

"Godsakes, who is your mother? Because I'd swear I couldn't raise such an image-obsessed, primping little—"

"That's enough." My father stood and touched my arm, kissing me on the forehead. "Your mother and I have some business to manage today, darling. And you haven't visited Georg and Margarita for ages."

I exhaled. "Yes, Father, all right."

I didn't grumble because I figured if I had to go to Georg and Margarita's, I could get them to tell me what was going on. They don't have children, and they don't really subscribe to the idea that children need to be kept in ignorance all the time. And anyway, I like visiting Georg and Margarita's because they have money and, unlike my parents, actually believe in spending it. They have the most beautiful wooden and white leather furnishings, and candy hidden in dishes throughout the flat, and a cream-colored BMW. Georg has old money, the kind protected in underground vaults dug before the war.

Georg and Margarita are at least twenty years older than my parents. They call themselves old family friends, but I know they actually met my parents in one of the smoky basement cafés where all clandestine rumblings happen in East Berlin.

When I arrived at their apartment, the manicured living room was as I had never seen it. I was immediately accosted by old-fashioned pop music blaring from the record player, books scattered on the floor, files strewn about coffee tables, and papers shredded in random piles on the carpet.

"What's going on?" I shouted over the music.

Georg looked up from where he'd started to rip up a copy of my mother's dissident newspaper, *Der Brandstifter*. He let the pieces fall from his hands and shot a finger to his lips, shushing me. He walked over, grabbing me by the arm and closing the door.

"We think they're on to us," Georg whispered close to my ear.

"You're being monitored?" I whispered back.

"We're all but certain."

I understood then that the music was meant to drown out electronic listening devices planted in the flat.

"How do you know?"

"Margarita misplaced her silver watch," Georg explained. "At the scene of a . . . well, an implicating crime."

"What crime?" I asked.

"I would tell you but your mother would flay me," he said. "We've searched everywhere for it. It was monogrammed. If she left it there, we are surely being watched, at the very least. Here, start ripping things up." He shoved a pile of papers at me, and I began tearing them up, lists and correspondence and a map of the world with red dots placed over random cities and towns. I saw the newspaper Georg had been about to rip, *Der Brandstifter*. Georg must not have known that I'm aware my mother writes this, or he'd probably have hidden it from me. I'd never gotten my hands on a copy before.

> *On Saturday night, the Eagle and the Nightingale infiltrated the annual Stasi Ball at the Palast der Republik. The Nightingale lured away the respectable and noted "family man," Senior Minister Lars Richenbach, where she deftly slipped an arsenic tablet into his drink and watched him fumble for breath until dead. Meanwhile, the Eagle, dressed as a waiter, did the same to as many as twenty champagne glasses. The Arsonist is pleased to report that the Senior Minister has gone on to face the wrath of the Creator he doesn't believe in. May he enjoy the warm climate in his new living arrangements, and may we rejoice that he will never block another citizen from fleeing to freedom again.*
>
> *GDR head of state and all-around party pooper, Erich Honecker, was among the first to discover his com-*

*rade's body, at which point he stood before the invited guests (after checking in a mirror to pomade his hair) and vowed, "We will eliminate the scum who committed this atrocity." Dear Erich, if we are scum, that makes you sewage. The apologist American ambassador and his wife also fell prey to the Eagle's and the Nightingale's arsenic cocktails before the night was done. The Arsonist has received word that the Eagle and the Nightingale snuck beneath the noses of those fearsome Stasi guards without incident.*

I immediately recognized the sarcasm of my own mother's voice in the writing. Georg must have been the Eagle, and that made Margarita the Nightingale. I hadn't heard about this on the news, but it's not unusual for the government to suppress information, especially an event that might incite dissidents.

The more I thought about what I'd just read, the more my hands shook around the newspaper. Georg and Margarita are murderers. They join my mother in that distinction. My father may be the only adult I know who hasn't killed someone.

I didn't think this was what the Cold War was supposed to be. Wasn't this meant to be a bloodless war? If anybody dies, it won't be on any battlefields, but beneath the rays of a nuclear bomb. It feels . . . old-fashioned, I suppose, to poison someone's champagne, to burn a building down around them. The world has moved on, but my mother hasn't.

- - - - -

November 12, 1986

After school, my parents were tearing through the house. Wagner blared from the record player and the living room was groaning with stifling heat. My mother crouched in front of the fireplace, stoking a blazing fire. She reached to the bookshelf and heaved an armload of books into the flames.

"Mother, what are you doing?" I asked.

My mother stopped jabbing the burning books but didn't turn to look at me. "Go ask your father," she said.

I ran to my parents' bedroom where I found my father leaning over their dresser, carefully placing folded socks into a suitcase sitting on the bed.

"Father, what's going on?"

"Ava," he said, smiling wanly. "Come sit beside me." He waited until I was seated before lifting a piece of paper from the bureau and offering it to me. "Georg brought this by today. It's been distributed around all the Stasi offices."

It was a small placard, printed with four faces—my mother, my father, Georg, and Margarita. Beneath, there was a fact sheet about the crimes they were each accused of. According to this, Georg and Margarita could be traced to fifteen deaths between them, including those of the senior minister and American ambassador who died of arsenic poisoning at the Stasi ball. My mother was linked to five, and my father was accused of being accomplice to each of my mother's crimes.

"We might be arrested any minute," he said. "We've decided it's time to attempt our escape."

"But they know your faces."

"Your mother will create fake papers with new names. We have to try."

"When?"

"Saturday," he said. "We need time to make the papers and get things in order. We're planning for several possibilities." He pulled out a map, marked with red dots like the map I'd ripped up at Georg and Margarita's. The dots marked cities scattered across the world. I spotted Geneva, Dover, a city in the Middle East, that tiny island off the coast of Italy that I always forget the name of, Melbourne, somewhere in the south of France, Buenos Aires, and a city in California.

"How will I fake being American?" I asked. "Or Italian? Or French?"

"We'll hide out for a while. Learn the language. And when they ask, say your German grandmother taught you to speak. We'll decide where we're going once we're out of the country. The Wall is the most dangerous part. If one of us is captured— well, we want to make sure they don't have any information to give."

"In case they're tortured, you mean."

"Yes," he answered honestly.

"But how will they know which rendezvous point to go to, if they're left behind?"

My father swallowed. "Ava, it's very important that you do exactly what I'm about to say. When you get beyond the Wall, you start running. Even if I'm behind the Wall still. Even if all of us are. Do not come back for us, understand?" My father's voice was firm, and there was something intense inside it.

I blinked. "Yes, Father."

"We've also decided it's safest if we pretend you're Georg and Margarita's child, just in the documents." I opened my mouth to protest, but he stopped me. "They'll be looking for a younger couple with a teenage daughter. We have to throw them off the scent. And it means that, if anything did happen, Georg and Margarita would be in a position to care for you without arousing suspicion. We'll still be a family, so don't give me that face. When we decide where we're going, you'll get a new name, too, and it's very important that your old name never be spoken again. Give it a little burial in your mind. Say a few words about how well it has served you. And afterward, forget you ever heard it."

"Why are you telling me this now?" I asked. "Why not wait till we get to our new home?"

"There is a chance—however small—that we could be separated. It's very unlikely, but I want you to be prepared."

"I'm not afraid," I said.

My father cocked a small, sad smile. "Oh, darling, no matter what your mother says, we must be afraid now. Wherever we go, the Stasi will be hunting us. Men like Werner, they won't just give up after we've crossed the border. We will be running for the rest of our lives, I fear."

I leaned back on the bed, my feet pinned beneath me. To any other person, this would have been terrifying information, but it sat somewhat satisfyingly in my chest.

I must be particularly suited to running.

# Pepper

*Human Anatomy*

Dear Ms. Eldridge,

Thanks for your prompt reply. I appreciate your advice about keeping my chin up, but in truth, I don't feel as though my chin will ever face upward again. You see, when I screw up and make an embarrassment of myself, I wonder, "Is this what my dad busted his hind to bring me to America for?" It is burdensome, being the sole source of hope for your entire bloodline. It makes me want to put my head down and sleep my life away. It makes me wonder what I would be if we'd never come here.

The times I miss Kuwait the most is summer. This is an unusual answer, because summertime in Kuwait is hotter than the asscrack of the sun. But that's when the country grows quiet. People empty out of the towns and head to where it's cooler and the beaches are cleaner and everyone goes swimming with dolphins (at least this is what I imagined, because we always had to stay in the summer for my dad's job). Before we moved away, I never thought about my country. America was inevitable from the time I was a baby. We spent all those years straddling Kuwait awkwardly, one foot on and one foot off, just waiting till we had the visas to go to the United States. But before we were to leave, I walked out of our house, onto the still warm pavement of the street, and looked to the east, where the palm trees and pointing fingers of high-rises and minarets were etched over the orange sky, where across the quiet morning, the call to prayer echoed from the loudspeakers on the mosque in town, the song weaving between buildings straight to my ears. It was so much that I found myself crying. I was sad about leaving, but mostly I was sad about the person I was leaving behind. Because surely, I would not be the same once I stepped off the plane. I wondered who I would be.

Ms. Eldridge, that little kid had such high hopes for himself. He'd go on to dream about becoming president one day. And this is why I can never point my chin in an upward direction again. Because the person I was in that interview with Petra couldn't be further from that dream.

In this essay I have chosen to speak about Human Anatomy. Is it not incredible the way my brain tells my fingers to type on my laptop and my fingers obey? A person begins to get the idea that they control their own body. That is, until suddenly when, without warning, their brain remembers Petra's interview, and their chest squeezes until there's a wondering if their heart is imploding. It is beyond unfair. I feel as though, as the owner of this body, I should be able to operate it as I wish.

But never mind, Ms. Eldridge. I don't need to dwell on Petra or the interview.

I have a brilliant new life plan, which is that I am going to avoid people for the next few dozen years. There was only one obstacle impeding my plan. That thing was called graduation. The school told me they would still let me walk in graduation with my classmates, but the idea made me feel like throwing things. I wondered what advice you would give me. And I realized the answer was straight in front of me. Research, yes? The scientific method and all of that.

My report is as follows:

Question: Will the consumption of expectorant have the desired effect of becoming so ill one is permitted to avoid graduation without arousing the suspicion of one's father who still has no idea that his son is a major screwup?

Ingredients:

One 4 oz. bottle of ipecac purchased from the Internet

One strong desire to avoid a pressing social engagement

One fully functioning stomach

Results: The subject took the recommended two tablespoons of ipecac, after which practically nothing happened, though the doorbell did ring and the postman dropped the mail through the slot, and the subject needed to fetch it as his seizure pug is known to chew the important bills. In the mail was a package addressed to the subject, Pepper Al-Yusef, and inside was an old paperback book that must have been mailed to him by mistake.

Foreshadowing: this will be important later, Ms. Eldridge.

On returning to the bathroom, still feeling zero effects, the subject determined the ipecac was likely old and diluted, so a second trial was conducted with:

One additional tablespoon of ipecac.

Results: It was not a minute later that the subject sensed something come alive inside his guts, a three-headed dragon-shaped thing that forced the subject to the floor, his face pressed against the tile, and commenced spewing liquidized Pop-Tarts from his gullet with the force of a fire hose.

His trusty seizure pug, Bertrand, bolted from the bathroom, proving definitively that he is the most pointless service puppy the world has ever known.

Fun Facts: Vomiting can be described as violent convulsions of the diaphragm, which causes stomach contents to be expelled through the mouth. This can be delayed if the upper esophageal sphincter refuses to relax.

Additionally, the word sphincter is humorous.

Vomiting releases endorphins into the bloodstream, causing the vomiter to feel pleasant.

After the vomiting finally subsided, many minutes later, I indeed did experience a sense of invincibility, a feeling that only people such as Superman and Iron Man and God feel. I have never felt this before, Ms. Eldridge, and the feeling was almost worth the vomit.

My dad patted my head and said he was sorry I was unwell but since I was better now and the graduation ceremony was probably already over, he was going to take advantage of the warm day to try to catch a sunfish, and I was left alone with nothing but my powerfulness, which was bigger than my body, bigger than my house, and begged to get out into the open air. I swished tea water from the warm kettle in my mouth and changed my T-shirt. Still feeling almost heroic, I swung the front door open to discover Shawn on the other side.

He took a step backward onto his phalanges (translation: his toe bones). There was a moment of wordlessness when Shawn patted his hair in the way he does when he's nervous.

"Everybody missed you today," he said.

Bertrand was pulling on his leash to go outside, but my brain was burning up with the last time I saw Shawn, when he yelled at me not to throw my life away, which was the worst thing anyone has ever said to me.

"Are you okay?" Shawn asked. "You look really pale."

"Why did you come here?" I said.

His eyebrows went up. "Are we not friends anymore? I don't even get what your problem is, other than me calling you on your bullshit, which I've been doing our entire friendship."

"Yeah, and maybe I am sick of it," I said, slamming the front door behind me.

"Well, then, fine. We're not married or anything. But you're not allowed to go all silent treatment."

At that precise moment, Bertrand pulled his leash out of my hand and squatted on the lawn directly in front of us, doing his unspeakables. I sat down on the porch and put my forehead on my knees, the feeling of powerfulness draining away from me.

"Dude, are you crying?" he asked.

"No," came my muffled reply.

"It's okay if you are."

"I'm not."

My esophageal sphincter, which had already been through enough today, clenched into a ball. I didn't know how to tell Shawn the truth, which is I don't want to be around him right now, and I don't know why. The closest I can get is that he is my best friend, but he's the best friend I had in high school. He could have been my best friend after high school, too, but that is not going to happen. Shawn's got his shit together, and I don't even have *shit* to get together. (This is figurative language, Ms. Eldridge, and not anatomically accurate. Please do not deduct points.)

"Some girl was looking for you," Shawn said.

I glanced up slowly. This was most definitely a sentence no one had ever uttered to me.

"I didn't recognize her," Shawn continued. "She wanted to know where to find you. She had a copy of your interview with a big red circle around your face, like a stalker."

This was extremely strange information to be receiving. "Well, did you get her number or anything?"

"No," Shawn said. "She could've been a psycho freak. I probably saved your life."

An irritated puff of air left my lips. "Why even come by if you didn't have anything real to say?"

"Oh, I'm sorry to bother you. You're obviously *so* busy."

I felt the vessels in my face burn with hot blood. "You don't know everything about me, Shawn."

"I actually *do* know everything about you. Like how the only reason you're acting like this is because you got your pride squashed by that bitchmeister Petra and now you're acting like someone else. Someone who shrugs."

I scoffed. "Shrugs?"

"Someone who doesn't give a shit. But giving a shit is practically who you are. I know you're embarrassed about what happened, but that's what you do. You tell your secrets to a perfect stranger."

"You make me sound desperate," I told him.

"Well, you kind of are," he said.

I stood, unconsciously pushing out my sternum as I'd seen male gorillas do. "You wanna get off my porch? If all you're going to do is insult my soul."

"If you're gonna be offended by everything I say, sure, I'll leave. I'm missing my own graduation party being here."

"Well, you wouldn't want to miss your *party*." I said this as though having a party was only something eight-year-old girls do. "Actually, I think I'll just leave," I said, and pushed past him down the street, Bertrand following behind.

My heart was aching, the ventricles and the arteries, the blood even, tugging at me to go back to where my best friend was standing, hands limp at his sides. You know what that feels like? When you can hear every cell in your body scream in their shrill, miniature voices to turn around, and you ignore them?

It feels like being a complete asshole.

I wound my way to the boardwalk and found myself heading to the Cyber Café. You may have seen it, a long rectangular space that's totally dark inside but for computer monitors and purple neon light strips running along the ceiling. Most of the people here are teenagers, playing Shieldcraft, who breathe through their mouths and could generally use some Chapstick.

Just as I was pushing through the glass doors, I heard some notes from the karaoke joint next door. Someone was absolutely butchering "Karma Chameleon," and the sound was making me pause.

It's hard to explain why I did what I did next. My muscles were still feeling punchy, my mind muddled from the conversation with Shawn, and my judgment must've been impaired because it occurred to me that I could do a way better job at singing than the idiot screeching from the karaoke bar. I'm a badass. I have an esophageal sphincter to rival the gods. I could make everyone throw their underpants at me, which sounded disgusting but was also the sign of a true rock star. If Shawn heard about it, even he'd have no choice but to respect me.

I turned away from the Cyber Café and wrenched open the karaoke bar's glass door.

Inside, sprawled out on vinyl couches, were several sunburned tourist families, most with some kind of aquarium-related item pinned to their person. The guy standing up onstage appeared to be the dad of some extremely embarrassed-looking pre-teens.

"Three bucks a song," said the bored-looking DJ, a girl with a shiny black bowl cut and a stud in her nose, leaning near a computer.

"I—I don't know what to sing," I said. Clearly, I hadn't thought this plan all the way through.

"I'll do a random selection from the greatest hits."

She wiggled her fingers at me and I fumbled in my back pocket for the money. When the dad finished his song, the DJ leaned down toward a microphone. "Everybody please welcome Kaylynn, singing a medley of songs from *Beauty and the Beast*."

I perched on a sticky-looking couch beside a family whose young daughter leaped to the stage, singing and spinning around in a purple dress. Now that I had a minute to consider what I was doing, I didn't know if it was the best idea. I mean, Shawn wasn't even here. And, as I scanned the room, there was not a single person whose underwear I'd even want to see, let alone have flung at me.

"Up next singing the disco classic 'I Will Survive,' please give a warm round of applause for . . . Pepper?" the DJ girl said uncertainly, reading the card where I'd written my name.

A smattering of applause rang out. I stood and pulled on

Bertrand's leash a few times, but he didn't want to leave the comfort of the couch, so I went on the low stage alone.

Piano strings started tinkling, and above, a spinning light scattered multicolored circles across the stage. On a screen in front of me, the first line of the song appeared, and disappeared just as quickly. I started singing along, and the true horror of my decision crashed around me. I was getting about every other word ("Crumble . . . die . . . survive . . . hey hey!"). In the near audience, the girl who'd just been singing Disney songs looked at me with a horrified expression, her mouth hanging open and a row of little crooked teeth visible.

Just when I was hoping some ancient god would throw a lightning bolt into the karaoke place, just to end this disaster, the door burst open. Standing in the doorway was not an ancient god but a redheaded girl, haloed by the setting sun. She strode into the room and held out a rigid finger bone, directly aligned with my forehead.

"IT'S YOU!" she shouted, so loudly her voice was picked up by the microphone on the DJ's podium.

Everyone in the place turned to look at this weird, pasty girl.

"Excuse me!" she shouted. "I need to talk to you. Can you turn that off?" she asked the DJ.

The DJ scoffed but halted the music.

"You're Pepper Al-Yusef," the girl stated.

The disco lights still whirled in my face, painting me with stained-glass colors. "Um," I said into the microphone. "Yes."

"I've been reading about you," she said, holding up the copy of the *Complacent Sparrow*. And there, just like Shawn described, my face was circled with red marker.

I always knew I would be famous for something, Ms. Eldridge, if not for becoming president then for something equally cool, such as body-building or Olympic-level badassery, soon to become an official sport. However, I was not expecting my rise to fame to be so soon, and certainly not from that article.

"Can I help you with something?" I asked the girl, in my politest tones, once we had stepped outside. The girl was clearly unhinged. I had to be delicate. I needed to not hurt her feelings, and also avoid being stabbed.

"I can't believe I found you," she said. Her eyes roved over my features as if she were trying to memorize them.

"Oookay," I said. "How did you find me?"

"I went to your school and talked to your friend, the cranky one, and he told me you hang out at the Cyber Café. You weren't in there, but then I heard the singing from next door, and when I checked it out, there you were."

The girl was rising off of her feet a little with every other word, and I saw now that she had a cast on her foot, white, with no signatures.

"Sorry," I said. "Who are you?"

Her forehead creased. "My name's Molly," she said slowly, as though I should know that. "I was sent this." She held up my interview again. The words "HE HAS THE ANSWERS" were written beneath my face. This was a very strange sentence. Most often, I don't even have the answers to my math homework. A precarious feeling was working its way through my chest.

"So," she said, "you have some answers for me?"

I shook my head. "I'm sorry. I don't have anything for you."

The girl's features changed in microscopic ways, ticking beneath the surface like something mechanical, so I knew she was trying really hard not to show what she was actually feeling.

"Are you okay?" I asked her.

"Yes!" she snapped, her cheeks filling with pink. "Actually, no, not at all. My mother sent me this, and it's the first clue I've had in years, and you *must* know something." Her eyes grew desperate, and for some reason, at that moment, something clicked together in my mind. I had memorized her features, in a weird way, staring at a photograph in a gold frame that had hung on the wall of my house most of my life.

She looked exactly like her father.

"You're—" I gasped. "You're Molly Mavity."

She stared, unblinking.

I let out a breath of a laugh. "I've been wanting to meet you for a long time."

"So, what do you know about my mother?"

"I—nothing! Only that she killed herself in France." All of the details of Winston Mavity's personal life had circulated on the news after his arrest.

"She didn't kill herself!" Molly shouted.

"All right," I said, taking a step back. "Then I don't know anything about your mother. But I knew your dad, like it says in the interview."

Her eyes twitched to the *Complacent Sparrow* in her hand. "My dad?"

"Yeah, the American soldier," I said, nervous that this information was going to make things worse. "He saved my life when I was born. That's why I always wanted to meet you. I'm alive because of him, and you could say you're alive because of him, too."

Her face remained fierce, and I winced, waiting for her to snap.

"You think this . . . this man in this interview, who saved your life, was my dad?"

Fact: The human voice is caused by folds in the larynx pushing together and forming vibrations when breath from the lungs is passed over it. The girl's larynx made her sound perplexed and angry all at the same time.

"I know my dad fought in the Gulf War," she said. "But I never knew he saved anybody's life."

"Well," I said, "he did."

She looked around the street. "You're positive you didn't get any kind of clue, like in the mail or something?"

"I never get anything in the mail—" I cut off, remembering earlier today and my vomiting experiment. "Actually, wait. I got a book in the mail this morning."

"A book?" she asked, as though a book was something to be

really hopeful about. "What was it called? Was there a note?"

"I don't know. It was just a book. I figured someone mailed it to me by mistake."

"Take me there," she said. "Right now."

As we walked the several blocks to my house, I snuck small sideways glances at Molly, at the sliver of her hard-set pale face, at the poof of her hair that rose off her head like waves of intense thought. Ms. Eldridge, did you know you can tell lots about someone, based merely on their face bones? Truly, you can pick up a skull, Hamlet style, and discern their gender, and their family history, and even if they ate a lot of meat. Because I'm a scientist, I could tell, just by examining Molly and the arrangement of her cheeks and her jaw and her mouth, something I think she keeps secret from everyone else:

Molly Mavity may just be the saddest person in the universe.

Molly squinted in the sunlight and lowered her eyes to Bertrand where, at our feet, he was making the constant stuck-drain sound of his breathing.

"This is Bertrand, by the way. He's my seizure pug."

"You have epilepsy?"

"A little bit," I said.

"A little bit of epilepsy?"

"Epilepsy which isn't anymore so much bad." This girl was freaking me out. My English always sucks balls when I'm nervous.

"Why is he a pug?" she asked.

"He was born a pug."

"But aren't seizure dogs usually golden retrievers or something?"

"Oh. The organization that gave him to me apparently got a surplus of pugs after the county busted a puppy mill operation. He was supposed to be some rich lady's lapdog, but instead he works for me. In a way."

My dad's car and his rattling tin boat were absent from the driveway when we arrived at my house. Inside, Molly's eyes skipped from the enormous fish tanks to the kitchen table where the book lay, still in the torn envelope.

"*The Arsonist,* by Ava Dreyman," she read, pronouncing the last name like "Dry-man," then started flipping through the pages. "My mother never talked about this. I wonder why she wants me to have it."

The cover illustration was of a match burning with a huge, tear-shaped flame. The page edges were bright yellow, like old books are sometimes.

"But your mother's—"

"She's not dead. Why does everybody say that!" With determined calm, she took a breath. "My mother is not dead. You know how you just know some things? In your bones, deep down into your marrow?"

Marrow: a substance that lives inside each bone in the human body. It is pink and important. I didn't read the whole Wikipedia article, but I figured out pretty easily that marrow has nothing to say about dead mothers.

"Well," she continued, "I can say with complete certainty that my mother is not dead."

"All right, let's go with that theory," I said. "Why would she want you to have this book?"

Molly stuck her lips out. "This girl, Ava Dreyman, she'd be about my mother's age. Maybe . . ."

"What?"

"Maybe this girl is my mother."

"Did your mother look like this?" I pulled the book from her hands and showed her the back cover where a photo of the teenaged Ava Dreyman was printed. The girl's heavy bangs hung just over her eyebrows and her head was slightly turned, as though distracted by something out of frame.

"Sort of," she said. "Maybe. It's kind of hard to see with her hair covering her face. But I know she's involved in this somehow. You're just gonna have to trust me on that."

I paused, not saying what I wanted to say, even though every nerve within my frame was aching to point out how little sense her theory made.

I handed the book back to Molly. She sat in my dad's dusty armchair and started reading, and I got out my laptop and did a search.

"*The Arsonist* was first printed in 1989, several months before the fall of the Berlin Wall," I read aloud. "The diary documents the life of teenager Ava Dreyman, one of East Germany's most well-known historical figures. Chronicled inside are Dreyman's final years, before she was martyred inside of a torture chamber at the hands of the Stasi, the East German secret police. After its publication, Dreyman became known as 'the Anne Frank of the Cold War,' a symbol of the resistance that, among other factors, motivated the people of both East and West Germany to bring down the Berlin Wall."

I typed the word "martyred" into an online dictionary.

Martyr: an individual who is put to death or endures great suffering as a result of a belief, principle, or cause.

"Why's it called *The Arsonist*?" I asked.

She flicked through the beginning of the book. "It looks like Ava Dreyman's mother burns down a government building."

"Is her mother even a very important character?" I asked, scrolling through the Wikipedia entry. "It says here she disappears after the first couple of chapters."

Molly just shrugged and kept reading. I scrolled to the bottom of the page. It said the diary cuts off right after Ava is locked in a Stasi torture chamber. She's just been stabbed by an officer named Captain Werner, who sits opposite her at a table like he's enjoying some afternoon tea. *"Please excuse the bloody fingerprints covering the page. He wanted me seated, and when I said no, he got me seated by shoving the knife in my ribs."*

This Ava girl was intense, Ms. Eldridge. How she managed to record all this while slowly bleeding to death, I don't know.

"I don't think this book has anything to do with you or me," I said. "I've never even heard of this lady. Someone just bought it online and the seller mailed it to the wrong address."

"You're wrong," Molly said, a blazing look in her eyes. "Look."

She held the book open to the frail title page. In red, someone had written, *Molly and Pepper, here is where to start.*

My skeleton started shuddering. Molly's mouth opened into the barest of smiles. "See?" she said. "You did have the answers."

"But . . . what answers?" I asked. "To what questions?"

She considered this. "We should start by reading the book."

"Yeah," I said, less certainty in my voice. My eyes fell on her face, how peculiarly she looked like her dad. "I should show you something."

I went into my dad's bedroom, past his bed draped in the embroidered bedcovering that he brought from Kuwait, and pulled open his bottom dresser drawer. I fumbled beneath a pile of folded scarves of my mother's. I do not like touching them normally because they cause my backbone to shiver, but I had no choice. My fingers found the cold edge of a framed photograph.

When I brought it back to her, Molly studied it. My father's face was covered with the black lines of oil, Winston's was unmovable and fierce, and at the center, the sleeping bundle of me in my father's arms.

"They're almost our age here," she whispers. "I always pictured my dad so much older."

I squinted at the photo. I'd always viewed my dad in this photo as a grown-up, but Molly was right. He was young here. The idea was, for some reason, startling.

Though I cannot imagine a future for myself, the one thing I now know for sure is this: One day, I'll look just like him.

I put the picture back in the drawer, facedown.

# Molly

Pepper,

On the day we meet, I walk back from your house and think about myths. I've grown up around myths, and I guess you have as well, what with the story of your birth. My myth was about how my parents met. My mother had read about my father, Winston, in a newspaper, the soldier who returned from war with oil in his lungs and sand-burned eyes. She recognized something so deep and charged in his photograph, she knew that she needed to meet him.

My mother had read all of the Nancy Drew books. She knew how to persuade people that she belonged someplace merely by the way she walked. This, as it turns out, extended even to breaking into military hospitals. She bought a candy-striper dress and sauntered right through the front door.

My father lay in a bed in an empty ward, his eyes covered with gauze. His face was rippled from the heat of oil fires. His red hair was growing out of a buzz cut.

The sound of my mother's footsteps echoed over the ward's vinyl floor.

"Who's there?" My father's voice rang out across the room.

"My name's Clarisse," she replied.

My father was silent for a long moment. She was standing near him now, and he reached out, his fingers touching the empty air.

"Nice to meet you, Clarisse," he said.

"Nice to meet you, Winston."

This is the myth that made me.

But how does that myth, of a girl so in love with a picture, she'd break into a military hospital, connect to the people I grew up around? Before we left for Nice, they could barely have a conversation without a strange, unnamed tension creeping in.

"Where'd you go last night?" my mother would ask, after he started coming home with brown sickles of gasoline beneath his fingernails.

And my father would stare at his oatmeal, and his silence would say everything there was to say.

"You smell like smoke," she'd say coldly.

"So do you," he'd reply. My eyes darted between the two of them, uncomprehending. My mother didn't smell like smoke. She smelled of lily perfume and salt water.

When they thought I was asleep, that's when they really fought. I'd find them, sitting in our straight-backed kitchen chairs, heads leaning together, whispering angrily. They never yelled. Somehow, the whispering was worse.

*The Arsonist* is a kind of myth, too. This book turned a girl into something unreal, someone we talk about as though she wasn't once a living person who breathed through lungs and ate with ordinary molars and walked with the same bones that we all have.

When I open the front door of my house, my aunt is sitting at the kitchen table beside Marty. My aunt's hair is a darker shade of red than either mine or my father's, tied back in a bun, and she's teaching Marty how to do something with a cookbook.

I sit in the kitchen chair beside him. "Going to cook us something?"

"Turkey linguine," Marty says.

"Yum," I say.

"You want to know something? I once bought an entire truck of turkeys with a false check," Marty says. "I got arrested and thrown in the slammer, and it was there that I met Ronnie Reagan. First thing he asked me—what did you think you were gonna do with all those turkeys?"

"Marty, is that story true?" Auntie Ro asks, because she can't stop doing her job, even though Marty's not her patient anymore.

"Partly," he says. "At least partly, it is."

"What part?"

He considers. "I've eaten turkey before."

You've never met Marty. He's sixty-something with a neat gray beard and wiry hair that I imagine could grow to Einstein-level proportions if he didn't clip it.

"So what happened the other night?" Auntie Ro asks me. "With Margaret and the girls?"

"Nothing," I say.

"Nothing? Even though you came tearing through the house, without Margaret, even though I expressly instructed her to keep you by her—"

"Margaret's younger than me. She shouldn't have to be my babysitter."

"She's not your babysitter, she's your family. I wouldn't want any of my kids walking around downtown at night alone."

I don't say anything about the fact that Margaret disappears fairly regularly to have sex with boys she meets in the smoking area of the public school parking lot.

"Oh, and Molly, I want you to finally clear out the storage locker," my aunt says. "No more evading. I'm tired of paying fifty bucks a month just to store your dad's old junk."

When my father was arrested, all our belongings were packed up and put in a storage locker. The house on Syracuse Road was sold to cover his debts. That was almost five years ago.

"And you need to visit him, at least one last time," my aunt continues. "You're never going to get another chance once he's dead."

I shut my eyes and dig the heels of my hands into my eye sockets. The best word to describe my aunt is blunt. Blunt like blunt-force trauma.

Marty leans over and gives me a gentle shove with his shoulder. "What's that book you've got?" he asks, looking at it on the table. *"The Arsonist,"* he pronounces, scratching his fingernails through his beard. "Never heard of it."

"Have you read it, Auntie Ro?" I ask.

"Everyone read it when it came out," she says. "It was a best-seller."

"Did my parents ever talk about this book?" I ask.

My aunt narrows her eyes as if wondering why I might be reading a book about an arsonist. "Not that I remember," she says.

After dinner, after Marty departs on the bus and he leaves me with a little nugget of his strange wisdom ("Keep your chin up. Your auntie likes you, even if it seems like she only loves you."), I go up to my room and finish reading *The Arsonist*. Then, I go back to the beginning and read it again into the early hours of the morning. I stare at each word for at least three seconds, try-ing to decode what my mother wants me to understand.

Pepper, I can't figure it out.

I carry the book in between my teeth as I climb up from my window onto the roof. It's still dark when I sit on the roofline, legs stretched before me, but there is something in the colorless sky that hints at dawn. I pull my phone from my cast where I've taken to storing it, and start searching online for Ava Drey-man. There are plenty of conspiracy theories, the most com-mon that the book was a complete work of fiction written by dissidents trying to unite an ambivalent East Germany to revolt against the government.

The most compelling piece of evidence for this theory is that Ava's original diary has never been located. Shortly after the first printing, it was stolen from the desk of Paedar Kiefer, Ava's former boyfriend.

But according to records and many firsthand accounts, Ava Dreyman *did* exist. She was born in a hospital in East Berlin on December 8, 1972. She attended school, and was a member of an amateur volleyball league. Her schoolmates even say they saw her carry around a white leather diary.

I turn on my phone's flashlight and flip through the book again, to the last page, where Ava is killed. A poisonous, dark feeling fills my chest. This girl was our age, and she died alone and afraid. It happened years and years ago, but it feels real, even now.

I turn the page and spot something I missed before, a note from the editor. When I see what someone has written there, all of my blood floods my face, turning my cheeks hot.

A thick line of red marker is drawn around a sentence near the bottom. It reads, *"Who killed Ava Dreyman?"*

"Oh my God," I say. My body freezes and, like a switch being flicked, an explosion of hot adrenaline stiffens my veins. I read the editor's note from the beginning.

*We are left with so many unanswered questions about the death of Ava Dreyman. All reference to her in official documents disappears after she fled the Berlin Wall at age fourteen. We do know that in 1989, at age seventeen, Ava returned to the GDR under the name Sally Bailey. She was subsequently taken to a torture chamber where, according to her diary, she was stabbed with Captain Heinrich Werner's bone-handle knife. No body was ever discovered. (The Stasi routinely performed clandestine cremations, and it is a popular theory that Werner used a crematory furnace to dispose of her remains.) Werner, one of the most infamous members of the Ministry of State Security, fled to Argentina soon after the Wall fell.*

*Who killed Ava Dreyman? At the time of this printing, no arrests have been made in Ava's death, though an official police investigation was conducted soon after reunification.*

My fingers tremble as I dial your phone number.

"Hello?" you croak. I can tell you've been sleeping.

"I've found something," I say.

I can hear sheets rustle through the phone. "What did you find?" you ask in a kind of annoyed way that reminds me it's not even light out yet.

"A message," I say slowly, "from my mother." I read the passage aloud, repeating the line circled in red. *"Who killed Ava Dreyman?"*

Your breath crackles against the phone speaker. "Your mother wants us to find out how some girl from Germany died?"

"Yeah," I say. "I think that's exactly what we're supposed to do."

You go quiet for a while. "But, it already says this Captain Werner guy did it. Ava describes him stabbing her."

"If it was that easy, then it must not've been him," I say. "Or—maybe it *was* him, but there's never been enough proof."

"So, we're just supposed to find a phone book from Argentina and call up an international fugitive?" you ask. "Do you even speak German?"

"No," I say. "But he probably speaks English, right?"

"Eh," you say. It's a reluctant sound, which makes me wonder if your next words are going to be something like, *Good luck with that.*

But you clear your throat. "Okay," you say. "I'll see what I can find. But in the morning. Need sleep now. Good night." The call clicks off.

The sun peeks over the horizon behind me, catching on the bay and reflecting back at me, so I have to squint, unexpectedly. I close my eyes, and sunlight bleeds through my eyelids anyway until it feels like all of my insides are being warmed. My mother's face comes into my head, and for the first time in maybe months, my mouth turns up at the sides in a smile.

"Good night."

# Ava

November 20, 1986

Today, Paedar walked me home from school, through the tall apartment blocks of Friedrichstadt, all colored in a mosaic of newspaper grays. A row of pigeons was cooing in the window frames of a concrete apartment block. Why they have to make every new building from concrete, I will never understand. The whole walk Paedar had been glancing over at me in the soft-eyed way he does when he's about to try to kiss me. Most of the time I let him because everybody knows he's the handsomest boy in school, though my mother's Hitler Youth comment isn't far off the mark. His hair is almost white and his eyes are a kind of light blue that would be cold in a different face.

"My parents are acting strange," I told him.

"Stranger than usual?" He laughed at his own joke and steered us toward the park where I knew he'd push me against a tree and rub his soft face against mine, but I grabbed his wrist.

"They're talking about getting out of Berlin for a while."

He halted. "For how long?"

"Maybe forever."

His mouth fell open. "Forever!"

"It's not good here for my family. The Stasi are asking questions."

"But, Ava, you can't just leave. My heart would never recover."

I shook my head. I have no pretensions that Paedar is the great love of my life. He's a distraction, a nice one, with his straight teeth and hair parted with a metric precision. But I think it might be impossible to love someone with no flaws. Like trying to climb a mountain with no footholds.

"Paedar, your heart will be fine," I told him. "In a month you'll find another girl."

"How can you say such a thing?" he said. A furrow had formed between his eyes, cleaving his perfect forehead in two.

"Don't just stand there," I said, annoyed. "I have to be home in ten minutes."

"I refuse to go on until you promise me you'll stop this silliness. Even if your parents leave, you can't go with them."

"And where am I supposed to go? I can't live on my own."

"We'll run away together. Into the forest, like lovers from a story. Anything, just so long as we're together."

Paedar is the kind of person who takes the job of being fifteen very seriously. He isn't going to miss a single opportunity to act like it. He clutched my hands in his and kneeled.

I wrenched myself from his grasp. "Paedar, don't be dramatic. People will stare."

He stood, his eyes blazing with blue ferocity. "Ava, you don't understand!" he said. "You own my heart. No—more than that. You set *fire* to my heart."

I stopped trying to lean away. He looked idiotic, but there was also something sincere inside his pained expression.

"I set fire to your heart?" I repeated slowly. "How are you alive with your heart on fire?"

"That's how your heart is supposed to be," he said, "engulfed in flames. I've never been so alive. I'll die if you go."

My eyes wandered to his chest. There, yes, I could see it behind the rafters of his ribs, an orange glow that got brighter with every heartbeat. I lifted my hand to hover above his chest. It was warm. *Hot.* I had to whip my hand away and resist the impulse to blow on my fingers.

"And me leaving would—do what? Make your heart go cold?"

He nodded vigorously. "And hard, like metal. I'll never love again."

I could imagine myself then, striking the flint wheel of a lighter, holding it to Paedar's heart, ablaze behind charred ribs. I made this fire. And there has never, not ever, been a greater feeling. My mother, even, couldn't have felt anything like this when she crawled into the basement of the government building and set the place aflame. Not even the Stasi can possibly feel anything like the feeling of this arson.

"You're right, Paedar," I said. "I'm sorry for being callous. I should have taken your feelings into consideration."

His eyes widened hopefully. "So you'll stay?"

I shook my head. "It doesn't stop the fact that if my family has to leave, so do I. But, I'm glad you told me. It'll be your parting gift to me."

His face crumpled again. "Don't leave, Ava, I beg you. You can stay with my family. I'm sure mother wouldn't mind."

I laughed. "Your mother?" And if his wan blue eyes looked a little hurt, I didn't care. I don't like to think of people as disposable, but it was clear that this boy had done all he was ever going to do for me. They say people come into your life to teach you something. I'm certain this is the lesson I was meant to learn from Paedar, a sense of what I'm capable of.

When I walked to my house, Paedar told me he would stand vigil on the sidewalk until I turned onto my street. I didn't glance back at him, books clasped between his joined hands. I knew it would've sent a little jolt through his heart, and that would've been too easy. It would've given me no satisfaction.


November 22, 1986

It's been, perhaps, twenty-four hours since I saw my father's brains explode out the side of his skull. Since that moment, the world has been tuned like a television to black and white and gray. Georg's hair, black. Mother's skin, white. The inside of father's head, gray.

And, finally, there was red.

We drove to the checkpoint like we'd discussed, in two cars, my mother and me riding with Georg and Margarita because that was the plan. The air smelled like burned-off petrol and rotting leaves. I could sense that we were nearing the Wall from the way the air pulsed with electricity, the follicles in my hair pulling a little to the West. Sweat bloomed in bullets along Georg's forehead. Mother fiddled with the nail on her thumb, peeling off a jagged sickle. She let it fall to the immaculate carpet of Georg's BMW. They'd changed the license plates so that, with luck, it wouldn't be recognized.

When we turned a corner, the Wall surprised me, just as it always does. The tall concrete sheets fit together perfectly, rails of barbed wire strung up in Y-shaped metal frames on top. To climb over would be to throw oneself in a sausage grinder. What a death, I thought, just picturing it.

I remembered the story of a man who worked on the Wall. He was alone in the world save for his only daughter. One day, his daughter ran out into the street and was killed by a car. In the night, when no one was about, the builder carried his daughter's body to the Wall and placed her inside a concrete frame. He poured concrete around her. A meaningful grave for any East German. If it really happened, it was twenty years ago. She could be in there right now, a bubble-shaped space around her bones where the flesh has rotted away. If the Wall ever comes down, what will they think, finding the bones of a girl encased in so much ancient concrete? I suppose it doesn't matter. The Wall will never come down.

Georg pulled up to the checkpoint. He rolled down his window and a guard approached from his glass-walled booth. The guard combed through our faked identity papers with his dry fingers and nodded his head, which meant that he believed we were truly a West German family returning home from visiting relatives. He walked in front of the car to drag the rumble strip out of the way. Georg nudged the car forward so both of its wide eyes now stared into the West.

Behind us, the other guard had begun shaking his head at Father's papers. This meant a seal was in the wrong place or the paper wasn't the correct weight. He waved over our guard, who left the rumble strip skewed in a diagonal across the pavement.

They opened Father's door, and when he refused to get out, they lifted him from the car by his armpits, rumpling his charcoal business suit. He looked skinny in their large hands.

The wind whipped the loose cloth of the suit. The flapping sounded like a gunshot.

And then, a shout. A struggle.

A real gunshot.

A hand holding a black gun.

A gray bullet.

Into the space above Father's white ear.

He keened back, eyes closed, spine arched. What is it like to watch your father fall down and never get up? It is cacophony. It is silence. It is the entire black universe falling down with him. The world might end. The earth might fall into the sun. It should, shouldn't it? The world has no business going on turning.

Mother opened her car door and ran to Father, kneeling beside him. The rough asphalt rose to meet her knees and ripped her black stockings to reveal two pale knees, white like onions.

I stared out the back of the BMW, sitting up on the backseat, and watched my mother thrashing in the arms of those men, her elbows crooked around their elbows, their faces creased with strain.

She saw me then, staring at her, and she must've known there was no going back. We were separated forever.

"Go, Georg!" Margarita shouted. "Drive!" Georg pressed the gas pedal to the floor, and my forehead smacked the glass of the rear window. The pain was black. The tears were white. The BMW bucked over the skewed checkpoint roadblock. My mother's mouth was open, but I knew she wasn't speaking, or crying out. Hers looked just like my mouth, hanging silently in an O.

The road flung us to the left, and my mother disappeared. The Wall on this side was covered in graffiti of every imaginable color, though I could barely take it in. I was screaming out the back window, my eyes burning with the afterimages of what I had just seen.

"Sit down, Ava!" Georg screamed. "Are you trying to get us pulled over?" I sunk down into the black leather of the seat, my teary eyes distorting the city out the window. On one panel of the Wall, outrageous yellow graffitied flames crept upward, emanating from a stenciled match with a brilliant red head. Scrawled across the flame in jagged black, *"Verbrennen sie es zum boden"*—Burn it to the ground. Yes. Burn it to the ground.

But how do you burn a wall made of concrete?

As we sped onto the autobahn in the direction of the Helmstedt-Marienborn checkpoint, our last barrier to freedom, I wondered aloud why we didn't try to get help from the West Germans, but Georg told me we could still be extradited. We had to put miles between us and the Wall, the Stasi. We stopped only once for Georg to quickly change the license plates on the car again and hand us new identification papers, burning the old ones that claimed we were West German. Now, we were American tourists, on a leisurely drive across the country. My name, my life had changed so many times in the past few days, I wasn't sure who I was now.

When we reached the checkpoint, the guard there peppered us with questions, and I said "yes" and "no" the best I could, letting Georg answer in his unaccented English. The guard even rummaged through the trunk, finding only our suitcases. Before we'd left, we'd torn the labels off of all our clothes and washed them in contraband soap, so that they smelled nothing like East Germany.

The gates opened for us. For now—for the moment—we are free.

Hours ago, when I saw my father killed, my heart became hot in my chest, burning and slippery, and the heat slid up the back of my throat like acid. But, as our car crossed the fields and small industrial villages and vacant smells of West Germany, my heart cooled. Stiffened, like molten metal hardening. Now, it is solid. It doesn't even make a tick. I fear it never will again.

# Pepper

*Personal Safety*

Dear Ms. Eldridge,

I appreciate your recent response to my last essay. I will certainly be wary and on guard because these events are, as you say, extremely bizarre. After all, as far as my reckoning can stretch, there exists not a single soul who knows both Molly and me beyond her father, but Molly won't hear any mention of him being the one behind this. "It is impossible," she says.

I also appreciate your reminder to not be deviating too far from the assignment requirements. It's just that I have much in my chest that is weighing on me heavily, crushing my heart and lungs and ribs and whatever else is inside there. But I will try harder with the facts. For instance:

Fact: Captain Heinrich Werner is one of the most famous Stasi men to ever exist.

Fact: Everybody on Earth knows he is a killer.

Fact: The most well-known person he killed is Ava Dreyman.

What if I were to inform you that everything you know

about Captain Werner is incorrect? Prepare to be taught some mystical informations, Ms. Eldridge, that you will never in all your days forget.

Now for the topic at hand: Personal safety. I think this is an interesting subject, though you may know more about it than I. You can see I am asking about the scar on your forehead again, of which you have yet to tell me the origin. Did it happen in a street fight? An industrial accident? Or perhaps the result of that game magicians play where they throw knives at people's heads? I always thought that was a supremely stupid thing to be doing, risking one's life to prove the throwing skills of a man in a purple satin shirt. I hope that isn't the case as it may cause me to lose a fraction of respect for you, Ms. Eldridge.

Anyway, personal safety. The government recommends that children should never enter a stranger's house, especially not one they suspect is an internationally wanted murderer. Today, I tested the truthfulness of this precaution.

Research Question: When interviewing a famous murderer, what are the chances one will become murdered, too?

I decided to test this question with the help of my research partner, Molly P. Mavity, aged seventeen. Her qualifications are:

1) holding three-fourths of a high school diploma
2) having read almost all the books in the world,

including *The Arsonist* and all the Harry Potters. (I've only made it through the first forty pages of *The Arsonist*, so this should come in handy.)

On Sundays, I help my dad at the mechanic shop where he works. I have to stand by while rich people tell my dad how to do his job, and also that if he scratches their paint they will report him to Homeland Security. So, you know, normal take-your-kid-to-work stuff. I mostly make runs to the supply store and clean oil off of car parts. My dad is meticulous, and he cares for his work with the same attention he does his fish tanks, and so I like helping him, even if the customers are rude, because it makes me feel good about my dad, which strangely makes me feel good about myself. This morning, though, I was in the back room on the shop's computer. I was not playing a game or watching videos about cats who can surf. Quite surprisingly to me, I was doing *scholarly research*. Read that sentence again. Has your jaw fallen off your face onto the floor? Mine too!

I dialed Molly's number at ten in the morning, which I hoped wasn't too early or too desperate of me, but that was as long as I could wait because I am an academic and the desire for truth was pressing on my mind.

"Pepper?" Molly asked.

"I have something," I said. "I've been doing research at my dad's shop. About Heinrich Werner."

"Did you get a phone number?"

"So much better," I said. "I got his home address."

"But he lives in Argentina."

"*Lived*," I said with all the panache of a satin-shirted magician. "He lived in Argentina until 1998 when he moved to Carmel-by-the-Sea for reasons that are currently unknown."

"Carmel?" Molly asked. "That's not that far from here."

"I know! I can possibly use my dad's car. I told him I was doing summer school." Ms. Eldridge, this was the only way that I could explain the reasons I was typing at my computer all the time now.

"But you graduated from high school already, didn't you?" she asked. "You shouldn't lie."

"Well, it's not exactly a lie," I said. "I'm finishing up some . . . assignments."

"Oh, okay. I'll meet you at your dad's shop."

When Molly texted that she was outside, I opened the shop door to find her sitting on the bus bench on the street corner, her good ankle hooked over her casted foot. She was wearing Bermuda shorts and a stretchy teal headband that pulled all her orange curls away from her forehead.

Once we were buckled in to my dad's Oldsmobile and Bertrand was installed on the backseat, I turned the car around in the parking lot. "Maybe you could duck," I said. "My dad thinks I'm going to the library to write."

Molly scrunched down, peeking out over the window to where my dad was hunched over the hood of a blue Volvo. "Is that your dad in the cowboy hat?"

My cheeks started to redden. "Yeah."

I sped out of the parking lot into the street. "You can sit up now."

She slid upward and clipped on her seat belt, adjusting her leg so her cast was stretched in front of her.

"How'd you break your foot?" I asked.

She paused for a long moment. "I guess it was just one of those things."

"Okay," I said slowly. I supposed that it had to be a real embarrassing story, like she tripped while practicing the dance routine to "Time Warp" from *Rocky Horror Picture Show* (not that I'd know anything about that, Ms. Eldridge).

"Good job on finding Werner," Molly said. "You must have mad Internet skills."

"Well, yeah," I said. I thought it would be too creepy to tell her that I developed my immense Internet prowess from all that time spent trying to find her dad. "I searched for Georg and Margarita, too, but couldn't find anything. Werner was easy, though. He's been living under his real name. That's weird, right?"

"Yeah," she said. "I saw on the History Channel that a ton of Nazis changed their names after World War II and moved to South America. I figured the Stasi would do the same."

I turned onto the winding, two-lane highway to Carmel. I always liked this road, the way sand dusts the asphalt and the ocean stretches so big, the only thing you want to do is pull over and stare at it for a million years.

"So what do we think?" I asked. "Is Werner Ava's murderer?"

"Well, he's definitely a murderer. That was his job. 'Storm Wolf,' and all," Molly said, making quotation marks with her hands. "Ava never actually says who stabbed her. It could have been some Stasi underling. But, she's in a torture chamber with Werner's knife in her belly and Werner seems to be the only other person in the room. So it doesn't look good for him."

Bertrand interrupted our conversation by hacking something up deeply from his throat.

"Did you know that Pliny the Elder recommended drinking gladiator blood to cure epilepsy?" Molly asked.

"Who's Pliny the Elder?"

"A Roman author."

"Did it work?" I asked.

"I don't know."

"Well," I said, "let's give it a try. Screw finding Werner. Let's go find some gladiators."

Her eyes raked across my face. "You've got epilepsy medicine, right?"

"Yeah."

"Good," she pronounced. "Pliny the Elder lived two thousand years ago so you're probably better off with that. And you've got your pug."

"Yeah, Bertrand's a real professional."

"Hey," Molly said, turning her body to face me, "I've been wondering, where'd you get the name Pepper, anyway?"

"I don't know. My dad's called me that since I was born."

"My mother used to call me *petit chou*, a little cabbage," Molly said, her voice sounding kind of far away. "In French, it's an endearment."

"We sound like really dumb comic book characters," I said. "The cabbage and the pepper, out to solve an epic mystery."

She breathed, and the way it came out sounded a little like a laugh.

I slowed to pull into one of the fake-rustic roads of Carmel. Molly navigated us through the winding streets of mossy-roofed houses and wooden picket fences, until we arrived at a massive gold-colored house rising from a rock outcrop. I parked by the curb a couple of blocks away, just in case this guy was fully psycho and could track us by my license plates.

At the shining wooden door, I paused. "We're about to knock on the door of a murderer," I said. "I just realized that."

"Eh," Molly shrugged. "I guess it's no different than visiting my dad."

She stepped up and knocked quickly, twice. A long moment passed then, on the other side of the door, a lock slid with a clunk. The door creaked open a few inches, a chain stretching across the opening, and I could make out a wrinkled eye. A heavy floral scent unfolded from the house.

"What?" the man asked in a gruff voice.

"Are you Heinrich Werner?" I asked.

"Usually," he said, and I could see his mouth now, a deadened flat line. "Unless you're here to sell me some religion. If so, there are no Werners at this address." It's usually hard for me to tell if someone has an accent, but his was so strong and German-soaked, I could practically smell it on his breath.

"We want to ask you about this book." Molly held up *The Arsonist*.

Werner's face darkened. He receded back inside the house a little. "You from one of those websites? Bloggers?"

"No," Molly said. "We just have a few questions."

"What questions?"

"This one," Molly said, holding *The Arsonist* open to the editor's note where the words *"Who killed Ava Dreyman?"* were circled in red.

He scoffed. "That's what everybody wants to know."

"Well, it's an important question," I said.

Werner cocked his head, for the first time looking at me. His eyes lowered to the porch, where Bertrand was licking his privates with a squelching sound. "Who are you?" he asked me.

Molly paused. "We're, uh . . . business associates."

"And your business is this?" Werner barked from the gap in the door. "Learning what happened to Ava?"

"Yes," Molly said, nodding eagerly.

"Well, you have come to the wrong place. Good day."

The door slammed with a noise like a slap.

"There's our answer," I said.

"No," Molly replied, a determined scowl settling on her face.

"I'm not giving up. He has to come out. For food and stuff."

"You are suggesting we . . . besiege this man?" I had learned about this concept in Master Quest. I once laid siege to Shawn's castle and he didn't speak to me for a week.

"Besiege, yes," she said. "That's just what we'll do." She sat down with her back against Werner's front door.

I sat beside her, and Bertrand wedged himself between us. This was a strange thing to be doing, sitting so familiarly against the door of a known killer. A front door is a very personal thing, I realized in those moments. It was in some ways like I was leaning against a body part of this man Werner.

"What if he's one of those old people who stockpiles crackers and don't leave their houses for like a month?" I said.

"He's not that old." Molly dug into her backpack and pulled out a package. "Want some beef jerky?" she asked. "Or do you have to eat only blessed food?"

"Halal? Not really," I said, taking the jerky.

I looked out at the tree-lined street beyond Werner's driveway. "So here's something I've been wondering," I said. "After your dad went to prison, did he leave you anything?"

Molly's jaw worked mechanically away at the jerky. "Only a bunch of junk, all the stuff from the house I grew up in. My aunt's been bugging me to go through it all since she has to pay for the storage locker. But I've told her I'd rather have my innards eaten by wildcats."

"That's . . . intense," I said. The only thing my dad will leave me is a rickety boat and two dozen fish trapped inside Plexiglas tanks. For some reason, this realization made me feel like my lungs were being stomped on. "He really left you with nothing?"

"Well . . ." her voice petered out. "Not exactly."

"What?"

"A lookout tower?" she said, like it was a question. "On the beach."

"Not that old wooden thing that looks like it's about to fall over?" I asked. Everyone knows that tower. It's been circled in caution tape for years. I always wondered why it hadn't been torn down. "I didn't think anyone owned it."

"It belonged to my dad. And now it's mine, I guess. Or it will be. After." She squinted, though the sky was overcast.

"That's got to be worth an absolute fortune. Beach property on Monterey Bay."

"The beach is public property, not my dad's," she said. "This newspaper tycoon owned the beach back in the day. In the eighties he tried to sell it, but no one had enough to buy it. It was worth, like, a hundred billion bucks or something. So, he built these towers on the beach and sold them. He still owned the beach, but other people owned the towers. And my dad bought one with his inheritance from his dad's death. He hated his dad, so he decided to blow it all in one big, frivolous move. Like a middle finger up to heaven, he called it."

I looked over at her. "Why is your tower the only one left?"

"When the newspaperman died, he wrote in his will that he

wanted the beach donated to the state of California. And after that, most of the people donated their towers. They weren't exactly secluded getaways anymore. Eventually, each tower was donated or demolished or collapsed. All except my father's."

"Huh," I said. I interlocked my fingers, pressing my thumbs against each other. "Molly, I've been thinking. Are you sure this whole thing isn't related to your dad somehow?"

At that moment, the door behind us was wrenched open. I fell backward and looked up at the pressed pants and tilted head of Heinrich Werner.

"What do you think you are doing?" he exclaimed. "Get away from my house!" This was the first time I was seeing Werner's entire presence, and he was maybe even shorter than me, but his backbone was so erect, he looked fifty feet tall. This is the point when I started becoming genuinely concerned for the fact that:

a) Werner never formally admitted that he *didn't* kill Ava Dreyman which,

b) doesn't matter since even if he didn't kill Ava, he most certainly *did* kill other people,

c) a lot of them.

My bowels suddenly grew weak.

I was ready to spring out of there, and Bertrand was following my lead, pulling on his leash and thrashing around on the paving stones. But Molly jutted out her upper lip like a fearsome warrior. "We're not leaving, and neither are you, until you talk to us."

"Yeah," I said, mustering some courage, squaring my stance as much as possible while being unbalanced by a flailing pug. "You're being besieged."

Werner's face was set so hard, I thought he could have a future as one of those people who break cinder blocks with their jaws. "I should call the police," he said. "You're trespassing."

"But I'm thinking you will not," I said, and I'm not really sure what came over me. I was inebriated with Molly's confidence.

"And why is that?" he asked menacingly, and my courage dribbled away.

"I don't know," I said quickly. "Only, the police could cause problems for you. With your checkered history and all."

Werner clenched his teeth so hard I thought he might break his face. "If I killed her, why haven't I been convicted? For that matter, why haven't I been *arrested*?"

Molly shrugged. "Not enough evidence."

"*No* evidence, in fact. No matter how much those Internet hooligans want to, they can't prove I was the killer. Even the GDR subscribed to the concept of habeas corpus. No body, no conviction. I refuse to waste my time with you any longer," Werner said, pushing past Molly.

"What about the knife?" Molly asked. "What about the knife that Ava says killed her? According to the diary, it was yours."

Werner turned. He paused, shifting his weight. "Oh, that knife. You know, there has been ceaseless speculation about that knife: It was made from an elephant's tusk; it has been in my family since the Middle Ages; it once belonged to Hitler. All rubbish." He cocked his head to the side. "Would you like to see it?"

My heart began making a crooked thump in my chest.

Werner reached into his inner jacket pocket and whipped out a knife.

"Holy crap!" My sneakers skidded backward, urging my body as far from the knife's point as possible. The way he held it, casually with fingers loose, his mouth kind of smirking, was the creepiest part. He knew how to handle a weapon.

While I was backing up, hands up in the international symbol for "Don't stab me, dude!" Molly just stood there. All crime prevention experts in this world would be slapping her silly at her blatant disregard for her own personal safety.

"Molly, let's go!" I hissed.

"The bone-handled knife," she said, her voice filled with awe.

I couldn't prevent my mind from picturing the knife diving into my stomach, into all the organs I only learned existed because of the last essay I had to write (wink wink, Ms. Eldridge).

"*Verwenden Sie . . . ,*" Molly said, peering closer to the knife.

"What?" I hissed. "Molly, let's get out of here."

"*Verwenden Sie nicht in Zorn,*" Werner said. "*Use not in anger.*" He tilted the blade to show the German words etched into the metal. "It was tradition in my family for a boy to have a knife. My father wasn't a violent man and he hated the idea, so when he bought the knife for my fourteenth birthday, he had it inscribed with those words."

"Your father gave you this knife?" Molly asked, looking into Werner's face. Her forehead was crumpled. "The same one you had in Ava's diary?"

He held her gaze for a long moment, then said, "Yes."

"How . . . fascinating," I said, backing slowly away. "But we need to be leaving."

Molly was still surveying Werner. "You know what I don't get?" she asked, her head turned to the side. "After you stabbed Ava, you left it sticking out of her side as she wrote the last entry."

"So?" Werner asked. I have not read that far ahead in the book yet, Ms. Eldridge, so I wasn't sure what Molly was getting at.

"What kind of specially trained Stasi operative leaves a prisoner with a potential weapon?" she asked.

"A very poor one, it would seem," he said, in a way that sounded almost amused. "And since you know so much about what I've done with this knife, shouldn't you be leaving?"

"I have more questions," Molly said.

"I've answered all the questions I'm going to answer. You need to leave." Werner moved toward us, leading with the knifepoint. "Now!" he barked.

Something sparked alive in Molly at that moment, because at last she backed away and, with skittering steps, started running down the driveway and across the street, toward the car.

Bertrand's nails scrabbled the pavement at my side. A constant muttering of "oh God, oh God, oh God," came from the back of my throat. I hefted Bertrand into the backseat as his tiny legs are shaped like buffalo wings and don't have the thrust to negotiate his body off the ground, and I started the car, my muscles jangling so I pushed too hard on the accelerator with a screech and the smell of burned rubber.

"Can you explain to me what just happened?" I asked.

I felt Molly turn her steady gaze on me. "I'm thinking . . ." she trailed off. "I'm thinking that Werner didn't kill her."

"Um, did we meet the same guy?" I asked, my voice high-pitched. "The guy who looks like he cooks children in his free time? The guy who waved a knife in our faces?"

"Didn't you hear him?" she asked. "He totally didn't stab her. He would never have left her with that knife, even if she was bleeding to death. And I read all about him on the Internet. He was raised by a single mother."

"So?"

"That whole story about his father buying him the knife when he was fourteen—that was a lie. He never knew his father. His mother never remarried."

I spread my fingers wide on the steering wheel, absorbing what she said. "So, who gave him the knife?"

"I don't know. And I don't know why he lied." She looked at me, and I could almost see how hard her blood was beating in the flushness of her face. "He told us that story on purpose."

I was coming to an idea. "D'you—d'you think he was giving us a clue?"

I could feel the full force of Molly's stare as I faced the highway. "Yes," she said slowly. "I think that's exactly what he did."

"But why?" I asked.

She pursed her mouth like she wasn't sure. Finally, she spoke. "You were asking before about why he didn't change his name. Maybe he doesn't want to be like those Nazis, who hid from their atrocities. Maybe he wants to make amends."

I shook my head in disagreement. "He's a war criminal," I protested. "It's like, look up villain on the Internet. There's him."

"It's gotta be more complicated than that. Think about it. The entire world thinks Werner killed Ava. If it wasn't him, and he's been quiet about it all this time, he must have some reason. Whoever actually killed her has sworn him to secrecy," she said. "Threatened him, or blackmailed him."

I began nodding because, truthfully, I didn't want Werner to be the killer. That would mean this whole thing would end right here. I may not be going to college, and I may not play basketball, or be in DECA. But right now, Ms. Eldridge, I am doing something. I am changing history.

# Molly

Dear Pepper,

All day after we visit Werner, I think about my mother. I can't help it. When she drifts into my mind, I always imagine her floating in the air. If she jumped like everyone says, that's what she would've looked like. For a moment, she would've been cradled by blue, suspended, like a ballerina flung into a jeté, her straw-colored hair wafting behind her against the teal sky.

I almost never think about the next moment, the one they say destroyed all of her in a single swift moment, splintering her bones into matchsticks.

I don't think about that moment because I know that it didn't happen.

"Molly," my aunt calls upstairs to my bedroom. "Dinner."

I hobble down into the gold-lit kitchen and sit at the oak table next to Marty, who is at work on his secret project. He is wrestling knitting needles the size of his forearm into a mass of yarn, a huge blanket rolling over his lap. Marty has told me exactly nothing about this project, even though he's been working on these blankets for as long as I've known him.

Today's blanket is blue with white stripes. I reach out to thumb a loop of the yarn. Heavy and rough, like fishing net material. "It's a sweater for a whale," I venture.

Marty laughs. "Keep guessing."

"Hmm," I say. "You're going to cover up the nude statues in all the art galleries in California."

"I would never," he says. "People gotta be nude if they wanna be nude."

"Amen to that," Margaret mutters from the corner of the room, where she's got her long legs doubled beneath her chin, the glow from her phone lighting up her face.

"Are you ever going to tell us what these are for?" I ask Marty, touching the blanket again. Sometimes, I'm sad that he hasn't let me in on the secret when I know it must be important.

Marty smiles his wide grin. "It's a surprise."

"A surprise for who?"

"For you!" Marty laughs. "For Monterey. For the world."

"Marty, you're one kind of special," Margaret says, rolling her eyes.

"Margaret, quit being such a b-word extraordinaire," I say.

"B-word?" Margaret scoffs. "You can say bitch, Molly. I promise it won't burn your mouth."

"I know. I refuse to call you one because that's what you want me to do."

"Marty, I take it back," Margaret says. "Molly's the truly special one around here."

"Molly *is* special." Marty agrees with a nod.

I smile. Marty's my best friend for a reason. To him, I'm not a weirdo. Marty once told me that he thinks I'm better than pie à la mode. Everyone should have someone in their life who thinks they're better than pie à la mode.

Auntie Ro stands near the kitchen counter and clears her throat. "Molly, we need to talk about your dad's . . ." she trails off. "About what's going to happen to your dad."

I cross my arms. "I'm *not* going."

"This isn't about what you want, Molly," my aunt says. "It's about being there for your dad on his last day on Earth." She didn't really know my father growing up, only being cousins, and so she treats him with an objectivity that I've never come close to. We've had this conversation a dozen times already, and the answer is always "no." The answer is sometimes "hell no." The answer has once been "not in a million fucking years," but I got in trouble for that.

"*Rosanne*," Margaret says from behind her phone, "it's not like he thought about Molly when he went around burning houses and murdering people."

"It's happening, Molly," my aunt says, ignoring Margaret. "Soon. And you'll regret it your entire life if you don't see him one last time."

I feel my lips sinking in between my teeth. I think that

if I sit in this room for one more second, I will start to tear apart cell by cell until there's nothing left of me but a sheen in the air.

I jump up, grabbing my backpack.

"Where are you going?" my aunt asks.

"The storage locker," I say. "Like you wanted, remember?"

My aunt purses her mouth. "All right, but take Marty with you. That storage place isn't in the safest neighborhood."

Outside, the sun is approaching the horizon and draws long shadows across the world. It's only about a twenty-minute walk, even with my cast, so we decide not to bother with the bus.

"Cheer up, kiddo," Marty says. "Cleaning is great for the soul. It's not good to be holding on to things you've outgrown. How's that foot holding up, by the way?"

Marty gives me a knowing look, his eyes all sparkly beneath his overgrown eyebrows. Here's another thing I never told you: My foot is all healed now.

I had an appointment to get my cast taken off before school let out, but I ditched it. When my aunt asked me why, I told her I wasn't ready yet. Don't judge me, Pepper. There are people who get their gallbladders removed and then save them in glass baby food jars. This is way less weird. I've just grown used to my cast. I don't want to give it up.

"I like it too much," I tell Marty.

"Ah," he says. "Maybe it's for the best. You haven't thrown yourself offa any bridges since you got your cast."

"Marty, I've already told you. I didn't throw myself," I say. "I was pushed. By a train."

"And you were up there for what? The view?" He wiggles his eyebrows at me.

He's making a joke, but I can't smile. "I guess I wanted to think about . . . before, you know?" I say. To my surprise, my voice warbles a little. I don't want him to think I'm about to cry so I clear my throat loudly. "That used to be my house, across from the train bridge."

I take a shuddering breath and Marty nods like he understands. "What do you think about what my aunt said?" I ask him. "About my dad? Do you think I should visit him?"

"Your dad?" He palms his balding head. "I don't have any thoughts, not really. Just that—you shouldn't judge people before you get to know them."

"When do you plan on getting to know my dad?"

"I didn't mean me. I meant you."

I look up into Marty's liver-spotted face, my forehead crumpling in confusion. "I think I know him better than anybody."

"That's right," Marty says. "You *think* you know him. Kids, they don't always know their folks like the rest of the world does. He wasn't always bad, was he? Your mom must've loved him. There could be something in him that you're not seeing."

I shake my head. "Whatever good in him is gone now."

"You never know, kid," is all Marty says.

Marty and I find the storage place in a large dusty asphalt lot, and walk through rows of metal storage lockers. When I find my dad's, I fit the key into the big silver lock and pause. My gut churns as I picture the space beyond that door, what might be hidden in some unopened box or suitcase, something dark and festering, something the police might've missed.

I slide the door up.

It's completely dark inside, so I turn on the flashlight on my phone and hold it over the threshold, the circle of light catching on a mountain of crumpled cardboard boxes and black plastic trash bags. The air smells like memories, half-forgotten.

Marty whistles. "That's the stuff of a lifetime."

I take a pad of Post-its from my pocket and look for anything worth keeping. All the furniture can be donated, I think, as well as the boxes of dishes and magazines dated five years ago.

I rip open a garbage sack full of my mother's wardrobe. I plunge my hand into the soft shine of these fancy, fine things, made of silk and cashmere, little buttons of mother-of-pearl. My mother never went cheap on clothes, even when everything else in our house was falling apart. "A lady needs to look the part," she'd say. I push a "Keep" Post-it into the black plastic. She'll want these when she comes back.

I rummage through every cardboard box, every garbage bag with papers hastily shoved inside. In a milk crate, I find photographs. They are water damaged and stuck together in a stack. The top photo is of my parents, standing together in the lookout tower, the dark waters of the bay black beyond the open balcony. My father appears as a blurred shape and is kissing my mother's cheek. Her mouth is open slightly as though in surprise. I have never seen my mother like this. She tended to arrange her face in a mask, every feature sitting exactly how she ordered them. Even the strands of her blond hair obeyed her.

"Your mom and pop?" Marty lifts the photograph from my hands and studies it. "See what I mean?" he asks, handing the photo back to me. They look happier in that photo than they ever did in real life. They look like they might actually love each other.

"No," I say, placing the photo in my backpack. "I don't."

In the farthest corner of the storage locker, where none of the sun from the doorway can touch, I go through the final plastic sack full of my own clothes from when I was twelve. They smell like childhood, like milk and cotton. I push the sack aside. It falls heavily to the floor in a cloud of dust, and I see what it had been sitting on top of, a huge brass-edged, black trunk. I grab the trunk's warped handle and wrench it up.

Inside, all I can discern are newspapers, pages and pages of them in messy stacks. "MONTEREY POLICE FLUMMOXED BY SERIAL ARSONIST," a headline reads.

I push the top one aside. "HISTORIC CANNERY BURNS

TO GROUND," says another. "ARSON SUSPECTED IN OLD TOWN WAREHOUSE FIRE." I shove each page away and find more and more newspapers advertising my father's fires.

Something acidic is clawing up the back of my throat.

One of the newspapers doesn't make sense, and I have to stare at it for a long moment to figure out why. The paper is warped and yellowed with age, and the words are in a different language. In clunky typeset, the words *"Der Brandstifter"* stretch across the top in ink so thick it bends the paper. The words prickle at the back of my mind. *Where have I heard those words before?*

A colorless photo stretches across the front of the newspaper, depicting a building that has been burned down.

"What've you got there?" Marty asks, glancing over my shoulder.

"Some kind of newspaper."

"Ah, *sprichst du Deutsch?*"

"You speak German?" I ask, turning to look at him.

"Only a little," he admits. "I picked up some from my grandparents."

"*Der Brandstifter,*" I say. "Do you know what that means?"

He thinks hard. "The Fire Raisers. Or the Fire Starters . . ."

As Marty says it, the meaning arranges itself in my mind, and the knowledge floods my veins like something hot. The newspaper begins to quaver in my fingers.

*Der Brandstifter* was the name of the subversive newspaper Ava Dreyman's mother printed in East Germany.

*Der Brandstifter* means *The Arsonist.*

This shouldn't be here. In a storage locker in Monterey. Among my father's things. But, somehow, it is. And I have to face the unwanted truth, becoming clearer by the second:

You were right, Pepper.

My father is involved somehow.

He has been all along.

# Ava

November 23, 1986

The morning after we escaped the Wall, I woke in a gas station parking lot on what must have been the French side of the border. The car was parked in view of motorists filling their cars with gasoline. It was barely dawn, and I was alone in the car. Beside the gas station there was a roadside café. I guessed Georg and Margarita had gone inside to get breakfast.

My muscles were stiff from sleeping crinkled up on the backseat. I hadn't allowed myself to touch the left side cushion, where my mother could still be sitting if I pretended.

I opened the back door, stretching my feet to the ground. My kneesocks sagged around my ankles, and I stopped to pull them back under my kneecaps. The air above was orange with light from the blooming dawn sun, still buried beneath the horizon to the east. A fan of geese flew above, honking their loud song. I stood for several minutes, watching them fly off into France. Freer than I've ever been.

I walked into the café and heard the people there talking, some with German in their accents, some French. My eyes rested on

every red-topped table where the diners ate breakfast. Georg
and Margarita weren't there.

Outside, I asked the gas station attendant if she had seen an
older German couple wearing plaid and tweed. She nodded.
"They picked up a rental car a couple of hours ago. Paid in
cash. They seemed in an awful hurry."

My face turned bloodless. I teetered on my feet and walked
back to the BMW. I sat in the driver's seat, too short to see
much over the steering wheel but the broad, yellowing sky. I
became certain that something terrible had happened. Perhaps
Georg and Margarita spotted a Stasi officer and had to flee.

If they'd left me a note, they would've had to hide it well. I
unhooked the silver latch on the glove box and riffled through
the things inside. I threw a couple of empty, expensive cigarette
cartons and the insurance information to the floor.

I grappled beneath the front seats. Beneath Margarita's was
a small yellow notepad she'd been writing on. There were only
a few pages left, all blank, affixed to the cardboard by a skin of
glue. I threw the notebook on the ground.

My mother would scream right now. She'd stamp her feet
and wail and light something on fire and let the entire world
know exactly how she felt. I've always been the other way,
poised, never letting people view the inside pieces. But at that
moment, I could feel myself shedding what little composure I
had left. Unconsciously, I began gulping air like I was starving
for it. I was alone in a country where I didn't belong.

It was then that my eyes caught on the notepad, lying where I'd thrown it to the floor. Shadows crossed the surface of the paper—indentations, I realized, from where Margarita's firm grip had imprinted letters on the page. Swiftly, I secured a pencil from my book bag and rubbed it against the paper. Letters assembled themselves beneath the lead.

*Monterey.*

A lightning bolt of memory shot through my mind. It was the name of a town, one of the rendezvous locations on the map my father had showed me: Geneva, Dover, that tiny island off the coast of Italy that I always forget the name of, Melbourne, somewhere in the south of France, Ahmadi, Buenos Aires, and a town on the coast of California. Monterey. This was the place Georg and Margarita had decided to flee to.

I pulled my atlas from my book bag, traced my hand over the slick pages, and let my finger rest on the tiny pock of a city on the Pacific Ocean. I felt myself calm, my breath returning to normal. For now, I wasn't thinking about the bloody spray that had flown from my father's head. I was thinking of a plan, and the sea, and how I was determined to find it no matter what.

I packed everything I could into my book bag, taking only the barest necessities from my mother's suitcase, and abandoned the car. I couldn't stay there; it was the first place the Stasi would look.

My parents had given me a third of their money after they'd emptied the bank accounts, gobs of creased marks that I changed for a smaller packet of francs at a kiosk by the gas station, and I was grateful for that now because it was obvious I had a very long way to go. I bought a ticket aboard a rickety train that jostled with every turn, past fields of countryside. For a moment, I saw the geese, only a crooked wire on the horizon now, but I could still hear their voices.

November 25, 1986

I knew I could catch a plane to America in Paris. The station that my train pulled into was hot and sweat-smelling and the air tasted slightly of metal. Everyone walked around with alarming efficiency, stepping precisely around the homeless men and women sitting in rags against the walls like crumpled paper. Rather than try the sticky mess of the Metro, I decided to walk to the Gare du Nord, where I figured I could take a fast train to the airport.

Outside, a cold and slick brown rain fell and gave life to the grime that covered everything. The smell was like the decomposed parts of a very old pond. Even in the rain, there were people everywhere.

I walked through streets, the limestone symmetry of shops blending into one another in the blurry evening light. I passed a cathedral with a line of stone saints set into the facade, their fingers held out as though about to bless some dirty peasant. Some of them looked up at the ceiling of the sky like there really might be a god up there.

I was starving by the time I picked up the heavenly smell of meat roasting, coming from a cart on the street. From where I stood, I glimpsed bratwurst turning over an open flame, a man in a grease-soaked apron jabbing at them periodically with a fork. My stomach doubled over from hunger, but how could I buy anything? I knew hardly any French and I wasn't dumb enough to try German. Suppose the Stasi had already covered France with spies?

I hovered nearby, waiting until a paying customer ordered. Just as the man in the cart offered the sausage to the customer, I snatched it from beneath his nose and slapped a bunch of francs down on the counter. The cart man shouted after me.

*"Je suis désolé!"* I shouted the apology over my shoulder, taking bites as I ran.

Only then, I heard something else behind me. Footsteps, striking the pavement like hammers. I looked back and nearly choked on the mouthful of food. Someone in a dark coat was running after me. *It couldn't be him,* I thought. Surely, it couldn't be. I wound through the streets, down a big boulevard bisected by oak trees, past monuments that I didn't know the names of.

"Ava Dreyman!" Captain Werner's voice barreled through the trees. I didn't need to look behind me to know he was close. I could hear the spray of pebbles from the path beneath his feet, conscious of the hard slap of my flat shoes, jarring my shins and the jelly inside my knees. I made a wrong turn and found myself in an alley that ended on a brick wall. When I turned around, he was already blocking the only exit.

Werner approached slowly once he realized I was trapped.

"What do you want?" I gasped.

"I found you at the scene of a fire that took the lives of four government officials. We can easily pin you to those deaths."

"You know I didn't set that fire."

"Who did, then?"

"My mother." The words were out of my mouth before I could stop them.

Werner smiled. "If you don't return to clear your name, you're guilty forever. That's how this works. If you run, you can never come back."

"Good," I said, my voice strangely forceful. "I'm never coming back anyway."

"Don't be so quick to give up your home," he said. "I guarantee you'll regret it."

He made a motion with his hand, just a hint of movement, really, but surely it was intentional because my eyes followed his fingers to his hip, beneath his coat, where I noticed the outline of something small, shaped like a gun.

I couldn't breathe. I should've been screaming, but I could do nothing but stand still and quiet.

"You—you can't kill me," I told Werner. "This is—this is not how I die."

Werner chuckled. "You've figured that out?"

"Of course," I said, somehow willing bravery into my voice. "It would take something much bigger to kill me."

"Like what?" Werner laughed. "A lion? A tank?"

"Or a hurricane," I agreed, trying not to shake. "Or a tornado, or a tsunami."

"No mortal is up to the task?" he asked, amused.

"No."

"Not even yourself?" he asked, cocking his head to the side. His expression was teasing, the way he looked the night of my mother's fire, when he joked about me not making it past the dogs, but his voice was cold. "Could Ava Dreyman kill Ava Dreyman?"

My fingers felt the brick wall behind me. My eyes twitched down to the place my fingers touched. A brick was missing, a hole where the mortar had sloughed away.

"I know where your family was headed, when you tried to escape," he said. "You're looking for the ocean, I can tell."

"You know everything."

His lips bent into a slim smile. "My mother told me an old folktale when I was young. She said, 'Did you know that when you look out into the ocean, really look, you see how your life will end?' I tested it and she was quite right."

I grimaced. "Why would you want to know that?"

"Because every moment until my death is really mine. And I'm much more peaceful for it."

"So, how do you die? Warm bath, sharp blade?" I asked, my voice an attempt at nonchalant.

He laughed. "Not quite. It's unfortunate. You'll never get to see the ocean now."

He took one step toward me. Then another.

When I pictured the ocean as a child, it was a great, dark, undulating thing that had always scared me. Now, though, the idea made my heart beat faster. I wanted to see the ocean.

I wanted to live.

I pivoted and ran at the wall, hooking my foot in the empty space, and hauled myself upward as Werner shouted behind me. I swung my leg and landed on the other side, and didn't stop running even after I could no longer hear him.

The streetlamps cast orange circles across the road and cold rain splattered down. I followed the streets north, past policemen who stood in the traffic monitoring cars, past bakeries pushing the smell of cake into the air.

I kept running.

Later

It was a strange series of events that got me onto the plane I'm on now, gliding over the black of the ocean. It was almost like the path was lit for me when I arrived at the massive, statue-crusted Gare du Nord. I waited for a girl who looked like me, same height, same dark hair, walked behind her and slipped her passport out of her purse without her realizing.

Today, I will cross the ocean and tomorrow, I will find Georg and Margarita. Tomorrow, I will discover America.

# Pepper

*Foreign Language*

Dear Ms. Eldridge,

I am very used to speaking languages. More than most people, I'd venture. My brain has been a translation machine for a very long time. My last year in Kuwait, I took classes in English from a British woman with beautiful dark skin, and she was pronouncing every word with an elegance that I appreciated, a kind that I still attempt to mimic to this day.

Around this time, I had a friend named Sunjip who taught me some Hindi. He had glasses the size of these big inflated American apples we get at Walmart. Nobody wanted to hang out with Sunjip because whenever anybody tried to talk to him, he stuck out his tongue and held it there for long minutes, staring at the person until the thing hanging from his mouth appeared less like a tongue and more like a piece of flesh torn from his enemies. But something about Sunjip I liked, so I gave him my dehydrated lemon snacks one day and he crooked his pinkie finger around mine and declared us friends.

"What's the worst thing you know how to say in your

language?" I asked him once, when he and I lounged on the school's courtyard benches in the abrasive midday sun.

"*Behen ke takke*," he whispered, a creepy smile filling up his cheeks.

*Behen ke takke*: Go suck on your sister's balls.

I thought that was the very best insult I had ever heard.

When we arrived in Monterey, my dad insisted we speak only English, so my remaining Arabic is just shreds and pieces that cannot be assembled back together without considerable effort. My first language is disappearing, and my second language is never going to fit just right. If you look at things a certain way, you could say that, to me, everything is foreign.

I spent the afternoon after Molly and I visited Captain Werner mowing the lawn, Bertrand a panting lump in the shadow of the porch, and by the time we came inside for cold tea, my entire body was a sweat factory. My dad sat at the table in the kitchen, tying lures. I fell into a chair beside him and grabbed a hook to start tying.

My dad wiped his wrinkled forehead with the back of his hand. "God, it's hot," he said.

I took a big swallow of cold tea. "Maybe someday we get an air conditioner," I said.

"We don't need one here," he said. "We are from Ahmadi. We can handle the heat."

"Okay, Baba. Never mind." I don't ask my dad about Ahmadi anymore. A seriousness overtakes him that makes me afeared of his answers. Ahmadi means images of worn-out sneakers melting on the desert sands, birds dropping dead out of the smoke plume, and my father crying out all the water he managed to drink because he couldn't stop thinking about my mama.

"The last time I felt this hot was the summer you were born," my father said. "We'd just moved to the new house and your mother was pregnant with you. She was the most beautiful thing I had ever—"

I closed my eyes hard because I knew what was coming, the story I'd heard one million times, the picture of her lying there, and the knowing that I killed her somehow, the way she was alive and moving one moment and in the next was perfectly still, and the tears that would squirm out of his eyes and make me squirm in my chair. And so, utterly without thought, I slammed my hand on the table and said, "God, Baba, stop!"

The room went silent, the only noise his fish tanks burbling in the corner and Bertrand's sniffling from the floor. My dad's hands fell to the table, fingers still pinching the neon threads in the start of a knot. "You don't want me to talk of your mama, Ibrahim?"

"Not—" I was shaking my head. "Not like that."

He nodded and attempted to tie the lure again. I watched his fingers, which were creased and accustomed to work. They tried and tried to tie the threads around the hook, but the knot was flaccid and not wanting to be tied. Over and under, over and under. He tried to tie that lure for something like five minutes.

I took the hook from his fingers and finished the knot. We sat there, staring at it, the green threads sprung up in the shape of regret. (That's me being poetic. Really it was in the shape of kelp.) Our throats ached to be saying something.

When my phone began ringing in my bedroom, I flew from the room to answer it.

"Can you borrow your dad's car again?" Molly asked, without preamble. I could hear traffic rushing past on the other end of the line.

"Where are you?" I asked.

"Walking back from my dad's storage locker," she said. "Can you get the car tomorrow?"

"Maybe. Where are we going?"

There was a considerable pause. "The prison."

My heart squeezed for five whole seconds, then let go all at once. "All right," I said. "I will ask my dad."

When I walked back into the kitchen to ask about the car, my dad was standing above one of his tanks, doling out chunks of freeze-dried worms into the water like coins to a wishing well, his face calmed like it gets when he is watching his fish and thinking about my mama.

When I picked Molly up the next morning, it was almost dark still. She said she wanted to get an early start because it's a couple hours drive to the prison and visiting hours start at eight. The sun rested below the horizon, but it still managed to color the whole sky a kind of dusty pink. There was a summertime chill in the morning air.

I drove onto the highway that would take us away from the ocean, toward the dingy, dry parts of inner California. In a moment, the sun edged over the land, and I had to push down my visor to block the band of blinding orange.

"You been to the prison a lot?"

"A few times," Molly replied. Her fingers wouldn't stop playing frantically at the black metal zipper on her backpack. I think she was nervous.

"What are you thinking about?" I asked.

"I'm wondering . . . why does your dad wear a cowboy hat?"

That's not what I'd been expecting. I had forgotten she'd even seen my dad at his shop the other day. "Why do you want to know that?"

"Don't know." She shrugged. "There are a few Muslim students at Keller and some of them wear hijabs, but none wear cowboy hats."

"We are not Muslim," I said, then shook my head, because that's not the total truth. "Well we are, but not a hundred percent. It's complicated to explain."

"What percent Muslim are you?" she asked. "If you're not a hundred percent?"

I considered this for a moment. "I think I am fifty-three point seven percent Muslim."

"What's the other part?"

"Pizza."

She peered at me, and her fingers stopped fidgeting with her zipper. "You are fifty-three point seven percent Muslim and forty-six point three percent pizza."

"That sounds about right."

A little bit of a smile began pushing up her mouth.

"What are your percents?" I asked her.

"I am a hundred percent white."

"White isn't a culture," I said. "White is a type of bread."

"Then I am a hundred percent bread."

"I mean, what countries are your people from?"

"My mom could only trace our roots back a couple generations, so she wasn't really sure. Her maiden name is British, though. And my dad's Irish on every side, times infinity, but we've been here for a long time. I guess I don't have a culture."

What a relief, I thought, to have no culture. To be default. To not have to explain why your father wears a cowboy hat.

Just then, my phone buzzed in the cup holder. Molly picked it up.

"Text message from Obi-Shawn Kenobi," she said.

It seemed early for Shawn to even be awake, let alone texting. "Can you read it?"

> "Pepper-dude, call me ASAP. I've got some phantasmagorical news. You will kiss me. Not really. But really."

"Should I reply?"

"No," I said firmly.

"You don't wanna know what the news is?" she asked.

"I don't care what it is," I said. I looked down and noticed that Molly was back to fidgeting with her backpack. "So are you gonna tell me why we're going to the prison?"

"I need to ask my dad about something."

I could tell from the way she was buzzing with nervous energy that she didn't relish the thought. "Why not just call him?"

"I need to see his face when he answers my questions." She cocked her head to the side. "He lies."

I parked the Olds in the tumbleweedy parking lot of the prison. Inside, I held Bertrand while passing through the metal detector, and then we were escorted into the large visitation room scattered with blue plastic tables. Winston Mavity was one of the only inmates there. He wore a black T-shirt with black drawstring pants and handcuffs around his wrists. The skin on his face was pocked and scarred. His hair was buzzed close to his head, and from his face grew a red, slightly over-grown goatee. Even still, he was recognizable as the man in my dad's photograph. There was such a feeling in my heart, seeing him. Because even though this man is a murderer, he is also the reason I am alive.

His stare, when it fell on Molly, was an intense, burning,

laser beam of a thing. I don't think he even realized anyone else was in the room.

"Hey, Red."

"Hi, Dad," she said. Her mouth had become a small crease at the bottom of her face.

"What happened to your foot?"

She shrugged. "Fell down."

He moved his head to the side with a twitch. "Shouldn't do that."

Everything they said felt like listening to a language I barely had access to. It was English, sure enough, but the meanings were different, so much history behind every syllable, so much trembling inside a single glance. I held my breath, afraid to interrupt.

"You look so grown up," he said. "I would've hardly recognized you."

Molly looked away. Something solid lived inside his stare, and I realized how much heavier Molly must feel sitting in his presence. Even I did, just being next to her.

I sat still as I could, trying not to draw Winston's eyes to me, taking shallow breaths of the astringent lemon-scented air.

"Have you heard from Mom?" Molly asked.

"Mom's dead," he said, hard, like two gunshots.

Molly was quiet. She was waiting for him to remember that she believed her mother was alive.

He sighed, rubbing his goatee. "No, I haven't heard from Mom. Why?"

"Because I have."

Molly pulled the paperback copy of *The Arsonist* from her bag and set it on the table.

If she was hoping for a reaction, she got it. The skin around Winston's eyes puckered in one quick motion. He put out a hand, but only let it hover over the book, breathing through his nose in bursts. Finally, he let his fingers fall to the cover, then wrap around the spine, pressing the book between his thumbs, as though testing the strength of it.

Winston looked up. "Who sent you this?" he asked.

"I think Mom did," Molly said slowly.

"She would never do that." His nostrils flared like an angry animal.

"Why wouldn't she?" Molly demanded. Her fingers gripped the table's edge.

The breath coming out of Winston's nose turned to short puffs, and soon he was crying, a keening sound that made me want to slap my hands over my ears.

"Why is this book important?" Molly asked. "What is it about this book?"

"You'll never understand, Red," he said, pushing tears away from his eyes with creased fingers. "And you shouldn't. She would never want you to know about this."

"I've already read it," she said. "And none of it means anything to me. But it means something to you, I can tell."

He looked up at her. "Whoever sent this isn't looking out for your best interests," he said forcefully, his face shiny with tears.

"Whoever sent it to me wants me to find my mother," Molly said. "*Dad*, do you know who killed Ava Dreyman?"

His face went vacant. "She was killed by the East German secret police," he whispered. "Everybody knows that."

"And it has nothing to do with you?" Molly asked. Her face was wadded up in disbelief.

"Of course not."

"Then why did I find this with your things?" she asked as she pulled an old newspaper from her backpack. The paper was inside a large plastic Baggie, like evidence. I leaned forward to examine it. The words were in a different language—but something about the image on the front was familiar. I couldn't figure out what.

"Where'd you find that?" her father asked, a small scowl settling over his features.

"In a trunk, with other newspapers."

"What do you want me to say?" he asked, his face clearing, his shoulders thrown back again. "There's no big explanation. I was interested in *The Arsonist* back then, like everybody was. I found this at a yard sale. I collected old newspapers—"

"DON'T LIE TO ME!" Molly shouted. Everyone in the room snapped their heads toward her. Inside my chest, my heart nearly strangled from the noise. "You're not gonna lie to me anymore. You're not gonna treat me like a child. Because I'm not one anymore! You—you walked out on my childhood. You don't know me at all."

Implosion: the feeling of stuff bursting apart, but on the inside.

That's what it felt like, watching Molly in that moment, like she was collapsing swiftly and with the force of a bomb.

Winston Mavity gave no indication of caring. "You probably think I flew all the way to Germany and lit that fire," he said, his finger stabbing *Der Brandstifter.* "You think I'm some kind of monster, Red. But you don't know me, either. And that's how it's going to stay." He stood. "Guard! I'm done here."

"N-no," Molly said, her voice low and terrible. Her forehead crinkled up. "No. You don't get to walk out like this. You sit back down and"— She wasn't crying, but her words burst forth from her mouth like sobs. —"and give me answers."

He stopped in his tracks, casting her one serious glance. "I'm your dad, Red. I have to protect you."

"When have you ever protected me?" Molly screamed. "You never once thought about me! Not when Mom disappeared, not when you were burning half of Monterey to the ground. You're a parent. That was supposed to be your job. And you messed it up!"

A guard arrived at the door, held out a hand to usher Winston through. The door clanged hard behind him.

I turned to watch Molly, her mouth open, breathing hard,

shock shining from her eyes. Then, she blinked twice, sat up straighter, and pressed her lips together, suddenly calm. I was startled by how easily she could put herself back together after being smashed like a teapot. I thought, only someone who's been demolished many times can do that so quickly, so efficiently.

"He's going to die soon," Molly said as I drove away from the prison, her arms crossed tightly over her chest. The day had become hot, the air leached of moisture. "How does it benefit him to be so secretive? It's unnecessary now."

She stared straight ahead out the windshield.

We passed a sign for restaurants at the next exit. "You hungry?" I asked.

"Sure," she said, sounding exhausted.

I got off the freeway and followed the signs for Dot's Diner, which turned out to be a squat, glossy, red-enameled building with a jukebox.

We slid into opposite sides of a vinyl booth. "So what was the deal with that newspaper?" I asked.

Molly reached into her backpack and pulled out the faded, wrinkled newspaper she had shown her father. She handed it to me, and I pored over every strange, backward-looking word.

"It's a copy of Ava's mother's subversive newsletter. Pretty unbelievable, right?" Molly asked.

"Do you think your dad lit this fire?" I asked, pointing to the front page.

"I don't think so. He would've been, what, fourteen? Plus, Ava was pretty explicit that it was her mother who lit that fire."

"You're sure he's never been to Germany?" I asked. "How else would he own a copy of this newspaper?" Neither of us was believing his story about buying it at a garage sale.

"He hates to fly," Molly said. "I don't know if it was just a post-traumatic souvenir from serving overseas, or if he's always been that way. But that's how my mom knew we'd be safe from him in France. He'd never follow us."

"That's why she took you to France?" I asked. "To get away from him?"

"She never told me in any direct kind of way. But yeah."

"Either way," I said, "your dad has to be in on this quest. We know that now, right?"

Molly lowered her menu and glanced at me. "Not necessarily."

"But he freaked out when you showed him *The Arsonist*. And kept talking about 'the truth.' Doesn't that mean that he knows what the truth is?"

"I already told you. He lies. You can't trust anything he says."

An elderly waitress in a pink-checked outfit came to our table to take our order. She glanced at Bertrand, who was on the vinyl seat beside me, with something like disdain. I made sure to adjust his reflective vest that read SERVICE ANIMAL ON DUTY, before ordering a burger and fries. Molly got the corned-beef sandwich and apple pie à la mode. In my pocket, my phone buzzed, but I ignored it. More texts from Shawn, I was sure.

The waitress scribbled down the order and left. Molly was biting on her thumbnail, a million miles away.

"Are you going to be there? When he . . . you know . . ." *Dies,* I wanted to ask.

Molly bored her eyes into the tabletop. "I'm busy that day."

"With what?" I asked.

"Literally anything else."

"I'll go with you, if you want."

She let out something that might've been a laugh, the way it made her shoulders bounce up and fall back down. "I don't think so."

"Why?"

Her nose scrunched up a little. "It's seeing someone die," she said. "Not just that—being killed. That's pretty extreme for anyone."

I thought about Molly, alone in the prison when her father dies. I thought about Winston Mavity, how he had saved my life. How I was tied to them both.

*I'd still go,* I thought to myself, but I had the sense to keep quiet.


After I dropped her at her house, my phone buzzed in my pocket. It was another text from Shawn. I shook my head. The kid just wouldn't give up.

> "Pepper, I know your knickers are still in a
> twist, but I've made it up to you. I scored you
> a date with PETRA FUCKING MIRKOVSKY. Consider

```
this my seppuku moment. A more selfless act was
never committed."
```

When I got home, I had to Google "seppuku."

*Seppuku*: when Samurai in ancient Japan fell on their swords for the sake of honor.

Shawn really is a shithead, isn't he, Ms. Eldridge?

# Molly

Hey, Pepper,

Everyone always wants to know whether there'd been signs that my mother would disappear. People don't leave without a trace like that. And I usually say, "No, my mother was *steadfast*," which was a word that always made me think of ocean liners. She was like an ocean liner, locked onto her course, never leaving but for regularly scheduled departures.

But, that's not the whole truth of it, Pepper. When I was little and the feeling of my father got too suffocating inside the house, my mom and I would sit in the backyard. We'd watch freight trains rattle past on the bridge, thick with graffiti, and sometimes we'd spot a hobo, sandwiched between boxcars, the wind ruffling his hair. My mother would say, "We should do that, Molly. Run away," and I took it so literally that I plotted out our entire journey. We could ride the Union Pacific line all the way to the Gulf of Mexico. My mother's face lit up. "Rent a catamaran," she said, her eyes roving across my map hungrily. "Fish for our meals. Nothing but us and the ocean."

Watching her, the far-off look in her eyes, my mouth formed a frown. This was the first time she had shown me the hidden place inside of her that longed to get away. Maybe children aren't supposed to see the secret people their parents are. It was like a crack of light between curtains, and it terrified me.

What might other people be hiding, if I didn't even fully know my own mother?

What might I be hiding?

After we return from the prison, I walk down to the library, through a part of town edged by evergreen trees, and wander to the nonfiction section in search of *The Arsonist*. I'm itching to be doing something for the quest, and I've exhausted the Internet. As I locate a copy and lift it from the shelf, I notice that it looks different from the copy you were sent. The picture of Ava Dreyman has been enlarged and set against a backdrop of a burned-out Stasi building.

I begin flipping pages. Everything looks the same except for the beginning where, instead of the editor's letter that accompanied the first printing, there is an updated letter written by Paedar Kiefer.

*A Note on the 20th Anniversary of the Publication of*
The Arsonist

*Twenty years have passed since Ava Dreyman's bloodstained diary found its way to my desk in Friedrichstadt. I was living in the dormitories of Spree University with four flat mates. Visitors were constantly coming and going, so I can't be certain who left the diary there. What I know is this: On the morning of February 23, 1989, as I was returning from the gymnasium, I found it sitting on my desk's bare wooden surface.*

*I knew immediately to whom the diary belonged. Years ago, I had seen Ava carrying it with her when we walked home from school. Inside the front cover, I discovered a photograph of a young girl with Ava's heavy brown hair, the author photo on the front of this book. A letter accompanied the photo, typewritten on a crisp, ivory card. No signature.*

Dear Paedar Kiefer,

This is the diary of Ava Dreyman, who died in a torture chamber on sublevel three of the Ministry of State Security Building in East Berlin, GDR, on the evening of February 22, 1989. You have been tasked with spreading her story. Let it burn those cowards who contributed to her death and the deaths of unspoken others. You have been given the job of ending this war, Paedar Kiefer. You owe it to Ava.

*I must have read the note a hundred times. My mind would hardly allow me to believe that Ava was dead. I felt a mixture of emotions: sorrow at Ava's death; anger at Captain Werner; and confusion. I was eighteen. Why had I been given this unimaginable task? And how would I orchestrate such a thing?*

I did the only thing I could think of. I went to the television tower where Ava described meeting the resistance in her diary, and in my mouth held the password: Summertime, a phrase the dissidents used to refer to a time when the Wall would be gone, when everyone in the East would step out from its shadow into the sun. The man I encountered at that meeting spot never gave me his real name. He said to call him Sandman, "Because I work at night and give people dreams."

Sandman's apartment was small and Spartan. The wallpaper had been ripped away. The ceiling was bare of tiles. "Makes it harder for the Stasi to do B measures." At my confusion, he explained. "B measures is bugging—you know, listening devices and pinhole cameras and such. And A measures is wiretapping. That one's easy to avoid. I stopped using a phone years ago." Sandman was bearded and grizzled and looked how I imagined someone might after surviving a nuclear winter. I realized, for the first time, that some people among us really had been through a war. I had believed the Cold War was a situation of bureaucracy and paper. But Sandman looked every inch a soldier.

I began to see the Wall as Sandman and the other freedom fighters I met saw it. I began to understand why they carried the word "summertime" around in their mouths like something sacred. When you shelter plants from light, they shrink and shrivel and die. Walking back after meeting Sandman, I saw it in people's faces. They were withered. I always thought of the Wall as a necessary inconvenience. Now, I began to see it as a straitjacket.

When I visited the next day, Sandman had printed over two hundred copies of Ava's diary. I was staggered by the mountain of them in the middle of the floor. The book was about the size of my outstretched hand, the spine held together by staples. He had managed to get the photo from inside the diary printed on the cover. He titled it, The Arsonist: The True Diary of Ava Dreyman, Martyr and Freedom Fighter. Ava would've loved the drama of it. Since Ava switched to writing in English halfway through the diary, Sandman had translated it, but with that done, he could run copies in his mimeograph as fast as he could crank. Our next task was to distribute them. Some of Sandman's friends went out with me, covertly placing The Arsonist on movie theater seats and tables in cafés. Sometimes I would stand behind walls and watch people pick it up and begin reading, their faces creasing. A thousand copies made their way into the mailboxes of East Berliners over the next week.

Sadly, Ava's original diary was stolen from my dormitory desk soon after the first printing, and has yet to be recovered. I believe someone who had a personal interest in undermining Ava's story stole it. The Arsonist must have scared the state security, particularly the Stasi captain Werner, who fled from the GDR soon after the diary was published.

But the diary's disappearance hardly dulled Ava's legacy. People stood openly in the streets with their copies. Sandman kept printing more, and I ran myself ragged delivering them across the city, but I had never felt so alive. In almost nine months, the Wall was torn down to the chant of "Ava! Ava! Ava!" Her memory burned in the air that night.

In the twenty years since its first printing, Ava's book has continued to have a life of its own. The Arsonist has been the subject of intense literary debate, a made-for-television movie, a plaque in Alexanderplatz, and a formal investigation by the unified German government in 2005 (in which DNA matching Ava's was recovered from a crematory oven inside of Stasi headquarters). I have written books and articles, given dozens of interviews, and all the while, I've only been able to repeat the maddening truth: I don't know who placed the diary on my desk. I don't know why they chose me. It's the greatest mystery of my life and, as my life advances, I have become certain that the truth will never be revealed to me. All I can say is that I'm grateful. The Arsonist introduced millions to the girl I knew

*and loved, the martyr who never gave in, even in the face
of incredible adversity, even up to the moment of her death.*
    Paedar Kiefer
    Berlin, Germany
    February 2009

I close the library copy of *The Arsonist* and slide it back on the shelf. It crosses my mind that Paedar isn't so different from you, the way you both received copies of *The Arsonist* from some unknown person.

I sit at one of the library computers and research Paedar online. He's in his forties and blond, with bright blue eyes and a serious mouth. It says that, after the Wall fell, he purchased and preserved Ava's old apartment, though he keeps it closed to the public, only allowing it photographed for special occasions. He's published a bunch of books about his time with Ava. It seems like that's his main occupation.

Hours later, when I trudge back home, Marty and my aunt are clinking pots and pans in the kitchen. I can hear my aunt explaining how to use a garlic press, and Marty responding, "Wow, that is truly the most versatile of instruments. I wonder if it works on almonds."

In the living room, Margaret sits curled up inside an armchair, engrossed in a book. Which is strange, since Margaret says reading is for people who can't make friends. (One time,

I told her, "Joke's on you because books *are* my friends." For obvious reasons, that didn't go over very well.) On the carpet, discarded, is a large white envelope. I bend to pick it up and see that it's empty, torn open at the top. The return address is Atwater Federal Prison. It's addressed to me.

"What is this?" I ask, turning to Margaret.

"What?" Margaret responds without looking up.

"This envelope. It's addressed to me."

"Oh, yeah, that came earlier today. There was a letter inside." She reaches beneath the chair cushion and hands me a crumpled note.

"*Dear Red,*" it reads, "*I hope this answers some of your questions.*" I run my hand inside the envelope. "What else came in this?"

"Right here," Margaret says, swinging the book she's been reading from her fingers.

I snatch it from her. "You opened my stuff?"

"Easy," Margaret says. "I wasn't going to *steal* it. I just wanted to see."

I examine the book, but it's not a book at all. It's a journal with a soft leather cover and gold edging, most of which has been worn away. My heart shudders for a moment when I imagine it's Ava Dreyman's diary, the one that was stolen from Paedar's desk, but when I leaf through it, I see the writing is all in English.

I turn the journal over. On the back cover, etched in gold, are the letters W.L.M.

"It's my father's," I say under my breath.

"Winston . . . Lunatic Mavity?" Margaret ventures.

"No," I say sharply. "His middle name's Leonard."

I flip through the notebook and scan the pages covered in handwriting, sometimes blue ink, sometimes black, sometimes in blunt pencil.

"Looks like notes," Margaret says. "Made no sense to me."

I open it to a random page. It's covered with sentences that don't go together.

*Which way to concourse C?*

*I can't lift that alone. Will you help me?*

*Seventy-five? I thought it was eighty.*

*I'm sorry.*

*I'm really sorry but I can't.*

"What is it, do you think?" Margaret asks. "Part of his trial, maybe? Like a psychological exercise?"

I shake my head, folding back the creased cover. "It's from a long time ago, I think. Maybe before I was born."

"In Criminal Justice freshman year, I learned about how in the seventies and eighties, they'd drug criminals and place a pencil in their hand and try to hypnotize them into a memory. They were actually admitted as testimonies in trials."

"Do you think that's what this was?" I ask. "Hypnosis treatments?"

Margaret hitches her shoulders up in a shrug. "What did he mean by '*I hope this answers some of your questions?*'"

"Who knows," I say, scanning the journal again. "That's

just like him, calling something like this answers."

"So . . ." Margaret says, "are you ever going to tell me what you're up to with that boy who dropped you off the other day in that rattling Oldsmobile death trap?"

I look up at her. "You saw that?"

"Is he your boyfriend?" Margaret asks. "No offense, but I didn't think you were into guys. I figured you were just smooth down there like a Barbie."

I'm used to Margaret's mode of communication by now. It's like a game. The more uncomfortable she can make the other person, the more points she gets.

"We're working together on something," I say.

"'Working on something'—is that what the kids call it now-adays?" she asks, her eyebrow cocked playfully.

"Shut up, Margaret," I say. "Why do you care? Shouldn't you be out with your friends, riding motorcycles off of cliffs or something?"

"Why's it so suspicious that I'm curious about my cousin and her new boyfriend?" Margaret asks.

"It's not like that," I say. "We're just—"

"Don't say 'friends,'" Margaret says. "You don't have friends."

It's nothing she hasn't said a million times, but her words still bruise.

But then, Margaret looks at me with an expression I don't recognize. She looks . . . *nice*. "If I swear I won't make fun of you, will you tell me?"

I know the only reason Margaret's talking to me—the only reason she ever voluntarily spends time with me—is because she's bored and doesn't have anyone better to hang out with. I sigh, because I might regret this. "You remember how you dressed up as Ava Dreyman at the Women's Studies dinner party? That guy—Pepper—and I think maybe Ava Dreyman didn't die the way everybody says."

Margaret's eyes narrow. "So, you guys are getting together to, what? Have a book club? I knew I had nothing to worry about."

"Exactly," I say. "Nothing to worry about."

I flip open the journal again, sifting through my dad's strange sentences.

"What does your book club entail, exactly?" Margaret asks, picking at her fingernails.

"We're trying to track down anyone who might know something about how Ava Dreyman really died."

"That seems unlikely," she says.

I nod. "A bit. But, short of going to Berlin, I don't know what else to do. There might be somebody around Monterey who knew her. Georg or Margarita, someone she met while she lived here."

Margaret nods, her lips pursed in concentration. I think she's going to add something meaningful, maybe even provide some idea neither of us had considered. Instead, she slaps her thighs, stands, and says, "This is lame. I'm going to play laser tag. Peace."

"Of course," I mutter, and turn my eyes back to the journal.

# Ava

November 26, 1986

I have arrived in America. From the airport, I took a taxi into Monterey and stared out the window at the wide roads and open land, rows of metal windmills and scrubby neighborhoods nestled between hills. No place on Earth could look less like East Berlin.

Once, I glimpsed the ocean, but only for a second.

The taxi driver dropped me off downtown because I didn't know where else to go. I walked around for a time, peering into shop windows and watching families stroll past. Eventually, I found a place on the sidewalk, where I've been for hours, staring down at the street where little bits of shredded tissue paper from some celebration are stuck. I picked up a piece and smoothed it out on my outstretched finger. It made a perfect mold of my fingerprint. I thought of Werner and scrubbed it into a ball between my thumb and forefinger, just in case.

November 27, 1986

I woke up to a flashlight held to my face. I covered my eyes from where I lay on the sidewalk, squinting up at a policeman who was speaking strings of sharp words that I didn't under-

stand. He grabbed me by the shoulder and made me sit in the
sticky backseat of his car that smelled of years-old sweat.

At the police station, they put me in a chair in a glass-walled
office where I met two policemen who looked like they were
dressed for dinner, one in a beige suit and an older one, aston-
ishingly, in powder blue.

The beige one crouched before me. His face was handsome
like an actor's, but an actor who only gets small parts playing
the main character's silly brother or the dumb guy who hilari-
ously fails at getting girls. "What is your name?"

I understood him. I had some English from school, though
it was mostly random verb tenses and flash cards of numbers
and vegetables.

"Ava Dreyman."

He asked something I couldn't make out, something I think
might've contained the word "parent."

I shook my head. *"Ich verstehe es nicht."*

"She's speaking German," the blue one said, standing.

"You speak it?" the other asked.

"From the war," he said. War. Somehow I knew that word.

The blue one pulled his chair near me. "Ava is your name?"
he asked in German.

I nodded.

"Are you lost?"

*"Ja,"* I replied in German. "Something terrible happened
when we left Germany. I, well—"

I considered what to say. I couldn't tell the truth. They'd look up Georg's and Margarita's names and lock them up for what they did to the American ambassador and his wife. Or they'd alert the Stasi somehow. "I'm looking for my parents. George and Marie Bailey." Georg had picked his new name from some old movie.

The officer wrote something down on a scrap of paper and handed it to the beige one, who left the room and returned a minute later.

"George and Marie Bailey moved to Monterey recently from Baltimore," he said. "The records say they have a fourteen-year-old daughter named Sally."

I felt all of the breath leave me in relief. It was like my father told me—Georg and Margarita had claimed me as their daughter in the paperwork.

The sky was still completely dark when they drove me to Georg and Margarita's house, a little whitewashed place with a picket fence. I noticed a street sign—Ponderosa Avenue—and the neighboring houses, small but neat. The beige policeman knocked on the door three times, hard.

Georg answered, wrapped in a maroon dressing gown. His face darkened with surprise.

"Mr. George Bailey?" the beige one asked.

"Y-yes," Georg sputtered.

"Recognize this little lady?"

Georg's eyes rested on my face for only a moment. "Of course," he said, his features calming. "Our daughter, Sally." Georg conversed with the men in immaculate English, and I caught enough of their conversation to guess what they were saying.

"She seemed unwell," the blue one said. "She said her name was Ava, that she was German."

Georg darted a glance at me, eyes hot. "Sally gets—confused on occasion."

Margarita entered the room then, pulling her hair loose from curlers, fat chunks of blond hair falling away with a sleepy bounce. She let a curler fall from her hand to the laminate floor when she saw me. Her mouth fell open.

Georg grabbed her arm. "Look, Marie, our daughter is back."

Margarita's face stretched in surprise.

"Can you explain your daughter's condition?" the beige one asked. "I've never heard of this disability before. Speaking a totally different language, and quite fluently."

"She's suffered delusions all her life," Georg said. "We have her birth certificate if you're interested."

"She was very close with her grandmother," Margarita said. Her English was much less smooth than Georg's. "I was born in Switzerland, and my mother taught Sally to speak German." The officer scribbled this on his pad.

"We will be needing to see that birth certificate. And your green card, Mrs. Bailey."

"Certainly, certainly. Marie, dear? Will you . . ."

Margarita was already walking to an ivory-colored safe in

the corner of the sparely furnished room. She spun the metal dial and extracted a manila folder. Inside, I knew, were three birth certificates they'd paid for, one for Mr. George Bailey, one for Mrs. Marie Bailey, and one for Sally Bailey.

The men glanced over the fake papers, touching the holographic seal on each one, shiny in the yellow living room light.

"Did you serve?" the blue one asked, glancing up from Georg's birth certificate.

"Serve?" Georg asked.

"In the war. You're the right age."

"I—I did. Proudly fought."

"What was your count?"

"My count? I'm sorry, I've gotten such little sleep lately."

"How many Krauts did you kill?"

I sucked in a breath. Georg had served in the war, but as a German soldier. He'd gone to the Russian front, lost three toes from frostbite, and got an Order of the German Cross for his trouble. He loved Germany with the entirety of his old heart.

"Twelve," he said. "Before the foot injury sent me home."

"I got one hundred and fifty. The most in my regiment."

Georg looked away. "Well done."

"Well, these seem to be in order," he said. "We're sorry to have bothered you Mr. and Mrs. Bailey, and so late at night."

Georg nodded stiffly. "We're just happy to have Sally back."

"You do know," the beige one said, "there are facilities for people like her."

"Oh," Georg said, eyes dragging across me. "That shouldn't be necessary."

When they were gone, Georg hissed at Marie to pour him a Scotch. He drained it in seconds and ordered her to fix another.

"Goddamn it, Ava, how did you find us?"

"Your notebook in the car said Monterey. I knew you must've had to flee. And my father—" At the mention of him, hot tears welled in my eyes. "My father told me to go to the rendezvous point no matter what. Werner found me in Paris and I only just escaped."

"Werner?" Georg barked. "You might've led him here, as well. This would never have happened if Mirka and Hans hadn't insisted you be linked to us in the paperwork. And now you're tied to us good and proper."

I blinked back my tears. A realization slowly poured itself into my head. "In France—you left me on purpose."

"Oh, don't look so hurt, Ava," Georg spat. "We were never supposed to take you without your parents. You were an extra piece of luggage that we could no longer carry."

The words were a blow across my face. "You were our friends," I said, my voice trembling. "My mother and father— they said I'd be safe with you."

Georg's face turned hard, and he swatted the air with his open hand. "We are living in a very different reality now, girl. We spent nearly every cent getting American papers. We can't start over again. And your little stunt with those detectives, telling them where we're from—suppose they look into it. Even if they find nothing, the Storm Wolves could start poking around here. They have ways of finding people, Ava, that you cannot even begin to understand."

Georg motioned his meaty hand toward Margarita, who led me to a guest bedroom. When I turned, she had closed the door, locking it behind her.

December 2, 1986

These past few days, I've understood Georg and Margarita to be very different people than I had once believed, and I see now that the signs were there all along, the way Georg can silence Margarita with a dartlike glance, the steady stream of liquor they both consume, the muttering that never seems to stop, which I can hear even through the door of this pastel-colored bedroom.

"The damn Americans, why were they at that party?" Georg muttered. "Everything would have gone off without a hitch if that goddamn ambassador hadn't been visiting."

"They were there, Georg," Margarita snapped. "They drank the champagne like the others. There's no changing it now."

"If they realize it was us, those detectives will be back."

"I told you it should've been Santiago," Margarita said. "Even Buenos Aires, with all the troubles there."

"Like some Nazi fugitives?" Georg spat. "We were freedom fighters. We changed the tide of the war."

"We poisoned some two-bit politicians and an American ambassador and his wife. As far as I can see, nobody's rushing to pull the Wall down in our name."

"Those fucking idiots will never pull the Wall down. Not in a thousand years. The GDR will be the empire Honecker wants, and not for any other reason than the entire country is a bunch of backward-facing sheep-brained cowards."

"We could've had a life here," Margarita said wistfully.

I heard the heavy thunk of a glass set down on the table. "We still can."

"How?"

Georg didn't answer. The room was loud with the sound of his thinking.

December 7, 1986

The orange juice didn't look strange. If I had examined it closer, I might have noticed a dusting of white particles on the surface, or felt the granules between my teeth. If my mother were there, she'd club me in the head for being so easily duped.

Georg and Margarita watched me over the breakfast table until I drank the entire glass. Every dish was laid out a little too deliberately, the silverware aligned with the edge of the table at exact degrees, and now I can picture Margarita waking up early to get the table setting just right so I'd suspect nothing.

The first thing I noticed was how long it took me to blink. My eyes closed slowly and it was an effort to prize them open again. A thought rushed into my head, but by the time it was delivered to my lips and tongue, I had forgotten what I'd been planning to say.

"Ava, how are you feeling?" Georg asked, his voice high with tension.

"I—" I tried to say, but my jaw felt like a cloud, floating free of the rest of my face. "I feel strange."

"It's working," Margarita said.

They stood from their chairs and Georg pulled me to standing, too. I watched my arms swing drunkenly at my sides.

Georg ushered me from the kitchen, into the chill early morning air, and flung me into the backseat of their beat-up car—not nearly as nice as the BMW they owned in Berlin. He and Margarita were silent in the front seat. After some time, by the smell of fish and salt, I knew we were driving to the ocean.

My first view of the ocean was white. My vision was hazy, and a frothy blanket of mist curved over the edge of land. The only person on the dock was a man. He wore an official-looking uniform of thick navy fabric. Perhaps a security guard. Georg marched me toward an iron boat, bobbing inside the fog like a toy inside a child's bubble bath.

On the boat, I looked between Georg and Margarita. "Where are you taking me?" I tried to ask, but the words came out in mushy German.

Georg leaned close to me, so near that I got a whiff of his

aftershave from the day before. His cheeks were untrimmed and he smelled sour and day-old, and I guessed he hadn't slept all night, waiting for me to wake up, to drink that orange juice. "Somewhere you can get better, Sally," he said in a loud whisper. A dull panic coursed through my veins.

When the boat slowed and nudged a dock, we climbed some precarious steps built into black rock, slick with sea spray, up to a place that looked like a crumbled old castle, though there was no reason I should've thought that. I have seen real castles and none of them are made of moldering rust-colored brick, none lit with giant halogen bulbs. None of them must be accessed on a guarded boat.

The uniformed man led us into the lobby of the large brick building and rang a buzzer on the counter. From behind a wired-glass partition, a woman with dusted gray hair emerged.

Georg and the woman began to converse, discussing something in English that fell through my brain like a sieve. My mind was trying and failing to determine what we were doing in this place, my thoughts like a lighter being clicked, the thumb of my mind rolling over the flint wheel again and again but refusing to catch.

The older woman looked to me, then. She walked to where I was standing and bent over a little to be eye level with me.

She asked a question in garbled English. My brain couldn't grasp her words. I looked to Georg and Margarita, who were watching me, holding their breath.

"*Wie bitte?*" I asked.

The woman repeated herself, louder this time.

"*Ich verstehe nicht,*" I told her. *I don't understand you.*

"See?" Georg asked, and I finally understood that he was telling her the same story he told the police.

"I am not lying," I said in rough English. "I am not crazy. I am from German Democratic Republic." But the words left my mouth clumsy and slurred.

The woman went to a desk and gathered some papers, handing them to Georg. The words "seventy-two hours" left her lips many times, cutting through the fog inside my brain. At last, Georg nodded, scraping a hand over his jaw.

"Is there a place we could say good-bye in private?" Georg asked the woman.

"Of course." With a hand, she indicated a small, poorly lit room nearby. Georg and Margarita walked me inside and closed the door behind us.

They began whispering in German, their mouths touching each other's ears so the woman beyond the door could not hear. "They will hold her for three days for evaluation," Georg said. "The drugs won't last that long," he said, glancing toward me. My eyes darted between the two of them.

"My God, Georg, they could figure it out," Margarita said, her voice a frantic whisper. "What if someone here speaks German and starts listening to her?"

"I don't know," he croaked. His eyes were stretched wide.

"We are paying them," Margarita said, her fingers shaking. "We are paying them all we have left. We'll be eating salted cabbage and beef tongue like paupers. All because Hans and Mirka couldn't follow the plan."

"My father's dead," I said. The two of them turned to look at me. "It's not that he couldn't follow the plan. He died."

It took me a moment to realize that tears were flowing down my cheeks.

Georg's features became sharp. "If only that hadn't happened," he said. With a decided motion, he reached into his jacket. In his fist appeared a small silver knife. "Things did not need to be this way."

Georg held the knife up in the air and I took a clumsy step backward. "You—" I slurred. "You leave me alone!" *This can't be the way I go*, I thought. I told Werner it'd take an act of God to kill me, and I meant it.

A dull smile played over Georg's frenzied features. "The knife isn't for you, Ava," he whispered. The fingers of his free hand traced the muscles beneath his rib cage.

"Georg, what are you doing?" Margarita gasped.

Georg's eyes were focused. He lifted the knife high, flashing in the air, and plunged it through his immaculate white shirt. He let out an unconscious, guttural scream. Margarita's hands flew to her gaping mouth. Georg wrenched the knife free, a saucer-size bloodstain already soaking his shirt.

I watched him, my limbs totally limp, as he pressed the

knife's naked handle into my hand, closing my fingers around it. I let the knife fall into the quickly growing puddle of blood on the floor. Georg grabbed my hands and slathered the flowing blood from his side onto my open palms.

He did all this with a steady industry, teeth flexed around his bottom lip. And then a switch flicked on his face, and his features contorted.

"OH GOD!" he screamed in English, so loudly I thought he could've woken all of California. "SALLY, WHY!"

Margarita started screaming, too, catching on. "Someone come quick! Our daughter, she's killed my husband!"

The old woman busted through the door, and behind her were several others, dressed in white nurse outfits, and guards in navy-colored uniforms. I stood paralyzed, my hands held in front of me, bloodied, my jaw hanging off its hinges. And a knife at my feet.

They've placed me in a small room. The walls are brick and the metal door locks with a great shaking thud that makes the air shudder. I have a mattress on a spring bed, nothing else, and I am alone.

I heard them call this place Rake Island.

# Pepper

_American History_

Dear Ms. Eldridge,

I have been saving this essay, for it is about my favorite topic, one I know much about. America was founded many years ago by George Washington, who wore fluffy white wigs, who had bone-and-wood teeth, who never smiled because he was ashamed of himself. They say every president since has had something to be embarrassed about. Taft had a special bathtub made to fit his enormous girth. Lincoln had an Adam's apple which was said to look like a veiny kneecap protruding from his throat, and that's why he grew a beard.

I always wondered what my shame would be. I thought it would have been Petra's interview, but it turns out to be much worse than that.

Today, you are surely already guessing, I found it.

I was at home reading _The Arsonist_ when I came upon a scene that made me sit straight up in bed. What Georg and Margarita did to Ava—the stabbing and leaving her at Rake Island—I couldn't believe it so much that I called Molly right then.

"Did you read this part?" I asked her. "What her aunt and uncle did to her."

"Georg and Margarita?" she asked. She pronounced Georg *Gay-org*. "They weren't really her aunt and uncle."

"That is besides the point. He stabbed himself and blamed it on her. He is the worst villain of the entire book," I pronounced. "Why do not more people think it was him who killed Ava?"

"He was in California when she died in Berlin."

"Still . . . I am bookmarking this idea."

"Can I come over?" she asked abruptly.

"To my house?"

"Yeah," she said. "I need to show you something."

It was so hot inside, what with my father's refusal to buy an air conditioner, and the heat was making the fish tanks smell like hot fish bodies and poop, so when she arrived I suggested we walk to the park on the corner. It was deserted as it was so hot and most people were probably by the water.

We sat on the edge of a dented merry-go-round, Bertrand lying down on the burned grass with a thump. I had played on this thing with Shawn when we were in the sixth grade, me lying in the middle of the flat disk, and him running alongside it, spinning me around and dying of laughter.

Molly held out a notebook and wrapped her fingers around the chipped pink railing as I read. She was frustrated by it, I could tell, because the little line had formed between her eyes.

"How is this answers?" she asked. "Not a single sentence in here makes any sense."

I thumbed through it, my eyes trying to assemble the broken-up sentences. "Have you ever seen your dad with this?"

"No," she said. "But it's got his initials on it. W.L.M."

"It kind of tells a story," I said.

"Yeah," she said, "like a play with all of the character names removed. He wrote about food, played games, went for walks, flew in an airplane. And there's this part that seems to be about fire." She paged forward to show me.

*Fire? What for? I'm not sure.*

*Because it's dangerous.*

*Don't call me that.*

*I'm not.*

*Fine.*

*It was, a little.*

*All right, a lot. How's your hand?*

*Do you need a nurse?*

*Fine, then. It's your skin.*

She sighed. "I wonder if these sentences could be voices in my dad's head or something."

"Does he hear voices?"

She shrugged. "He never said."

I flipped through the book some more.

"He's talking to someone here." I pointed to a section around the middle of the notebook.

*You are the most beautiful girl I've ever met.*

*Maybe.*

*Where will you go?*

*Of course it matters.*

*Me? Somewhere warm. With beaches.*

"But then it all falls apart again," she says, turning to the next page. "'*Breakfast is at eight, scrambled eggs, or what they call eggs. I have my doubts.*'"

"Who's he talking to?" I wondered.

Molly shook her head. "My mom once told me that my dad changed a lot after they got together."

"How did he change?"

"Well, he started lighting buildings on fire for one."

I blew a lungful of air from my lips. I felt bad talking about Molly's dad this way. There was still a big part of me that wanted him to be the redheaded soldier who saved my life, who my dad had built up into a kind of superhero. "Why do you think he changed?"

She shrugged. "Why does anybody change? I guess over time he grew into a different person."

"Maybe your mom changed him."

She turned to look at me, her forehead frowning. "What do you mean?"

"Nothing, really," I said, because she was peering at me in a way that made me sense I had said something wrong.

"No," she said, her voice quiet and low. "What did you mean?"

I swallowed. "People can change other people is all," I said. "Like how I can't be around my friend Shawn right now because he makes me want to punch his face or cry or something, and I don't need that. Like how my mom said one thing about fish that messed up my dad in the head forever."

"And you think my mother did that to my dad," she said, her voice a sharp clap that ricocheted around the playground. She stood from the merry-go-round, arms crossed over her chest, eyes crumpled angrily. "Don't be stupid."

"I'm not stupid," I said. "Don't call me that."

"You're acting pretty fucking stupid right now," she said. This might have been the first time I'd heard her swear, and it struck me across the cheek like a slap. "My dad was probably writing this insane crap way before he met my mom." She held the journal up. "There was probably always something wrong with him."

I held my hands up before me as if to stem the flow of words coming from her mouth, shocked at how easily I had turned on the faucet of Molly's anger. "Okay," I said, my voice attempting to be low and even. "Okay, okay."

Molly was shaking her head. "You don't get to just say *okay* like that," she said. "Like we're done talking about this. My mother didn't plan on being married to someone like that." She leveled her eyes at me. "Just like your mom, actually. Your mom didn't ask to be cooped up in some house under an oil storm. Of course she tried to leave when your dad wasn't watching."

Something like a cello chord struck across the playground.

Something that made me feel burned and furious. "Don't talk about my mother."

"I can talk about whatever I want, actually," she said. "And it's not even the same. You've never even *met* your mother."

We were flinging knives now. We were aiming to kill.

I stood up then, so quickly and unconsciously it took me a moment to catch up with what my body was doing. "You think that makes it okay?"

"Of course it does!" she said loudly, her hands waving in the air. "I knew my mother for *twelve years*. Did you even know yours at all? Why do you think your mom did what she did, if you knew her so well?"

I opened my mouth, popping my lips like a dumb gold-fish. I didn't know the answer. I didn't know enough about my mother to even guess.

Molly set her mouth in a rigid line. "I know my mother didn't make my dad the way he is. She was a good person. She was kind and generous and considerate—"

"Then why did she jump off a cliff and leave you all alone?" I snapped.

The sound in the park was dead: the seabirds that had suddenly gone quiet, the dried summer grass, the air that had slowly choked on heat. And the two of us, covered with the wounds of our words.

Molly's mouth fell open, drawing in a silent breath.

I set my jaw and said the thing I had been skirting since

the very beginning of all of this. "Your mother is not the one who is orchestrating this, Molly. She's not the one who sent my interview to you. She's not the one who sent me the book. Because she died."

I watched the sentence plow through the air like a bullet. I could actually see Molly waver the moment it made impact. She stumbled backward a step. Her face wrenched painfully. "Stop saying that!" she shouted, grabbing handfuls of hair. Her voice was high-pitched, like a child's.

And I realized, when her mom was discussed, Molly was a child. She became twelve years old again, frozen in the moment her mother abandoned her on a cliff in France. And maybe, in the same way, around the topic of my own mom, I am a newborn, just barely alive.

This was the moment we've been plummeting toward, Ms. Eldridge, the moment in which I discovered my presidential-size shame.

Quincy Adams had his flatulence.

Truman had erectile dysfunction, so they say.

And Pepper Al-Yusef can be a real shithead when he wants to be.

I stood to make my exit, which was impeded slightly by Bertrand who wouldn't budge, and had to be lifted bodily from the dirt. (Exits are always less dramatic with a pug under one's arm, but I was still too red-faced to care.) I thought Molly might call after me, say she still needed my help with

Ava Dreyman's mystery, that she wanted to say sorry and forget about it. Just once, I glanced behind me. Molly was looking toward me, but when she saw me look back, her face became a hate-filled, bunched-up glare. My throat grew thick like I was choking.

I walked a whole block waiting for the hot pinpoints inside my tear ducts to fade. My hands were still shaking when I pulled out my phone and dialed the number Shawn had texted me. It rang twice.

"Hello?" came the soft voice from the other end.

"Petra?" I asked.

"Ibrahim," she breathed. "Shawn said you might call."

"Yeah."

"I expected it a lot sooner, though, I have to say."

"I—think Shawn's text was delayed or something. Anyway, do you still want to meet? We could have lunch tomorrow at the boardwalk."

"Yes," she said. "I would really like that."

"I'll meet you there. Noon?"

"Okay. Bye, Ibrahim."

"Can you call me Pepper?" I asked. "I like being called Pepper."

"Oh, sure thing," she said. "See you tomorrow, Pepper."

I hung up, squeezed my phone in my hand as tightly as I could, putting as many feet between me and Molly Mavity as possible.

# Molly

Pepper,

After our fight, it's like ten gallons of adrenaline have been pumped into my blood, and I feel like I could punch the lights out of a million bad guys. I don't cry. Instead, I think venom. I think, "I hate you and I hope you die." I think, "You're a prick of the highest order." More than ever, I want to be a comic book villain. I want to stretch to the height of the Manhattan skyline and fling cars around. I want you to scramble over the bucking concrete like an ant.

After a while, though, the blood in my body slows down so my veins are only barely moving. The feeling starts to shift, and suddenly I feel myself grow very small. I hear your words, repeated over and over again in different combinations.

*Why did she jump?*

*Why did she leave you all alone?*

*Why?*

*Why?*

*Why?*

*Because she died.*

You're wrong. You have to be, but that doesn't sweep away the ashy cloud above my head, the thing that, I'm only realizing now, has left me alone since I found Ava Dreyman's diary. Since we started looking for answers.

I stand from the merry-go-round, bending each limb deliberately. I feel like I just walked off of a battlefield. I look down at my body, feeling like I must have broken bones, like there should be blood dribbling across my skin.

But I am, remarkably, intact.

I walk down the street, shell-shocked, my throat raw and my skin feeling stretched-out and wrong. There's a sound in my head like when you hold a shell to your ear and hear the swirl and thrash of the ocean. That sound reminds me of my parents. My father would sometimes look at my mother in his measured way, and say, "Remember when we used to sit by the ocean together?" And her face would fill with such unexplainable sadness, I thought she would cry.

My mother never cried, though. It's where I got it from. Maybe another person would break down right now, but my veins are filled with Novocain.

My phone buzzes. I fumble in my pocket for it, certain it's you calling.

It's not.

"Hey," Margaret says on the other end.

"What's going on?" I ask. Margaret never calls. If she has

anything to say to me, it's in a text, usually something like, "Ro says go buy pasta sauce."

"You don't sound good. You sound like you're literally dead, actually."

"What do you want, Margaret?" I ask.

"I just wanted to ask you about the, uh, quest you're on."

My feet come to a stop on the sidewalk. Margaret might as well have said she wanted to ask me about alien autopsies or something. "What about it?"

"Well, I didn't have anything else to do this afternoon, and *Rosanne* kept telling me to do the dishes even though Marty was right there and that's kind of the whole point of his coming to our house, so I did a little digging about that book. And I found something. Some*one*, I should say."

"Who?" I ask, taking an eager step forward.

"I think I found Ava's godfather, Georg."

"Georg Winkler?" I ask, blinking away my astonishment. "*The* Georg?"

"Pretty sure," she says. "He lives in the boonies but he works in Monterey. He changed his name again, after the diary came out. I thought, since he chose his first alias from *It's a Wonderful Life*, he might do it again."

"What do you mean, *It's a Wonderful Life*?"

"Remember?" she asks. "Ava says Georg picked his new name from an old movie. George Bailey is the main character in *It's a Wonderful Life*."

"I never would've thought of that," I say.

"Anyway, I tried all the other character names and I found a match, an eighty-six-year-old man living outside of Salinas. He's called George Gower now. Mr. Gower's that old man who hits George Bailey on his bad ear."

I know I give Margaret too many chances to be a jerk to me. She holds out a lure and I bite, every time. It's honestly pretty pathetic. But my battle-torn heart is jerking to life at her words. The quest isn't over. My mother is still out there.

I start walking toward my aunt's house. "When can we leave?"

The streets are nearly dark by the time Margaret and I set off. When I meet her out front, I find her dressed all in black. The two of us hop in Auntie Ro's car, a white Civic that hugs the ground so closely, it feels like riding in a soapbox derby.

"All right, navigator, you ready?" Margaret asks. "Our man Georg works at the monoplex in Old Monterey."

"Got it," I say, holding up my phone where I've already looked up the route.

"Two girls on a mission," Margaret says. "Hunting criminals, seeking justice, capping fools."

"I'm not planning on capping any fools tonight," I say. Margaret is smiling, which makes me suddenly suspicious. "Why are you helping me?"

"Do I need a reason?" Margaret asks. "God, we're related,

why do you have to make it weird whenever I want to hang out with you?"

"Because you *never* want to hang out with me."

Margaret rolls her eyes. "I guess you could say I've begun to appreciate your style, after what happened with Brielle."

I look over at her, sensing for the first time a strangeness about her. She holds the steering wheel at the bottom with just her pointer finger, but the hand in her lap is wrapped in a bloodless fist.

"What happened?"

"You haven't heard?" Margaret asks. "I forget you don't do social media. Everyone's talking about it. Nobody will shut up, actually."

"What did you do?"

"I kind of—might've—hooked up with Grayson."

"You did *what*?" I ask.

"I know, I know," Margaret says guiltily.

"No, what does hooked up mean? You didn't—you didn't *sleep* with him."

"Jesus, Molly, you sound like a black-and-white movie."

I gape at her. "But he's your best friend's boyfriend."

"It was an accident."

"How does that happen by accident?" I ask. "How did his penis *accidentally* go up your vagina? Why were you naked in the first place? Did he fall on you or something?"

"I don't *literally* mean accident," Margaret says. "I mean it was a mistake. Now none of the girls will talk to me. And Brielle didn't even break up with Grayson."

"What?" I say. "That's so not fair."

"Right?" she says, incredulous. "*Thank* you. Grayson was the one who cheated, but I'm who gets punished. The patriarchy is *not* dead."

I consider placing a hand out to comfort her, but that seems too friendly for us. "I'm sorry, Margaret. Your friends—I know they're important to you."

Margaret's cheeks inflate and she exhales loudly. "It feels a little bit like right after my dad left. There's this giant thing, like a balloon, that fills up so much of your life and then, pop, it's gone and there's nothing left but a hole."

I feel a twang inside my chest. This was exactly the feeling I had when my mother disappeared.

If I looked, really looked, I think the mother-shaped hole that was punched out of me when I was twelve is exactly the same size today. Maybe bigger.

"So that's why I'm helping you," Margaret continues. "Because I have no friends. You and I finally have something in common."

*I have a friend*, I almost say, thinking of you.

But then I remember.

I roll down my window, the cool air washing over my face. I have always loved the old part of Monterey, these neighborhoods of Steinbeck and Doc Holliday, streets of canneries and the salt smell of the ocean coloring everything. It's a weekday, so there are just a few locals walking the pavement lit by pools of light from streetlamps.

"Here," I say. "Turn here."

Margaret pulls up into one of the few parking spots in front of a tiny art deco theater, the facade lined with diamond-shaped green tiles. A glass-cased ticket booth extends on to the sidewalk.

"We're looking for a man named George Gower," I say to the woman inside the booth.

"He's upstairs, in the projection room. He expecting you?"

"Yes," I say, already pushing through the glass doors. I run into the flickering darkness of the theater. A handful of people sit in the moldering velvet seats watching the screen where Charlie Chaplin roller skates around a toy store balcony. I climb a set of stairs at the back, the thunk of my cast echoing around the theater, and push the silent swinging doors at the top.

An old man sits in a metal chair, lit by the pulsing illumination of an old-fashioned film projector. The dull brightness from the screen shines on his face, wrinkled like a letter folded a hundred times. He looks like he might've stepped out from another era, dressed in a faded herringbone suit. He holds himself utterly still, the only sign of life his left hand, loosely feeding celluloid film into the projector.

"Georg Winkler?" I whisper above the winding music from the film.

The old man turns his watery blue eyes on me. "Nobody with that name here," he says, his voice dry and brittle.

"We know you're him," Margaret says from behind me. "The Internet does not lie."

"Go bother someone else," he croaks. "I'm not who you're looking for."

I take a step into the room. It's uncomfortably hot. A stippling of sweat has broken out on the man's brow.

"I'm trying to learn about Ava Dreyman," I say. "Maybe you could help me."

He flinches slightly. "I don't know who that is."

Margaret steps forward. "I looked you up online. Did you know your house in Berlin was flattened to build a mall?"

I eye Margaret, uncertain of where she's going with this.

"So what?" Georg barks.

Margaret shrugs, looks down at the black carpeted floor. "I'm just saying, a lot of time has passed. No offense, but you're old now. If you went back to Germany, you wouldn't even recognize it, and they wouldn't recognize you, either."

"And that's supposed to convince me of something?" he asked, his voice rising. "Reminding me that I'm old."

"It means they might forgive you," she says. "Have you ever even asked for forgiveness? Have you even tried?"

"Bah!" he exclaims, his mouth shriveled. "They will *never* forgive me."

My eyebrows dart upward. I could hug Margaret, which I've

never done except once when forced for a family photo. Just like that, she's gotten Georg to admit who he is.

"Why won't you just leave me alone?" he asks, shoulders slumped. The air is quietly buzzing.

"No can do," Margaret says. "Hey, how come your English is so good?"

He clears his throat roughly. "The same reason Ava spoke it like a native by the end. We were both held captive in this damn place. Her on that island, and me in a camp. Not a mile from here." He sees the confusion pass over our faces and adds, "People forget there were POWs carted here from over the ocean during World War II. Half the roads in town were built by Nazis. There wasn't much for us to do but haul rocks and learn English."

Margaret's eyes stretch in surprise. "Did you know about that, Molly?"

I shake my head, my stomach a tightening knot.

"Doesn't surprise me," he says. "Nobody wants to remember their own bloody history." He leans forward and grips a film canister in his fingers, loosening the top and pulling out a new roll of film.

"But—" I ask, sorting through what Georg just said. "But if you were a prisoner here, why would you come back to this place?"

Georg shakes his head. "It would be the last place they'd think to look for me. And I was right. They never found me."

"And Margarita?" I ask.

"She hasn't been Margarita for twenty years," he says, suddenly looking deflated. "Marie died five years ago. Cancer."

I pause. "How did you learn Ava had died?"

"Same as everybody, in that damn book." He slaps his hand down on his knee. "If there was ever a question of me going back to Germany, it was dead after that book was published. I can never use my real name again. She may not have killed my body, but she effectively killed Georg Winkler."

"No offense," Margaret says. "But I have a hard time feeling any sympathy for you, dude."

"You got Ava locked up to save your skin," I say forcefully. "How long did she have to stay on the island, everybody thinking she was crazy?"

"Bah, things were different then," he says. "You have to see it through the perspective of someone who constantly feels the itch of a sniper's sights on the back of their head." His fingers graze his neck like he's swatting away a bug. He glances at the film reel, slowly winding down inside the projector. "The movie is almost over. Tell me what you want to know, and leave."

I take a quick breath. "I want to know who killed her."

"I don't know if you'll ever find the answer to that," he says quietly. "All of us who knew her, we're dropping like flies, and every day it's harder to remember her face. The only thing I know for certain, it wasn't Werner. He had a reputation for killing, yes, but what purpose would he have had to kill her?

If she was killed in the torture chamber that night, it was by some young grunt. A trainee. More likely, they made her drink strychnine or starved her to death in a cell."

"But everybody knows that Ava was stabbed with the bone-handled knife," I said.

"That knife," Georg breathes. "That knife is not what you think."

"I know," I tell him. "I already figured out it didn't belong to Werner."

"You're right," he says. "That knife belonged to Ava."

My head reels back. "What?"

"Her mother gave it to her when she was a little girl. Her parents fought about it. I'd never heard Hans raise his voice before. You know the inscription? *Use not in anger.* He had it printed there. I remember the argument he and Mirka had afterward. She said of course Ava would use it in anger, if the time came, it was a knife after all."

My brain is still rearranging itself around the image of the bone-handled knife in Ava's fist. "But—it's her diary. Why wouldn't she mention it was her knife?"

"She left it out," Georg says. "Or someone took it out."

I blink. "You think the diary was tampered with?" I ask. "But why? To frame Werner?"

He nods. "Finally you're catching on."

"Who would want to frame him?" Margaret asks, turning her gaze on me.

"That's the question. Because in that question lies the answer to the one you're searching for." He drags in a long breath. "Who actually killed her."

"What if . . ." Margaret says.

"What?" I ask.

"Well, it seems like the most obvious thing is that she killed herself," she says. "Don't look at me like that, Molly, it fits. She got arrested and put in a prison cell, alone with this knife. She must've been desperate. She killed herself and framed Werner in the diary."

A poisonous feeling floods my veins. "Who placed the diary on Paedar Kiefer's desk to publish, then?"

"Maybe she hired a courier service?"

"And how did she arrange that from inside a torture chamber?" I ask. "And how did *Werner* end up with her knife?"

"Maybe he was the one who found her body?" Margaret muses. "And he took the knife as a kind of souvenir. It totally adds up, if you think about it."

I am shaking my head, refusing to accept that as a possibility. "No. Why is that the one thing that people will never drop?"

"You're not talking about Ava now, are you?" Margaret asks.

I stare Margaret down, incensed that she would take this moment and make it about my mother. I am thinking of the things you said as well, right now, and I almost feel like throwing my fist into her throat again, like I did on the boardwalk.

"You seem very certain of things, girl," Georg says in a whisper.

I turn to look at him. He's holding his pale eyes to mine.

"You take a lesson from Ava," he says. "You want to know how to navigate life? Don't live and die by the beliefs you had when you were young. Everything changes, that's what you learn when you've lived as long as I have. The worst crime you can do to yourself is to forget why you chose the path you're on, but keep walking down it anyway."

Several things are happening quietly in this moment. The screen has turned to black, and from below, the sound of moviegoers pushing off from velvet seats and pacing across the sticky floor to the exit. I clutch my hand tightly, the image of my mother floating through a turquoise sky inside my head.

And beside Georg, the celluloid film has run out. It is flicking against his open palm, over and over and over.

# Ava

The sound when they slammed the door of my room echoed in my head for what felt like hours. They put me in a canvas jacket that tied my arms around my torso and only took it off just now when they passed in a plate of food. Justified, I guess. I didn't go with them easy.

The walls are brick and constantly damp. Someone has been watching me. There is a plastic flap in the door of my room. It whines whenever the person opens it, gazing in with a blue eye. Closes the flap. Leaves.

Date unknown

The blue-eyed person opened my door today. She said to call her Nurse Keating. Her face is angular and direct, with brown hair that falls straight down the sides of her face. She is younger than my parents, could almost be a university student. She unbuckled and removed the straitjacket I'd worn for days. I shook out my arms, letting the blood return to them.

She held her palm to me, gesturing for me to stand. I studied it from where I lay on my mattress. I stretched my body to standing in the clothes they gave me—yellow cotton pants and a shirt with buttons, soft like pajamas—and ignored her hand.

I walked between her and a barrel-chested man in a uniform, my stocking feet sliding on the dark stone corridor. "Keep an eye on her," the woman told the guard. "She's got violent tendencies." I almost chuckled at this.

We passed patients' rooms, and some had wheedled the little plastic flaps on their doors open and stared out with their roving eyes, touching me with the shine of them.

"Quickly now!" a voice called from down the hall. Wind rippled through an open door where a red-haired nurse stood, ushering in patients who had been enjoying some kind of outdoor recreation. "Everyone inside."

I paused for just a second, breathing in the smell of the sea, and darted through the open door. The guard grasped my shoulder, but I pulled from his grip and began sprinting ten, twenty, thirty paces over the vegetation and closed-in walls of trees, until I came out onto the black-rock plane of the outer island. I slowed for just a moment to take in the view, testing what Werner had said, that you can know your own death by looking at the sea. My heart was beating at the edges of my vision, and my eyes frantically traced the sparkling expanse, but before I could see anything of my death, I felt myself plummet to the hard rock. Breath left my lungs with an *oof*. The barrel-chested guard had tackled me, pinning me down.

"Get off me!" I shouted, struggling, heart beating through my chest against the porous black rock.

I thrashed my head to the side and saw the woman with the blue eyes nearby, panting, hands on her hips, her cheeks flushed. "Take her inside," she said, and then kneeled beside me. "Try that again, and you'll get worse than a straitjacket."

I wiped grit from my cheek with an open palm.


Date Unknown

Nurse takes me to her office at random times each day, her arm clasped firmly around my elbow, though I attempt to pull away from her at every opportunity.

She asks me questions in English, the same ones over and over, to the point that I have started to recognize the pattern of syllables, and can even respond sometimes with my own, though never in the way that she wants.

The first time I got her to crack was after three days of English-only questioning.

"What is your name?" she asked.

I stared at her, unresponsive.

"What is your name?" she barked again. "What is your name? What is your name?" She slammed her hands down in frustration. "*Wie heißt du?*"

My head shot up. I wasn't sure if I'd actually heard her correctly.

"*Ich heißt Ava,*" I whispered.

Nurse frowned. "*Nein. Du heißt Sally.* And your parents are George and Marie Bailey and you're here because you have done a terrible, terrible thing. You tried to kill your father."

"*Nein, ich habe das nicht getan.*"

"In *English*," Nurse snapped.

I sighed. "No, I did not."

"What happened then, Sally?"

I shook my head because it would have been impossible to explain in English, and I knew—she would never believe me, anyway.

Date Unknown

Time on this island feels like what I imagine an ocean current feels like: persistent, washing over everything in an undulating way that draws me out farther even if I don't want it to. This is how they control us. Not the straitjackets or the drugs that Nurse has threatened me with. It's the endless days with nobody to talk to but nurses and the people invented by our own minds.

A person will almost do anything to feel like they've accomplished something that day.

A couple days ago, I shouted until I lost my voice. Yesterday, I bit the inside of my hand and made a red circle on the floor.

Today, when the meal slat opened, I lay on the floor with my feet angled up above my head. When the guard slid the tray inside, I slammed my feet into it so it launched directly into his face.

Nurse berated me, which made a thump in my chest, at least. Something was happening. When she looked away for a moment, I took my opportunity, pushing past her out into the corridor. I ran farther this time, past the medical building, where two old nurses stood smoking, over the black rock, to the edge of the island where the basalt falls away into the ocean. I made my swimmer's stance, sprang up so my body arched high, and fell into the sea. It was a mistake coming to California. That's what I was thinking as I plummeted through the air gracelessly. I will get back to Germany, where I belong, where my mother is in some Stasi prison, but alive, I know it. I will find her and free her even if I die in the process.

The dark water shocked my body, and I fought hard not to pull a lungful of it inside me. I struggled against the muscle of the waves, and fell under the choppy black ocean after only a few seconds. Strong hands of a guard pulled me to the surface, and I squirmed against him, though I was freezing. "Piss off, you *Scheißkerl*! You piece of shit!"

Back in my room, two guards held me down, and I struggled as they injected me in the bend of my elbow with some liquid that made my veins tight and hard. My fingers straightened on their own, joint by joint, as though reaching for something.

They left me to lie on my cot all day, paralyzed and restrained to the bed with wide nylon straps, the cold ocean water gradually drying from my hair. My door stayed propped open, the guard on patrol checking on me often, which allowed me a view of the hallway. A parade of people walked past, each with something grotesquely strange about them. The woman in patient clothes with the cleft palate so severe her face looked like it had been cleaved in two with an ax. The teenage boy wearing a pencil over his ear who had a hole in his chest the size of a fist so you could look straight through where his heart should have been and see nothing but the air behind him.

The worst was the face I recognized. My father, a spatter of brain matter and blood suspended in the air to the right of his head, frozen in place like a paused video of rain. The bone of his right eye was missing so the eyeball hung from his head impossibly.

I don't speak German out loud anymore. But only because my mind can barely fathom what words are. Even now, am I really writing with my hand or am I rubbing my pupils against the paper and painting nonsense on the lines? I can't speak, and the size of my voice presses me to my cot so I can't even move from the weight of it.

Date Unknown

Maybe I am getting better. Maybe they've just drugged me for so long they've convinced me I belong here. I wonder if my mother is going through something like this. The Stasi are almost as good as the nurses at making you admit you've done something wrong.

Nurse got me speaking English, finally. She promised to take me off the medicine. My vocabulary is so small that I speak to her like a child, but she looks satisfied.

Of the parade of mangled people, only my father has

remained. He stands silently in the corner, looking almost like he did the last time I saw him, if I could only ignore the place where the gunshot blew off the side of his face. Still, he has the same quiet way about him, the same watchfulness. I've taken to talking to him in my mind.

"How did I end up here, Father?"

"You ought to practice your English," he replied.

"Even in my own head?"

"Especially there. You're going to need it."

"How do you know?"

"I'm your father," he said simply. "You should listen to me."

It's not disconcerting speaking to my father with half his brain lolling from his head. I've grown used to it, to the way he's always around, the way he politely turns to face the wall when I change clothes, how he dodges out of Nurse's path when she visits.

"Never leave, Father," I said.

"I wouldn't if I could, darling."

Date Unknown

Today, Nurse allowed me recreation with other patients for the first time since I arrived. She marched me through a heavy-hinged wooden door into a long room painted pale mint. Several card tables were scattered across the bright space, and a semicircle of couches surrounded a large television. A dozen patients, most much older than me, sat around the room.

I could sense Nurse behind me, watching. I shuffled over the creaking floor past a sectional sofa with four or five people, to a window in the far wall. I stared past the metal mesh inside the glass. No ocean, only a thatch of dense vegetation.

I looked up at the sound of footsteps in time to see a lady with a pile of ashy hair charge at me, a noise in the back of her throat like an angry bull. She rammed her sharp hip into me until I moved from the window.

"Melody, that's not your window," Nurse said, jogging up to the woman. "You have to allow others to share it."

Melody didn't respond, only pressed her face against the glass and stared out the diamond shapes the metal mesh made.

The swinging doors opened. I looked over in time to see someone holding a yellow ball of yarn trip heavily through the doorway and fall hard to the floorboards. Sprawled on the splintered wooden floor was the teenage boy I'd seen outside my room, the one with the hole in his chest. The one missing his heart.

The yarn he'd been holding had fallen from his hand and rolled over to my feet, the color bright against the dark-stained floor, like the sun crossing the sky.

Heavily, the boy dragged his legs beneath him and stood. Most people wore slippers, but he had on a pair of tattered sneakers. He was wearing a plaid dressing gown over mint-green pajamas. The aftereffects of the drug were still making my vision hazy, and when I stared at the boy's chest, I could see the hole where his heart should be, but only if I squinted. Our eyes met for a brief moment, his eyebrows shooting up his pale face, perhaps surprised to see that I was around his age. Everyone else here is much older.

My father stood nearby. He gave me a significant look.

"Talk to him," he said.

"I hardly speak his language."

"You think that matters?" he asked.

I glanced at him sideways. "What do you know? You're dead."

"I may be dead," he said, "but you're not."

I dragged in a breath, then lifted the yarn ball from the floor and strode toward the boy, swallowing down a feeling of dread.

"Are you all right?" I asked him in blundered English, the words hanging thick like German soil in the air between us. He was taller than me and I had to look up to see into his eyes. His face was broad and deeply freckled. "You're not . . . hurt?"

The boy paused, then pulled a tiny notebook from the front pocket of his robe. He held up a page where a sentence had been deeply penciled.

*I don't speak*, it said.

I felt my mouth go round in surprise. "You mean you're—" I nearly said the word in German—*stumm*—but I couldn't think what it was in English.

He flipped to a blank page in his notebook and wrote. *Mute*.

"Did—did something happen to your throat?"

He shook his head. His expression had turned guarded.

"Something happened to your . . . head?"

*That's what they think.* He ticked his head toward the nurses on the perimeter of the room.

"What do you think?"

He shifted his pale eyes to the side, considering this. *I think I'd talk if I had something to say.*

"I always have something to say," I proclaimed.

And then he wrote something in his notebook again. I watched him pencil each word before he turned the notebook out to me. *Are you a knitter?*

I shook my head, confused. "No. Why do you ask?"

*You seem very attached to my yarn*, he wrote.

I looked down to the yellow ball of yarn that I'd been wringing in my fingers nervously. I passed it to him, my face prickling with a flush.

He took the yarn in his hands, and when I looked up at his freckled face, one corner of his mouth was smiling.

"What is your name?" I asked.

*Everyone calls me Lido*, he wrote. *What's yours?*

My eyes slid behind me to where Nurse was standing, watching us. I put my mouth near Lido's ear and whispered, "I think I'm called Ava."


The Next Day

"I've seen cases like yours," Nurse told me today. She held her hands clasped on her desk. "Many times."

I cocked an eyebrow. This hardly seemed likely.

"Girls reach an age when they get tired of their ordinary lives," she said. "They want to skip the next four or five or six years when they have to live in their parents' houses and go to school. They want to jump straight into adulthood where they think they'll suddenly become something different. Something *extraordinary*. They want to cast off the Sallys and become Avas. But you can't change who you are."

"But you are happy to change me yourself," I said.

"I'm not changing you, Sally. I'm introducing you to yourself again." Her eyes were steel. "So, what is your name?"

"Ava Dreyman."

"No," she said firmly. "Your name is Sally Bailey. Say it."

"My name is Ava Dreyman."

Nurse's face seemed to fall into shadow. "There are other ways we can do this, Sally. I'm aware that you keep a diary. I know you write in it as a mechanism for advancing your delusion. Anybody could see that I'd be justified in removing it."

My body froze. "I wouldn't do that, if I were you."

"Oh?" she asked, in a voice that was disturbingly sweet. Her eyes were too round, too blue. "I will do whatever it takes to rehabilitate my patients. You already know about straitjackets. What about isolation chambers?" She made a small noise in her throat like a question. "I've read some very persuasive case studies. Or, we can try more medication—a sedative, perhaps. Now," she said, "what is your name?"

Her eyes burned into mine. My vision went blurry from tears.

I swallowed hard. "Sally," I spat.

Nurse's smile pinched her lips. She scanned her notes. "Did you enjoy your time with the other patients yesterday?"

I leaned back in the chair, staring at the water-stained ceiling. My mind was still turning over the idea of isolation chambers. I thought things like that only existed in the GDR.

"Ava, someone's speaking to you," my father said. He was standing, straight-backed, against the wall.

"I don't want to talk to her," I told him, out loud.

"Who?" Nurse asked, because of course she hadn't heard my father speaking. "Melody?"

"Why not, Ava?" my father asked. "This woman is trying to help you."

"She thinks I'm crazy," I said.

"Try to be patient with Melody, will you?"

"Well, you know the truth, don't you?" my father said.

"Yes," I replied.

"See?" Nurse said brightly. "You're making so much progress. What did you enjoy most about your afternoon?"

"Nurse can help you see Lido again," my father said.

"Lido?" I asked, blinking up at my father.

"Lido's a nice boy," Nurse said, nodding.

"He might be important," my father said. "I have a feeling."

"He can't even speak," I said.

"Give him a chance," Nurse said.

"Give him a chance," my father said.

I nodded.

Date Unknown

In the morning, I woke to the sound of Nurse unlocking my door. It was much earlier than our normal sessions, but I was too sleepy to protest when she walked me down the hall. When the corridor forked, I expected to turn left, toward her office, but she steered me to the right. I'd never gone this way before, and my heart constricted as I pictured what lay beyond, rooms of shock treatment equipment and straitjackets and vials of evil medicine.

"Where are you taking me?" I shouted, trying to twist from her grip. "I've done nothing wrong. You can't do this!"

Nurse turned her smiling face on me. "Why, Sally, I'm only taking you to breakfast." She shoved open a door that led into a dining hall, lined with tables where patients ate porridge and eggs, and tiled on every surface, even the ceiling. I hadn't known this place existed. Until now, I had been eating meals in my room.

Nurse lightly nudged me into the dining hall.

The tables were sparsely occupied with patients who mumbled together in drugged, patched-up conversations. I saw Lido sitting at a long table, alone but for a middle-aged man in a navy fleece robe. The man was leaning close to Lido's ear, talking fast and conspiratorially.

"It's like I says, Lido, it's like I says, you can't trust 'em, they're out there and there's no fighting 'em when they come for yous."

Lido glanced up as I sat down.

"Who's she?" the man asked. His eyebrows curled out from his head at least several centimeters.

"I'm—" I began, twitching my eyes to where Nurse was watching me from the wall. "I'm Sally." If Lido thought it was strange that I was using a different name today, he didn't indicate it.

The man chewed on his mouthful of eggs as though weighing whether to believe me. "She all right? She *capisce*?"

Lido scribbled something in his notebook. The man read what Lido had written and turned back to me.

"Pardon me." The man straightened his arm. "Call me Hamish. Martin Hamish. I'm a good friend of Lido's and Lido tells me you're a friend of his, so I guess that makes us allies."

I shook his hand. Some of the nurses, standing like stiff paper napkins along the edge of the room, bristled at us touching.

"How are you finding our little island paradise?" Hamish asked.

I mulled my words. "It smells like rotten seaweed," I pronounced slowly. "And I rarely sleep. Someone screams all night long." The screams had woken me up every night so far, a screeching animal noise that I couldn't block out, even if I jammed my pillow over my ears.

Hamish's eyes squinted. "You got an accent of some kind, I can tell," he said. "What's your story?"

My eyes twitched up at Nurse. "I grew up in Baltimore."

"Naw, I'm good with accents. It's the way you swallow your r's, we don't do that here. Your accent's German. Maybe Dutch."

"My grandmother was Swiss," I said. "She taught me to speak."

He peered at me hard for what felt like a whole minute. "That would explain it," he nodded finally.

An attendant brought out two matching bowls on a tray, one filled with scrambled eggs and the other with porridge, and set them in front of me.

Hamish leaned in. "You know they drug the food here."

"Really?" I glanced at Lido and he shrugged, like he wasn't sure if Hamish was telling the truth.

"Oh yeah. Everybody's got different cocktails. That's why you never serve yourself. Back in the old days, we didn't get pills, just sugar pills sometimes to trick us into thinking it was lithium. All kinds of miracle drugs they's concocted lately, they say. Gonna make all of us perfickly sane, so they says."

I leaned forward, looking into Hamish's dark eyes, my voice low. "You don't know a way out of here, do you?"

"Why would we want out?" he asked, a little too loudly. "This place is easy street. It's an asylum—you know the root of that word? A *safe place*. We get warm meals, and the nurses even tell you stories if you ask them." He shoveled a mouthful of porridge into his mouth. "Mmm, tastes like sanity."

Lido was laughing silently, but I didn't find it funny. I pushed my tray of food away.

"I do not belong here," I told him.

"Wise up, girlie. You belong here as much as I do," Hamish said.

"I'm not crazy," I said.

"You don't have to be *crazy* to be crazy. Take me—I got problems with reality, but I got good genes, too, relatives who survived the very first Shoah. My grandfather escaped the old country with three babies and a nine-months-pregnant wife only to die of—can you guess? Piece of Russian space junk, crushed his skull like one of those baby oranges. Life's never certain, you know?"

I scoffed. "I know myself, and I know I'm not like these people." I cast an arm around the room at the other patients, with their stretched-out T-shirts and slack jaws. "Half of these people don't even know where they are. Or *who* they are."

Hamish's eyebrows raised up high. Lido's pencil clattered from his grip to the table. His face had gone still, and something in his gaze made the air vibrate. I knew I'd said something very wrong.

Lido picked up his pencil, wrote something in a rush, and pushed his notebook toward me, scowling. *They're my friends*, it read. I felt my stomach hollow out at his narrowed eyes.

And then, Lido stood from his seat and left the room.


Date Unknown

Today for recreation they allowed some of the patients to go down to the rocks by the water. I haven't been outside since my last attempt at escape, however long ago that was. It's clear that swimming to shore is too dangerous. For now I am biding my time, thinking on a plan to get across the water, and then to Germany, to my mother. I'm constantly searching for unlocked doors, for a nurse to be careless with the keys to the armored boat parked at the dock.

The freezing sea air flooded the holes in my skin, and the fog was up to the land's end so I couldn't see the ocean but for the lip of it ringing the island, dark and dashing itself against the rocks. Nurse stayed a step or two behind me, my constant shadow.

The rock shelf was dotted with patients shuffling in slippers over the sharp black surface, staring down into the tide pools. I spied Lido, meandering across the rocks in his tattered sneakers, still wearing his green pajamas. Funny how they dress us like that, as if at any moment we might drift off to sleep.

My father sat on a rock outcropping, the unshattered side of his face pointed toward the salt spray of the ocean. He nodded toward Lido, where he stood silhouetted against the fog. He's been urging me to make things right with Lido for days.

I walked up behind Lido. He must have heard me slipping around on the rocks, but he didn't turn. "It looks like you could jump in and not fall," I said, gesturing to the fog that was billowing up over the land.

He looked out across the ocean, not answering me.

"You know, sometimes I wonder if this place is even real," I said. "I heard a fairy tale once about an island that was really a speck floating in an old man's soup bowl."

Lido's face remained so still, I thought he might not have heard me. I moved to stand directly in front of him, so he was forced to look at me.

*What do you want?* he wrote.

My eyes fell to the tattered sneakers he wore, pulling apart at the seams. "I want you to tell me why you don't wear slippers like everyone else."

Lido twiddled the pencil between his fingers and scribbled a reply. *Why do you care about my shoes?*

I shrugged. "They look . . . interesting."

*I spent all my allowance on them before I got here. They're Nike Tailwinds. Fastest shoe in the world. I bought them two sizes big, so I could wear them forever.*

His eyes held a kind of unstoppable pride, though, to me, the shoes looked like they belonged in the trash. I wondered how long Lido's been here. Years, I'd guess, by the state of his shoes.

"You're a runner?" I asked.

*I wanted to be, once. I wanted to be the fastest man on Earth. My face on all the newspapers and Wheaties boxes.*

"What use are fast shoes here?" I asked. "It's an island. Not many places to run."

His smile faded. *If I need to run, I'll be ready.* He held his notebook out for only a moment, then took it back, stuffing it into his robe pocket. This was a clear signal that he didn't want to talk to me anymore.

I felt like walking off. Talking to somebody shouldn't be such a chore. But my father was watching us, and he wore that look that told me he was expecting my best behavior. So I tried again. "I'm sorry about what I said the other day. Really. About the other patients."

His face tightened. *You're not sorry*, he wrote. *I can tell.*

I could feel all of my features wad up in the center of my face, angrily. "Well, I'm *not* like the others. Truly. I do not belong here."

Lido stood and wrote roughly in his notebook.

*None of us belongs here*, it said. *In the outside, people think this place is a trash can, except it's for human beings. They send us here so they don't have to think about us anymore. Just like your parents did. You're no different. You're garbage just like the rest of us.*

His words sunk into my rib cage like a blade. I took a step backward. "You don't know what you're talking about," I said, my voice a guttural noise. "You don't know a thing about me."

*You don't know a thing about me, or any of us*, he scribbled.

"Thank God for that," I spat, and stormed off.

# Pepper

*Geometry*

Dear Ms. Eldridge,

Everything has changed since last I wrote. I was unspeakably despondent and now? I am a thousand things, smashed together. I'm writing this very hurriedly because I am currently hurtling down the freeway in a taxi. Bertrand is in as excited a state as I've ever seen, because even he must know we're headed to the airport, and everyone finds the airport exciting, even if the air there smells like other people's mouths.

The topic today was supposed to be geometry, a class I almost passed (but for all of the tests that I failed) so I feel pretty confident writing about this. But that will need to be interrupted by another topic, the reason that I am about to hop on a plane to someplace else.

The events began yesterday when I was heading downtown for my date with Petra Mirkovsky. Shawn and I met behind the French fry stand kitty-corner to the aquarium. Bertrand scuffled at our feet, searching for wilted fries among the concrete.

"You couldn't have dressed up a little?" Shawn asked when he saw me.

"Nice to see you again, too, Shawn."

"No offense, but this is *Petra*," he said. "Petra *Mirkovsky*, sacred daughter of the Mirkovsky dynasty of car salesmen and local news anchors. This is Monterey's elite. You don't wear nasty ripped jeans to a date with Petra Mirkovsky."

I hadn't even thought about what I was going to wear. I'd spent the day too absorbed in reading *The Arsonist*. (I've not yet made my way through it. I just got to the entries written on Rake Island, how that Nurse woman insisted on telling Ava that her name was not her name. Can you believe that?) The fact that I can even say the sentence "I was absorbed in reading," should indicate to everyone that something has changed with me, Ms. Eldridge.

"And that Ewok in Training shirt is at least five years old," Shawn continued. "Do you smell? Come over here so I can smell you."

I batted him away. "I thought you didn't even like Petra."

"I don't," he said. "But I do know that she only dates, like, hip photography guys and bass players and stuff. Which is why it would've been awesome if you had, I don't know, showered in the past week."

"Well, if you're such an expert in wooing women, maybe you should go out with her." Shawn made a face like he couldn't believe I wasn't jumping out of my skeleton with joy right now, and this fact was odd to me, too. The more I tried to figure out why I wasn't happy, the more a point at the back of my mind started to pinch, a little niggling worry that I could not swat away.

"I'm going to take that as a sign that you're nervous," Shawn said. "As well you should be. You will need to be the most charming, wittiest, funniest Pepper you have ever been. Personally, I think you peaked around eighth grade, but maybe the pressure will work for you."

Shawn was freaking me out. "Well, at the very least, I'll smell like French fry grease and dead fish. What woman could be resisting that?"

"You're right," Shawn said. "We need to air you out. Come on, it's almost time to head down there anyway."

We walked toward the wharf where Petra and I had agreed to meet, and I had to cradle Bertrand because there were so many people around (when he is accidentally trodden on, he screams like an old woman, and that was to be avoided for many reasons). I spotted Petra through the crush of tourists, wearing a pink sweater with a raccoon face knit into the chest and a plastic bow stuck to the side of her head. She scanned the crowd, stretched up on the very tips of her toes.

"All right, dude," Shawn said, clapping me hard on the shoulder. "I think you might have a real shot with this chick."

"This is Petra Mirkovsky," I said. "She doesn't even like me."

"You might be wrong about that. She texted me when you didn't call her right away. She was worried I might've given you the wrong number."

At that precise moment, Petra saw me and waved in my direction.

"May the Force be with you," Shawn whispered, disappearing into the crowd.

Petra hugged me and pressed her cheek to mine, like she was kissing me but not. It was making the pinched place at the back of my mind squeeze even tighter.

"You are a sight for sore eyes, Pepper Al-Yusef," Petra said, smiling with her small pearly teeth. "I missed seeing you around school."

Looking at Petra, I was thinking about geometry, how symmetrical her face was, how the triangular window between her lips formed a perfect equilateral. Ms. Eldridge, I bet you figured that, once I got a little perspective, I'd see Petra not as the beautiful creature I once imagined her to be, but as the regular girl she really is. You would be wrong. Petra was still gloriously pretty, her blond bangs a rounded cylinder on her forehead, her blue eyes smiling and soft.

Petra may have been waiting for me to say that I missed her, too, but the words were lodged in my throat. All the symmetry and too-neatness of her meant something, but I couldn't tell what yet.

In my arms, Bertrand opened his wrinkled mouth and let out a small, dainty burp.

Petra smiled. "Want to get a bite to eat?" she asked.

"Yep," I said.

We ambled up to the row of shops and restaurants and exchanged a few awkward words about where we should go. I didn't want to suggest any place in case it wasn't fancy enough, and Petra didn't volunteer anything, either, so we decided on a touristy Chinese place that everyone knows sucks because it doesn't have a real name, it's just called "Chinese Restaurant."

Petra ordered some tofu thing. I got orange chicken and rice.

The picture of the orange chicken in the menu was the same exact color as Molly's hair. I dashed that thought aside. I wasn't supposed to be thinking on Molly Mavity any longer.

While we waited for our meals, I drank my Coke too fast and immediately regretted it because now I had nothing to do except stare across the table at Petra. Neither of us could find anything to talk about other than the pigeons walking around on the floor, steering clear of Bertrand.

"How can that not be some kind of health code violation?" Petra asked, her nose wrinkled.

"I like them," I said. "They add character. I think every restaurant should have animals. It's friendlier."

"Some restaurants have tanks with lobster," she said. "Although I guess you wouldn't like that, what with your dad's fish tanks and stuff."

My stomach lurched that she had brought up anything she learned in the interview.

"I guess," I said.

"Well, I think they're gross," she said. "Pigeons, I mean. I read an article about how they could cause the next plague."

"If it was my restaurant, I'd use it to my advantage," I said. "Imagine how much it would save on the cost of chicken."

Petra stared at me for an eternity of moments. She made a cringey face like she'd just watched the joke walk into traffic and get creamed by a semi truck.

"So . . ." she said, drawing out the word, "are you coming back to school next year? Your friends told me you didn't graduate."

"I'm still determining," I said. "Just weighing my options."

I didn't want to tell her about these essays, Ms. Eldridge, or about the quest. I didn't really want to tell her anything.

She nodded. She must have sensed something was different, and I guess I was sensing that, too. I never would have thought a date with Petra Mirkovsky could go this long without me trying to forcefully pour my heart into hers.

"Pepper, you're really quiet."

I nodded. "I guess I am just thinking about things."

"Like what?" she asked. "What have you been doing this summer?"

"Just lots of . . . reading," I said.

"I saw you one day, like a week ago."

"Where?"

"Dot's Diner. With a girl," she said, looking away. "I was by the jukebox. You looked at me a couple of times, or your eyes did, but I don't think you saw me."

"I didn't." The confused pinch in my brain got suddenly worse.

"I thought you might've been mad at me," Petra said.

"Why?"

"The interview?" she said. "Everybody thinks I used you to get into NYU."

"Oh," I said. "Didn't you?"

Her cheeks reddened a fraction. "Well, I didn't necessarily expect you to volunteer so much personal information, but you knew it would be printed, and how could I censor those parts?" She paused. "That's why I wanted to meet with you today. I wanted to apologize for all that." And then, quieter: "I never meant to embarrass you."

"I know," I said. And I meant it. Petra had only ever wanted an interview. I was the one who wanted something else.

Slowly, the confusion at the back of my mind was clearing. Petra was perfect like round numbers are perfect, like pi is perfect in its infinity. That had not changed in the weeks since I'd left Hoover, but she was just another person now, and that person didn't make me feel anything anymore.

We split the check and left the restaurant.

Petra squinted against the sun as we walked down the crowded street. I glanced around the teeming mass of tourists and spotted Shawn sitting on a park bench about twenty feet away, holding a newspaper like a spy in an old movie. He let one side of the newspaper fall and gave me a thumbs-up. I could see him mouth the words, "She wants you, man!"

I almost laughed until I saw that the newspaper he was holding had a big story about the execution of Winston Mavity. It was a week away, and the appeals had been dropped. He would not fight to live.

My mind landed on Molly again. I wondered how she was taking the news.

Petra adjusted her purse strap on her shoulder, and there was a silent moment that seemed to ask whether the date would end here, in the middle of this gum-covered sidewalk. I turned my eyes away from her expectant face and glimpsed something that made all other thoughts freeze inside my brain.

A woman in the crowd with slick dark hair. A woman whose face I had memorized.

A woman who shouldn't be alive.

She wore a businesslike skirt and high heels, and even though she looked twenty years older than her picture, it was absolutely, undeniably her. Her shoes made a sharp clop against the pavement. She shouldered through the slow-moving crowd, past where Shawn was sitting.

"What are you looking at?" Petra asked.

"That lady," I said. "She looks familiar."

I started following the woman, tugging on Bertrand's leash and pushing through the stream of people, knocking into shoulders. Someone stepped on Bertrand's foot and he let out a high scream like a Southern belle, so I had to bend to pick him up, but I managed to keep my eyes locked on the back of the woman's head.

"What are you doing?" Petra asked, and I looked back at her for a second, long enough to see saw Shawn rise from the park bench.

"What in the flaming *fuck*, Pepper?" I heard him say over the din of a million passersby.

My heartbeat quickened, and for a quick shuddering second, there came a blast of silence. Just me, and a dog shaped like a Hot Pocket, and inside my eyeballs the image of the most remarkable sight I've ever beheld.

Ava Dreyman.

Alive.

# Molly

Dear Pepper,

I fiddle with my cell phone, dialing the number, then deleting it a thousand times. I have been debating whether to make this call, but after our fight, Pepper, and after meeting Georg, I am anxious to continue the quest. I need to find the answers.

I hit Call.

"I wish to speak to Heinrich Werner," I say.

"Is that right?" Werner answers in his solid, German-tinged voice. I'm on top of the roof of my aunt's house again, where I know I won't be overheard.

"And who may I ask is calling?" he asks.

"Molly Mavity," I say. "We spoke recently, outside your home."

I hear Werner grunt. "Can I ask how you got my number?"

"The Internet," I say simply. I had to use my aunt's credit card to pay one of those creepy identity-selling websites to get it. "I wanted you to know that I met with Georg Winkler."

"You are aware that you do not get a prize for collecting us all," Werner says.

"Georg told me the knife belonged to Ava," I say. "Explain."

Werner chuckles. "I don't have to explain a thing to you."

"How did Ava's own knife kill her?" I ask. "And why do you have it? Why did you say it was yours? Who are you protecting?"

He goes silent, and I fear that he's hung up on me.

"Nothing is simple about East Germany." His voice becomes quiet. "That is what the conspiracy theorists don't ever understand. Do you know the expression 'History is written by the victors'? That's never been truer than in the GDR. We were the best secret police the world has ever known. The KGB? The SS? Bah! Sloppy imbeciles. To be a member of the Stasi was all I ever wanted, and now I'm supposed to look back at those years with regret? If I'd been born in America, I would've been the kind of cop you see on one of those TV shows. But I was born in the German Democratic Republic, and I became a villain."

"You killed people," I say. "You made them disappear, and didn't even let the families hold funerals."

"That was the machine, not me."

"You were part of the machine," I say.

I hear him sigh loudly from the other end of the line. "I really must be going now. Good luck with your goose chase. You ought to get out of the house. The bay is beautiful today."

The line goes dead.

I stay on the roof, letting the sun beat down on my face, and I can practically feel it multiplying my freckles.

In my hand, my phone vibrates, and I think for a moment Werner's calling back. But it's not his name on the caller ID.

"Pepper?" I ask, my stomach clenching slightly.

"I'm at the boardwalk. You'll never guess who I'm looking at right now." Your voice echoes across the phone line, into my ear.

"Who?" I ask.

"Ava Dreyman."

You tell me the rest in a blur. I climb down the roof in a way that can only be described as reckless, hanging from the gutter and swinging onto the porch, and begin sprinting bare-foot down the hot pavement of neighborhood streets, past the 7-Eleven and the pool on Hacienda Street that's still shut down for repairs, until I finally see the bulging blue of the bay. My naked foot slaps over the hot, rough pavement of Cannery Row, but I barely register any pain. I scan for your face in the crowd.

The place is a swarm of tourists and office people on their lunch breaks and soldiers from the Presidio in reflective vests out jogging in groups. I collide with the shoulders of a dozen people who shout out in surprise, but I don't apologize.

I can't.

I am holding my breath.

I scan the storefronts until I see the Chinese restaurant, tucked beneath a skywalk that connects two canneries. As I approach, a woman with a wave of black hair hanging down her back walks out the front doors.

My feet slow. The woman reaches into a leather purse and checks something on her phone. It's strange, after everything, to see Ava Dreyman in the flesh, liberated from the black-and-white world of her photograph.

"Molly," you shout across the crowd. You sprint to me with Bertrand in your arms, and a boy and a girl tagging behind you.

"That's her," I breathe. "That's really her. How can it be her? She's dead."

"Let's worry about that when we catch her," you say. "Come on."

I follow the top of Ava Dreyman's head through the crowd, edging forward as a group of summer camp kids pour out of the Cannery Row museum, an adult shouting, "Don't let go of your buddy!" I try to push through them, but there are too many, and they're all connected at the hands like a human cat's cradle. When I look up again, I can't see Ava. I swivel my head around and I've lost you, too.

I feel the panic rising up my throat.

I know at this moment that I must keep it together. If I lose it now, I will never find Ava again. I run back to the Chinese restaurant. The bundle of bells around the door handle slams against the glass. A teenage boy behind the counter looks up.

"A woman was just here," I stammer. "Her name is Ava Dreyman. Black hair. Skirt suit."

The boy squints. "And what should I do with that information?"

"Do you—do you have a home address for her?"

He scoffs. "Customers generally don't leave their addresses."

"Or a credit card receipt?"

"We're not in the business of handing over credit card information."

I step closer to the counter. "Isn't there anything you can do?"

"For a stranger looking for specifics about a customer's identity?" he says, full of sarcasm. "Pretty sure that's against the law."

My breath is coming faster now and the hot ginger air inside the restaurant is making my cheeks flame. I dash back into the teeming street, hoping maybe you've found her, but when I see you, you're alone, standing on a bench and scanning the crowd.

"Shit!" I shout. "We just had her. She was *just* here."

"I'll make a round of the block," you say, running off into the crowds.

I'm too preoccupied with keeping myself tethered to this place on earth, with pulling air into my lungs because it's gotten suddenly difficult. Heat is creeping from my face down my neck, and I know I am very close to tilting on my axis. The girl you were with before comes running down the street with your pimply friend. I take a few steps backward and accidentally knock into a little boy wearing one of those "Hairy Otter" T-shirts they sell at the aquarium gift shop, and he goes plummeting to the pavement. His high-pitched wail shatters my ears, and I cover them with my balled-up hands.

And now I can hear the girl asking, "What on earth is wrong with her?" and your friend saying, "Mental problems?" and the girl responding, "Oh," which is just one syllable and shouldn't stab me like it does. I fall to the pavement, the little boy no longer screaming. No, now I'm screaming and coming as close as I ever come to crying, my screwed-up face aching, every muscle in my body rebelling against the barriers of this mind, and I forget all I ever knew about coping mechanisms. Coping mechanisms don't bring back Ava Dreyman. They don't bring back your mother.

"*Shhhhhhh.*"

Cool hands press to either side of my head.

"*Shhhhhhh.*"

I open my eyes and stare straight into yours, Pepper. You are kneeling on the pavement beside me. You are expressionless but for your lips opening to make the soothing "*shhhhhhh*" sound. I start to breathe again in time with the noise you're making.

"I'm sorry I said those things to you," I say after a minute. "I'm so sorry."

"It's all right," you say. "I'm sorry, too."

Just then, the pimply boy touches you on the shoulder. "Pepper, do you want to explain what the shit is going on?" He looks down at me. "You're that weird girl who found me at Hoover, before school ended. You were looking for Pepper."

"My name's Molly."

"How fascinating," the boy says, turning back to you. "Pepper, are you gonna tell me why you abandoned a date to chase some lady through the streets?"

"I'm wondering the same thing," the beautiful girl says.

"You're on a date?" I ask.

"I'm sorry, Petra," you say, lifting your hands away. "It's . . . a very long story," you say, and then you turn back to me. I sit up on the pavement, my legs bunched up beneath me. "I found something," you say.

"Ava?" I ask, though I know it can't be. She's gone.

You shake your head. "At the Chinese restaurant there was this kid behind the counter and he was extremely rude to my face, but then his dad came out and asked if my name was Pepper or, uh, Molly. He gave this to me."

I notice for the first time what you're holding, a small manila envelope. On the front, our names are written in red Sharpie.

"Open it," I breathe, and you tear open the envelope in a quick motion.

My mind can barely make sense of the contents, shaking in your trembling fingers. Two plane tickets to Berlin. Leaving from Oakland tomorrow, returning two days afterward.

But even bigger than that is the business card printed with the address to a bank in Berlin. At the top, the words *Muriel Weisz* have been circled by a line of red Sharpie.

"Muriel Weisz," I say. And then, "Ava Dreyman is alive."

You start grinning, your face parting completely so I can see your back molars. "How's your schedule tomorrow?" you ask. "You up for some international travel?"

I smile, and we both laugh like I haven't in ages, a big,

gut-busting laugh, and pretty soon there is nothing that matters but us because we know we're part of something bigger than ourselves. We are on the path of Ava Dreyman.

"Where's Petra?" Shawn suddenly asks.

We look around the milling crowds. She isn't there anymore.

Shawn shakes his head. "Well, you royally fucked that one up," he says. "Your one chance, ruined. And not even to mention my seppuku moment which you have *completely* disrespected."

Just then, you wrap your hand around your mouth. I wonder if you're going to cry or curse yourself for letting that girl get away. Your eyes start to fold over themselves, but I realize you're laughing.

"That was the worst date in history," you say.

"I thought she looked very interested," the boy mutters.

You shake your head, still grinning.

"You just threw away a shot at Monterey royalty," the boy says. "Why are you so happy?"

"Come on, Shawn," you say, clapping a hand on his shoulder. "Let me tell you a story. Have you ever heard of Ava Dreyman?"

He scowls. "I don't want to hear it," he says, in a huff. "I don't want to hear anything except an explanation about why you're such a dumbass."

Shawn walks off, but when I look at you, your face is still beaming. You heft Bertrand from the pavement. "I wonder if puppies need passports."

# Ava

Date Unknown

I was dreaming about my father again last night. Sometimes there are no images, just the sound, the single ricochet of that gunshot. It doesn't matter that he's still here, with me. The memory of that sound will haunt me the rest of my life.

Tonight, I woke suddenly and at first I thought it was because of the dream. Then, I heard the screams.

The screams start at the same time every night. The walls are heavy so the sound, when it comes, is only a faint wail. It's not the normal screaming of the patients who carry on like they're practicing a musical instrument. This is true terror.

I am starting to wonder if I'll ever get out of here.


Date Unknown

I haven't sat next to Lido and Hamish in the cafeteria since our fight. I'm an expert at the silent treatment. Weaker people fold after a day or two. Not me. Stubborn, my mother called me. Hardheaded. I call it steadfast. I call it tough. Whatever I commit to, I stick with, forever. Even if it kills me a little.

Even if I feel a stab somewhere above my stomach each time I look over at Lido's table.

At breakfast, I was sitting with Melody and an older man named Gus, who always wears military medals pinned to his undershirt. He slips food into his robe pocket when the nurses aren't watching. He reminds me of the stories my mother would tell about her parents, who grew up during the Depression.

Once, I gave Gus a muffin wrapped in a cellophane wrapper from my tray, and he made a gruff noise of thanks. He and Melody don't talk much, which is fine with me.

At breakfast, I felt someone tap my shoulder, and turned and looked into Hamish's face. He sat heavily onto the bench beside me, holding out a thick green scarf.

"That's not mine," I said.

"He made it for you." Hamish inclined his head back, to the table where Lido kept his gaze intensely averted. I took the scarf, rubbed it between my thumbs. It was soft and woven with an intricate design of leaves.

"You're a deliveryman, then?" I asked.

Hamish cocked an eyebrow. "Only special deliveries," he said. "You ought to talk to him. He says you had some kind of bust-up on the rocks."

A warmth was prickling through my fingers where I held the scarf, and it radiated out to the rest of my body. Still, I set my shoulders. "What'll you give me if I talk to him?"

Hamish squinted in surprise. "What do you want?"

"I want a favor," I said. I thought it would be helpful having an ally if I'm going to get out of here. "Not now. Sometime in the future. When I need one. Do you agree?"

Hamish turned his head to the side, as though weighing my words. "Lido's a real good kid," he said. "Don't seem to me like anyone ought to be compensated to spend time with him. But sure, Sally. You take your favor."

I held out my hand for Hamish to shake, then stood from the table and walked to where Lido was sitting. He had his arms crossed.

"Thank you for the scarf," I said formally.

*To keep you warm*, he wrote. *It's almost winter.*

"That's very nice of you," I said. "But I'm afraid I can't accept it." I held the scarf out to him.

He blinked a few times, his eyebrows frowning in the middle of his forehead. *Why not?* he wrote.

"It's not usual to exchange gifts when at war."

His eyes rounded, as though trying to determine whether I was joking. *We're not at war.*

"I think we are," I said.

*Fine*, he wrote. *I'd like to issue a peace treaty.*

I stuck out my chin. "What are the conditions?"

*That you take the scarf*, he wrote. *And sit next to me.* His pale eyes were smiling.

I looked at his notebook, where he'd penciled the words so deliberately.

"You're not going to insist I apologize?" I asked.

*Would you agree if I did?*

I lowered myself onto the bench, thinking he knew me a little better than I thought.

There was a tangle of blue yarn on the table's surface. Two knitting needles fashioned from driftwood protruded from it.

"What's the story with this knitting?" I asked.

He shrugged, like it was obvious. *I like to make things*, he wrote.

"Why?"

*My mom taught me.* A smile touched his mouth briefly. *I started because it was just something to do, but now I like the idea of making the world a little more colorful. Everyone has something I've made now. I want to see this place completely covered in yarn.*

Nearby, my father and Nurse leaned against the wall, in mirrored poses, watching. I glared at them. I wish they'd both get a life. I turned to Lido and I saw he had written something in his notebook.

*So how did you end up here? On Rake Island.*

I let out a breath. "It is a long story."

*I'm not busy*, he wrote.

"Maybe I am," I said. "Maybe I have important things to do. Movies to see. Men to buy me drinks."

He rolled his eyes, then wrote. *I don't see anyone lining up.*

I scoffed. "You're here, aren't you?"

*Tell me how you got here*, he repeated.

I turned to look behind me at Nurse again, close enough to catch me if I jumped up and tried to run from the room, but not close enough to hear anything above the dull echo of patients' talking.

I moved myself closer to Lido's ear and started, slowly. "I am from East Berlin. My mother is still there, a prisoner. I am going back for her." I told Lido about my home, about Captain Werner, about the checkpoint and my father and the gunshot, about my plan to escape. I felt lighter, just saying the words. Lido starting chewing on his lip and turned his broad, freckled face right at me.

"Do you believe me?" I asked. "Nurse thinks I'm delusional."

He paused. *I believe you*, he wrote, finally. And I knew, from the look in his pale eyes, that he did. Relief plowed through me.

"In my dreams, I hear gunshots," I told him, my throat tightening, forcing out the words even as my father stood nearby, the result of those gunshots standing out quite clearly from his skull. "Even in the daytime. My brain replays the sound and I feel afraid, just like I did in that moment."

Lido nodded, retrieving his stub of a pencil and pad of paper before writing, *I don't like loud noises.*

"Why's that?" I asked.

He put his pencil to the notebook and began writing *My father,* but quickly dashed it out, scribbling over the words until the paper puckered and ripped.

*I hear shouting,* he wrote. *Not even words, just angry shouting. I can't get it out of my head.*

"What's it feel like?"

He looked into my eyes before he wrote.

*Like going crazy.*

Date Unknown

I came into breakfast today and was disappointed to see that Lido wasn't there. Hamish was, though. Hamish is nowhere near as tolerable as Lido, and he fills every moment with conversation, so much that I think I will learn every English word in the dictionary just by listening to him.

"Hey, Sally, want a cigarette?" Hamish pulled out a pack from inside his shirt, holding it against his chest so the nurses wouldn't see. A book of matches was pinned to the cardboard pack by the cellophane wrapper. "Here, take one."

"Better not," I said. "My father would kill me." I looked over to where he was sitting on the radiator.

"So would mine. Doesn't stop me."

"Hamish!" One of the harried, white-robed attendants stood by the swinging door. "You're scheduled for an eight o'clock consultation. Hurry up!" Hamish stuffed the cigarettes into the inner pocket of his robe and patted it with his hand.

"Coming right along, sir," he said, mock bowing. "Anything you say, sir, anything at all."

- - - - -

Date Unknown

Today Lido and I met at the rocks, though it was windy enough to strip paint from walls and we were some of the only patients outside. I'd wrapped the green scarf Lido gave me around my neck. Lido sat down next to me in the shelter of a rock shelf and pulled several books from his robe.

I flipped through each one with chilled fingers while my mind opened like a mouth, wanting to devour every page. On the cover of the final book, *Fahrenheit 451*, there was a man formed out of pages from books being ravaged by yellow fire. My eyes traced the peak of each flame. I hadn't realized how long I'd gone without seeing fire. I felt almost hungry for it.

*Have you read it?* Lido wrote.

"No," I said, opening the book. The first line made my heart quiver. *It was a pleasure to burn.* Of course, an image of my mother came to my mind.

Lido told me you have to build up privileges here, and that he's earned them all, including access to the island library.

*They don't give books to people who jump into the ocean,* he wrote, the fold of a smile in his cheek.

"I'll throw you in the ocean," I said. "See how you like it."

He smirked. *Not if I throw you first.* He reached to his left where there was a tide pool, gathered a handful of water, and threw it at my face. I screamed a high-pitched girlish shriek I haven't let loose since I came to America. I stood and kicked at a puddle, spraying him with water. He grinned and hopped across the rocks in his Nike Tailwinds, and then he took off running, his notebook flying from his front pocket like a seagull flung around by the wind. I chased after him, but it was no use. His long legs pumped under his dressing gown, and the black rock sprayed up beneath his feet like an Olympic track. He ran like he could've kept running forever. Like he really could have been the fastest man on Earth.

### Date Unknown

"You need to be careful with Lido," Nurse said today.

I'd been gnawing on my thumbnail. I looked up into her unlined face, my hand falling to my lap. "What do you mean?" I asked.

"He's fragile," Nurse replied.

I blinked at her. What was she talking about?

"Just be . . ." Her eyes swept the ceiling. "Be gentle."

Gentle. I was never taught to be gentle. When I sang, I did so loudly. When I played sports, I had to win, otherwise what was the point? My mother would never tell me to quiet myself for a boy. She would tell me to never change for anyone, because the people you change for are the people who control you.

My eyes found my father, reclining on Nurse's desk. "Not likely."

### Date Unknown

I've grown used to the motions of time here, like a current pulling me constantly deeper. Each day seems to pass slower than the last. I eat in the cafeteria, and walk beside the ocean, and talk with Nurse, building fabricated sand castles of stories about my life before. My English has legs now, growing stronger every day. I am going to try writing in English as much as I can, too. Perhaps if I try hard enough, she'll let me out, though it's likely no use. Georg and Margarita are paying them well to keep me locked up.

On the rocks today, the air was awash in pollen from flowers growing in the cracks in the black rock. Lido had spent the afternoon trying to teach me to knit, with difficulty.

He set the yarn aside and pulled out his notebook. *Did somebody put your fingers on backward?* he asked.

I rolled my eyes. "Maybe you're just a poor teacher."

*I'm a great teacher,* he wrote. *I've taught half the people on the island.*

I read his words, then unconsciously tracked the horizon with my eyes. It was growing darker.

Lido'd scratched something into his notebook. *Why do you do that?* he'd written. *Look out over the water like you're searching for something?*

I pursed my lips. I didn't know what to say. I still look at the ocean, to see how I'll die, but all I ever see is water. I couldn't explain it in a way that would make sense, I was sure. Not to him, or anybody.

"When you try to talk, what stops you?" I asked him instead.

A shade drew across Lido's face. I thought he might clam

up, but he grabbed the nub of his pencil and wrote. *They call it selective muteness*, he said. *But it's not me who selects it. It's something else. It's got this vise grip on my voice.* He mirrored grabbing his throat, like he wanted to reach in and drag something out. *Sometimes I think it was stolen. Like in a fairy tale.*

I looked away demurely. "Maybe you have to kiss a beautiful maiden to get it back."

He laughed soundlessly. *Let me know when one shows up.*

He was smiling a small, mischievous grin, but as he looked at me, his smile fell away. His eyes pressed into mine.

*You must know you're beautiful*, he wrote.

My breath caught in my throat. I didn't say a word. I felt my body going very still, as though afraid to frighten away the moment. Beyond, thunder broke across the water like drumbeats.

*But you're a terrible knitter.*


Date Unknown

Lido didn't come down to breakfast today, or lunch, or recreation time. I stood at our spot by the water, waiting for him for an hour. I cursed myself silently. This never would've happened back home. Boys always waited for me.

I searched for Lido inside, stopping first in the TV room, a small glass-domed atrium with a scattering of potted plants. In a few wooden chairs, patients watched a news program on the antennaed TV. They were whispering quietly, not watching the program, the energy of the room prickling with a strange tension. Worry began spidering up my spine. Something was wrong; I could sense it. I turned to leave, when the news anchor's staccato voice grabbed me.

"President Reagan continues to face Soviet and East German backlash for the statements he made on his most recent trip to West Berlin."

My body turned toward the screen, where the American president stood in front of the Brandenburg Gate, a sea of people pooling before him in the hundreds. The crowd's cheering crackled through the TV speakers, and the sound shot through my limbs like a shiver.

The president cried out, "Mr. Gorbachev, tear down this wall!"

The people in the audience screamed. I felt every muscle in my body seize up. My hand crept slowly to my mouth.

"You okay?" a middle-aged patient named Jonesy asked me.

"I'm fine," I said, swallowing hard, straightening my backbone. "Have you seen Lido?"

Jonesy's eyes shifted to the ground. "You should talk to Hamish about that."

A cord of dread struck within me. I darted to the game room where Hamish was playing solitaire with a bent pack of cards.

"Where's Lido?" I asked, slamming into the table.

Hamish leaned back, sighing. "Lido's room was raided," he said. "They took everything—his blankets, his knitting needles, his piles and piles of yarn. Plus all the stuff he's made for other people."

"Why?" I asked.

"Old Gus, you know him? The guy who's been here since right after Pearl Harbor?" I nodded—he was the one who sat with Melody, who wore military medals on his underclothes. "Well, Old Gus died today."

My face wrinkled with confusion. "But what's that got to do with Lido?"

Hamish swallowed heavily. "The old man hung himself, from the sprinkler pipe in the center of his ceiling. He used the scarf that Lido knit him to do it."

I didn't speak. I found I couldn't say a word.

"So, the powers that be told Lido no more of that," Hamish said. "No more knitting or teaching. Can you imagine? What's he s'posed to do with all that time? It'll kill him, watch if it doesn't. He's got so little left."

This made me pause. "How do you know that about Lido?"

"We're in group therapy together."

"Aren't you supposed to keep that secret?"

He tossed up his shoulders. "I have problems with impulse control. They should expect I'm not a very good secret keeper."

I knew Hamish was capable of talking utter nonsense, but this time I decided I would believe him. "Do you know how he ended up here?"

"Oh, the classic story," Hamish said. "The old man is a real bruiser. I saw him visit once. Tough guy, the kind of man feels he's gotta be the biggest and the loudest to get respect. When

Lido was little, he'd cower from his old man, and his dad'd fly off the handle, like, and shout 'Don't you trust me, son? I ain't gonna hurt you!' And sometimes his dad'd swing a baseball bat with all his might and stop it an inch from little Lido's head, and whenever Lido would flinch, his dad would start shouting 'Don't you trust your old man? I'm not gonna hurt you! I'd never hurt my own son!'"

I had stopped breathing *"Scheiße."*

"Yeah, real nice guy. Well, this happened a few more times, but by now Lido was coming on eleven, twelve years and growing bigger, and one night when his old man grabbed him, Lido did what he did. Clocked him good in the skull with one of those titanium baseball bats. And he hasn't said a word since."

Hamish's words stung me all the way through to my bones. I glanced at my father, his expression pained, holding the unbroken side of his face in his hand.

"Lido's the best of us. Most of us, we's lost causes, but our Lido's not like that," Hamish said. "So whatever you do, don't go bringing up baseball bats. Or scarves. He's breakable."

Hamish's words echoed what Nurse had said, about Lido being fragile. But I was shaking my head, my mind tracing over how young Lido must have been when he arrived here, how even after living in darkness all these years, he still emitted so much light. Lido's not fragile. Lido has the strength of someone who has taught himself to survive.

"Hamish, I don't think you know a damn thing about Lido," I said, standing. I drew my eyes to his surprised face. "I'm calling in my favor. Do you still have those cigarettes?"

I found Lido on the rocks. Out above the ocean, a storm was fumbling over itself in great, dark clouds, but here, a beam of fresh sunlight was hitting Lido exactly. He stood with his back to me, facing the churning obsidian-colored surf, the wind running its fingers through his hair.

"Lido," I said hesitantly. He lifted his gaze to mine. His pale eyes seemed nearly bled of color. "Are you okay?"

He shook his whole head, hands folded over his face. I was afraid to touch him. Something about the rigid way he held himself, I thought if I did, my fingers would come away burned.

He was scribbling something in his notebook.

*Gus*, he wrote. *He'd be alive if it wasn't for me.*

My forehead furrowed in confusion. A sound came from my throat that made it clear how ludicrous I thought this. "That wasn't your fault," I said. "You can't think you caused that."

*If I'd never given him that scarf, this wouldn't have happened. If I wasn't here, he'd be alive.*

"What are you talking about?" I scoffed. "People don't do that just because someone gives them an opportunity. You do that because you hurt too much. Because—because your mind lies to you. He would've found another way."

*Why are you yelling?*

I hadn't intended to raise my voice. I licked my lips, salty from the wind blowing across the water. "You need to be strong, Lido. You did nothing wrong."

*He was like me*, he jotted quickly, almost like he'd blurted it. His pencil hovered over the paper for a long moment. *Gus had been here forever. Most of his life, definitely. I always thought, that'll be me one day.* He paused writing, his face tense. *Looking at him was like looking into my future.*

"Lido, how could you think that? You're nothing like him."

He was shaking his head, writing something else in trembling thin penmanship. *I'm afraid.*

"Why—"

He shook his head again curtly, cutting off my question. *I'm always afraid.*

He turned his back to me, his whole body coiled against the abrasive wind.

Before we fled the GDR, I'd always thought of fear as a passing hurt, a moment, a single panicked pang in your heart at a sound in the night or a shadowy figure on the street. But I know now that fear can wrap around a person, swallow them. Can make them hear gunshots in their sleep. Every day, my mind retraces my fear like a tongue against a missing tooth, because it's almost as if my mind likes the pain. I saw now that this was Lido, too. He was cushioned in fear.

I took the matches from my pocket. Hamish had handed them to me with a confused expression on his face, but he didn't ask questions. If he had, I wouldn't have told the truth, which is that, lately, I've been remembering the things my mother taught me, and realizing she might have been onto something. I held the matches up so Lido could see them.

"Lido," I said. "I think I can teach you to not be afraid."

He threw a hand up as if to bat away my statement. I took a step closer, the spray from the ocean dampening my slippers.

"I'm telling the truth," I said.

He turned, holding his notebook in curled fingers. *You don't know what you're saying,* he had written. And then beneath it, he slowly printed, *How?*

"I can teach you to be powerful," I said. "You can only fight fear by yourself for so long. You need a weapon against it." I slipped my hand into his and tugged on his arm. He paused, then followed and we walked inland, behind a rock shelf where the ocean mist couldn't reach, gathering brambles and dried driftwood as we walked. He looked at the pile with suspicion.

"Are you ready?" I asked.

*What are you going to do?*

"I won't do anything," I said. "You will." I took out the matchbook Hamish had given me and held it between my fingers.

I struck a match against the flint paper. A flame quavered in my grip. Lido followed the light with his pale gaze. My mother was right. Fire is a kind of magic. Behind us, through the overgrown needles of a thousand cypress trees, was a hive of people, slowly consuming the time they had left, as if the clock isn't always ticking. Sheep, my mother called them. But out here, against the surging sound of surf just beyond these rocks, I held a flame in my hand, something so alive, I knew, finally, what my mother saw in it. The flame looked like her. It burned just as brightly. It worked just as quickly. I realize only now, writing this, that my face must have worn the same expression she had on the night she burned down that Stasi office building.

She taught me about fire so I could fight back. Now, I was teaching Lido.

I dropped the match to our feet where it fizzled in moss. Lido pulled his lips into his mouth, his jaw set hard. *This won't work*, he wrote. *It's going to take a lot more than a match.*

"My mother always told me, when they lock you up, when they take away your voice, become an arsonist. When you light something on fire, you're also burning down the bad things in yourself."

Lido seemed to sigh, making a small, reluctant shake with his head. *Give me the matches*, was all he wrote.

I thrust the matchbook out to him and he slid a match against the flint paper. It flared to life with a *whoosh*. Lido placed the match on the dead brambles at our feet and they took flame gradually, the fire twining up the stalks with slow, orange efficiency. I showed him how to stack the wood, and the blaze expanded, turning blue and green from the salt. The flames leaped higher than I had planned and Lido stood too close, the wind whipping tendrils of flame near his body, but he didn't back away.

His mouth gathered up seriously. *Do you still want to escape?*

My breath caught in my throat. I looked over at my father, standing far from the fire, buffeted by the wind. He was thinking of my mother, I could tell, living behind that Wall still. "Yes," I said. "More than ever before."

Lido's hand trembled as he wrote the words, *I want out, too.*

The air in my lungs all came out in a stream. "Why?"

*What you said, about how it's impossible to run on an island. You were right. I want to run again. I want to go to a Dodgers game. I want to eat a frozen chocolate banana like they sell on the boardwalk. I just—*

His forehead furrowed as he looked across the rock shelf toward the hospital buildings. *I just don't want to die here,* he wrote.

I was nodding, the blood in my veins pulsating from the flames, from the idea of leaving this place. Something like a plan was formulating in my mind, put together by the image of Gus hanging from a sprinkler pipe in his room.

"We can start a fire, set off the sprinkler systems," I said. "One in my room, one in your room, to create confusion. They'll have to evacuate us, unlock all the doors. And in the chaos, we can steal the keys to the boat. We can make it to shore."

*When?*

"Soon."

A grin flooded his face, and a feeling of pride formed in my chest at the sight of him, burnishing amid the smoke and embers wafting through the air. His gaze fell hotly on mine, and the gaze was made of sea air and the whipping wind and tears and the ashy hotness of that fire, that fire, that glorious fire washing over us, never burning us.

## Date Unknown

Tonight, we escape. We put everything in place this morning. In Nurse's office, as she was scanning some document, my fingers checked for the thousandth time that I had the matches in my front pocket. Like a magnet, her eyes ticked upward, straight to my fingers. Her mouth pursed.

"Hand it over," she demanded. "I know you've got something."

I reluctantly pulled the matches from my pocket. "I just . . . found them. I was about to turn them in. Somebody could get hurt."

She took the matches in her hand. She frowned, then, gradually, her features softened. "I haven't told you this enough, Sally, but I'm very proud of you. You've come so far."

She stood from her desk and wrapped her hands around my shoulders, squeezing in what was probably her idea of affection. I had to fight my body from stiffening against her touch. I couldn't betray how badly I wanted to get away from her, how much I hated her.

I found Hamish during lunch. "I need more matches," I told him.

"How many cigarettes did you smoke to burn through those so quickly?"

"My nurse found them," I growled.

"Nurse Keating? That Rottweiler?" He whistled.

"So it would seem," I said. "Now, are you going to hand them over?"

Hamish's face was thoughtful. He reached into his front pocket and pulled out a new book of matches. "Whatever you're planning," he said. "I hope you know what you're doing."

I smirked at Hamish. I almost pity him. This time tomorrow, he'll be playing Scrabble in the rec room. And Lido and I?

We'll be gone.

That Night

I don't want to write what happened tonight. I don't want to imagine it, the burning bed, the unstoppered smoke, the tracks of ash beneath Lido's nose from where he tried to breathe. He'd tried and tried to breathe but—

I have to write this down. I must remember what I've done.

When I thrust the flaming paper to the smoke detector in my room, I expected water to spray down immediately. I stretched my arm as high as my shoulder would allow, standing on tiptoes on my wooden chair, but the flames turned the paper to ash and no water spurted forth.

"Damn," I whispered.

I ripped another page from my diary and lit it again. When the paper burned down to nearly nothing, a blaring alarm started drumming through the walls. Water at last flung from the ancient pipe, brown at first, then gushing clear. Shouts rang out. I hopped down from my chair and heard nurses and doctors unlocking doors. My door unlocked with a click.

I poked my head into the hall, where nurses were helping patients out of their rooms, water gushing from the ceiling like a shower. "Line up neatly in the hallway," I heard someone command. "We will evacuate to the administration building."

"We're going to die!" Melody shouted, covering her ears.

"Nobody's going to die," a nurse said, guiding her to the open doorway where another figure ushered others outside.

I fought my way through the teeming hallway, through the freezing water showering from above, through the nurses, through the swarming patients holding hands to their ears against the alarm, in the direction of Lido's room.

My footfalls faltered when I heard screaming. A blond nurse stood at the end of the corridor.

"Help!" she shouted, her voice sounding strangled. She fumbled with keys, trying to find the right one.

Smoke unfurled in a thick bank of fog from beneath the door. Lido's room. He was in there. Beyond the door came the wood snapping noise of fire. My muscles wavered. I thought I might fall like a dummy with its strings cut.

The nurse unlocked the door and a mountain of smoke tipped from the opening. I shoved past her and held my breath as I rushed into Lido's room. *Please, please, please*, I chanted in my head. The air in the room was caustic and hot, and blood rushed to the surface of my face. An orange tongue of fire glowed at the center of the room, devouring Lido's bed, blackening his blanket, peeling back like a rotten banana peel. My stomach hollowed when, at last, I saw Lido, sprawled in the corner, limbs bent and loose.

My lungs burned with the breath I was holding. I touched his chest, feeling for movement. There was none. I couldn't let myself think what this might mean. I was frozen to the spot, when a blade of white cut through the smoke. It was the nurse's white-uniformed presence, pushing past me, pulling Lido by his shirt. I grabbed his ankles, and in a moment, we were standing in the shower of sprinklers in the hallway. My lungs screamed as I finally pulled in a breath.

"He needs oxygen," the nurse said, in a frantic tone that made my heart squirm. We lifted him by his shoulders, his entire body limp, and dragged him toward the cool night air pushing in from the outside. Every shuffling step, a hope bloomed in my mind: The sea air would revive him. The smoke would fly out of his lungs and he'd breathe.

In the night air, we set him down on the rough rock surface, and the nurse ran toward the medical building for supplies. I fell to the ground beside Lido, pressing my trembling hands to his face.

"Wake up, Lido," I whispered.

His head lolled on his neck, eyes closed. The wind was whipping around us, cutting through my light clothes. Ash speckled his skin, and his face was flushed unnaturally crimson. All around us, nurses ran and patients screamed, and above all, the siren still blared. My heart was smashing around in my chest, and tears came to my eyes, a sob breaking through my mouth.

"Lido," I wept, doubling over him.

He cracked his eyelids, and my heart lifted for a moment. His eyes drifted around unfocused, then he leaned to the side and vomited.

"Sally!" I turned and saw Nurse running toward us.

I felt light-headed with relief. "Help me!" I cried to her.

She bent down to inspect Lido, pressing shaking fingers expertly to his chest, peering in his nostrils and throat, his eyes. His breath came in a struggling stream, the sound like a whistle, and I knew then that something was so broken in his chest, it may never heal. Lido grasped Nurse's coat, pulling in a whining, ragged breath. The full weight of what I had done smashed down on me. I looked over at my father, his forehead pinched with fear. Lido was—Lido was dying. My fingers shake as I write this, hours later.

Lido was dying because of me.

I touched his chest, where it jerked beneath the pearlescent buttons of his pajamas. My face crumpled and tears overwhelmed my eyes, falling uncontrollably.

"I'm sorry, Lido," I gasped. "I'm so sorry. It's all my fault."

I felt Nurse stiffen beside me. She turned her hard gaze to me. "You did this," she hissed.

She looked at me as though I was the dangerous girl Georg and Margarita had said I was. Only now, weren't they right? I'd killed the one person here I cared about. My body burned with pain.

"You—you were getting better," she said, barely audible above the siren. "Why would you do this, Sally?"

I focused my tear-drenched eyes at her, a fury kicking inside of my chest. "Don't call me Sally," I said. "That's not my name. My name is Ava Dreyman. And you will never tell me it's not."

Nurse recoiled as though I'd struck her.

The blond nurse appeared with an oxygen tank, just as someone frantically shouted Nurse's name across the black rock expanse. She stood, casting one last glare at me, and ran into the night. The nurse secured the mask to Lido's face and listened to his heart with a stethoscope.

I felt Lido's hand touch mine. Slowly, he unfurled the fingers of my fist. I lay my fingers flat and watched as he placed something there. A small ring of keys. My eyes widened. When he'd grabbed Nurse, he must have stolen them from her pocket.

He traced a finger along my cheek and pulled back my

sleeve, revealing the clean skin of my arm. He drew a word on my forearm with ash.

*Go*, he printed. The sight of it kicked something to life in my chest. I looked into his eyes for a moment, before they grew foggy and slid backward beneath his lids.

I placed his head down gently, memorizing the look of him amid the black canvas of rock and overgrown greenery, red-faced and cloaked in smoke. My eyes fell to the spot where I'd once been able to gaze through his chest, where his heart ought to be. Barely visible, I saw a flicker of flame in that dark cavern where once there had been nothing.

In my chest, I felt it, too.

# Pepper

*Physical Fitness*

Dear Ms. Eldridge,

You will not be believing Germany. It is crowded, even more crowded than the Oakland airport, and everyone rides a bicycle, and you can buy schnitzel on the street corners. Schnitzel is like the best fried chicken I have ever had, better than KFC, better even than the Vietnamese place in Seaside. I was enjoying my time so much here in Germany, it almost took the edge off of discovering that, in *The Arsonist*, my favorite of all the characters, Lido, is maybe dead. I gasped aloud when I read it.

"You're only just now getting to that part?" Molly asked.

"I am reading very carefully," I replied. "For the purposes of the quest. Does he come back at the end?"

"It's not like a novel," Molly replied. "Ava never saw him again."

I had to try very, very hard not to hurl the book into the path of a train.

But back to the subject at hand. I'm supposed to be talking about physical fitness, which I will get to eventually, but first I need to tell you about Germany.

Fact: The Germans are loving their beers so much, they have bars on every block like we have Starbucks, and they are badly wanting to pass the beers off on young people who are not legally allowed to drink in their own country.

Fact: Ms. Eldridge, it would be very irresponsible for a person such as myself to be consuming alcohol considering the sensitivity of my mission. However, when it was presented to me, I thought, "Ms. Eldridge would not wish me to waste such an opportunity for action research," so with your blessing, I consumed some beverages but not more than several.

Fact: German beers are tasting much better than the yellow cheap beer the Horsemen secure for social functions.

I apologize for failing to inform you of my destination in my previous e-mail. I was certain you might consider telling my father, and that would have been very detrimental to my mission. My dad believes I'm spending the next few days camping with Shawn, and Margaret has told Molly's aunt that Molly is at the library.

"Your aunt will not believe you. You cannot spend three whole days at the library," I told Molly once as we were arriving at the airport.

"You don't know me very well," Molly said.

The people at the airport check-in counter nearly lost their minds when they scanned my Kuwaiti passport, and then my American Disability Association card, as though they weren't sure whether to "randomly select" me for a strip search or offer me a wheelchair. In the end, Molly and I got to skate through the boarding process because I'm considered a "valued special-ability passenger," which also meant that Bertrand got to ride on my lap during the flight.

"I'm excited," Molly said when we were seated. "Sauerkraut is really good for your gut flora."

"Your what?"

"The microbes that live in your gut. If you didn't have them, you'd die. Altogether, they weigh like five pounds."

Already I was learning so much.

The plane ride was a little frightening for Molly as she hadn't flown since she returned from France after the tragic . . . disappearance of her mother. (Ms. Eldridge, I employed an ellipses there to subtly demonstrate that I don't really believe that Molly's mother is disappeared.) She kept staring down at her passport, showing a picture of her twelve-year-old self, facial features magnified inside a miniature face. This was making me realize how little time has passed since then.

I stared out the window over the expanse of land below. Strange, I thought, to be moving so swiftly over America. Where it wasn't cloud-covered, it looked green and beveled and the color of dark dirt. It looked like anywhere.

When we changed planes at JFK, it was early in the morning and still dark. Bertrand fell asleep and oozed from my lap partway onto Molly's, snoring loudly. My eyes itched with tiredness but I didn't want to sleep, so I got out a bag of Cheetos I'd retrieved from a vending machine and poked Molly.

"It feels like we should be a lot more prepared than this," I said. "I don't even have an adaptor for my phone."

"My mom said before we left for Nice that everybody should just drop everything and get on a plane at least once in their lives." She shut her mouth so her bottom lip kind of crumpled beneath her top lip. "Anyway, I bought a plug adaptor while you were in the bathroom so you're all right."

Molly had us talk over the plan approximately one million times. "Okay, so we're going to land around eight a.m., then we'll grab something to eat, and then we head straight to the bank on the business card, because that's obviously where we're supposed to go first." She drummed on her lap with the business card, stamped with the name Muriel Weisz.

I nodded. "And once we follow those leads, we'll go to the Cold War Museum, because they have an Ava Dreyman exhibit and maybe there'll be something there." That was my contribution to the plan, Ms. Eldridge. I'd found out about it with my ninja-strength Googling skills. That is a kind of physical activity, right?

When the plane landed, my five pounds of gut flora and I were practically dancing in my seat. We were going to solve the mystery! We were going to make all our dreams come true! (I know I am overselling this, Ms. Eldridge. It's called hyperbole and the ancient Greeks loved it.)

I can hear you already: "Pepper, this is great about the fried chicken and the gut flora and the underage drinking, but don't you have an essay on physical education to write?" Okay, fine. But I think you'll agree it's ridiculous to write about physical education when I'm a fine physical specimen who doesn't need a class to teach me buffness. Gym class means being told to do torturous things like dodgeball, and flag football (which I object to because I've touched way too many butts by accident that way), and worst of all *running around the track*. Who does this outside of America? This is an invented thing. In most countries, exercise means working in a factory or going out to hunt a wildebeest, not running around a stupid concrete circle. For this reason, I do not see the purpose of gym class, a point I informed my gym teacher at Hoover of all the time. This might be the reason I did not pass gym.

As for my essay, this is the best I could do:

*Today, I traveled halfway around the world, and even though I've been here for an hour I've already walked around half of Berlin, and I sweated like a professional wrestler because it was incredibly hot the entire time, and now my foot has a blister.*

I know this essay is too short to receive credit, but if you take into account all my body has been through just since I started this project, Ms. Eldridge, I've done the equivalency of like five gym classes.

Consider me physically educated.

# Molly

Hey, Pepper,

For a while, it was very tense here at the hospital, by your bedside. We were all holding our breath so much our lungs may have suffered permanent damage. But, now, the tension has bled away a little, and what's left is So. Much. Boredom. You just lie there. There isn't even a machine in the room that monitors your heartbeat and goes *beep . . . beep . . . beep*. There's just your respirator sucking away in the corner, and Shawn, who has taken to whispering in your ear.

"What are you doing?" I ask him.

"Telling Pepper dirty jokes," he says. "I figure if I can make him laugh, maybe his whole system will jump-start and he'll wake up."

"Okay," I say. "What's one you're telling him?"

He leans forward. "What's the difference between snowmen and snowwomen?"

"What?" I ask.

"Snowballs." He cracks up for a whole minute.

Thank God you don't laugh. I would've been really disappointed if you'd woken up for that.

- - - - -

After we arrive in Berlin, it's like I can't open my eyes wide enough. We take a train from the airport into the heart of the city, and I try to take in every pockmark on every building, watching the concrete sprawl of industrial parks around the airport peel back to reveal the city. The historical time period seems to change every few blocks—the facades of buildings shifting from old brick to communist concrete to ancient marble to modern glass—and I picture all the bombing and destruction that must have created this patchwork place. Most of all, I scan every person's face, hoping I might catch a glimpse of Ava Dreyman or, even better, my mother.

We get off the train and grab some food from a street cart and eat quickly as we walk the few blocks to the address on Muriel Weisz's business card.

"This is Potsdamer Platz," I say, looking up from my phone. We've arrived in a modern section of the city shaped like a square. On all sides, we're surrounded by glass and metal buildings and the rushing of cars forking off in different directions. In the center of the square, people dart in and out of a huge, glassed-in enclosure reading "Bahnhof Potsdamer Platz." It looks like a subway entrance. "I read about this online," I say. "This was the center of Berlin, right between the East and West. It was a no-man's-land when the Wall was up. Nobody could go here."

You sweep your eyes around us. "I'm glad they brought it back to life."

Muriel Weisz's bank is located just off the square in a glass building, at least twenty stories high. We enter alongside a bunch of men and women in dark suits and shoes that sound like a herd of deer in the marble-plated lobby. You wrap Bertrand's leash tightly around your fist.

My heart is palpitating with how close we are, a dangerous kind of knocking behind my ribs that makes me fear I might be putting my internal organs at risk.

Behind a large desk in the center of the lobby, a man dressed in a suit waves us over. My cast makes a thunking sound against the floor as we approach. He asks something in German and when we shake our heads, he tries again in English. "Do you have an appointment? You'll need to sign in." He indicates a clipboard on the counter.

My brain does a massive flip. "We, um, have an appointment," I say. I pull Muriel Weisz's business card out of my shorts pocket and hold it out to the man.

He looks us over. We do not look like people who would have an appointment at a bank.

His eyes flick back to the business card. "She's on the fifth floor. Please sign in here," he says, pointing to the clipboard. We jot our names and quick-walk to the elevator.

At the fifth floor, we step out into a wide expanse of cubicles laid out in precise rows, divided up by glass walls so we could see all the way to the windows.

"There's like one million offices here," you say, awed.

"Maybe we should split up," I say.

"Nuh-uh," you say. "That's the first rule of horror movies. Don't split up."

"Pepper," I say. "We're in a bank. How many horror movies happen in banks? We'll meet on the grass out front afterward."

You scoop up Bertrand, who has been desperately trying to eat the leaves off a potted plant. "Fine."

You and Bertrand take off in one direction, and I go the opposite, walking through rows of cubes. We are so near to answers, Pepper. My blood is rippling with excitement. It's a Christmas morning kind of anticipatory feeling, because inside this building is a woman with the name Muriel Weisz, who might hold the answer to everything.

It's the feeling of finding out what happened to Ava for real.

It's the feeling of seeing my mother again.

I allow myself to think about the first thing I'll do when I find her. We'll go out to eat at a fancy restaurant with oysters on the menu. She hated the taste but ordered them whenever she had the chance. "I'm looking for my pearl," she'd say. "I'll sell it and we'll be rich. Richer than a queen."

*We'll find your pearl, Mom*, I think. *We've got all kinds of time.*

The space is filled with German voices and the machinations of a copy machine and the clicking of computer keys. Sunlight slants through the windows, shooting across the office floor at the exact moment that I see her.

Ava Dreyman is standing twenty feet away.

Her hair is in a ponytail, sleek like water from a garden hose. She's leaning over a man's desk, pointing to something on a computer screen. Her mouth moves and German words pour out. Her mouth, a determined line, slightly underturned, is just like the one in her photo.

"Ava Dreyman?" I whisper. She seems to hear, like how you always hear your name being said, even in a noisy room.

The skin on her forehead gathers up. I take a couple of steps toward her.

"Ava Dreyman." This time, it leaves my mouth ecstatically. A laugh pops from my lips. I look around for you, but I don't see you anywhere.

The woman levels a hard gaze on me. "*Nein*," she says.

My feet fumble and make a loud scuff against the carpet.

"It's you," I insist, and though the woman has wrinkles darting crookedly across her forehead and lips covered in dark red lipstick, I've never been so certain about anything as I am about the fact that this is Ava Dreyman. "You're Ava, I know it. Don't—don't pretend you aren't."

The woman shakes her head, her mouth tugging into a frown. "You've mistaken me with someone else," she says in thick English. And just like that, she grips her elbows in her hands, and walks quickly away down the corridor.

I don't think, I just move. I dart forward and grab her by the shoulder.

"You're lying," I say, the sound coming out louder than I'd planned. "You *are* Ava Dreyman."

She gives her head a frustrated shake. "Oh *Christus*, this always happens," she says. "People—young people, especially—insist I'm Ava Dreyman, based on nothing more than an old photo. Well, you can just leave me alone. Ava Dreyman is dead. I'm not who you're looking for."

"Who are you then," I ask in a measured voice, "if not Ava Dreyman?"

"Muriel Weisz," she says, like it's the most obvious statement in the world.

"And you've always been Muriel Weisz?"

"You are welcome to check my birth certificate if you would like."

"But you—you look just like the photograph."

"Yes," she says exasperatedly. "It's a likeness, I won't deny it. But I'm not her."

At this moment, I'm thinking that the universe cannot be so cruel. I am *inches* from Ava Dreyman, and she should be able to answer all of our questions. But it's another dead end. A firestorm has begun inside my brain. My mother, who felt so close only a moment ago, close enough for me to imagine the perfume she always wore, close enough to let myself imagine the oysters and the pearl, is suddenly slipping from my grasp.

Ava—or Muriel—turns to walk away. She is slipping through

my fingers. She's leaving me alone. Just like my mother did.

No.

*No.*

"No!" I shout. My voice comes like a bullet, tearing out of my throat. The muscles in the woman's face jump. My fists ball up and the workers in cubicles turn to stare. "NO! You—you're lying. Do you have any idea how *sick* I am of being lied to?"

The woman's mouth is frozen half-open.

There is an earthquake in my limbs, Pepper. Can you feel the tremors on your side of the office floor? "You are going to tell me the truth," I breathe, "right now. Or I will . . . I will hurt you. I will. Believe me, I know how."

I step toward her and the woman backs up, her eyes darting around.

And just like that, something comes loose, all the skin on her face collapsing. "He warned me this could happen."

"He?" I demand. "Who?"

"I don't know his real name. Only that he calls himself Boy Scout." Her eyes dilate with fear. "He's going to kill me. He's never spelled it out but I know he will. I—I swore I'd never talk about this."

"You're talking about it right now," I say desperately. "Tell me. Tell me what you know."

"*The Arsonist* is . . . not what people think."

"What do you mean?"

"It's a hoax," she blurts.

Without meaning to, I stagger backward. I have to push my hands down hard to the sides of my legs to stay upright.

A *hoax?*

"We should go somewhere private," she says. She pulls her phone from the pocket of her skirt, checking the time. Numbly, I notice she's got the same type as me, the same phone a billion people on the planet have. "I can give you ten minutes before I need to get back to work."

She grabs a can of Diet Coke and a key card from her desk. In the elevator, she punches in the button for the roof. I want to barrage her with questions but I jam my tongue between my molars and wait. When the doors pull back, we step out into the open air. We're not very high up, but there's a view through the taller skyscrapers to the city beyond. I can see the patchwork of ancient marble and jutting metal buildings and yellow trams dissecting Berlin through the screwy winding streets below.

I sit beside Muriel on the edge of a fountain encrusted with teal tiles. She sets her phone beside her and opens her can of soda, taking a long swallow, then nods. "Well, let's get this over with."

"That really is you on the cover of *The Arsonist*, isn't it?" I ask.

"Yes," Muriel says. "But I'm not Ava Dreyman."

I shake my head, uncomprehending. "How—" I sputter. "How did it happen?"

"How did a photograph taken of me at nineteen end up on the cover of one of the most famous books ever written?" She chuckles. "I was young and it was the eighties, just before the Wall fell, and I had placed an advertisement in the local paper: *model and actress looking for professional assignments*, along with the pertinent information about my appearance, height, skin color, age, like you did back then. Only ever got one call, a man asking me to pose for a photograph. Just one photograph, he said, and it might not even be used." She's said all of this quickly, and I wonder if this is the first time she's gotten to tell this story.

"The photographer didn't know what it was for, either, but we both got paid. I didn't think about it again, not until those pamphlets appeared and people started chanting Ava Dreyman in the streets." She takes a shuddering breath.

"And when *The Arsonist* came out?"

"I had to go into hiding, practically. Cut my hair short, looked awful, but I became paranoid about keeping reporters away. I moved to the West as soon as possible. I still get funny looks."

"Why can't you just tell people it was you in the photo? That it's you on the cover of *The Arsonist*?"

Her mouth forms a frown that seems well-worn. "Because there are people out there who still badly want my silence. The man who hired me for the photo called me at my new address after the diary was published. I don't know how he got my information. He sounded nice at first, thanked me for my time, but then he made it clear what would happen if I ever revealed the truth."

"So this guy's been blackmailing you all these years?" I ask.

"Not exactly," she says. "There seems to be at least two men involved. The man who hired me for the photo sounded older. Distinguished. I pictured gray hair, I don't know. It was a different man who called to threaten me afterward. He calls himself Boy Scout. He's in contact regularly. He—he tells me what he'll do if I ever reveal the truth."

"What does that mean?" I ask. "That more than one man would call you to make threats?"

"What do you think?" she asks, shifting in her seat. "There are a lot of people who want to keep the world from knowing that it's me in that picture. You said you're tired of being lied to. Well, I'm tired of people threatening my life. And it's all to do with this *Arsonist*. I can tell you this much: The three hundred marks wasn't worth it."

She presses the home button on her phone, checking the time, and sets it on the edge of the fountain. It occurs to me again that our phones are the same model. An idea flickers to life in my mind.

Muriel drains the last mouthful of her soda and stands. "Now can I be left in peace?" she asks. "You need to keep all of these things to yourself. People's lives are at stake here." She lifts the phone from the side of the fountain and slings her purse over her shoulder.

"You were in Monterey last week," I call after her.

Muriel glances back at me. "So?"

"So I'd bet that wasn't the first time you've traveled there."

"I have business there, on occasion."

My eyes narrow. "Do you meet Boy Scout in person or is he smart enough to hide his identity?"

"I—" Muriel opens her mouth. She casts a guilty look at the ground. "I go to a dead drop. Cash, in exchange for my silence. He won't do electronic wire transfers. Paranoid it'll be traced to him, I assume. I fly to the same place every year. I've never seen his face."

Muriel walks away, disappearing behind the doors of the elevator. I stay seated, my mind filtering everything I've learned. Someone wanted Muriel to stand in as Ava on the cover of *The Arsonist*, and now she's being threatened—and paid—by someone called Boy Scout. Who would want to hide the fact that Muriel Weisz's face has been standing in for Ava Dreyman's for all these years?

And if Ava's photo was faked—what else in the diary might be fake?

I feel as if I've just run a huge distance. My heart is only now slowing down to a normal pace. Bad thoughts are starting to seep in. My mother isn't here. She's not waiting behind a door, ready to be revealed like a prize on a game show. My chest grows more constricted with every breath.

I walk to the edge of the roof and gaze down at the street below. If my mother jumped from the cliff at the Château de Nice, she did so from a height like this. There'd be no surviving a fall like that. I close my eyes and imagine it. She would have wavered in the air a moment,

silk blouse flapping,

hair floating,

her every cell suspended above the earth,

nothing to pin her down anymore.

A long time passes, and I realize slowly that you must be waiting for me. I head toward the elevator, pulling Muriel's phone from my pocket. Maybe she'll think it was a mistake that I took her phone and she took mine. I type in the passcode I saw her enter earlier and click on her contacts. I scroll a few times, then see what I'm looking for.

Boy Scout.

The number listed there is only six digits long. I've seen these before. They're text-only lines, like companies use when they send message alerts to customers' phones. I open up an Internet window and Google the number, but I can't find who it belongs to.

Curious, I open up a text message. My thumbs hover over the phone's glass screen for a moment.

I run the phrase "We need to meet," into Google translate, pray it sounds like authentic German, paste it into a text message, and hit send.

# Ava

December 25, 1988

I had to walk around Monterey for hours to find Georg and Margarita's house. The fronts of the homes on Ponderosa Avenue looked dingier than two years ago. Now, the lawns were all dried up yellow carpets. Strings of cheap electronic Christmas lights hung halfheartedly over doorways. When I finally found the house and stood before it, I felt a pulse of anger, remembering what they did to me. I wanted to hurt both of them. I thought I could.

From behind lace curtains, an orange light glowed. I jiggled the locked door handle.

"What's that?" I heard a woman call from inside.

The door swung open and Margarita stood before me, a thick glass of whiskey in her hand. Her face went blank with surprise. I pushed past her into the room, slamming the door behind me. Georg sat in an armchair with a flannel blanket over his legs. An artificial Christmas tree sat in the corner, covered in neon baubles. He looked up with a start from the American sitcom he'd been watching. On a side table, the remains of a meaty dinner sat beneath dirty silverware.

I snatched the serrated steak knife from Georg's dinner plate and pressed it into his throat, leaning hard on his thigh with my knee.

"Ava?" he gurgled in shock.

"Where is she?" I demanded. "My mother. Where?"

"What are you talking about?" Georg sputtered.

"You're mad!" Margarita screeched, her hands by her face. "I'm phoning the police!"

"You do and your husband gets a knife through his throat." Margarita froze. I faced Georg, watching the serrated edge of the knife indent his flesh. "Where is she?"

"I—I don't know," he sputtered. "She hasn't been in contact."

"But you must have some idea."

"We have no idea!" Margarita shouted in her thin, broken voice.

I pushed the knife deeper into Georg's neck, a bead of blood forming along the metal.

"Please . . ." he cried. Tears blurred his blue eyes. This guy fought on the front lines in the war. He killed Allied soldiers. I thought he'd be tougher to break.

"Have you tried contacting her?" I asked. "Have you looked at all?"

"No, but—"

"Why not?" I growled.

"It would have been too dangerous," he said. "We had a hard enough time convincing these people we were American.

Making inquiries about someone in East Berlin would have placed suspicion on us."

"You were supposed to be her friend," I snapped.

"It wasn't just the Americans we feared. That Stasi man, the captain . . ."

"Captain Werner?" I asked, my blood turning icy at the memory.

"Yes, Werner. He'd been searching for us. We heard from a friend in the West that the Stasi had blanketed the television and radio with our names. We're wanted fugitives! If Werner knew we were here, he'd hunt us down. That's his specialty."

"I remember," I said.

"Then you know it would be suicide to look for Mirka."

I could've killed him. Just pushed a little harder on the hilt, turned the blade a hair to make sure I carved through an artery. Margarita would be easy compared to that big band of fat around Georg's neck. But I know what violence does to a person, how it ruins you long after the act is done. I looked at my father, where he was standing beside the darkened window.

I took a shuddering breath. "Do you have any idea what it's like wondering whether your own mother is dead or alive?"

"You must not delude yourself about her, Ava," he said. "The Stasi, they would not be forgiving of a woman like her. After a month, she would have outlived her usefulness."

"Don't say that," I shouted, the knife shaking in my fist. "She

could still be in prison. Or she could've gotten out. She'd—
she'd be looking for me."

"If she were free and she wanted to be found, she would
have by now."

"The Wall—"

"The Wall wouldn't stop your mother. The Wall still stands,
but the people are stirring. The government is trying to tamp
down an uprising as we speak. They're grasping at straws, letting people watch television, opening up the borders more. She
hasn't been in contact, which means one of two things: She's
dead, or she doesn't want to be found."

His words mirrored my own darkest thoughts. But I can't en-
tertain the idea of leaving her. I've tried, and every time I do I
remember her face. "Open up the safe," I said, motioning my
head toward the white box on the wall. Margarita looked from
me, to her husband, to the knife in my hand. "Do it!" I screamed.

She jumped a little and wound the combination on the dial,
unlocking it with a clunk. I lifted the blade away from Georg's
throat, standing in the middle of the floor, purposefully flicking drops of blood onto their white carpet.

I grabbed all the money from the top shelf, packed neatly in
a cream-colored envelope.

"I assume you still have my American papers?" I asked.
"Must keep up the pretense of having a lunatic daughter."

"It's in the folding file," Georg said. He was rubbing his neck,
blood coming away in his fingers.

I riffled through the accordioned cardboard file and found the passport for Sally Bailey. The girl in the picture is so young. Did I truly ever look like that?

"I trust you won't be calling the police, *George*," I said as I stepped out the front door into the night.

A few blocks away, under a streetlamp, I tossed the steak knife into the weeds beside the road and thumbed through the cash, counting.

It's enough. It has to be.

# Pepper

Dear Ms. Eldridge,

My seizures have always been brought on by stress. I can sense one moments before it is about to occur. There is a charge in the air, like the static before a lightning storm. Except the static is inside my head.

I have been feeling the static lately. Hovering right behind my ears, and sometimes Bertrand looks at me strange out the corner of his bulbous eye and I wonder, though he has always been utterly useless, if he senses it, too.

All my seizures do is make me tired, a deep kind of tired, like my brain has run a marathon, and I sleep for days afterward. At any other time in my life, if I lost days to sleep, it wouldn't have mattered. But for the first time, I can't afford to drop off into a days-long slumber. So I pretend I don't feel the static.

After I searched the office floors, looking for Ava Dreyman and finding nothing, Bertrand and I circled back to the lawn in front of the bank to wait for Molly. It was now ten minutes after we said we'd meet. After fifteen, then twenty, then thirty more minutes, I was growing panicked.

I tried calling Molly's phone, but no one picked up.

My breath was coming raggedly, and I had to pace around to contain the tornado of crap that was flinging around in my brain. Or worse? A realization of the full quantity of the trouble we were in had just hit my forehead with the power of a water balloon. Do I call the police? What if someone kidnapped her? What if she's in a European death dungeon right now? Is this what a panic attack feels like? Spots were covering my vision, and I was thinking that I needed a paper bag like I've seen in movies.

"You look like you're going to pass out."

I turned to see Molly squinting up at me in the sunshine. She was panting hard, her face red and exerted. At the sight of her, my heart did a relieved kind of faint, like a swooning lady. Bertrand let out an excited bark.

"I found her," Molly puffed. "I found Muriel. And she's not Ava—She just posed for the picture—And now someone's threatening her—He calls himself Boy Scout—And I stole Muriel's phone—So we can contact this guy—And catch him—And make him tell us who killed Ava Dreyman—"

My stomach was fizzing nervously, like I'd just done the Volcano Challenge. (This is a game the guys at school play sometimes. You drink a bottle of Coke, then a package of Alka Seltzer. If you don't go to the hospital with internal bleeding, you win.) "You want to catch the guy who's threatening her?"

"Yeah," Molly said, like it was obvious.

"He could be Ava's killer. We have to think this through."

"We're only here for another day and a half," she pleaded. "We need to get some answers before we fly back home."

"Okay," I said. "But we must treat this delicately. Like a bomb that might explode. Be very, very careful."

"Okay," she said. "But if he texts back, I'm going to meet him."

I silently hoped this Boy Scout would not respond. To change the subject, I reminded Molly of the next step in our agenda—the Cold War Museum.

We set off along the riverbank. The air was steamy and warm, and it seemed as though everywhere people were stretched out on the grass looking like beached whales. Many men are shirtless here, and even a few ladies. Sufficing to say, I have seen much too much German skin today.

The museum was a slick-sided black box. We paid our five Euros—strange-colored bills with politicians' faces that I did not recognize—to the woman at the front desk and entered the air-conditioned building.

We toured rooms containing the equipment of the Stasi. An officer's gray dress suit. A camera with a button on the lens for clandestine photo taking. A necktie with a listening device sewn in. I swear, Ms. Eldridge, these guys would've been funny if they hadn't been so scary. They actually *used* this crap. There was also a wall with jars filled with orange scraps of fabric, which I read on a placard contained the smells of dissidents who the Stasi could sic their dogs after. They collected *smells*. What a bunch of nutbags.

Molly's face had gone a lifeless noncolor. I could tell she was filling up with the sadness of this place, the neighbors spying on neighbors, the aftersmell of fear and paranoia.

We shuffled ourselves into the exhibit, called "Undying in Death: Remnants of the Life of Ava Dreyman."

I walked around, taking in the mannequin with one of Ava's school uniforms, and a reproduction of the big cream-colored BMW that Georg, Margarita, and Ava escaped Germany in.

Molly's attention had been grasped by a glass case full of photographs of Ava's parents. Her mother was severe-looking with a short haircut. Her father appeared soft-eyed and sleepy. There was a copy of his death certificate, which according to the plaque listed his cause of death as "cranial trauma."

And there was a photo of Paedar. It showed him as a teenager, his blond hair scored with comb lines. His irises were made of blue like a frothy sea, and his skin was ultrapale. Ms. Eldridge, he looked like milk, if milk could be a person. I asked Molly what he was doing with his life now.

"I read online that he goes on TV and gets interviewed a lot," she said, her eyes trailing across the photographs in the case. "And he writes. About Ava, mostly. He just had a new book come out, I think. And apparently he purchased Ava Dreyman's apartment after the Wall fell, but it's not open to the public."

Why would a guy buy his dead ex-girlfriend's house, even

if she was famous? Creepy, right, Ms. Eldridge? Or maybe sad.

There was one photo of Ava as a young girl. It was colorless and showed her at about four or five, wearing a buttoned dress. She stood inside a living room, of the same apartment Paedar now owns, I suppose, hands on her hips, smiling so wide, it seemed to overtake her whole face. I felt my throat grow tight. I wanted to reach through time and pluck her out of that photo, take her by the hand and walk with her to safety.

Along the back wall, the photograph that everyone thinks is of Ava was blown up to the height of the ceiling. It's grainy and unfocused. On purpose, I realize now. Her blank eyes stared ahead, the irises the height of my stretched hand.

"Can you believe it?" Molly whispered. "That's not her."

"And the whole world thinks it is. We're some of the only ones who know the truth." The feeling was sort of like pride, I think. In class, I was always the last one with the answers. Now I was ahead of seven billion people. "Ava was real," I said. "Or, at least, this exhibit seems pretty certain that she is. Why not just use a photo of her on the diary?"

"I don't know." Molly was shaking her head. "What I don't get is how everyone who knew Ava really believed the photo was of her. I know it's not great quality, and Muriel probably looked something like Ava, but still."

Automatically, my eyes found the photograph of Paedar again. His pressed shirt, his teeth gleaming in a grin.

"Hang on . . ." I said aloud. My mind was chasing a thought

that was moving away almost too quickly to catch. "Someone sent Paedar the diary, yeah?"

Molly nodded. "It was left on his desk with a note to publish it."

"And Muriel's photo was printed on the very first copies."

"Yes . . ." Molly said, drawing out the word like she hadn't caught on yet. "The photo was included with the diary."

"So, Paedar must have known the photo wasn't really of Ava. Why did he print the book with Muriel's photo? And why hasn't he told the world that's not Ava Dreyman?"

When I looked at Molly, her body was tensed. "Paedar's hiding something," she said. "We need to find him."

"Whoa, what now?"

Molly's eyes had taken on a bright, burning gleam, like she was formulating a plan. "We're here for one more day. We've learned something *huge*, but it doesn't really tell us anything. And Boy Scout hasn't responded," she said, checking Muriel's phone for the one thousandth time. "Paedar is the only other person who might know what happened to Ava."

"So, we find him. And . . . ?" I asked. My gut bacteria started wriggling.

"Talk to him," Molly said. "Convince him to give us some answers." She used Muriel's phone to navigate to Paedar's website.

"I found this earlier but wasn't sure we'd have time to go," she said. "He's appearing at a bookstore in Berlin tomorrow for a reading."

"Let me see," I said, taking the phone and scanning the page. "What are the odds of that?"

The look on Molly's face was fierce. There appeared to be something hot cooking inside of her.

"You're really thinking—"

"Yes," Molly said. "I'm going to go talk to him."

"What do you mean, 'I'?" I swallowed. "What about me?"

"You . . ." she started hesitantly. "You're going to break into Ava Dreyman's apartment."

"Uh!" I exclaimed. "I am to do *what?*"

"You've broken into the Hacienda Street pool before, right? Paedar's hiding something. He purposely published a fake photo of Ava with the diary. And he owns Ava Dreyman's old apartment, which he keeps closed off to everyone. Why? What's he got in there that he doesn't want the world to see?"

"I don't really think—"

"Please," she said, half-frantic, half-pleading. "He's got to have . . . letters there. Correspondence with Ava maybe. Something." The skin around her eyes was crinkled up with desperation. "We're here for one more day. I just—" She broke off, and I could tell she was picturing her mother. I was getting good at telling that. I was afraid, Ms. Eldridge, if you want to know the truth. Afraid of the disappointment Molly was hurtling toward. She was on a collision course, and there was nothing I could do.

I nodded. "Yes," I said. "Of course. I will help you."

# Molly

Dear Pepper,

On our second morning in Berlin I watch the sun rise through the dingy glass of our hostel room window. The space is misty with the breath of twelve other travelers, and the only sound this early is the creaking of bunk beds. You're asleep on the bunk across the aisle from mine, clutching Bertrand to your chest like a teddy bear. I want to wake you, because right now, I feel strangely lonely. I'm surrounded by people, their small noises in my ears, the unwashed smell of them in my nose, but an ache thrums through me so suddenly, I have to press my forehead on the sweating window glass. Maybe, until my mother comes back, I will always feel this alone.

Sometimes, I wonder if missing her will ever fade, or if I'll go my whole life fearing the grip of it, squeezing me so tightly, it takes everything in me not to scream. You can tell, can't you, Pepper? Even asleep in your bunk. I am eroding. I am one of those planets that's already disintegrated, held together only by gravity. What happens when the gravity gives out? What happens when I have no more hope left to hold on to?

You crack your eyes open, stretching your body. Bertrand yawns so huge, he looks like Pac-Man.

"Morning," you mumble, rubbing your eyes with the heels of your hands. "Have you been up for a while?"

"Not long," I say, even though I spent most of the night feeling as though something else had taken over my muscles, my bones, a mechanical energy that was focused on one thing: finding the truth.

It's today, Pepper. Today, we're going to learn the truth.

"Well, I'm going to enjoy my final moments in a bed outside of a prison," you say.

"You're not getting arrested." At least, I hope you're not going to get arrested.

Bertrand burrows farther beneath the covers until he's hidden but for his tail. "I'm glad you have confidence in me."

"I actually don't," I tell you. "I'm just saying that to make you feel better."

I thought that would make you laugh, but your eyes go slightly bugged-out. "Great."

"I'm kidding," I say. "You know how to break in places. You've done it before."

"We hopped the fence at the Hacienda Street pool and sometimes broke into the locker rooms when one of us needed to pee. But those doors were held shut with like, chewing gum. It wasn't hard."

I watch you, giving you a long moment to say the words I'm

anticipating, that you want to scrap the whole idea. You stare at your feet.

"I'm going to need breakfast," you say, at last. "I'm going to need, like, a metric ton of breakfast."

"Yes," I agree, relieved. "Breakfast first. Crime second."

We find a café and order eggs and German sausages, the sight of which makes Bertrand wheeze so loudly, I think he's going to pass out. I have about three coffees, which is probably a mistake because my nerves are drilling inside my head like tiny jackhammers, but I need something to do other than talk over the plan for the billionth time and check Muriel's phone for a text back from Boy Scout. Finally, it's time to leave for the bookstore.

I search for directions to the bookstore on Muriel's phone. The route has us walking down a stretch of busy road with a wall running the length of the sidewalk. The wall is long and separates us from the river, like someone's stretched out a concrete curtain as far as we can see, and scrawled all over it with murals and graffiti. We pass a section painted with an image of the Israeli flag, and an enormous stenciled picture of two politicians French kissing. You stop in your tracks, pulling up on Bertrand's leash, just as a crowd of tourists approaches, a tour guide leading the way.

"Molly," you say, your face stretched open all surprised. "I think this is the Wall."

I crane my neck upward, eyes washing over the concrete face of it. "This is the Wall?" I ask in disbelief. I spread a hand out to touch the eroded surface, the caked layers of paint. Nearby, several tourists from the tour group take selfies.

"It's smaller than I imagined," you say. Quietly, I agree with you. It's not even twice my height. I'm used to picturing the Wall as mythological, like the labyrinth that even a minotaur couldn't break out of. But now that I can touch it, I wonder how something so small could have hurt so many people.

"I guess we have to imagine it with guard towers," I say, nodding up at it. "And spotlights, and razor wire and dogs." You grimace. "It didn't need to be tall to work."

People died here. Ava's dad was shot here. Now that I know what it is, this place feels weirdly like walking on a cemetery lawn, only one skirted by traffic and pedestrians and carts selling key chains and French fries.

We come to a stop across the street from the bookstore. Outside, there's a chalk sandwich board on which Paedar's face has been drawn. My muscles begin quavering, and I have to clamp my fingers into fists.

"Well, this is my stop," I say. "You have directions to Ava's apartment on your phone?"

You look as though you're pushing down a surge of nausea. "Can I really do this?" you ask.

My heart does a little sympathetic origami fold at the look on your face, Pepper. I want to reassure you, tell you I believe in you, think you can do anything, but who says stuff like that? So I point at you and say, "Here's what we're gonna do. Kneel down."

You look at me like I've just requested Bertrand's hand in marriage, but, on the scummy sidewalk, covered in the dark circles of old gum and unreadable stains, you kneel.

I point at your shoulders in my best approximation of a sword. People passing by crane their necks to stare, but I ignore them.

I clear my throat. "This fifteenth of August, in the city of Berlin, Germany, let you henceforth be known as Sir Pepper the Brave." I move my hands in a combination of the sign of the cross and the phrase "thank you" in American Sign Language which I learned in school. "I bestow upon you the abilities of stealth, sneakiness, and burglary. Let your steed, the noble Bertrand, guide your path."

You smile, eyes still closed. "I feel all tingly," you say. "I think it worked. I'm definitely a ninja now."

I hold my hand out to help you stand. You hold on to it for a moment, my fingers warming from yours. "Let's do this thing."

You grab me in a hug, and I freeze before closing my eyes and hugging you back. My throat goes a little tight, thinking about the danger we might be walking into. And then you've let me go, and you're leading Bertrand away, down the sunny motorway, several bicyclists speeding past you and cars running in a stream of traffic noise and car exhaust, and the world continuing to turn, unaware of what we're about to do.

I take a breath, and walk across the street toward the bookstore, trying to push down the churning in my gut. I tell myself that we are doing the right thing. I'm about to meet the person who knew Ava Dreyman better than anyone else alive. And if he has nothing to hide, you'll be fine, and we'll both leave Germany unscathed. But even so, dread hangs in the air around me, cobwebby, coating every surface.

I push open the door to the bookstore, a tiny place with creaking wooden floors. Near the cash register stands a pyramid-shaped display of Paedar's book, *Der Brandstifter Leben*.

*Der Brandstifter Leben. The Arsonist Lives.*

Nobody seems to be around, not even any employees, but I hear a voice from the rear of the store. Somehow, I know exactly whose voice it is. The muscles in my legs grow weak as I make my way through the store, to an open space where about thirty chairs are arranged in rows. In the front of the chairs, standing with a microphone in his hand, is a middle-aged man in a tan suit, his blond hair parted on the side.

Paedar.

I take in the details of him—the way one shirtsleeve sticks out from his jacket, the noise as he clicks his teeth together while speaking. *He's real*, my mind sputters. Of course Paedar's real, but after meeting Muriel, I don't trust the reality of anything right now.

I sink into a seat in the back row, trying to catch my breath. Only about ten of the seats in front of me are occupied. Paedar speaks in German, so I can't understand a word, but there's something nice about his voice. At various points, he causes the small audience to laugh, and he laughs, too, like we're all together having an intimate party. Could he have killed Ava Dreyman? I try to picture it, but his smiling face won't allow me to.

At the end of his reading, a few audience members approach Paedar to buy a copy of his book. I hang back, waiting for the others to leave. Then I near his signing table, a nervous shudder returning to my limbs.

His eyes are icy blue, just as Ava described. A vein bisects his forehead so symmetrically, his face looks like it was cast out of a mold. He smiles at me and says something in German.

"Sorry, do you speak English?" I ask.

"Of course," he says. "I was just asking who I should sign the book to."

"Oh," I say. "It's Molly."

After he's signed the title page, he looks up, considering me. "You're not German, I take it?"

"No."

"You're not even European, I'm guessing. And yet, here you are in this bookshop of all places."

"Yes," I say, and my palms have begun to sweat.

He stands. "I find it beautiful, that's all," he says. "The things that bring people together. We are all just organisms, charting our own individual journeys through the world. That our paths should cross with anyone is a miracle."

"I'm just . . ." I say, but he interrupts me.

"One moment," he says, pulling a small flip notebook from his shirt pocket. "I need to write that down."

My eyes trail around the bookstore awkwardly as he transcribes the words. He closes the notebook between his hands and gestures to me. "Unforgivably rude of me to interrupt you. Go ahead."

"I was just going to say, I'm here because I'm interested in Ava."

His face splits open in a smile. "I'm always amazed at how far Ava's story reaches. Every corner of the globe. I think she would have liked knowing that."

He reaches for the book he signed and hands it to me. The inscription reads, "Molly, if you like this one, check out my other published works," and the name Paedar Kiefer signed below in a scrawl. He stuffs some papers into a canvas satchel, a bookstore employee shakes his hand, and they exchange a few words in German.

Then he's making for the exit and I follow right behind him, my cast making a thunk against the wooden floor.

"You will need to pay for that!" a bookstore employee calls from the cash register, indicating the copy of *Der Brandstifter Leben* in my hands. Hurriedly I fumble in my pocket for some Euros, smacking them down on the counter and hurling my body outside. My eyes scan every direction. The pavement is crawling with cars and bicyclists, and the sidewalk teems with pedestrians. I don't see Paedar. I hood my eyes with a hand, searching. If he's on foot, he should be close, but say he got into a taxi? My breath starts huffing like Bertrand when I glimpse a golden-haired head in the crowd. It's him, walking down the sidewalk, the Wall a colorful backdrop behind him. My knees weaken with relief.

"Wait, Paedar!" I shout above the traffic noise. I hobble toward him as he turns, a question on his face.

"Did I forget something?" he asks.

"No, I just—" I begin, uncertain of what I should say. "I was wondering if I could—could interview you. I'm doing a project on Ava Dreyman."

He frowns, and my mind starts blinking with ways to keep him here. "You'd be doing a huge favor for your biggest fan on the planet." I smile sweetly, and his eyebrows raise. I take a breath, winding my fangirl dial up to full blast. "Do you have any idea the impact your work has had on my life? On the world? To even have a moment of your time would mean everything to me."

Paedar pauses, and then smiles. "A quick coffee," he says. "We can walk while we chat."

He points toward a café nearby and orders a coffee that looks like thinned tar in a tiny paper cup, and I ask for something called an Eiskaffee which, from the photo on the menu, looks like it's made of ice cream and chocolate shavings. We take our to-go cups outside and walk down the humming city street.

"So," I say. "What was she like? Ava?"

He takes a sip of coffee. "I'm sure you know Ava very well, having read her diary. I'm curious what you think."

My eyes drift down the cigarette-strewn pavement, spotting

the section of the Wall we saw earlier. I remember the way Ava described it, humming with electricity. Even knowing that, she wasn't afraid to escape. "I think—I think she probably had a very good idea that she'd change the world someday."

"I think you might be right." He makes a close-mouthed smile. "You young people always cut right through things. I like that. You see the truth without the fog of the past."

"Do you ever wonder what Ava would be like if she were alive today?" I ask. "Would she have kids?"

He chuckles. "Oh, gracious no. Ava would've been the worst mother. She was self-centered in the best way. She could only be bothered with the things she found interesting."

This strikes me as a little unfair. "You only knew her when she was fourteen, though," I point out.

"Well," he says, "yes, I suppose that's true. You know, sometimes I do wonder if she's not out there living somewhere. Having a life."

I turn to look at him. His face is weirdly expressionless. "What makes you say that?"

"Nothing particularly. Only . . ." He sighs. "When someone you love dies, you want more than anything to think they could be alive. You trick yourself into believing the most outlandish stories. For a while, every time I walked through Grotewohl Park, the place we used to go after school, I could swear I saw her. I liked to imagine her existing somewhere, on an island or some remote town. Anywhere, just . . . alive."

Paedar has thrown a dart precisely at my heart. Because sometimes, I picture my mother on an island, too, or in a cabin in the forest, or in an apartment in a city, waiting for the right time to return to me. My breath hitches in my throat, and I'm suddenly foggy from pain. But it's obvious that Paedar doesn't put stock in these daydreams.

We stroll to a denser part of the city, passing over a road spanning the Spree River, beyond the biggest church I've ever seen, hulking and domed in corroded green metal. Across the street is an open pit where construction equipment is pulling down the jagged metal remains of a massive structure.

"What building was that?" I ask, pointing to the construction site.

"Ah," Paedar says. "That used to be the Palast der Republik. Ava used to talk about how ugly that building was. She said she'd love nothing more than to see it destroyed. Well, Ava, you got your wish." His eyes pinch, as though he was looking at something bright. "Sometimes I can't conceive of how young we were. Being so full of confidence, you think you can take on entire governments. The world even. That was Ava." He says it like he's not sure whether to be impressed or sad. It makes me realize something I hadn't quite understood until now: Paedar's grown up. And Ava? She'll always be a teenager.

My eyes rove across the construction site, the dirt pit and jutting metal bones, and try to imagine the bronze glass structure I'd seen in pictures online. "They're demolishing it?"

He nods. "After the Wall fell, nobody could agree what to do with these old government buildings: tear them down and forget what happened or preserve them as memorials. They went through the same thing with Hitler's palaces."

"What do you think they should do with the GDR buildings?" I ask.

His bites his bottom lip before responding. "Tear them down," he says. "They're doing nobody any good now."

"Why not keep them as a reminder?" I ask. "Of the things that happened here."

"And that'll make people feel better, constantly being reminded of that pain?"

I frown a little, in confusion. "But you make a lot of money reminding people about the past."

Paedar makes a startled laugh. "That's one way of putting it. But people can avoid my books if they desire. Those who have to walk past this place every day don't have that option. It's not possible to move forward with constant reminders of the past."

"You don't think the world needs to remember?" I ask.

"I was wounded worse than anybody when they murdered Ava," he says. "I can safely say I don't want to be reminded of that any longer."

I go quiet a while. My face must betray my confusion because he turns a quizzical gaze on me. Paedar purchased Ava Dreyman's old home, for God's sake. His job is to literally be an expert in her life. If he truly doesn't want to be reminded of the past, why is he still talking about Ava Dreyman after all this time?

A grenade launches from my mouth before I can stop it. "Is that why you used a photo of another girl on the cover of *The Arsonist*? Because you don't want to be reminded of Ava?" I can almost see the words arcing through the air, exploding.

"What did you say?" Paedar asks, a deep line scoring the space between his eyes.

My heart cowers. "The—the photo on the cover of *The Arsonist*, the one the entire world believes is of Ava Dreyman," I say, my throat quavering. "It's not really her."

Paedar breathes a dismissive note. "That's absurd. A conspiracy theory."

I throw my shoulders back. "The woman in that photo is named Muriel Weisz," I say. "And you must have known it wasn't really Ava the second you saw it."

His face turns suddenly thunderous. "You shouldn't talk about things you don't understand," he says quietly. The look he gives me makes my gut twist.

"I—I know a lot more than you think."

A ringtone sounds out from Paedar's pocket. He motions for me to wait, then lifts his phone to his ear.

"*Hallo?*" he asks. The voice on the other end crackles through the speaker.

Paedar instantly pales.

"*Der Alarm . . .*" he says, before getting cut off by the voice.

An alarm? A lightning bolt forks from the top of my head to the soles of my feet. *Pepper.*

Paedar speaks rapidly in German into the phone, then hangs up. I can see the scribbles of red veins in the whites of his eyes.

"I—I need to be going home now." He turns back, face ticking upward into a fake smile, sloughing off his icy demeanor instantly. "It was a pleasure meeting you. You know, you have something of Ava about you—an indomitableness of spirit. She'd like you."

I don't smile back. As Paedar rushes off, something is working away inside of my head.

My hand wheedles Muriel's phone from my pocket. It enters her passcode. Opens the text message to Boy Scout, the one still not replied to.

"Turn around," my fingers type, almost without my realizing.

They press send.

They tremble in the air.

*Ping.*

Inside the pocket of his jacket, Paedar's phone alerts him to a text message. He lifts it out, fingers tracing the glass surface.

He turns to face me.

His blue eyes are hurricanes.

And, at once, Paedar turns and runs.

# Ava

January 9, 1989

I arrived in West Berlin this morning. The last time I saw it, right after my father was killed, my eyes took in nothing of this city. Now, I drink the place up, this colorful, fun-house version of the East. Behind all the doors of these apartments, they can watch whatever they want on television, and they never have to hush the person on the other end of the telephone because they think they've heard the click of surveillance. This place smells like freedom.

From the airport, I took the U-Bahn to Friedrichstraße Station, one of the only places where westerners can travel into the east. Even underground, it was obvious when we passed beneath the Wall. The brightly lit Western stations were replaced by dark tunnels. The people on the train grew quiet, like they could feel the change in the air. I felt myself carefully readjust, so I sat up straight. I was entering the city of my childhood. What would it think of me now?

At Friedrichstraße Station, I followed the crowd of people up a set of stairs, toward the border checkpoint. I looked to my father, who stood nearby, his eyes passing over the faces of all these West Berliners. It did not escape me that, this time, we were attempting to get in, not out.

"Almost there," I told him. Several people turned to look at me, and it occurred to me that they were staring not only because I'd spoken to my father, who of course none of them could see, but because the words I'd uttered were in English.

At the glass-walled booth at the top of the steps, I passed over the passport that named me as Sally Bailey. The guard scanned my photo before sliding it back to me.

"*Willkommen*," was all he said before looking past me to the next person in line. I stayed rooted to the floor. "What?" the man barked. He wasn't Stasi, just some ordinary checkpoint operator with dense stubble and tan dress slacks.

"Aren't—aren't you supposed to question me?"

"You've been watching movies?" he asked. "The border is looser than my socks now."

I stared in disbelief. "I can just come and go as I please?"

"Well, when you put it that way," he grumbled. "What is the purpose of your visit?"

"What?" I asked.

"The purpose of your visit," he repeated. "Are you slow?"

"I'm American."

"That explains it."

I felt myself bristle. "I'm just visiting."

He peered at me like he found this idea suspicious. He looked down at my passport again. "Bailey," he said. "That's an English name. How do you explain how fluent your German is?"

"My grandmother taught me," I said. "She was Swiss."

He nodded.

"And my parents," I said, emboldened. "My father died at the Wall."

"You must be very proud," he said drily. "People everywhere love those stories. Seems everyone's had a cousin who was shot, an uncle who was detained. Take your papers. Welcome to the beautiful German Democratic Republic. I hope everything is as you expect it to be."

I stepped outside of the station and into the tepid sunlight of the city. How was it that everything appeared so changed after only a few years? Satellite dishes have bloomed over rooflines like mushrooms clinging to trees, audaciously facing west. Plaster has sloughed off the sides of brick buildings, and nothing looks as sturdy as it once did.

Perhaps it isn't that this place has changed.

Perhaps my eyes have changed.


I decided the first person I'd visit would be Aunt Kruger. I was amazed to find her living in the same apartment.

"What happened when you were detained?" I asked when she let me inside the dusty confines of her front parlor.

She frowned a little, her loose skin puckering. "They thought capturing me would flush out the damned arsonist they were spending so much energy searching for." She sparked a lighter as she attempted to ignite a cigarette. "Too bad they were right. They flushed her out, didn't they? Just as they flushed out your father's brain matter."

I glanced over to where my father reclined in the corner, his brain matter currently suspended from the side of his head prominently. He studied Kruger's face as though taking inventory of the new lines, the gray tiredness that had collected below her eyes.

"Sorry for the colorful language, dear," Aunt Kruger said. "Old writerly habits. They kept me in a cell in *Hohenschönhausen*. I don't think many of the prisoners I was with ever got out."

"Dead?"

"That or still inside. The Stasi are patient men."

"My mother's in prison," I said. I gave her a look that I hoped conveyed I was not entertaining the possibility that she was dead.

"And you're planning on getting her out." Aunt Kruger drew on her cigarette. "Don't ask it of me, dear. I have nothing left to give."

My heart plummeted. "Then tell me who I can go to for help. Who knows where she is?"

Kruger's eyes shifted around the dusty room. "There's a man. He has a network, but he's very underground. Your mother used to sell him lithographs and typewriters." She taps her cigarette into an ashtray. "They call him Sandman."

"Sandman," I repeated. The name sounded familiar. Perhaps he was one of my parents' subversive friends, weedy academic types with tab collars and thick glasses. "How do I find him?"

"I've heard that if you stand by the television tower and say the word 'Summertime' to the right man who happens past, you'll be taken to him."

I grasped Kruger's hand, grateful, and stood, eager to be on my way. "Thank you, Aunt Kruger."

"Dear," she said. "Your parents wouldn't want you in danger. Don't do anything your mother wouldn't do."

I glanced at my father, standing silent beside the door, and I knew we were both thinking about my mother, the things she was capable of. "I won't."

January 15, 1989

I have stood vigil beside the TV tower every day for nearly a week. I've been sleeping in cheap hostels, trying to stretch the Winklers' money for as long as possible. I was forced to purchase a heavy wool coat at a charity shop because I was freezing out here, waiting all day for one of Sandman's men to walk past. I believe I have looked into the face of every person in East Berlin, an endless litany of cold-chapped lips and gray eyes. Only the punks look even the littlest bit alive in their studded jackets and dark makeup. (They risk a lot dressing like that. The Stasi target the punks almost as much as real dissidents.) The people are stirring, Georg told me. The fires of revolution are beginning in the furnaces of their chests, but all I see are people who are very good at being controlled, of tolerating one more indignity, always just one more.

Their faces are hard like ice. I wonder if they will ever, ever thaw.

Today a bland-looking man a couple of years older than me stopped by the tower, lighting a cigarette, cupping his hands over his face against the wind. He was dressed so unexceptionally that I might've missed him if I hadn't been looking hard at every person that passed.

"On a clear day it makes a cross in the noonday sun," I said to the man, as I had to several others before.

He leaned back and stared up at the mirrored ball of the TV tower, the grandest symbol of the GDR's might, a tower so brilliant and high and sparkling, they would see it in the West and envy our industriousness. From here, it looked like a shadowed moon atop its spire, barely glowing in the sunless afternoon sky.

"You know what they call that in the West?" I asked. "The cross?"

He shook his head.

"The Pope's revenge," I told him. "For all the churches the GDR demolished. Has a ring to it. The cross shows up better in summertime."

He nodded, dragging on his cigarette. "What do you want?" I knew he meant with Sandman.

"I need help finding my mother," I said. "She was captured three years ago."

"We don't help just anybody," he said. "Besides, we've each had a loved one detained."

"Sandman knew my mother," I said. "She made typewriters. She had a newspaper, *Der Brandstifter*."

The man's forehead wrinkled. "Your mother wasn't—"

"Mirka Dreyman," I said, keeping my voice low. "And my name is Ava Dreyman." I realized it was the first time in years I'd claimed my own name so clearly, so out in the open. My pulse quickened.

"You got out?" he asked. "We assumed you were detained or killed, like your parents."

I paused, stunned for a moment to hear that my parents' fates were apparently common knowledge. "I got out," I said simply.

The man chewed on his bottom lip. "Come with me."

He walked me to a nondescript apartment block not far from where I grew up. There was no elevator, so we trudged up the flights of concrete stairs in cold-lunged, winded silence. The man used different keys to open the three locks, then knocked.

"Nighthawk," the man announced to the door.

"What's the capital of the GDR?" a voice called from behind the door.

"Honecker's backside," the man said.

The sound of several dead bolts sliding echoed into the hallway. The man who opened the door looked about thirty with a bushy beard and eyebrows. He wore a hole-ridden knitted cap and faded gray sweater. He stood before a table littered with tiny mechanical parts. In his hands, his fingers absently fiddled with a plastic block I guessed was a co-opted listening device.

"This girl says she's Ava Dreyman," the boy who'd brought me here said. "Mirka's daughter."

The man's eyebrows shot up. He studied me, placing the listening device on the table.

"Welcome, Ava," he said. "Call me Sandman."

January 18, 1989

"You say you want to find your mother," Sandman said. I've been granted asylum inside his apartment, in a frigid bedroom with no window, bald wooden walls, all of the insulation stripped away. "What you haven't told me is how you propose doing this."

"That's where you come in," I told him, pacing in front of his desk. "How would you break into a state prison?"

He leaned back in his desk chair, cupping a chipped mug of dark tea. The room was dim, illuminated only by the bare filament of a single lightbulb.

"I wouldn't," he said. "And believe me, I've thought about it. My wife is inside. I wouldn't risk the lives of my people attempting it." He must have seen my expression, downcast, because he sighed and put down his drink. "My wife did nothing illegal. But that's the way with them. If they can't get their target, they grab the closest person. At least she's alive, as far as I know."

I crossed my arms. "I won't accept that this is impossible."

"You sound very much like your mother," Sandman said. "And that is not intended as a compliment. Your mother was reckless. So were the Winklers. Those of us left have survived because we're careful. You will not find me burning down buildings or planting arsenic in champagne unless the payoff is guaranteed. I've been trying to free my wife for a year and I still have no idea in which prison she's being held. Your mother could have been transferred out of Berlin by now."

"We could infiltrate the Stasi headquarters," I said. "They must have files on her."

He leveled his dark eyes at me. "That, little one, would be a suicide attempt."

"'Little one,'" I repeated. "You know who called me that? That Stasi captain, Heinrich Werner."

Sandman's bushy eyebrows darted upward. "He orchestrated my wife's arrest."

"He knows where my mother is," I told him. "I am certain of it."

Sandman smiled in a way that betrayed his skepticism. "And so you'll ask him out for a drink and he will reveal all, I assume?" Sandman asked. "You're charming, but you are not that charming."

"You don't know the half of me," I said, my lips pressing into a smile. "I think I have a plan."

- - - - -

January 23, 1989

For the past several days, we've practiced. Drilled. Talked strategies until our muscles quiver from wanting to dart from the flat and do the thing already. The first man I met, the one in the brown coat who goes by Nighthawk, will be accompanying us, as will the woman I've been rooming with, Phoenix, who, as far as I've seen, does little but stare, hard-eyed, out the living room window. Her brother was killed at the Wall, years ago.

"Our goal is what?" Sandman asked, during one of our many planning sessions.

"To lure out Captain Werner," I said, my hands grasping in my lap from nerves and giddy excitement.

"And?" Sandman asks.

"We kidnap him," Phoenix says, her eyes bright and flashing. "And preferably kill him."

"And then we *interrogate* him," Nighthawk corrected. It was a strange thrill, hearing the others discussing my plan.

From the corner, my father watched me with his half-exploded face. I didn't meet his gaze. He wouldn't approve of any of this, but I'll apologize to him afterward.

After I get my mother.

"Most importantly, what will you do?" Sandman asked, looking toward me.

"I will not show my face to anyone important," I said with reluctance.

"Yes," Sandman said. "It's inadvisable for you to accompany us at all. Your pretty face will be recognizable to most high-ranking Stasi officers. If they see you, they'll know you're here for your mother. She will be transferred, perhaps killed. When we nab Werner, you will be far, far away, yes?"

I swore to it, though it tasted bitter in my mouth.

Excitement drums through my limbs. Soon, we will depart for the Palast. I want to look into Werner's black eyes. I want to show him what I can do to a pale, weak body like his. To show him how much like my mother I can be.

January 27, 1989

Today, the four of us dressed in gray and black clothes that will absorb light and trod our way through the frozen slush covering every surface of East Berlin, to the Palast der Republik, the GDR parliament building made of caramel-colored reflective glass. When I was little, I told my parents I wanted to taste it. It looked like candy to me. Walking through the early morning, I thought it looked like a powder keg, ready to ignite.

We darted inside between shifts of security guards patrolling the ground floor. It was a heart-thudding kind of thrill to walk here, where meetings are held with two thousand politicians at a time in cathedral-style seating, where, all those years ago, Georg and Margarita poisoned the American ambassador with arsenic and champagne.

I couldn't help craning my neck once we entered the cavernous entryway. Clinging to the ceiling was an array of massive lightbulbs the size of bowling balls. "Erich's lamp shop," I'd heard people call it, after Erich Honecker and his gaudy taste. In darkness, the bulbs were merely round shadows above.

We passed the stage that had been erected for tonight's performance of the East German National Ballet. On the back wall hung a wood carving of the beard-covered silhouettes of Lenin, Marx, and Engels, surveying us disapprovingly. I stuck my tongue out at them. Nighthawk saw me and laughed silently.

In front of the stage, I halted, overwhelmed with the importance of this place. I stepped onto the low platform, where Honecker stands when he addresses the members of government, and scanned the rows of empty seats. I understood how Honecker could command such confidence. Anyone would, with that many eyes watching. I set Paedar's heart on fire with ease. I wondered what I could do with an audience of thousands.

On the edge of the massive room, Sandman jimmied a silver lock with a pick, and a piece of the wood-paneled wall opened to reveal the auxiliary maintenance hatch. We crawled through, down a tunnel, and up a narrow staircase until we arrived at our destination—the catwalk, a metal structure fifty feet above the ground. I peered down at the velvet seats where we'd just walked through the semi-open drop ceiling, honeycombed with light fixtures and wires. My first thought was, *This could work.* A low hum of elation came to my ears. *Mein Gott, this could actually work.*

"We'll set up here," Sandman said, crouching down on the metal support of the catwalk. "This entire room is made of kindling. If the walls aren't filled with asbestos, we might get the whole thing to come down."

"And if they are?" Phoenix asked.

"Well, at least we'll color the sky with smoke." He allowed himself a wry smile. "Either way, this is sure to be a night none of them will ever forget."

Later

Around seven, members of the government, the military, and the Stasi started arriving in the hall below. The four of us lay on our stomachs on the catwalk, observing the gaudily dressed officials and their wives trickle in. Sandman pointed out the important people.

"There's Erich Mielke," he whispered, indicating a thick-waisted man with hollows of bald skin peeking through his puffy chestnut hair. "Head of the Stasi. They call him 'the Master of Fear.' Pah, I'm more afraid of his terrible haircut."

"Werner's boss," I muttered.

At that moment, the man himself entered the room. A cold sliver of ice fell down my throat. Werner wore a crisp black suit, his dark hair combed precisely in the way I remembered. My breath felt tight in my chest. On his lapel, his silver Storm Wolf pin glinted but otherwise, he was unadorned of medals. He didn't need to wear them to garner respect and fear. I balled my fingers into a fist to stop them trembling.

Werner swept his eyes around the hall, and even from above I could see his gaze rest momentarily on each exit. He stared at the maintenance door practically hidden in the wall. Sandman and I traded glances.

"Don't worry," he said. "We're foolproof."

The performance began after President Honecker made a speech about the *might* of our nation and the *import* of our duties and the *rightness* of our efforts to create the perfect empire, all to uproarious applause.

"It's like they really believe what he's spouting off," Nighthawk whispered.

"They do," I heard Phoenix grunt.

Honecker's head, hallowed in a band of receding hair, had begun to shine under the heat of the lights. It had grown stifling up on the catwalk, as well, even in the shadows. Sweat had begun to prickle on my forehead. I shifted uncomfortably.

Honecker's speech concluded and he took his seat in the front row.

The lights dimmed for a blessed moment and, in the darkness, the room cooled. A hole of light appeared on the stage and grew to encompass a dancer in the red stretchy bodysuit. He lay prone, barely breathing inside a mist of artificial smoke. Bullets lay scattered over his crimson body.

This was Germany, half dead after war.

Slowly, the dancer dragged his feet from beneath his body, a cascade of bullets falling to the stage, the hard noise filling the auditorium.

This was Germany deciding to live.

The music started, blaring horns and percussion, shocking the senses. The rest of the history of the GDR spelled itself out across the stage in full propaganda form. My veins grew tight. This was the country that ruined my family. During a quiet gap in the music, I heard sniffling from below, the sound of crying from those overwhelmed by the glory of the GDR's story.

"This is fucking depressing," Nighthawk whispered.

I sputtered a laugh, and at that moment, the music died.

Sandman darted me a severe look, but the audience's attention was quickly diverted by a new addition to the stage, a ring of gray-clad dancers with linked arms.

This was the Wall. The place my father was killed.

The audience applauded.

Sandman lifted his hand in a signal and stood to a crouch. Slowly, the rest of us followed him, securing our duffel bags, unzipping them carefully, centimeters at a time. Our moment had arrived. Time to flush Werner out.

My bag shifted from the catwalk. My heart launched into my throat and I caught the bag in my fist before it could fall to the seats below, but not quickly enough to stop it colliding with the hanging bay of spotlights directly below us.

*BAM!*

An industrial lightbulb exploded over the audience, the sound of shattered glass tinkling through the air, and a spray of light hung above the crowd like a firework. The audience gasped, craning their necks. The dancers stilled their waving limbs and the room went quiet.

I darted my eyes around frantically, and Sandman and the others threw me a series of horrified looks. Cold dread doused me as I realized none of them knew what to do, either. My mother would know.

My mother wasn't here.

But somehow, in that moment, I knew what she'd tell me to do. I had to become her.

"THE ARSONIST LIVES!" I bellowed down into the silent hall.

My throat reverberated with the shout, and my heart began to pump faster. I reached into my duffel bag and pulled out a handful of GDR state newspapers. I flicked my lighter and lit the bundle, and when they caught fire in a plume of inky smoke, I let the flaming bouquet fall. They cascaded below, splitting apart into embers that looked like the most beautiful stars I'd ever seen.

I'll never forget the sight, as long as I live. Or the sound of screams echoing from below.

Soon, the others followed. In almost no time, it was raining fire-soaked papers, sparks spraying in every direction. Fire was pulsing my muscles excitedly, and I could see it jump a little beneath the surface of my skin.

"Look at them run!" Nighthawk exclaimed. Stasi officers and their wives scrambled from their seats, jockeying to avoid the falling embers. I spotted the red-clad GDR dancer covering his head with his arms and running from the stage.

There was something like justice in the air, alongside the smoke. Years from now, these people will carry the scars of this night still, where coin-sized embers burrowed into their vulnerable skin, and every time they glance at that spot, they will think of me. They will think of everyone they shot on the borders, everyone whose throats met the teeth of dogs while attempting a run to freedom, everyone rotting inside prisons.

I have stamped myself on their skin. They will never be rid of me.

I pulled another match, lit the flame.

Ignited the papers in my fist.

Watched them burn.

# Pepper

Dear Ms. Eldridge,

All I remember from my physics class at Hoover is the constant feeling of my brain hurting. Here's an example of a law of physics that I had to copy off the board:

*The line integral of the magnetic flux around a closed curve is proportional to the algebraic sum of electric currents flowing through that closed curve.*

What in the actual crap? It sounds like they made that using a random word generator. Someday, everyone will realize that physicists are punking everyone and really they're, like, slam poets in disguise who say things that sound cool but don't make any actual sense. When I wasn't feeling completely confused by physics, I was smacking my head with how obvious it was. "An object at rest will stay at rest unless a force acts upon it." You only have to look at Bertrand to see this law in action.

Speaking of things in action: Today I committed a grievous crime. I believe it is called "breaking and entering," though I broke very little. I did *enter*, however. I entered an apartment that I was, strictly speaking, not legally allowed to, and apparently in Germany that holds a prison sentence of up to thirty years. What!

I was to break into Ava Dreyman's apartment, which is now owned by one Paedar Kiefer, in order to see what he was hiding in there, because he must be hiding something, or so Molly figured. I know, it was a tenuous plan, but feedback is not necessary at this point. I already know this all too well.

From Alexanderplatz, I followed the directions on my phone for Bötzowstraße, the street where Ava's old apartment is. The whole time, I eyed the apartment blocks punching holes in the sky, which are large and ugly and were built with the intention of withstanding a hundred nuclear bombs. I was so nervous, every organ in my body was balled up like paper.

Ava's old neighborhood was a nice one, surrounded by lots of trees exploding with green leaves, except for the fact that a lot of the buildings' faces were scrawled over with graffiti.

My plan, or what I had of one, required patience and acting like an inconspicuous and totally innocent person who just so happens to be wearing a hooded sweatshirt and a baseball cap and sunglasses and carrying a crowbar inside my sleeve that I purchased on the walk over from a hardware store called Stop Hammer Time, which I found on the Internet and will write a favorable review for because of the name alone. Bertrand wore his hoodie, too, since he is a very recognizable pug with unfortunately conspicuous nipples.

We waited casually beside the locked front entrance, trying

to look like we belonged, the whole time my stomach going acidy from fear. When a woman exited the building, we strolled through the open door, attempting to look natural, which was impeded somewhat by Bertrand suddenly balking at the doorway and refusing to budge. I hauled him into my arms as he tried to squirm away.

We climbed the stairs to the twentieth floor, so many flights that I had to carry Bertrand halfway because he was acting like he was going to die from exertion. "God, Bertrand, you suck," I hissed. Bertrand let out a wheeze in reply.

The corridor on Ava's floor was lined with wood paneling and illuminated only by little lamps at eye level, emitting blobs of muted orange light. I walked until I found a door with metal letters spelling out 2034. Ava Dreyman's apartment.

My heart was bashing around in my chest like it wanted to escape. I was standing before the door leading to history. All of our answers were beyond it.

Except when I tried the door, the knob wouldn't budge. Destiny was being elusive. That's okay. I had a plan.

You know how in movies, when they want to show you something that takes place over a long time, they do it in a "montage"? Just imagine you're watching one right now. Let's put some peppy music in the background, like "Wake Me Up Before You Go-Go." I know all the lyrics because it's the song my dad sings when he's trying to get me out of bed. Anyway, your dashing leading man, Pepper, runs at the door and ricochets off like a rubber bouncy ball. Pepper then kicks at the door and grabs his foot in pain, hopping till he falls over. An old man approaches from a nearby apartment, and Pepper, lying on the ground, pretends to be groping around for a lost contact lens until the old man leaves. Pepper then tries his crowbar, knocking at the knob, the hinges, but the crowbar is as useless as Bertrand, who is barking at the door like it will help.

The montage ends with Pepper sitting down in the hallway, panting.

Do you know what saved me in the end, Ms. Eldridge? Physics! After nearly dying from exhaustion, I remembered a lesson that Mrs. McLintock, my physics teacher, taught us about torque. This is when the force you apply to something is magnified farther away from the rotation point. I know, I know—you're probably wondering, Hey Pepper, how are you recalling this information with such ease when you set the state record for worst grade in a physics class (cough . . . seven percent . . . cough)? It is because Mrs. McLintock wrote the symbol $\omega$, on the board about fifty times when talking about torque. I had to clench all of my muscles not to be laughing the entire period, because that symbol looks like a certain piece of anatomy that boys like to graffiti on the walls of school bathrooms. I was sore for a week after that class. I grew like three abs.

Anyway, so I realized that, in this equation:

torque = the crowbar, and

the rotation point = the door hinges, and

$\omega$ (ha ha ha ha) = Pepper's powerful man muscles, pushing on the crowbar.

It was most efficient to apply the torque far away from the hinges. This must be why I've always somehow known that the doorknobs on hobbit houses make no sense. Anyway, I started prying the crowbar between the door and the frame, so hard my wrists started hurting, and my biceps were bulging out of my shirt (at least, I assumed). But, soon, it started to budge! Slowly, with tons more strain and pulsing of my muscles, the locks became like teeth, cutting through the old wood of the frame. The door came splintering away and flung open with much $\omega$.

Physics! Turns out those nerd poets were actually onto something!

My feeling of euphoria lasted for about five seconds. Five wonderful seconds to savor my accomplishments, and the lactic acid already pooling in my muscles like the nectar of the gods. The apartment smelled like old things and looked like a scene from a black-and-white movie, so I knew this had to be the right place. It was as if the whole space had been holding its breath for years and years, unchanged since the day Ava left.

And then the nerves took hold, spidering out of my heart and into my lungs. I wasn't exactly sure what the cause was at first, other than having just become a criminal, but soon I figured it out. A beeping was coming from my left.

Every muscle of mine locked in place. Slowly, my eyes

inched toward the sound, across the patterned carpet, up the wood-paneled walls, to a white box beside the door, where a red light flashed. It was an alarm. Why, *why* hadn't it occurred to me that Paedar would have an alarm?

Answer: Because Pepper is a Grade-A idiot.

I understood then what true, frozen panic looks like. It looks like a teenage boy realizing he's going to be arrested in a T-shirt with a death metal unicorn on it.

My brain started performing a Ping-Pong match inside my head:

| | |
|---|---|
| Should I run away? | No, I'm here for the mission! |
| But the alarm! I'm scared! | So am I! |
| *Uncontrollable screaming.* | *Uncontrollable screaming.* |
| *Screaming mixed with sobbing.* | |

Wait, remember, dude, you're a ninja!

I was a ninja! I figured I had like five minutes before the cops arrived. I sprang into action, running to the kitchen, which was covered in tan-patterned wallpaper. I started wrenching open cabinets while, at my feet, Bertrand got so excited that he started twirling around in circles. I searched through the drawers, throwing silverware all over the floor, and even broke a few plates because I was a criminal now. I spent a ton of time sifting through that one random drawer every house has, filled with twist ties and change and old rubber bands that had lost all their elasticity. My brain may have actually begun sweating. Like, I felt the little rivulets running down the inside of my skull. I couldn't figure out what to do. This was an impossible mission. What was I even looking for? What did we even think Paedar might be hiding here?

I looked beneath all of the furniture, which was hideous and weird, in shades of brown and dark yellow. I searched the master bedroom, but it was so bare and sparsely furnished, there wasn't much to see. The alarm echoed throughout the apartment, each beep jacking up my heart rate even more.

Bertrand followed me as I ran into a small bedroom with yellow walls and checkered lace curtains. I halted, realizing where I was. It seems important to note that I'd never been in a girl's bedroom before, and it wasn't anything like I'd imagined it would be. Namely, the girl whose bedroom I stood in was dead.

This felt like someplace . . . holy. Ava was just an ordinary girl when she lived here, but knowing what she'd become, I felt the sort of quiet peace you get when you enter the cavernous, geometric space of a mosque, like I've done when it's Ramadan and my dad gets the urge. I placed a hand on the surface of her bed, the soft ivory blanket slightly pilled. On the wall, there was a framed picture of a pressed daisy and a shelf with some children's books. I pulled one down. It looked like a German version of Nancy Drew.

I turned toward Ava's desk, which sat against the opposite wall. I pulled open the top drawer, and old charcoal pencils rolled around beside a writing pad with green-tinted pages, covered in math equations that I took to be homework. This had to be where she kept the diary when she first got it.

*Beep. Beep. Beep.*

The beeping had grown louder, or else my subconscious was knocking against my eardrums to tell me to *get the eff out of there*. I had no idea how much time I'd spent spacing out in Ava Dreyman's bedroom, but it was too much. At this point, the voices in my brain were all screaming:

RUN! RUN!        RUN, YOU NUMBNUT, RUN!

I darted back into the kitchen and took one final look around, eyes scanning each drawer, each cabinet. It looked like the kitchen had barfed its entire contents all over everything. I had this pressing feeling that I was leaving behind *something* important in all that mess, but I had no idea what.

My eyes landed on a bunch of red plastic forks scattered across the floor. They looked like something you'd bring to a picnic, but the sight of them made the world grow quiet and muffled, and even the beeping receded to the background. A strange feeling percolated inside my brain. I glanced at Bertrand, thinking for a moment it was a seizure, but no.

It was a realization. A key turning inside my mind.

"Hey," I said aloud. "Didn't Ava's mom melt down plastic forks to make the logo she put on all her typewriters?"

Bertrand panted at me, his tongue uncurling from his mouth, which was his way of saying "Yes!"

I had to close my eyes to capture it, the feeling of thoughts

lining up perfectly like dominoes and falling into place one at
a time.

"And didn't she hide her typewriters inside the brick wall
between the kitchen and the bathroom?"

Bertrand let out a soft, tiny bark, which was his way of saying "HECK YES!"

My fingers were stuttering as I traced the brick wall. I raised
the crowbar above my head, holding it there for a quiet moment
as I found a spot at eye level to aim at. With all the force I could
muster, I brought the crowbar down hard on the mortar between the bricks. A shock rang through my body. I slammed it
down again and again, until mortar started falling away in drifts
like snow. Bertrand stuck his tongue out and tasted the mortar
dust, which I thought was his way of feeling involved.

My shoulder began to ache. A lot. And my knuckles were
all bloody from all the times I'd swung and missed and raked
my hands across the brick. In summary, it's really hard to break
through a wall. But I kept going, Ms. Eldridge, because I was
a ninja now, and because I had an electric current running
through me that wouldn't let me stop.

When I'd cleared away a lot of mortar, I threw the crowbar
to the ground and scrabbled between bricks with my bloody
fingers (just want to point out that I have officially shed blood,
sweat, and tears for these essays). My breath was fast and choppy,
and I was now regretting my stance on gym class. I pried one
brick away and threw it in the kitchen, then another.

And then I saw it.

"*Ya salam,*" I said to myself. "Oh my God."

Behind the bricks was a cavern. It was clear, at once, what was contained within.

A choir of angels might have begun singing behind me. My throat grew thick, like I might unexpectedly begin to sob, and I nearly did.

Okay, maybe I actually did. Maybe I am still crying a little, from the sight of it.

Inside the cavern was a white leather diary.

Gently, I picked it up. It was better than finding a pharaoh's tomb. Better than a moon rock. In my hands, the cover fell open slowly, to Ava's final entry, where blood speckled the yellowed pages.

I felt as though I was holding Ava Dreyman's heart in my own hands. This was the greatest, strangest, most brilliantly wonderful feeling in the world, Ms. Eldridge. Everyone should make a discovery from within a secret hole in a wall at least once in their life. I believe we would all carry around a little more wonder in our chests if it was so.

It was Bertrand's growl that caused me to finally tear my eyes from the diary.

A man stood in the doorway, confusion and anger coming off of him like steam. For a moment, we just stared at each other, vibrating with shock.

"What are you doing in my apartment?" Paedar thundered.

I put my hands up in front of me. I don't do confrontation well, Ms. Eldridge. I'll do whatever it takes to stop someone from yelling at me. Especially if that person is a weird German man with hair that looks oddly like a blond wig. "I was just leaving."

Paedar's eyes swept around the room, his face twisted in confusion. "You broke my door! You—you broke my plates."

"I know—" I said, my heart dropping into my testicles. "I know, and I'm sorry about that. I'll pay you back."

He took a step toward me, and I took a shuffling step back. Close up, he was made out of sharp angles, leaner than in his teenage photo. His gaze came to a stop first on my face, then on the hole in the wall, and finally on the diary in my hands.

"What do you have there?" he asked.

Fear traced my nerves like a cold finger. I moved the diary behind my back.

"Give me that now," Paedar said, his voice growing loud.

"Why should I?" I shouted. I'd pulled a tiny amount of courage from somewhere and suddenly decided that I could fight him. My mind was flipping around at the possibilities— maybe I could throw Bertrand at Paedar and knock him down like a bowling pin. "This wasn't ever yours. It was Ava's. You lied about it being stolen all these years!"

Paedar's lips tightened and something clicked in his face, like hearing my words forced a decision in his mind. He reached into a nearby drawer and came away with a long knife with a thin curved tip.

Terror makes us do strange things, and I learned it turns me into one of those inflatable arm-waving men they have at used car lots. I screamed a single, piercing note and started flailing and lunging backward. Turns out, that strategy doesn't work that great against someone with a knife. All Paedar had to do was grab me by the shoulder and point the blade at my sternum. My arms froze. In fact, everything froze. My breath, my eyeballs, my internal organs. Even my blood became very cold and slow, like a Slushie.

"Please," I gasped, collapsing in his grip. I had to blink away a haze of white creeping across my vision, which I'm pretty sure was my life starting to flash before my eyes. "Don't kill me. I have to write an essay." I was as surprised as you, Ms. Eldridge, that this was the first thing that occurred to me upon almost being impaled on a kitchen implement. I think that alone deserves a passing grade.

"Give me that," Paedar said, snatching the diary from my hands. He gestured with the knife toward a door. "In there," he barked, yanking open the door, revealing an empty kitchen pantry. "Until I decide what to do with you."

He pushed me inside, Bertrand at my heels, and slammed the door.

Here is where we've been for something like thirty minutes. I cannot get in contact with Molly, because there is no service or WiFi here. I do not know if we are close to being killed or if the police are going to arrive. I've been shouting my lungs out and Bertrand has clawed and barked, too, but so far nobody has rescued us.

I am only able to type this on my phone. I'll click send when I'm done and hope it will go through the moment my phone picks up a signal again. My request is that you might be able to call 911, except the version for Germany, to report a crime happening currently. I know it's only three a.m. in Monterey, and you are likely asleep, but I've heard being a school administrator is a high-stress job and it's possible that you are still awake.

Since I stand the chance of receiving serious bodily harm in very short order, this is perhaps a good time to create my last will and testament.

I bequeath my seizure pug to my dad.

I bequeath my copy of *The Arsonist* to Molly Mavity.

I bequeath all of my Master Quest gold and crystals to Shawn, Wallace, and Reggie, to be divided equally among their night elves.

I am sorry to leave you hanging on a cliff, Ms. Eldridge, but I myself have no ideas as to how this particular chapter in my academic life will end.

Godspeed,

Pepper Al-Yusef

# Molly

Pepper,

I chase Paedar down the busy street as quickly as my jellied legs and thunking cast will allow, pushing past pedestrians, my blood pumping frantically in time to my drumming thoughts.

Paedar is Boy Scout.

And you, Pepper, are inside of his apartment.

Ahead, Paedar darts left suddenly, and my feet stumble. A man on a black moped honks and steers around me, and I almost trip over a woman with a dog on a leash.

When I look up, Paedar's gone.

I stumble forward, scanning the crowd. *No, no, no.*

The taste of the milky coffee is crawling up the back of my throat.

I look to Muriel's phone to search the location of Ava's apartment, but when I enter the password, the screen flares white, then dies. She had the phone disconnected. "Damn it!" I shout, and slam the phone down to the concrete where it shatters.

I race around frantically. I flick back through the conversation with Paedar in my mind, searching for a clue to the location of Ava's building. Where did he mention Ava going? The Palast der Republik, the TV tower, Grotewohl Park—

Grotewohl Park. He said that's where he and Ava used to meet. The park across from the apartment where she grew up. The place you are right now.

I dart down the street. "Which way to Grotewohl Park?" I ask to everyone I pass. I know I must look as crazed as I feel, my hair a frenzied cloud, my cheeks red, and the Germans look at me like I'm deranged. Finally, an older man points down the street and I take off running.

I have never run this fast before. I am afraid. For myself, but mostly for you. I haven't known anything like this fear for years. I haven't cared about anybody enough. I have been living in a kind of emotional colorblindness, but now I am seeing in brightest Technicolor.

I have to save you.

I run for what feels like ten minutes, maybe fifteen—however long, it's too much. You're trapped, Pepper. My chest feels like it's being skewered a thousand times when, at the end of the street, a green wall of trees rears up. I push toward it, my heart straining with every step. I run around the park, scanning each building. At last, I spot something, a plaque, so small I almost miss it. The words are in German, but AVA DREYMAN and the number 2034 are printed on the brass. At the front door, I press my hands onto all the apartments' intercom buttons. I hop on my feet, waiting. A buzzing sounds, and the front door clicks unlocked.

I throw myself up flights of stairs, to the twentieth floor, and hurtle down the hall, cast clunking, coming to a halt before a door that has been torn away from the frame. I hear muffled screaming from inside.

Bile rises up my throat like vinegar, and I feel I might drown from this nightmare, right then, in that hallway.

I push the broken door open and take a step inside. Every atom of oxygen hangs suspended inside my lungs, waiting. The apartment is dimly lit, the drapes pulled shut. Dust slants in from a single gap in the curtains, and everything the light touches is destroyed. Broken plates and papers on the ground, chairs upturned, drawers emptied. *What happened here?* I wonder. For a moment, that's all my brain will allow me to think.

"Molly?" your muted voice calls. All of the blood rushes from my head in relief. I step in the direction of your voice, toward a pantry door at the opposite end of the kitchen.

"Don't," a voice warns from behind me.

I turn slowly. Paedar steps out of the shadows of the living room, silhouetted in the darkness. A band of light pushing in from the curtains slashes across his chest, and a flash of silver in his hand catches on the sunlight. A knife. My throat constricts. I step away from him so quickly, and my back connects with the wall.

"Wh-what are you doing?" I stutter.

Paedar's mouth forms a scowl. In his hand, the knife rotates just slightly.

A thought flits through my mind that maybe I could get help.

I glance toward the broken-down front door. "Thinking of running?" Paedar asks, inclining his head. "What do you suppose will happen to your friend if you do that?"

"Don't you put a finger on him," I say, my voice murderous. In this moment, I might be capable of tearing Paedar apart into tiny pieces with nothing but my bare hands. "You let him go now."

"You're not in a position to be giving orders," Paedar barks. "This is a civilized country. You cannot come onto someone's property and take things that aren't yours. No, he will not be leaving here."

"*Molly!*" I hear your voice from inside the closet. "Molly, run!"

"I'll call the police," Paedar says, ignoring you. He takes a prowling step forward. I press into the wall even more. "I'll tell them two crazed kids broke into my house and tried to kill me. What do you think they'll do with you, then?"

"You'd really involve the police?" I ask. "I'll tell them you're Boy Scout. I'll tell them you've been threatening Muriel Weisz. About how *The Arsonist* is not what people think it is. Everyone will know what a liar you are."

Paedar's face pales. "You're so . . . smart," he says. "You've figured everything out. I suppose you are right. I don't have any other choice."

He dashes toward me, and I skitter backward but Paedar lunges with too much force. He slams me against the counter and I fumble frantically against him, pummeling his stomach, his neck, until I feel the cold edge of the knife press against my throat. I go still. Nausea crawls up my stomach. In the pantry, you're banging against the door, screaming.

Paedar presses the knife a little deeper into my neck, his hand shaking. I raise up on my toes to avoid the blade. A cold realization runs through my mind. He means to hurt me. He means to kill me. If my mother is really dead like everyone says, maybe I'll see her again. Soon.

"Just don't hurt my friend," I whisper, blinking away spots. Paedar's eyebrows fly up high on his forehead. "You can kill me. But don't hurt him."

I flinch backward, anticipating the blinding pain, the moment everything ends, and an uncontrollable, shuddering whimper claws from my throat, because I don't want it to end.

I want to live.

In a burst of desperation, I twist away from the blade digging into my throat. It takes only a single second for the blade to peel through the goose-fleshed skin of my neck. A burble of warmth erupts across my skin.

My mouth pops open in silent terror, a scream frozen in my mouth.

A bead of blood crawls across my throat, into the hollow of my neck.

"*Mein Gott*," Paedar chokes. The muscles beneath his face writhe. A hand flies to his mouth and his neck bobs forward. He rushes to the sink, a retching sound in his throat, and I watch him in shock as he empties his entire stomach into the stainless-steel basin, the knife slipping from his grip.

I race for the knife, grasping it in my fist. My hand finds the gash on my throat. I picture an ax wound, but when I pull my fingers away, they are covered with only a few drops of blood. I close my eyes and a sound claws out of my mouth, an unrestrained cry of relief.

The pantry door bursts open in a cloud of splintered wood. "TORQUE!" you cry, as you come barreling out, riding the momentum it took to break the door down. You spot Paedar standing over the sink, your eyes blazing.

"GET AWAY FROM MY FRIEND, YOU DOUCHE BAG!" you shout, and tackle Paedar to the ground like you're a football player. Bertrand's behind you, barking like crazy, nipping at Paedar as he collapses to the floor. I run forward, dread replaced by a surge of anger.

I hold the knife out in front of me with bloody fingers.

"Don't move," I shout, loud as I can muster. "Or you get five inches of steel in your femoral artery."

"His femoral artery is in his leg," you say. "I learned that recently."

Paedar doesn't try to get up. Instead, he goes kind of limp and his eyes cloud over with tears. His face is a broken up thing, nose sniffling, skin flushed red, mouth crumpled. All of his composure has washed away. "D-don't," Paedar pleads. "Please, don't hurt me."

"You were going to kill me," I say, gesturing with the knife.

"You are a crook and a liar," you shout.

I speak, lowly. "And you killed Ava."

"I did *not* kill Ava," Paedar says, his voice pained.

I lower the knife. "You didn't?" I take in his collapsed figure, limp against your grip. I can't decide whether I believe him.

He's shaking his head, tears streaming down his face, into his hair and onto the floor beneath him. "And I had no choice about Muriel Weisz. If people knew the photo was fake, they'd assume the diary was fake, too. I had a reputation to protect."

You shake your head, your face twisted like you want to sock him in the face. "That was more important than the truth?" you ask.

"I was trapped. You would have done exactly the same as me. Anyone would!" Paedar cries. "The photo came with the diary when it was placed on my desk. Someone called my number that day to say if I told anyone that photo wasn't really Ava, they'd do terrible things to me."

"Maybe you should have let them," I mutter.

"Why wouldn't they just find a real picture of Ava?" you ask. "It makes no sense."

"I never knew," Paedar says. "I imagined whoever sent me the diary wanted a photo of Ava to sell its authenticity. Without a face, would anyone care about Ava Dreyman? Her mother didn't believe in cameras, so there were hardly any real photos of her."

"You've had a lot of years to think up that excuse," you say.

Paedar lets out a strangled sound, and a sad, pinched expression washes over his tear-stained face. "I hated it, all these years," he says, his voice breaking. "Being in Ava's constant shadow. You should be allowed to outgrow your childhood. You should be allowed to cast off the person you once were. The mistakes—" He inhales a shuddering breath, tears falling from his eyes. "I am always on the other side of that Wall. For me—it is always the year 1989."

Paedar turns over and reaches behind him. At first, I think he's grabbing a weapon and I tense my grip on the knife, but instead he pulls a book from his waistband.

A white leather diary.

*It's not possible.* My brain tries to imagine some other explanation for a leather diary, well-worn and blood-spattered, in Ava Dreyman's apartment.

It can't think of anything.

I glance at your face, searching out an answer. "Is that—is that what I think it is?" I ask. You nod, and even given everything, a small smile pushes up your mouth.

"Have it," Paedar says. He extends it to me. "I can't carry it any longer. I don't want it. I never wanted it." He closes his eyes and breathes.

I think about your father, how he never recovered from your mother's death. About my dad, bruised by war in ways I don't think he even understood. I think about all the people

I've met for whom the past is a cloud, keeping them constantly in shadow.

I think about myself, then. About a single minute six years ago, at the top of a cliff on the Mediterranean Sea, that has held me suspended for so long. I take the diary from his hands, and even though we're in this enormous, nightmarish mess, when I look at you, you smile so widely, even the tips of your hair are touched by it. I can't smile, not yet, but a little breath leaves my mouth, awe-filled.

"What are you going to do with the diary?" Paedar asks. His face has grown strangely peaceful, his eyes detached and gazing at something in the far distance, inside of his mind.

My grip tightens around it. "Show everyone. Show the world."

Paedar pauses, considering this. "That is right," he says, and there is something like relief pouring off of him. He's been holding on to this diary for twenty years. He has been frozen in a country that no longer exists.

I feel the touch of your hand on my shoulder. You are standing, Bertrand beneath your arm. I stand and walk with you, the knife still in my hand, and take one final look at Paedar, lying unmoving inside the shattered remains of Ava Dreyman's apartment, looking like the survivor of a bomb blast.

I close the door behind me.

Pepper, I will make you tell me the story of how you retrieved Ava's diary multiple times, as I am barely able to listen at this moment. I carefully riffle through the diary to the end, where the pages are speckled with blood, where Ava describes being stabbed in the Stasi subbasement. Her bloody fingerprints mark the page. I flip backward some more, until I reach the beginning of Ava's English entries, and start moving forward again, stopping every page or so to read.

My attention snaps to a sentence on the top of a page. My scalp prickles, reading it.

*The night air is cool on my face but I can tell my cheeks are burning still, burning from the feeling of what we did.*

"Do you recognize this part?" I ask.

You lean over, scanning the pages, which are scrawled over with Ava's cursive writing. "I haven't finished the book yet," you admit.

My eyes skim down the page. "I'm pretty sure this isn't in any version I've read. And I've read this book *a lot*."

In my periphery, you pet Bertrand, your forehead as wrinkled as his. "What the heck does that mean?"

My breath catches in my throat. At once, I realize why Paedar kept the diary locked up for all of these years. "Someone cut them out," I say, feeling suddenly certain. "Someone didn't want the world to read this."

# Ava

January 29, 1989

The night air is cool on my face but my cheeks are burning still, burning from the feeling of what we did.

As the audience fled from the smoking auditorium in the Palast der Republik, we hurried to strip off our military jackets and baggy pants, revealing our dressed-up outfits intended to blend in with the night's guests. Sandman wore a pair of exaggeratedly large glasses, and Phoenix hurriedly arranged a frizzy brown wig on her head. I adjusted my knee-length black dress and a short blond wig. Even with his thick beard, Sandman looked striking in his tuxedo.

"Dapper," I said. But Sandman refused to look at me.

My throat reverberated from the words that I had shouted: *The Arsonist lives.*

"You put us all at risk," Sandman muttered as we sprinted down the stairs, his voice heavy with disgust. "Werner will have recognized your voice. He knows you're involved now. You know what that means."

A strained silence stretched after Sandman's words and my heart made a precarious thud. "Are you going to help me still?"

I asked to his back. "Help me learn where my mother is?"

Sandman stopped just before the maintenance hatch, turning behind him to look at me. The others were silent, waiting for his order.

"We need this to have been worth something," he said with reluctance, and opened the door so we could scramble out.

The auditorium was awash with chaotic noise. At least half of the audience was still hurrying from the room, covering their mouths and noses with sleeves or collars from the smoke streaming from burning velvet seats and carpet.

We pushed through the crowd toward the lobby, where the air was blurry from smoke. The light of a thousand enormous lightbulbs was barely distinguishable through the haze. Sandman was squeezing through the crowd near me, eyes darting around. I struggled to keep up behind him, sliding my way through the masses, when a hand latched onto my wrist.

I turned, and looked into the wide, blue eyes of Paedar Kiefer.

"Ava!" he breathed, his pale face stretched in astonishment.

A cold bolt of lightning struck my muscles. I glanced around the large space, too noisy for anyone to have heard. How could he be here? *Why* would he be here?

"You—" he sputtered. "You've changed your hair."

He looked older, and yet still wore the same stupid expression. "Paedar, let go of me," I said. I tried to pull away but his grip tightened.

"What are you doing here?" he asked. "What happened to you?"

I pulled my arm harder, the two of us ignored by the surrounding people, too occupied with shoving through the lobby toward the doors. "Now's not the time for catching up."

"I won't let you go," he declared. "Not until you tell me where you've been. I—I've missed you so much."

I spun around, looking out to where Sandman was shouldering himself through the lobby doors. Phoenix and Nighthawk had vanished. I felt panic rise like bile in my throat.

Paedar pulled me toward him.

"Don't touch me!" I hissed. With my free hand, I pushed him hard in the chest and wrenched my arm free. I turned and plowed into the crowd, Paedar just behind.

"Ava!" Paedar's voice cut through the frantic din around us, and several people swiveled to look: a bald Stasi officer, some diplomat. I thought I saw recognition wash over their faces, and my blood drummed in my ears. I lowered my head and surged forward, trying to slip quietly between shoulders.

"Ava, where are you going?" Paedar bellowed from behind me. "AVA DREYMAN! Come back!"

Every muscle in my body jumped at his words. Suited Stasi men spun around, craning their necks. A cold wave shot through my blood when I saw, behind Paedar, the dark head of Captain Werner, hawk-eyed, making his way through the crowd.

I threw myself forward, pushing people aside to shouts and gasps, running now, and not bothering to blend in.

"She's there!" a man's voice called. "Get her before she escapes!"

I made it to the door and sprinted into the night, gasping the clean air. Sandman materialized from the darkness and grabbed my arm, pulling me from the crush of people like a drowning person from the sea.

"Wait," I said to Sandman, slowing and looking back at the illuminated glass building. My muscles were pulsing with adrenaline. "Werner was right there—we can still go back and do this." Outside, hundreds of people in fancy clothes were scattering, the military-suited Volkspolizei gathering on the streets, pointing their guns into the faces of civilians. Nighthawk and Phoenix were nowhere in sight.

Sandman didn't reply, but gripped my arm tighter. He dragged me behind him and didn't drop my arm until we were on a bridge spanning the Spree, near a darkened residential street in a neighborhood I didn't recognize. I ripped my arm away from his.

"Why did you do that?" I barked. "We could've grabbed Werner. Don't give me that look. How could I have known Paedar would be there? I was following the plan."

Sandman's face was contorted with fury. "Do you have any idea how close you just came to death?" he shot back. "You would not have made it out of that place alive."

"It wasn't my fault," I said. "And anyway, we made it, didn't we? We can still complete the mission."

"You were *seen*," Sandman hissed. "They know you're back in Berlin. They'll figure out that you're after your mother. Do you think they'll allow you even the possibility to free her after that? She'll be under constant guard now, or else—"

"Don't say that!" I screamed. "Don't say—" *That maybe they'll just kill her now.* The unspoken words boomed through the night.

Sandman batted the air. "You want to know why I'm still here when your mother and the rest are in prison or dead? Because I don't take foolish risks. This mission is a failure. It's done. You're *done*. Good-bye, Ava."

"But—" I sputtered. "But you promised!"

He turned away and disappeared into the night, my only shred of hope, fading on the horizon.

I stood there for a long time, the river sliding beneath my feet like a black snake, a tattered girl in a city that is no longer hers.

February 1, 1989

I walked along the Spree for an hour, until the angry tears stopped spouting from my eyes and a deadly calm overtook me. I changed out of my dirty, sweat-drenched black dress, and back into the unremarkable outfit I'd worn earlier. With a bitter taste in my mouth, I let the blond wig fall into the river and shook out my dark hair. I set about looking for Ruschestraße, the street where Stasi headquarters is located.

I waited until morning to enter the sand-colored building, until men in suits made of thick synthetic fabrics marched to work, their medals clacking against their chests, the air filled with chatter about last night's events. They won't allow the story into the state newspapers, but I know every government employee must've heard the words "The Arsonist lives," passed around like a secret.

I walked through the main hall with confidence. That's all it took, nodding at the secretary, my shoes clipping along the floor sharply, like I wasn't afraid. I waited by the elevator for someone to enter—a harried man reading a report—and slide his key card so I could punch the button labeled "Records."

I found myself in a huge basement room containing ceiling-high cabinets on sliding casters, rows and rows of them, the contents of which catalogued every shred of surveillance the Stasi has ever gathered.

I cranked a handle on the end of the cabinet labeled "D," and it moved to the side, revealing a tight space, like a very narrow hallway.

I found the file labeled DREYMAN.

My father's death certificate lay on top. I flicked it away. He was standing next to me, running his fingers absently along the hundreds of folders, and there never was a question as to what had killed him. I found no death certificate for my mother. That didn't mean anything, but the ball of tension in my chest loosened slightly.

The first folder contained surveillance reports. Everyone my family knew—the kind old man with the incontinent dog who lived below us, the baker, the woman who walked her children in the park near our apartment—had reported on our activity for the Stasi. Most of the information was useless—the times my parents came home from work and descriptions of visitors to the apartment. A blond boy is described a few times walking with me in the streets, and I know that must've been Paedar.

The most precise reports were made by members of the Stasi. They were typed on perforated-edged paper.

*15:35 hours: "Princess" walks out of school with a male person. The two hold hands. The male person received the name "Boy Scout."*

*15:39 hours: "Princess" and "Boy Scout" walk through Grotewohl Park. Their conversation seems to focus on the activities of their peers. They arrive at a small grove of aspen trees. In the time from 15:42 hours until 15:47 hours, "Princess" and "Boy Scout" kiss violently against a tree which affords them some privacy.*

It goes on like this for pages and pages. I felt sick reading about the dozens of people, Stasi and citizen, who watched us and recorded the minutest, stupidest details of our everyday lives.

I checked over my shoulder at the door, still closed. I could see shadows flash beneath it. I had to hurry. Someone could walk in at any moment.

I opened the second file. My heart thumped faster when I saw that it seemed to contain a record of my mother's activity these last three years. Since September 1986, she has been held in *Hohenschönhausen* prison, cell 453. She spent the last six months in a deep segregation cell away from other inmates. Included were pages of sign-in sheets. Some weeks, Werner visited her five times, and the visits could last hours. My throat clenched. From the notes here, it didn't appear as though the torture and interrogation had returned any results. She never gave away the rendezvous points.

I had what I came for—*Hohenschönhausen* prison, cell 453—but a thought held me there. I scanned for the surveillance reports again until I found the one logged just before we attempted our escape.The meaning of it materialized like a truck of cement on my skull.

*On Sept. 13, 1986, at 16:34 hours, approached by "Boy Scout" with information that Dreyman family will escape tomorrow with false documents. Information considered extremely reliable. Recommend descriptions be sent immediately to all checkpoint booths.*

The words read like a vise tightening on my chest. I could almost hear my ribs splinter. The informer. The reason my father is dead.

Paedar Kiefer.


The records room door creaked open and I hurriedly closed the file and stuffed it randomly onto a shelf.

"What are you doing down here?"

If I hadn't just been squeezed to fragments by what I'd read, I might've fled, because the man standing at the door was one I recognized, even in the dim lighting. A man with black hair and small eyes.

Captain Werner.

"I—I got lost," I said in English, remembering to fake an American accent. "I'm sorry, I was looking for the administrative desk."

Werner walked down the aisle toward me, approaching slowly. *This could be it,* I thought. The moment Werner at last gets his way. He's had years to plan what to do with me. The only question is what method.

The space was small, the width of my shoulders. By the time he'd walked the length of the aisle, there was nowhere for me to go. Werner blocked the way out. "You've wandered quite a long way," he said.

"Well," I said, a fake smile budging up my features, "once I got down here, I thought, what the heck? Who gets to see a room like this? It's pretty neat." I clamped my shaking fingers behind my back.

"You're . . . American, I take it?" he asked.

I nodded vigorously.

"What is your name?"

"Sally Bailey," I said, my voice slipping just slightly. "I'm a journalist, with the *Monterey Herald*. Here to interview a Stasi officer. The Americans are very interested in what you folks get up to over here." *There's no way he's buying this,* I thought, my heart squirming, but I didn't let the plastic smile fall from my face.

Werner glanced down at his fingernails as though he had lost interest in the conversation. Did he recognize me? Did he hear my heart thumping in my chest, calling out my true name?

"The staircase on the other side of that door will take you to the main floor," he said. "You'd better hurry. This is a restricted area. Don't want you causing an international incident."

I managed a tight laugh. "Of course!" I said. Werner turned sideways, and I brushed past him as quickly as possible. I could feel the scratch of his suit on my bare arm.

I didn't fully inhale until I was outside. Once across the street, I bent over, feeling like I might be sick. I had escaped, somehow. I should have been celebrating the fact that my flesh hadn't been pierced with a bullet, but my heart was weighted down by what I'd read in my family's file.

Paedar had informed on my family. I couldn't understand it. He wasn't ever very passionate about the GDR's grand mission—at most, I could imagine him becoming a file-pusher in a government office someday.

I've learned where my mother is, though I'm appreciating now how little good the knowledge does me without Sandman's help. How can I possibly break in? And once I've found her, how will I get us *out*?

For now, I have a new mission. The reason my mother is in prison. The reason my father is dead. His name is Paedar Kiefer.

February 3, 1989

I found out where Paedar was living from the information desk at Spree University, a Protestant college favored by the city's few wealthy families, where Paedar's family had gone for generations. The pine-floored corridors of his dormitory were full of eighteen-year-olds who had never known a cold or hungry night and never would for all of their lives.

I followed the fluorescent-lit stairwells to the top floor where Paedar roomed with four other students. From beyond the door, I could hear the voices of boys laughing, an unconscious, vaguely naughty sound that I hadn't heard in years. When I knocked, the door opened and a smiling boy opened it. Paedar. His mouth gaped open as soon as he saw me.

"Ava?" he gasped. "You—you're here. I'm so glad you found me."

I let a little disbelieving laugh escape my throat. "Are you?"

"Of course I am!" He closed the door behind him. "I'm sorry about the scene I caused at the ballet. I just didn't want you running off again. I think about you every moment, Ava. Where have they been keeping you?"

"They?"

"The Stasi. You've been locked up all this time?"

I weighed his question. "Yes," I said.

"I feared maybe you wouldn't want to come back here. Lots of people who've disagreed with the government have moved away."

"Well," I said, "I had to come find you."

His face lit up a little. "Oh, Ava. I haven't seen any other girls since you left. Well, some, but even then, I couldn't forget your face. I couldn't forget how you made me feel."

I wanted to place my fist directly into his perfect cheek.

"Why don't we go for a walk?" he asked. I nodded to avoid speaking because surely he'd notice my anger cooking.

Paedar's university abuts the Spree River, and we traversed the stone bridges and river walls which cut the waterway into canal shapes. A little of the West has crept into the way some men leave the top button of their shirts open and women color their eyelids powder blue. Still, the people hold themselves high-shouldered and tense like they always have, and the mirrored ball of the GDR television tower still stands above the horizon like a surveilling eye.

We wound our way to the Palast der Republik. Behind its bronze mirrored walls, there was barely any indication that something had happened the other night.

"I certainly hope it wasn't overly damaged in that fire," Paedar said. "It's a glorious building, don't you agree?" A smile plastered his face.

"That building is hideous," I said. "Gold plating, chandeliers. It feels so old-fashioned."

His smile fell a fraction. "I missed you so much, Ava," he said. "I can't even describe it. It destroyed me when you left. But you're back now, and that's what matters."

"Paedar, don't distract me from my point," I said. It struck me how unpleasant it was talking to Paedar compared with Lido, and Lido didn't even have the advantage of speech. "This building is all wrong. Its walls are mirrored glass. They reflect outward, and make the people look at themselves, when what it ought to be doing is reflecting inside, so those Stasi and government men have to look at their own ugly eyes while they're working all day."

Paedar's face pinched in confusion. "Ava, what have they done to you? You never used to be so cold."

His eyes drew downward, to where my fingers clenched into tight fists. I put my hands in my pockets.

"They killed my father," I said, my throat gripping as tightly as my fists. "Right in front of me."

He grimaced. "I heard."

"So you understand. Why would I want the people responsible to move on when I never will? They should have to be haunted by my father's dead eyes in their nightmares every night." A pink color was pushing over Paedar's jaw and cheeks. I leaned toward him. "Do you see my father's eyes in your dreams?" I asked.

"Ava," he gasped, taking a step back.

"You informed on my family."

He shook his head. "Where did you get such an idea?"

"Don't lie to me," I spat. "You're a villain, Paedar. It might be years before the world changes, but someday people will know what you really are."

Paedar's face transformed in that moment. He didn't crumple or cry or beg my forgiveness, like I expected. His expression grew resolute, jaw squaring and shoulders pushing down.

"You're being irrational, Ava," he said with the certainty of a boy who's grown up believing that he knows everything. He turned his back on the building and stared out over the skyline where dark-colored buildings peeked over the treetops.

"These things—informants, the Stasi, the GDR—they're not black and white. They're gray. That's what you always said, *this place is so gray.* Well, you were right. Your mother? She wasn't a saint and you know it. She put your whole family at risk with her actions. And me? I did what I thought was right."

"So you admit it."

"I didn't want you to leave," he said. "After that day in the park, you looked so pretty, and every word I said was true. You had my heart. I would have done anything to keep you. I didn't know they would detain your family. I thought they'd just con-fiscate your car or something."

"And that's how the Stasi work?" I shouted, suddenly inca-pable of holding back my voice. "What kind of rewards did you get for informing on the Dreymans, Paedar? What kind of prizes, Boy Scout?"

Paedar reeled back a step, a hurt expression in his eyes. "You—you are truly not the Ava I once knew."

He was right. I am nothing like the girl I used to be, the romantic girl, who thought she could control the world with a wink and a smile.

I am someone who has learned that the world can be cruel, and that I can be, too.

"You never would have had me anyway," I told him. "You're nothing to me. You've always been nothing. A distraction. You had a crush and you killed my father over it. I hope you never forget what you've done."

I wrapped my hands around my middle to quell the shaking in them. I took off walking down the sandy pathway, toward the city.

From behind me, Paedar's voice traveled on the wind with the speed of a tram. "You can't just do what you did to me and expect everything to be fine!" he bellowed. "You destroyed me. You burned me up from the inside. And now look at me. My heart is dead because of you, Ava Dreyman. I hope you never forget what *you've* done!"

I turned back and stood paralyzed, watching his figure grow smaller as he walked away, a black swath in the hazy winter air, until his silhouette disappeared into the traffic of the street. His words hung inside my brain, repeated again with every footstep.

I don't know how I could have been so wrong about everything. My mother burned down an office building and it killed my father. I burned Paedar's heart and it did the same thing.

# Pepper

Dear Ms. Eldridge,

You may have recently received an e-mail from me notifying you of a crime happening inside Ava Dreyman's apartment, the crime being the fact that a knife-wielding maniac was holding me captive. I am hoping you have not yet read that e-mail because the threat has passed, and there is no longer any need to notify the police. I REPEAT DO NOT TO NOTIFY THE POLICE. The brave and talented Molly Mavity rescued me and Bertrand from Paedar's clutches. I am sorry if I caused you to have a cardiac arrest.

For today's essay, I will speak to you about psychology. That is, the study of why people act the way they act. Ms. Eldridge, I have no idea why people do what they do, like why my father wears a cowboy hat, or why you still refuse to tell me about the scar on your forehead. But I will do my best. Psychology is all about case studies, yes? Let us proceed.

Case Study #1: Two kids born on different continents have found themselves jumping up and down in a narrow alleyway in the middle of Berlin. Why do they do this?

Answer: It's quite obvious, Ms. Eldridge. We had just located Ava Dreyman's diary, and though Molly had a cut on her neck that needed first aid, we were safe and sound. We had electricity pumping in our veins, and Molly let loose a string of girlish giggles that I'd never heard before. Our chests were light as hot-air balloons. Even Bertrand stopped licking himself to jump around on his hind legs, the feeling in the air was so contagious.

Case Study #2: These two kids had suspected a forty-year-old fame monger of killing a beloved figure from history. Did he really do this?

Answer: I'll let Molly Mavity take this one. While I was leafing through the diary, she turned to me and asked, "Do you think Paedar killed Ava?"

I glanced at the place where Paedar's knife had slid across Molly's neck, now covered with a Band-Aid. The wound was superficial which is what matters, but I'm still not able to comprehend how close she came to dying. Earlier, Molly had told me about how Paedar's whole face had gone green and his mouth had folded up right before he vomited in the sink, all from the sight of a little blood.

"No, I don't think so," I told her.

"I think you're right," she muttered. "It's just like her, to make this a challenge." And the way she said it, with a mixture of pride and hurt, sent a pang just below my rib cage.

Case Study #3: A seventeen-year-old girl, the most logical, supersmart person I know, believes that her mother, dead for six years, is actually alive, and orchestrating an elaborate murder-mystery scavenger hunt. Why?

Answer: I don't know, Ms. Eldridge, and I'm sick about it. Maybe we trick ourselves into believing things because we so badly want them to be true. Some people imagine their fathers are alive even with a gunshot shattering his head. Others that their mothers are alive and in hiding, even when all evidence points to the contrary. And some people imagine they can become president.

At once, the humidity of the day broke open as warm, dirty rain started pouring down. Thunder echoed overhead. Molly stuffed the diary into her bag and we ran from the alley to the street, past people sprinting for cover. We found shelter from the rain beneath the awning of a coffee shop.

"We have to do something with the diary before we leave," I told her. "We can't keep it quiet."

Molly's face pinched in confusion. "But we just got it. Sending it off is basically us giving up on the mystery."

"It doesn't have to be."

"But what other leads do we have now?" she asked. "Other than knowing Paedar isn't the killer. We're no closer to finding out who it really was." Molly clasped the diary in her hands, running her fingers over the edges of the pages.

"It's not ours, Molly. It's theirs." I gestured to the people crowded beneath awnings across the street, sitting inside lit-up restaurants the size of shoe boxes, pouring out of a club where the air tasted like alcohol, their clothing wet and steaming.

Molly sighed. "Just let me hold on to it. Until the rain stops." She pulled the diary from her bag and opened it up to the back cover. My throat gasped.

"What is that?" I asked, pointing.

Inside the back cover, Ava had scrawled some kind of doodle, a large letter "V" in black pen. Beneath it was a single word written in her real, curling handwriting.

*Lido.*

Molly's mouth stretched open. "It's a clue," she said. "A clue to Lido."

After that, Molly didn't feel so terrible about sending the diary away. It didn't feel quite as final. It didn't feel like she was giving up on finding her mother.

Molly was even the one who suggested sending the diary to *Der Spiegel*, the premium newspaper here. Together, we wrote out an explanation in her notebook of how we'd come across the diary, and ripped the page free.

At the post office I found a large, padded envelope.

"Safe travels," Molly said as I slipped the diary inside. We sealed it up, along with our note, and paid an exorbitant fee for insurance and fast delivery.

And then it was time to walk to the train station that would take us to the plane that, somehow, we were to be catching in just a couple of hours to go home.

We crossed a bridge traversing some tram tracks and we

each slowed, instinctively, to take in the city opening up before us. The sky was a gray blanket trapping in heat, and tram wires stretched like clotheslines beneath the bridge, and the TV tower stuck out in the middle distance, the shape of an enormous needle. I closed my eyes, breathing in the smell of Berlin which the rain had woken up, cooking sausages and smog and beer and steamy heat. Sunset pushed through a break in the steamy cloud cover in a streak of pink. A strange feeling overtook me. Moisture had collected in most every place on my body, but I was feeling something like glowing. A feeling like I was belonging with these people, in this strange crack of time, in this strange confused city.

On the plane, Molly and I sat in companionable silence, independently digesting the events of the past two days. That's all the time that has passed, truly? It feels like an entire volume in the book of my life could be written about Berlin. I feel stronger. Not physically, but somewhere like my spirit. There is a feeling like I can survive anything now, because I've already survived so much.

Molly asked to see my phone where she had photographed every page of Ava Dreyman's diary. She flipped through them for a while, then zoomed in on the "V" from the inside back cover.

"What do you think it means?" Molly asked.

"Maybe it's the roman numeral, five. Five Lido, Lido Five. I don't know."

"Or maybe it stands for a place-name," she said. "A place

where Lido is." Though the flight attendants had said to turn off all mobile devices, she began running through the top Google results beginning with V. "There are a dozen towns beginning with 'V' in California—Van Nuys, Venice, Valencia."

"Why are you only searching California?" I asked. "If Lido's alive, he could have left California by now. He could be anywhere in the world."

She sighed. A single letter of the alphabet was not much to go on.

During our layover in Amsterdam, Molly and Bertrand and I ate vending machine pretzels and searched through my phone for news on *Der Spiegel*'s website about Ava's diary.

"Look!" Molly said, jabbing a finger at the screen. Though I could not understand a word on the homepage, the headline contained the words "Ava Dreyman."

"They got it!" I said, scrolling through the article, past scanned pages from Ava's missing diary entry. I stopped at a video of Paedar's face.

I hit play, and together we shared my pair of earbuds. The video showed Paedar standing outside of Ava's apartment building, holding a press conference. His face took up the entire shot, but the sound of snapping camera shutters indicated there were journalists surrounding him.

He wore a sharp blue shirt and spoke in German, so Molly set subtitles to appear on the bottom of the screen.

"By now you've heard the news," Paedar spoke, his eyes still raw looking. "But it's important that I tell you all with my own words. Like thousands of others who survived the East German regime, at the age of fifteen, I became a citizen informant. I alerted the Stasi to the plans of the Dreyman family's escape from East Berlin. And it is because of that choice that Ava's mother was imprisoned and her father killed."

The camera shutters started banging like crazy, flashes illuminating his face like strobe lights, and Paedar shuttered his eyes for a moment, taking measured breaths. "I have lived with the weight of that decision," he said, opening his eyes again. "I have lived with that foolish adolescent mistake for over half of my life. There is no apology great enough, and no one left alive to deliver it to. There has never been a day that I have not been sorry for what I have done, but I never knew how to admit the truth. Instead, I hid my actions from the world. When I received Ava's diary, I cut sections of it out to obscure my horrific deeds. For this, for fooling the world into thinking I am someone I am not, I might never forgive myself."

"I am donating the entirety of the Dreyman family apartment to the city of Berlin, with the goal that it be operated as a museum. And I am commissioning a new printing of *The Arsonist*, a complete and unedited edition. One the world deserves to read. All profits will go to running the Ava Dreyman Museum. And after those things are done, I will no longer speak about Ava Dreyman in public. I will let Ava's words speak for her." Paedar's eyes were shining like polished marbles, and he said the next sentence very quietly. "She did a better job than I ever did."

His face squeezed with anguish, but there was something else there, and it looked like relief. The journalists surrounding him began shouting questions. One broke through louder than the rest. "Why are you coming forward? Why now after all this time?"

Paedar's eyes were watery still, and his expression grew blank. I wondered, if you swept away Ava Dreyman from his life, who Paedar Kiefer even was.

He swallowed with difficulty. "It was going to come out anyway. But more than that, it was time." He paused for a moment, casting his squinting eyes around. "At a certain point, your conscience cannot carry a lie around any longer."

Paedar ducked his head and stepped out of the shot. The video stopped.

"The Internet is going to kill him," Molly said.

I shrugged. "But then they'll forgive him."

Molly looked up at me. "You think so?"

I nodded. Paedar was a douche bag for sure, I stand by that assessment. But *Der Spiegel* says there were maybe two million citizen informants in East Germany. You can't be angry at two million people, Ms. Eldridge. It's just impossible.

If Paedar hadn't lived in a society where it was encouraged to inform on others, he never would have done it. And what about what Molly told me Werner said? If he hadn't been born in East Germany, he would've been the kind of cop they make

TV shows about. I wondered about me, about the system that had decided I was a flunked-out loser. Given the chance, I'd already proven that I could be a hero, a detective, and excellent at breaking down doors.

For the first time, I wondered what else could I be, in different circumstances.

It was nighttime when we boarded our flight to Oakland, and televisions flickered on the backs of headrests, strange light pulsing within the dark body of the plane. "I was wondering something," Molly asked. "That girl at the boardwalk. You were on a date with her, right?"

"Yeah," I said.

"But you're not going to date her again."

I considered this. Perhaps this conversation would be awkward with someone else, but Molly's words weren't searching for something to make fun of, like the Horsemen can do.

"I don't know," I said, at last. I was very confused about Petra still. "Have you ever had a boyfriend?"

Molly shook her head. "No."

"A girlfriend?"

She smiled. "No."

"Do you think you want one of those things?"

She paused for a moment, and I thought it looked like the gears of her mind were working hard. "Not yet," she pronounced finally, and turned to look at me. "Margaret's friends think that makes me a weirdo."

For some reason, I wanted to catch Molly in a hug and squeeze until she believed that she's just fine, just like this. She would probably punch me in the larynx if I tried that, though, so I just said, "I don't think you're a weirdo."

"Okay." And then she turned toward the window and closed her eyes to sleep.

When the plane touched down in Oakland, it was with a little bit of sadness inside my chest that I stepped back onto American soil. While Molly bought a new phone from a kiosk, I watched the people strolling past, hearing their American voices for the first time in what felt like years. I caught a glimpse of myself in a plate-glass window. I looked rumpled and mustachioed and I hadn't had the opportunity to shower in some days. In summary, I looked no different than I did on the cover of *The Complacent Sparrow*. I felt my old skin fall back onto my body. I was not a badass here. I was not a knightly figure on a quest with Bertrand, my noble stead. Here, I am a high school dropout with questionable facial hair. Here, I am exactly the person Petra wrote about in her article.

In the taxi back to Monterey, a radio newscaster yammered on about the war in Iraq, which my father never talks about because his heart cannot take it, the knowledge of people like us being bombed to pieces. The newswoman switched to talking about Molly's father's scheduled execution. I had almost forgotten about it. I wondered if Molly had, too.

It's tomorrow night, Ms. Eldridge. Molly's father will pass away at precisely one minute after midnight. What an idea, scheduling the death of someone.

"Still not going?" I asked her.

She shifted her mouth to the side. "Not for all the lynx pee in the galaxy."

The taxi dropped me off first, and I said hi to my dad before lying down on my plaid bedspread and sleeping for the rest of the day, Bertrand quietly snoring beside me.

I was woken some hours later by the buzz of my phone on my nightstand. The caller ID read "Obi Shawn Ken Obi." I watched my phone shudder three, four, five times.

"Hello?" I asked, but before I got the second syllable out of my mouth, Shawn interrupted me.

"I know you don't want to deal with me because you've been on your period or whatever, but I've decided to forgive you about blowing it with Petra, and as a show of my forgiveness, I'm inviting you to a party tonight, organized by my sister, at the Hacienda Street pool, and you better not say no."

I took in a breath. "You're invited to a party?" I asked, disbelieving.

"My sister says I can invite three people," Shawn said, "since I suggested the locale."

"You know exactly where the party is. Why do you need permission to go?"

"She says I'd bring down the market value of the entire

thing. Anyway, I figured I'd invite you and Wallace. Reggie is already an official invited guest. That means I have a third invite. I thought maybe you could ask Petra."

I held in a groan. "I'm not asking Petra."

"*Dude*," Shawn said, "what happened with you two? You used to be in *love* with Petra."

"I wasn't in love with her," I said. "I was—something else. Could I invite Molly?"

"That girl from the boardwalk?"

"Yeah."

"Ehhh . . ." I could hear Shawn cringe on the other end of the line. "She was weird. I think if anybody could bring down the market value of the party worse than us, it'd be her."

"I'm inviting her," I said. "She'll probably say no anyway."

When I called Molly, she was quiet for a long time.

"A party," she repeated, splitting the word into two precise syllables.

"Yes."

"Do I have to dance?"

"No," I said.

"Oh," she said. "All right, then."

When I dropped by Molly's house, Shawn was already in the backseat, and the day had begun to cool. Molly had changed her clothes from this morning, into a pair of overalls with the shoulder straps tied around her waist. She rolled the window down and the wind ruffled the curls of hair that dangled down around her shoulders.

I was drunk on jet lag, and I felt like I was still existing in a little pocket of elsewhere. Molly existed in that pocket, too. While Shawn chattered about comics in the backseat, I glanced over at Molly, her eyes closed, the wind rushing over her face. We had shared something particular and important, I think, on that trip, and I wanted to hold on to the feeling a little while longer.

We stopped by Wallace's house last. Shawn high-fived him when he scooted onto the backseat. "It's a fine night and I'm ready to fuck some shit up," Shawn said. "And by shit, I mean my penis."

"Shawn!" I admonished.

"Oh, I forgot," Shawn said with an eye roll. "We're in mixed company. Apologies, milady."

"It's okay," Molly said. She smiled, and then her smile fell from her face so quickly I almost heard it shatter.

"What's wrong?" I asked.

"I just realized something," she said.

"What?" I asked.

Molly's fingers rested on the window frame. "My dad's going to be executed tomorrow."

Wallace and Shawn swiveled their wide eyes from Molly to each other.

"Fucking-a," Wallace breathed.

"I don't think my penis is going to be able to function after hearing that," Shawn muttered.

I braked the car in the middle of the street, the tires swerving slightly on the pavement. I reached into the backseat and smacked Shawn as hard as I could with my seat belt holding me to the front seat.

"Dude!" Shawn snapped, slapping my hand away. "What is your problem?"

"Everyone be quiet for the rest of the car ride!" I said, realizing how much I sounded like an exasperated suburban mom.

A car honked behind me, and I accelerated down the street again. I thought about asking Molly if she was okay, but I could tell by the way she looked out the window that she didn't want to talk about it, at least not with the Tweedle Dick and Tweedle Dipshit in the backseat. I turned up the radio to drown out the moment.

When we arrived at the party, it was already going. Electronic music was flying out of speakers perched on the diving board, and a massive crush of kids were down in the empty pool, jumping up and down to the beat.

Wallace jumped into the pool to join the party, but I stopped Shawn before he could run off, too. "You need to quit being so rude to Molly," I said under my breath, so Molly couldn't hear. "I'm serious."

"I know you're serious," he said loudly. "You're so serious, it's like I don't even know you anymore. What are you *doing* with that chick? Is this some kind of rebound from Petra? 'Cause if you want to get into her pants, just get it over with already."

My face started burning. I deliberately did not turn to see whether Molly had heard. I couldn't handle the mortification if she had. I said the only thing I could think of under the circumstances. "You're a dick."

Shawn shrugged, like he'd been expecting that. "I'm your best friend, Pepper, and if that means being a dick sometimes, that's just the way it's gotta be."

I stammered, feeling so angry I could not form words. Shawn walked to the edge of the pool. "Incoming!" he shouted, and launched himself over the bodies. Hands sprang up and carried him over their heads. After a moment, he was amalgamated into the crowd.

Molly and I stood beside the pool for a while, finding some cans of Sprite to share, watching the jumping crowd below. Several kids had Glow Sticks in their hands and a beach ball was bouncing between people's hands. On the speakers, a loud pop song smothered the night.

"I'm sorry about Shawn," I shouted, so she could hear me. "I don't know what his problem is."

She shook her head as if to say it didn't matter. "Looks like he's having fun," Molly said. I spotted him by the diving board, jumping up and down, off time to the music, his Panama hat flopping around his shoulders.

"That's my cousin, Margaret, next to him," Molly said, peering into the crowd. "That tall skinny girl. I didn't know she'd be here."

"With the bright green hair?"

Molly nodded.

"I think they're dancing together," I said.

Margaret and Shawn were definitely dancing together, their front sides basically smashed against each other. Margaret was about a foot taller than Shawn, but they didn't seem to care.

"Well, I guess they hit it off," I said.

Molly made a face. "I don't want to go down there," she said, looking into the crammed pit of bodies.

"You want to take a walk?" I asked.

Her shoulders seemed to relax at the suggestion. "Sure."

Through the darkness and trees, the bay and downtown weren't visible, though I knew both were in front of us from the way the salt in the air got stronger. The moon illuminated rows and rows of single-story houses and maple trees interspersed with palms. Bertrand sniffed the bushes running along the sidewalk before finding one to piddle on.

"If Ava had survived, where do you think she'd be right now?" Molly asked.

I shrugged. I honestly had trouble imagining Ava Dreyman living in the world.

We walked down to the beach, picking our way over dark rock outcroppings. "You know what kills me?" she asked. "That she didn't even *have* to die. The country was almost collapsed. Just a little longer and the Wall would've fallen."

I nodded. It was almost too sorrowful to bear, Ms. Eldridge. I had to look away from Molly's face and out to the crashing surf.

At the far edge of the beach, her father's tower was shad-owed against the moon-bright sky.

"Why is it roped off like that?" I asked. A huge perimeter around the tower was cordoned off with sheets of neon orange plastic mesh. At intervals, signs shouting "Danger!" and "Keep Out!" were posted.

"It's been condemned," Molly explained. She had a kind of wistful look, and I wondered if she was remembering all the times her family had come here before everything fell apart. "If it collapses, it could injure people."

"If it falls down, what happens to your claim?"

"It's gone. I only own the tower—the wood, the nails. If it falls, that's it. The beach belongs to the people."

"Why don't you just give it up?"

She was silent. She thought a long time, opening her mouth at one point as if to speak, then closing it again. "It's my dad's," she said simply.

"When's the last time you climbed up?"

"Before we went to France."

"Let's go up there," I said.

She looked uncertain. "I don't know."

"Come on. How often can I say to a girl 'Show me your tower'?"

She laughed, considering this, then nodded. "All right, let's go see my tower."

We climbed up the wooden staircase to the plywood door at the top. Molly keyed in the number to the combination lock on the handle and yanked it open. It took a couple of thrusts to push the plywood aside and when it finally gave, she staggered inside.

The tower room was an open space with a wide doorway leading to a balcony that looked out over the water. Wind funneled powerfully into the place, whipping Molly's hair around her head. Plastic utensils in a Baggie and a bloated roll of paper towels sprawled on the ground beneath a particle-board table. On the wall, beneath a metal thumbtack, a photograph hung inside a plastic report cover, infiltrated by damp. The photo was of Molly, her father, and what must've been her mother. Her mother had bouncy blond hair and a close-mouthed smile. She looked strange next to Molly and her dad, who appeared nearly identical: same darkly freckled faces, same wiry orange hair. You could put your hand over her mother and the picture would've made a lot more sense.

Molly stepped onto the small balcony facing the sea. The water stretched endless before her, choppy waves colored white by moonlight.

"They never let me stand here when I was little," Molly said. "They said it wasn't safe. It's almost funny now. This feels like practically the safest place I ever was in my whole childhood."

"You're feeling sad about your dad."

"I'm not feeling sad," she said. "I just wish I could've stopped this. If I could just try again, go back to the start, those people he killed would be alive, and even though he deserves it, he wouldn't have to die, either. None of this needed to happen."

"You know you're not to blame, right?"

There was a struggle in Molly's expression, as if she was fighting with an idea inside. "What if—" she began. "What if my parents were fine when they were our age? I've heard their stories enough times, the story of how they met. They loved each other more than I can even imagine," she said. And then, quieter, "Maybe my parents were fine before I came along."

I wanted to tell her that she wasn't responsible for what they became, but who was I to say? I know my parents were okay before I was born. At the very least, without me, my mother would be alive still.

"Why do they make us carry their heavy loads?" I asked, my mind touching on my father, and the fish he collects to honor a dead wife even though that makes no sense, and at the same time I wondered if the fish are the only things keeping him from sailing into the bay and letting his body fall over the side of his boat and sinking down all the way to the bottom.

I wondered what I could have done to stop him from becoming the way he is, and I know the answer is nothing, just as there was nothing Molly could've done for her father and mother. These people were broken a long time ago.

I turned to her. "Do you want to know something I've never told anybody?"

Molly nodded.

"For a field trip in eighth grade, we went to a museum in San Francisco. I thought the whole thing was boring because we had to fill in a worksheet as we walked around, but then I found these black-and-white pictures of people's heads, and over the top of their heads was another image. Double exposure, they're called. There was a girl with a city skyline sprouting from where her hair should be, and a guy with tree limbs coming from his forehead. I thought that if it were me, out of my head would be waves, crashing all over the place. That's what I think I maybe am, really, and nobody knows. I'm drowning inside and no one can tell."

Molly looked at me for a long time. It didn't seem like she was breathing. She reached out and placed her flat palm to the top of my head. She pressed down through the long curls.

"No one but me," she said. And the way she spoke it, I knew she felt the same thing I did.

I had never kissed a girl, Ms. Eldridge. I still haven't. Maybe I should've reached over and done it, because the air between us was buzzing and I know it would've felt nice to press my warm mouth to hers. But what I have with Molly doesn't need that. Her friendship is not a consolation prize. It is worth more than all of the diamonds in Master Quest. Maybe Shawn and Wallace and Reggie wouldn't understand, but I do. Because the waves in my brain were being slowly calmed by Molly's hand, and for a moment, the waters inside of me were peaceful.

# Molly

Pepper,

When I arrive home after the party at the Hacienda Street pool, I feel odd. Restless. I go to my room, close the door, and sit on my bed. I look at my books. I scan the spines, but don't feel like reading any of them. There's *The Arsonist*, but for the first time, I don't want to look at it. There is a feeling like something important was born tonight, in the open air of the lookout tower, and simultaneously something important is dying.

Once, just once, I Google whether my father has changed his mind about a last-minute appeal.

He hasn't.

My phone buzzes on the table. The caller ID reads Margaret.

"Hey," I say.

Noise crashes through the phone speaker, electronic pop music and voices shouting. "You need to leave my friend alone," a voice calls from the other end of the line. I know immediately that it's not Margaret. The voice sounds far away, like from the bottom of a well.

"What?" I demand. "Who is this?"

"I'm Pepper's best friend *for life*. I know him better than anybody. Better than *you*." I realize then that it's your friend Shawn. From the noise around him, it sounds like the party is still going. I can practically smell the tang of alcohol through the phone.

"Pepper has been weird ever since he met you. You're ruining him and you need to leave him alone!"

I feel my heart beating in my neck. "You're drunk," I say.

"Margaret's friends told me how you peed your pants with milk. You're a *freak*," he slurs. "You should know Pepper's only being your friend because he dropped out of school and the love of his life smashed his heart. And then you ruined his chances with her! He's only hanging out with you because he feels bad about himself."

I go very still, listening to this. I take each word in, feel it slide down my throat. I wonder if you can overdose on words.

"Shut up," I whisper.

"Is that Molly?" Margaret's voice echoes through the electronic music behind her. I imagine her head all strung with tinsel, her glittery cheeks reflecting the pulsing pink light. "Molly, where are you? You should come back to the pool! I'm so happy right now. I saw Brielle and Grayson and I didn't even care!"

Aftershocks of Shawn's words crash over me again and again. "Margaret, put Shawn back on," I tell her.

But the line goes dead.

I walk into my bedroom and lay on my bed, my stomach

churning. I try to sleep, even as the sun begins to fill the hallway with the gray light of morning.

All I can think is that I'm furious that I let this happen. I was such an idiot.

To think that I could be a different person from the one I'd grown used to being.

To think I could ever be something other than alone.

I distract myself, for the millionth time, by considering the inside back cover of Ava's diary where the inked *V* was drawn. I imagine Ava and Lido, what might have happened to them if she'd never gone back to Berlin. They could be living in this city right now. Maybe they wouldn't have kids, like Paedar said. Maybe they'd be one of those kidless outdoorsy couples who kayaks around the bay—

My eyes snap open, and I sit up in bed.

Monterey Bay is shaped like a "V."

I pull up a map of Monterey on my phone. Protruding from the bay, right where the two sides of the *V* come together, is Fisherman's Wharf. I've been on it a dozen times with my family. My tower isn't far from there.

I throw on my jacket and pad out of the quiet house.

On the waterfront, I sprint past restaurants and gift shops, and there are only a few people about this early, an old couple walking and sipping coffee from paper cups, restaurant workers unloading crates of fish and ice.

I walk onto the wharf, which in hours will be overrun with

tourists, and let my eyes stretch across it, to the nest of boats parked at the sprawling docks, their masts sticking into the sky like splinters. I walk to its end where it becomes a pier, sticking out into the bay. A lone fisherman has cast a line into the water.

In the strange morning light, the sky and the water are almost the same pale color, making the horizon look vague and blurry.

I walk the entire length of the wharf, scanning every surface. On wooden handrails, I read everything people have carved, initials and profanity. "HM loves JE," "Eff the machine," a few fish heads adhered to the concrete.

I walk back to the entrance of the wharf, and notice something on the concrete walkway that I missed before, shadowed by a railing. A single word, written in black block letters. The writing is faded and appears very old.

*Erinnern*

I don't recognize the word, but a feeling tugs at my brain and I enter it into a translation website. The word is German.

It means "Remember."

My legs turn to jelly. It could be Ava. I stand at the handrail and peer over the side to the shore and sea plants below, the aquamarine water slapping the rocks a short distance away. It isn't a high drop from where I stand. Five or six feet to the floor of the bay. At high tide, there'd be nothing to see but ocean water.

I lower myself to the rocks.

The light is dim under here, and it feels like a strange, secret room, smelling exactly like the color green. I can make out objects scattered over the bed of seaweed. Lost shoes and food wrappers and a couple of bloated books. I pick up a sheet of newspaper, but it's only a full-page advertisement for a furniture store, and the saturated paper falls to pulp in my hands.

And then I glance up.

There's something carved deep into the wooden crossbeam. I barely understand at first, because the words are faded, and they form the last phrase I ever would've imagined. The words are carved deep, like the hand that made them was determined to make them last the years.

## Winston ♥s Ava

I read it again, and again, and again.

Today is the day of my father's execution. I spend it walking around town for hours, until the fog burns off, until the buskers singing for tourist money come and go, until the seagulls get tired and finally fly off home. When the day is dwindling, I arrive at the white fence of my aunt's house. I lift the latch slowly, and the action lifts something inside my mind.

My father knew Ava Dreyman.

My father loved her.

My father would want to know how she died.

I am thinking that you were right from the start, Pepper.

The person behind this has been my father, all along.

My aunt stands in the kitchen when I walk in. She doesn't question where I've been all day, my hair and skin washed in the grit of the city and sea. Marty is knitting at the kitchen table, his rainbow swaths of fabric spilling out over the floor. His paunchy eyes are red from crying.

Auntie Ro stands with her hand on her hip. "Molly," she says, her voice firm. "You have one last chance to change your mind about not going."

I don't respond. I lift my aunt's car keys from the end table and go outside to wait in the passenger seat of the Civic, watching the sky bleed of light.

When we arrive at the prison, a guard takes us to a steel-paneled room where my father is waiting. My aunt sits in a chair against the back wall, taking my father in, the way his nose lilts to the left, the chapped crack in the corner of his mouth. Even now, knowing he'll stop breathing soon, he doesn't seem like anything other than my ordinary, broken dad. I feel the same way around him as I always have: heartsick, uncertain, tired, betrayed.

A shaving kit with a plasticized hand mirror sits on a metal table between my father and me. His face is pink as a newborn. The neck-length goatee he grew in prison is gone.

A guard takes the razor away, but my father asks to hold on to the mirror, looking at his face in the warped surface. It is the last time he will see himself.

The remains of my father's last meal sit on the table in front of him. The fork-shaped bone from a steak. Mashed potatoes pushed to the edge of the plate. "They give you the default meal if you don't request one," my father explains. "I never liked meat until I met your mother, did I ever tell you that? I was almost a vegetarian, didn't even like eggs, or my stomach didn't like the idea of them, but she was a carnivore if there ever was one."

A guard approaches then. "Your dessert," he says. "Bon appetite."

On the metal tray, the guard has placed a small carton of plain yogurt and a cellophane-wrapped cookie. My father peels back the wrapper and I see that the cookie is shaped like a shell. He holds it in his palm for a moment, then takes a slow, cautious bite. He doesn't look at me.

"Mom's last meal was yogurt and madeleines," I say, my voice low and serious.

My father silently eats the cookie, opens up the top of the yogurt, dips in a plastic spoon. His face is expressionless.

"That was—that was the last thing mom ate before—"

"I know," my father says.

I want to toss questions at him like throwing knives. *What do you know? What aren't you telling me?*

"I always thought that was strange," I tell him. "If she was going to kill herself, she would've wanted her last meal to be a feast. Five courses. Champagne. Go out in style."

My dad just blinks, finishing his yogurt. I want to slap it

out of his hands. I want to throw it against the wall.

The clock on the wall says it is nearly midnight. Almost time. I pull up the photo of the carving from the wharf on my phone. I place it on the table in front of him.

"Tell me what this means," I tell him.

His face could be smiling, but it's the kind of smile that shows what's going on inside his head is something terrible. "We said we would meet there, if we got separated. We would meet there when we were free."

His eyes clench shut.

"I loved her, you know." For a long moment, he is quiet, and I am not sure who it is that's sitting inside my father's head, Ava Dreyman or my mother.

A guard enters the room with a stretcher. Without a sound, he motions for my father to lie down because it's almost time. My father climbs up onto the cushioned surface. The balls of his bare feet hang off.

My father will never stand again.

"Maybe I'll be with you afterward, like her father was for her," he says. "Maybe I'll have another chance."

"What?"

"She never told me about that," he says. "That she saw him the whole time we were on the island together."

"Who?" I whisper, barely audible.

"Ava," he breathes.

It will be his very last word. I think he planned it that way.

"Who are you?" I ask, a quaver in my throat.

He reaches out for the hand mirror still resting on the table and holds it to his face. He breathes a full, deep breath, clouding the surface. With a finger, he spells out a word. I bite down on my knuckle to stop my teeth from rattling, from breaking apart my skull. The word disappears on the glass a moment later.

LIDO.

His red eyebrows are high on his forehead. They seem surprised all at once by what has happened to him, by the turns his life has taken, almost without his knowledge.

The guards begin strapping him down and wheel him from the room, into a sterile glass-walled booth, and somehow I end up on the other side of the glass, next to the family members of the victims dressed in suits and dresses and pallid faces, and I am the only one in that whole goddamn place without tears coursing down her face.

It happens too fast, what comes next.

I imagine I can smell the chemicals, the one that numbs and the one that stops the heart. The smell is coming from two syringes full of liquid that will soon be inside my father's body. Inside my own body, all the atoms are quivering from the smell. I dart from the booth, out of the fog of chemicals and the metal everything, past the guards who open the doors for me when they see me running down the hall. I slam out the front doors and run into the night, the black freeway to my left, the stars neon-green bulbs above.

I run in my Croc and my cast through the burned fields of weeds along the freeway. I can feel burrs poke through the holes in my shoe, but they don't register. Because inside the building behind me, my father's life is ending.

I scream, but not a scream anyone can hear. It is a scream my bones are making, and the wires in my brain, and all the wrongness inside of my body.

I cry, but not tears. I cry memories, droves of them, and they don't fall like normal tears. They lift upward, off the smoke-stack of my brain, in plumes.

# Ava

February 10, 1989

Today, I walked into a bar near the Palast der Republik. It was old-fashioned—dark-stained wood and dust-covered silver steins lining the walls. I'm old enough to drink here. I've never been old enough for anything before. The barman asked what I wanted and I said "Anything," so he plopped an easy, watery beer to the wooden bar. I drank half. I can't remember the taste.

I don't feel like a person anymore. I am so tired; my body feels more like something heavy that I have been tasked with carrying around. I am shredded and undone. I am pulling apart at the seams.

I let my hands fall inside my coat pockets. The fingers of my left hand brushed against something metallic. When I pulled it out, my loose fingers cupped a key.

Oversized, brass, industrial-looking. The word *Hohenschön-hausen* was stamped on it. It was a big word. A word that meant something.

*Hohenschönhausen* is the name of a high-security prison in Berlin.

Werner had brushed past me in the records room, close

enough to drop something into my pocket without me notic-ing. He *had* recognized me. He was leading me straight to what he knew I wanted most in the world. My mother. My fingers closed around the key, tightening so the metal edge gouged my skin. Though this must be a trap, my heart began pumping more strongly. I have never felt so full of direction, of adrena-line, of purpose.

February 14, 1989

It snowed last night, powdery particles that took ages to melt in my outstretched palm. I waited beneath an outdoor staircase until a guard left through the prison's back door so I could dart in. I felt it the moment I entered the dark doorway, floors and floors above my head: the vibration of cold suffering. Humans existing behind walls and bars. It will take decades to get that ringing out of my ears.

I found my mother's cell too easily. The halls were empty. I should have known something was wrong after I climbed sev-eral flights of stairs to cell 453 without encountering a soul.

My mother's door was made of metal, black with circles of rust growing through the paint like a disease of the skin. A small metal flap was hinged to the door at eye level.

The key felt heavy in my fingers.

I fit it inside the lock. The door creaked on its hinges.

There was no light anywhere—no window in her room but a small grate for ventilation—but somehow an otherworldly

grayness infiltrated the cell, and I saw her like you see something through a spyglass. She looked shrunken inside a utili-
tarian canvas dress. Her sharp elbows broke through the fabric,
and I wondered how the bone didn't break through the skin,
too.

Her hair was long. That was the worst part. She always cut
her hair short.

When she saw me, her expression wasn't joyful, or anything
like I'd expected. Her filth-covered face furrowed with extra
skin I didn't remember.

"Ava," she gasped, her lips trembling.

"I'm here to rescue you."

"Oh," she said, tears coming to her eyes. Her head began to
shake. "It's not safe here, Ava. This isn't what I wanted."

She wasn't making sense. I took her hand in mine, and was
shocked at the desiccated boniness. "What can you mean? You
didn't want me to find you?"

"You are in danger here."

I pulled on her hand. "Then come with me. We don't have
much time."

She seemed to rouse at this. Her head moved robotically
around her cell, as though there might be something there to
pack. The smell inside was starting to make my eyes weep. Her
cold fingers gripped my hand like a machine.

A clang of metal. A rectangular sweep of light. My mother
threw down my hand. "Get out," she whispered. "Run."

I turned to face the beam of a flashlight. My head whipped back at the flare of bright white. A man's voice shouted, "Grab her!" A man pulled at my waist, and I braced my hands against the doorway, and I hung there, palms cutting into the sharp steel framing the door. I was screaming, a different scream to the one I'd screamed three years ago when Georg drove away from the checkpoint and my mother's silhouette disappeared behind the Wall.

This scream could accomplish things. This scream could rattle the concrete of the Wall and turn it to dust.

It cannot be described, the feeling of the guard in olive polyester pulling me away from the doorway at last. The echo of my noise rang in everyone's ears, but it had done nothing. My final weapon wasn't powerful after all.

From down the hall, I heard my mother's weeping and the final, conclusive slam of her cell door.

"Take her to headquarters," the guard said. "Werner will want to meet this one. I'm reasonably certain it is the Dreyman girl."

"I almost feel sorry for you," the other guard said to me. "It's gonna take the grunts days to scour the floors after Werner's finished."

It's cold where they took me, this white-tiled room. There is nothing in here but a small table and two chairs. A square-shaped fluorescent light flickers in the ceiling. I can tell from the pressure in my ears that I am many feet belowground.

- - - - -

A few hours later

The man in the doorway had blue bags under his eyes. He wore a black suit and carried a bone-handled knife in his hand. Captain Werner. Please excuse the bloody fingerprints covering this page. He wanted me seated, and when I said no, he got me seated by shoving the knife in my ribs. I can look down at it now, only the white hilt visible as all its silver is buried inside my left abdomen. I can feel the tip of it touch my lungs. It makes a curious tugging sensation when I try to breathe.

He's letting me record this because I've told him I'll write a confession. He said if I did, he'd consider not killing my mother. I know he's lying, though what can I do?

He looks half crazed, sweat covering his face, his pomaded hair coming loose at his part in hanks of black. Nothing like the neat, precise Stasi officer I met the night my mother burned down the government office building.

"You've won the game," I tell him. "All it took was giving me everything I wanted."

His mouth forms a smirk. "I always knew you'd be easy to catch, Ava Dreyman."

"Easy." I laugh, then wince at the pang in my side. "Took you long enough."

"You're right," he says. "I've had informants looking for you all over the world. Traveled everywhere there was a sighting. Geneva, Jakarta, London. I never doubted I'd get you, though."

"But the Wall will come down. The people—"

"It's not over yet," he interrupts.

The pen is really shuddering in my fist now. I apologize in advance to whoever reads this. I could do so much better. My father taught me proper handwriting.

My father. He is slowly disappearing. Floating. His face is shining. He says he can stay for another moment longer. It'll be just another moment longer, he promises.

"Where did you go?" Werner wants to know.

"California," I say.

He nods. "I should have guessed."

"You're right," I say. "You should have."

"The ocean," he sighs. "Always the ocean. Was it worth it?"

"The ocean, no," I say. "The ocean is only another force that wants to control people."

"So you regret leaving?"

My breath is coming slower now. When I breathe too deeply, I taste iron and salt in the back of my throat. I can feel my teeth growing red. The Wall is killing me, like it killed my father, and so many others. But, it's not indestructible. I feel certain of that now as I watch blood fall away from my body, down the chair in sticky warm rivulets. I see the Wall in my mind, tipping sideways like I will tip in moments, stones pouring across the ground like blood.

I spit out a mouthful of red onto the tile floor and finally answer Werner. "I said the ocean wasn't worth it."

Lido. Perhaps alive. Perhaps breathing in the world still, a lone beacon on the surface of the earth. I can't stop thinking about Lido.

He was worth it.

And now I've arrived at the last moment of my life, the last words I will write in this journal. I am thinking about the first words of another book. *It was a pleasure to burn.*

More than anything, it was a pleasure to live.

*Editor's Note: Ava Dreyman's body was never recovered, and its exact location remains unknown. In 2001, forensic investigators found traces of her DNA inside sub-basement 3 and a Stasi cremato-rium in Stasi headquarters, the former German Democratic Republic.*

# Pepper

<u>*College and Career Readiness*</u>

Dear Ms. Eldridge,

This letter will be the concludance of my essays to you. The saying of this is with some sadness, some reliefs. I have completed twelve essays, and I suppose this should be the thirteenth, though I am in all ways not feeling up to snuff.

I have been leaving the subject of "College and Career Readiness" for last because I have never felt ready for either, and I'm not sure I ever will.

What do I know about careers, Ms. Eldridge? My father was a fisherman. Now he is a mechanic. And all I've ever wanted to be is president of the United States. For my whole life, everyone told me no, it is impossible. But if I'd told them doctor or engineer or anything but fisherman or mechanic, would it have been any more possible? So I made up a dream that was impossible, and enjoyed knowing that I was aiming higher than anyone. Even if I never did a thing, it made me feel like somebody just to dream it.

But now? I am starting to think dreaming false dreams is a crime against oneself.

Yesterday, Molly's father died. The Murderer-Arsonist of Monterey. The man to whom I am owing my life. She texted me this morning asking to meet. I wrote back, "Yes, okay," because I didn't know how to ask how she was feeling without things becoming out of control.

I opened my front door and she was already sitting on the hood of the car, her cast tucked beneath her ankle. The air had grown cool and dark-smelling. Summer is nearly over.

"It was my father," she said when Bertrand and I were close enough to hear. "You were right, Pepper."

"What do you mean?"

"His nickname when he was a kid was Lido."

"Lido?" I asked, my brain somersaulting inside my skull. "Your dad?"

Molly nodded. I sat on the car beside her, facing the house.

"Your dad never told you about being on Rake Island?"

She shook her head. "My Auntie Ro said my dad went to boarding school for most of her childhood. Maybe that's just what her parents told her. And he was a minor, so those records would have been sealed. I doubt even the military knew he was a patient there."

"So he eventually got off the island, after the fire. And if he looked for Ava afterward, he never found her because . . . because she died."

"And then he joined the army."

"And saved my life," I said. "And met your mother in the army hospital."

The story was coming together now, clearly, so that every puzzle piece fit. I looked into Molly's face, expecting tears, but her eyes were dry. She looked emptied, like a wrung-out sponge. "He had a totally different life before he met my mother," Molly said quietly. "I wonder if she ever had a clue. God, all along it never had a thing to do with her at all."

The seriousness in her voice was scaring me. She shook her head, hair flying down to cover her face. "I don't understand it."

I was feeling the same. How does someone like Lido— quiet, thoughtful Lido—turn into the man I met at the prison? It makes me afraid, Ms. Eldridge. It makes me afraid for the people we turn into when we don't even realize it.

"He was our age," I said.

My eyes started growing heavy with that wet feeling, and before I was knowing it, the wetness was covering my face. I pushed it away with my fingers.

"That's what kills us in the end, I think," Molly said, her face grayed with pain. "Not other people. Not knives. Not lethal injection—Lido was dead a long time before my father died. What kills us is what's inside of us."

I felt like taking her hand, but I wasn't sure that was the right thing to do so I pressed my palms together. "Do you wanna keep trying to solve Ava's murder?"

She shrugged her shoulders in a jerky way. "Not really much point now, is there?" she asked, and there was something hard in her voice. "Not when the person asking the question is dead."

"So the mystery's done?"

"Looks like it," she said, rubbing her eyes. "I'm starting to think it happened exactly the way everyone thinks. My dad—he didn't have a close connection to reality. Werner probably did kill her."

I was staring at my house, the squat dusty building in which I'd lived since we arrived in America. Even from out here, I could glimpse the topmost edge of the living room fish tank, burbling on the other side of the window. I thought about my father, and his grief, which was killing him even though my mother died almost two decades ago. There was no saving Lido, not anymore. But there might be a way to save my father.

"Molly, will you do something with me?" I asked, standing. "Something of utmost importance?"

She raised her head to look at me. There were blue half circles in the chicken skin below her eyes. She was tired, I could tell. So am I, Ms. Eldridge.

"I don't know," she said. "I have . . . chores to do at my house." This was not the reply that I expected. Molly's face was pinched. I realized then that, actually, her entire body looked pinched.

"Please," I said. "I need your help for this, very much."

She paused for a long moment, then nodded.

My father was asleep inside the house, so we had to work quietly. I dipped a couple buckets into the aquariums and filled them with silty water, then grabbed the big net and waited for the fish to trap their slimy bodies in the mesh. When the aquariums were finally emptied, they seemed to me like purposeless glass boxes, filled with churned-up dirty water. I belted the buckets full of fish into the backseat of my father's sedan, Bertrand sandwiched in between.

I glanced over at Molly, hair waving in wisps around her face. The air was warm inside the car and full with the end of summer, and I was strangely more peaceful than I had any reason to be.

At the boat ramp, I backed the boat into the water, Bertrand in his normal place on the prow. The waves were choppy in the wind. Molly held the buckets on either side of her knees, arms surrounding them protectively. I ripped the cord on the engine and steered us into the bay.

When I slowed the boat, Molly took the lids off of the buckets and one by one, I poured them over the side. Bertrand looked on, watching each fish dart away into the black water, the fringehead, the pancake-shaped sand dab. They never looked back.

The last was the ugly gray eel, curled up on the bottom of its bucket. "I hope I never see you again," I told him.

He stared up at me with his flat black-and-white eye and I'm certain he was saying the same thing. I tipped the bucket over the side and let his entire heavy existence fall into the water with a splash. His body uncoiled, stretched out dowel-straight, slithered away.

I am no fisherman, Ms. Eldridge. I never will be.

- - - - -

Though the wind was blowing hard enough to raw our faces, I steered us toward Rake Island. By now, Bertrand had curled up beneath a crocheted blanket near my feet, and Molly was huddled inside one of the plasticized anoraks we keep on the boat. The waves were too big to get close to the island, but we could look out over the black shape and imagine Ava and Lido, Ava and Winston, how their lives ended in ways that did not suit them.

"There's a boat," I heard Molly say, over the wind.

I shaded my eyes with a hand. "Where?"

"On the island, see?" She pointed to where the dense black rock tapered down to the water and stairs were etched into the cliffside. A white boat was parked at the dock.

"Probably the groundskeeper," I said. "My dad said it's a wildlife refuge now."

"Pretty nice boat."

Now that she said it, I noticed that it was worth probably a hundred of my dad's tiny tin dinghy. I flipped the flimsy wire latch on the tackle box and pulled out my dad's binoculars. "It's like a small yacht."

Molly reached for the binoculars and held them to her eyes. "A groundskeeper wouldn't drive a yacht, would they?"

"Molly, the mystery's over," I said. "Isn't it?"

"Yes," she said. But at the same time, she put down the binoculars and got out her phone, typing in the boat's license plate number.

Back on land, we hitched the boat back to the Olds. The buckets thudded into each other in the backseat, empty.

I had to park a block away from Molly's house merely to find a piece of sidewalk large enough to accommodate the car and the boat. The space between us buzzed uncomfortably. The sun was setting over the bay behind us, spilling over the black water in neon orange, and the air had grown crisp. The only sound was the click, click of the Olds's engine cooling.

I was preemptively sad. I think that's why I did what I did. I felt as though Molly could open the passenger door at any instant and never return. The final things had all been done. Ava Dreyman was murdered and that's all we'll ever know. Molly's father is dead and with him all the answers he might've given. The two of them were the only things Molly and I ever had in common.

"Do you still believe your mother is alive?" I asked, because I knew it would keep her in the car.

Molly's forehead pushed down. "Yes," she muttered. "I just can't believe she's not. My brain won't."

"Are you sure, Molly?" I asked. "Are you really sure you believe that, still?"

She turned to look at me. "Why are you asking me that?" she asked. "Why are you asking me that again?"

I looked away, not answering, not knowing what my answer would be. The silence was punishing.

"Well," she said. "I'd better be going."

"You don't have to," I said. "We could go get burgers. I could show you Bertrand's fry-catching trick."

"I don't think so," she said.

"Why not?"

She exhaled. "Did you know Shawn called me the other night? The night of the pool party?"

I felt my forehead crinkle. "No."

"He said you were only hanging out with me because you felt bad about yourself."

My entire body turned to face her, to detect whether she might've been joking. "What?" I gasped. "That's not—that's not the truth."

Every muscle in her face frowned. "So it's not true that right before I met you, you dropped out of school?"

"Well," I said, "that's true."

"And how about the fact that your heart had just been broken by that Petra girl."

"Also true, but that's not why I started hanging out with you."

"It's not?" she asked. "What would you have been doing this summer if those things hadn't happened?"

"I—" I thought about this. I would have gone to the Cyber Café to play video games. I would have held Master Quest tourneys with the Horsemen. I would have composed and deleted many e-mails professing my love to Petra.

"You wouldn't have been hanging out with me," Molly said. "I wouldn't be your first choice. I wouldn't be anybody's first choice. I've been called Milk Pee Mavity since I was twelve years old, for God's sake. I'm just pissed off that I didn't figure it out sooner."

Blood was flooding my cheeks, making me so uncomfortably hot, a headache was forming in my temples. "I'm pissed off right now, too," I said, my fingers tightening around the steering wheel.

She turned to face me, her freckled face creased. "What do *you* have to be pissed off about?"

"Shawn was drunk that night," I said. "He's a liar when he drinks. Why would you believe anything he says?"

"None of that matters, Pepper!" she snapped. "What matters is that you were only my friend because"—she clenched her eyes shut, then took a deep breath—"because you didn't have anything better to do with your time."

I was crying now, big, fat tears burbling out of my eyes, hot and salt-filled and surprised. "You are full of shit," I said. "You think I went all the way to Berlin with you, you think I went to the prison with you, just because I didn't have anything better to do?"

"You didn't have to do any of those things," she said, shaking her head, angry. "Nobody made you."

"I know this!" I said. "That is my point, exactly. I did them because I wanted to."

Her hair covered her face. In her lap, her fingers were prying at a piece of frayed skin around her thumb. "I don't believe you," she said.

The static feeling I get before a seizure was starting to fill my brain. From the center armrest, Bertrand was pawing my arm. I pulled him onto my lap and pushed the static to the back of my mind.

Molly looped her fingers around the door handle. I was so angry at her still, but I also did not want her to go. I didn't know how this had happened so quickly. "They're opening the pool up tomorrow," I said. "The one on Hacienda Street. The repairs are all done. We could go tonight, break in, be the first to use it. We could cover your cast in plastic wrap." My voice had turned high-pitched and pleading. "What do you say?"

She didn't move, except for her fingers which tightened on the door handle.

"Just say yes," I said.

"Why?"

"It would be . . . fun." Mostly, I could not imagine not seeing Molly again, not after seeing all of the things we had seen, after being united by something so important.

"We have no reason to go anywhere together anymore," she said. "The mystery is done, you said so yourself."

"Yes, the mystery is done, but—but you and me—" I could not finish the sentence.

"You and me . . ." she said, her voice broken up into pieces. "We were never friends."

Molly opened the car door. She slammed it. She walked

down the street, hobbling where her cast hit the ground, and entered her house.

I felt like shouting out. I felt like looking for a number to call, to report a problem, to speak to a representative, because surely this is not the way things were supposed to go.

Ms. Eldridge, maybe I don't know what I'll do with my life, what college I'll go to, what careers I will be having, but prior to today, I was very certain that Molly Mavity was my friend. It was one of the things I was entirely certain of.

Bertrand was pawing at my arm again, but I couldn't look into his watery black eyes. I couldn't do anything but drive home, concentrating fiercely on the white dashed line in the middle of the road.

I parked my father's car in the driveway and tore through the house looking for something to do, something to take my mind off of the slaughter that had just happened. I was no longer a friend of Molly Mavity. I was no longer on a quest. I was now and forevermore just Pepper Al-Yusef again. Ugly, unmotivated, flunked-out Pepper Al-Yusef.

Without realizing, I pulled open my father's drawer where the photo of Winston Mavity lived. I held it between my hands, taking in the hazy image of my dad, his face looking almost exactly like mine, unhandsome, unimportant, unpresidential. And beside him, the shorthaired mirror of Molly. Same broad cheekbones, same straight nose. If you looked at Molly and me through a slanted glass, we'd've looked just exactly like that photo.

I decided that I could not stand still a moment longer. I would go for a run outside, and I'd hop the fence at the pool on Hacienda Street, for the first time all summer filled with water. I would stand on the edge and rip the photo to pieces, the last evidence that said Molly and I ever belonged in the same universe, and let the pieces fall to the chlorinated water.

I twisted the brads on the cardboard backing of my father's golden photo frame and pried it up. I reached for the photo, and saw something I did not expect.

At the back of the picture frame, the photograph I was planning to rip to smithereens was obstructed by something, a small notebook with a thin black cover. I had never seen it before. My father must have placed it there years ago. And when I opened it, a heat filled my brain, so little sense was that minuscule notebook making. All at once, into my head came the statement that had been scrawled over my face on the cover of the *Complacent Sparrow* that had been delivered to Molly at the beginning of the summer.

*He has the answers.*

I did have them, all along, Ms. Eldridge. I didn't know it until now. I just needed to look.

# Molly

Pepper,

You are nearly caught up with the story now.

After our fight, I sit on the porch steps outside my aunt's house, head pressed to the wrought-iron railing, listening to the rattling sound of your dad's car disappearing down the street. A creeping feeling climbs through my body, forking in my throat. I feel like I have just lost something very important. *But I never had it*, I tell myself. *We were never friends.*

"I looked up that license plate number you texted me," Margaret says, plunking down beside me on the porch steps. I barely hear her. My ear is still tuned to the street, listening for your car, but you're really gone.

"The boat you saw at Rake Island?" Margaret continues. "It belongs to Heinrich Werner."

I turn to search her face, whitewashed in streetlight. "*That's* who owns that boat?" My mind goes a little off-kilter. "What would Werner be doing on Rake Island? There's nothing out there but birds and a bunch of abandoned buildings."

Margaret pauses. "Seems like a good place to hide."

- - - - -

I text you once, then again.

You don't reply.

I expected this, but it still burns like a lit cigarette in a spot above my heart. I never used to think a heart could actually hurt before. I was wrong about a lot of things.

Margaret goes back inside, and I climb up to the roof to examine the sky and the neighborhood of short houses with patches of golden window light coloring their lawns. Everything is quiet and dark from this high up. In the distance, I can hear the soft murmuring of the ocean. I sit like that for a long time, wondering if my mother, or even Ava Dreyman, could really be living on the island, if the answer has been sitting out there in the bay, all this time. I wonder what you're doing right now. Somehow, I feel certain that you're not sleeping, either.

My feet cross in front of me on the shingles. My foot is healed inside this cast. It has been healed for much longer than I've wanted to admit.

All at once, I stand. I descend the roof and, in the kitchen, find a pair of kitchen shears. In the dull light streaming in from the streetlights, I gnaw at my cast with the shears. It takes forever, but gradually I make my way down the side, around the curve of my ankle. I cut a final length at the open toe, and pry the cast away from my foot with a crack. My foot looks lifeless and pale, a finger-length scar stretching over the top, and another on the side. Six months ago, my foot was a purse, and my bones were coins. I was a rattled-up, broken thing. But, would you look at that. I can heal. I've done it, without even being aware of it happening.

In the mudroom, I push both my red Crocs on, the left one having sat disused for months, and walk into the street. Something drives me forward and soon I am running, testing out the strength of my knitted bones, and in no time a smile is spreading across my face at what I am capable of. It takes a moment for me to realize I am heading for your house.

I'm almost there when, far off, the sound of barking cuts through the diffused black night. I run faster toward it. It's a familiar sound. It's getting closer.

In the glow of streetlights, something is moving like a dart along the pavement. Something dun-colored and small.

Bertrand.

He runs to me and barks frantically. I have never seen him move so quickly, and the sound he's making is closer to a shriek. He dashes around, switching direction.

He barks again once more and tears off down the street.

"Wait!" I shout, and sprint after him. He leads me through the star-dappled streets, down alleys, around corners, like he knows exactly where he is going.

He is leading me to the Hacienda Street pool.

Bertrand tears through the parking lot, gravel spraying beneath his feet, and stands on his hindquarters at the chain-link fence around the pool, pawing frantically at the metal. He won't stop barking. I am still a block away, but even so, I see you beside the fractured teal light of the pool water, standing on the edge of the shallow end. Your body is strangely stiff, and when I get closer, I see that the muscles in your face and in your fingers are pulling in different directions. In one dreadful, elegant motion, you keel forward, knees collapsing, and plummet headfirst into the water.

Bertrand screams.

I run for the fence, shaking the gate in my hand but a thick chain is secured around the latch. I sprint around the building, trying the doors to the changing rooms but they're locked, even the concession stand door. My heart is fumbling like a tumble dryer. Finally, I cast off my Crocs, and fit my bare feet into the spaces in the chain link. At the top of the fence, I let myself fall to the cement, and I career into the blue water.

You have sunk all the way to the bottom of the pool. When I grip your body in my arms, you are moving vaguely, like a low electric pulse, and the water makes you weigh a ton. My lungs burn but I manage to propel us to the surface.

I drag your body to the pool stairs and onto the concrete. My hair is a heavy, saturated blanket around my head and my eyes are streaming from the chlorine, but I can see that your face is blue and your lips are a pale, bloodless color that I don't think I've ever seen before. Your mouth is full of water. A gash on your head burbles with blood, streaming into your wet hair.

I fumble for my phone, but it had been in my pocket and is

soaking wet and won't turn on. "Fuck!" I shout, smashing the thing on the pavement. I start compressing your chest with my hands, but I don't know if I'm doing this correctly at all. And then I start screaming, as loudly as I can. I don't know what words I'm even speaking, probably not even English but some invented language of grief.

The security guard's flashlight beam cuts across the night. He has a phone, and he makes the call, and I keep up the chest compressions, though beneath your bare skin, I hear popping noises that I am afraid means I am breaking your ribs, and within a moment, an ambulance comes, and the security guard lets the EMTs through the gate and they take your loose body away. Bertrand sits beside your head on the stretcher, licking chlorinated water from your hair. I don't ask if I can ride in the ambulance with you.

I can't sit there while they tell me you might be dead.

After the ambulance screams down the street, the air is too silent, the pool surface settled into a seamless blue sheet. The water marking the place where your body had been slowly dries. There is a smear of blood on the pavement. I cannot move. I feel like if I stand up now, it will somehow seal your fate. I have to conserve energy in case you need to draw some from the universe.

My eyes catch on something at the edge of my vision. The photograph of my wartime father beside your grief-stricken one sits discarded near the fence. I lift it from the concrete. By this point, Ava Dreyman had died, and so had your mother. These two men had just lost everything.

I wonder why you brought this out here. I wonder if you did it because you thought I might meet you at the pool like you wanted. Maybe, I think, my heart cramping in my chest, maybe you wanted to give it to me.

I find the picture frame to fit the photo back inside, and freeze. Against the glass, there is a small notebook. Black-colored and cheap-looking, only a few dozen pages inside. I don't understand why yet, but I am terrified of what's inside.

I open it, and my mother's face stares up at me.

My mind scrambles over it, trying to make sense of this image. She's young—younger than I've ever seen her, plumes of blond hair framing her face beneath a scarf, her mouth stretched in an unstudied smile. I look beyond the photo at the notebook beyond. I only read enough to see that the first page is marked "1989."

I snap the cover shut.

The air begins to fill with golden light by the time I enter your hospital room. Bertrand is curled up on your bed, between your legs in a small tucked-in bundle like a pill bug. He pushes his body under your hand on the sheets and heaves a huge breath.

I walk into the room tentatively. You're asleep, all of the muscles in your face loose. Your skin looks shiny and unnatural. Your mouth has settled into a frown.

Shawn sits beside you in a chair, head resting in his hands.

"How is he?"

Shawn's head jerks up. I realize he had been dozing off.

"They don't know yet. He's supposed to have another surgery later. Why would he go swimming like that? Why would he be there alone?"

Slowly, my hand comes up to my face. Then my other hand. I stand like that for a long time. I hear Shawn shift his weight.

"Hey. I just—I want to say I'm sorry," Shawn says, and though he's standing just on the other side of your bed, it's like I'm hearing him from a great distance. "About the stuff I said."

"It doesn't matter," I say, from behind my hands.

It's minutes before I let my hands fall. When I open my eyes, Shawn is gone.

Your head is wrapped beneath a cap of gauze, and it sits strangely on your neck. I touch your temple. Beneath the gauze, there is a ring of dried yellow color where they must've sterilized your skin with iodine. There's a choked feeling in my heart, realizing that you might never talk again.

Your father walks in the room carrying a Styrofoam coffee cup. He's got deflated circles beneath his eyes and wears the cowboy hat that you hated.

I wonder if he knows who I am, if he recognizes my father's face in mine. His eyes catch on the small notebook in my hands and his eyes widen. "Where did you get that?" he whispers.

I hold it up in the air between us. "I found it at the pool," I say. "It was next to the photo of you and my father."

He nods slowly, and I know now that he recognized me from the moment he entered the room. "Molly Mavity," he breathes. He closes his eyes. "Have you read it?"

I shake my head. I can't open that front cover again, Pepper. Not until you wake up.

"I promised I'd keep it safe for her," he says, then falters, as though struggling to choose the right words. "You were never supposed to find that. Nobody was."

I scan his face. A shadow collects beneath the brim of his hat, just over his eyes. "You knew my mother."

He nods. "We met in Ahmadi."

"What was she doing in Kuwait?" I ask. "She never traveled anywhere."

"I can't—I can't say," he responds, and it's not clear if he doesn't know or if something is preventing him from telling me.

I fold the small notebook between my hands.

There is a terrible, cold idea welling up in my chest.

The idea: that I didn't know my mother at all.

"You met both my father and my mother before I was born," I say, my brain struggling to accept this strange fact.

He shrugs with his mouth, like a frown. "It was—it was a strange coincidence. I think it must mean that, somehow, they were meant to find each other. That they would both come to visit the same house, my house, months apart."

My fingers find the photo of my mother inside the note-book's front cover. A few curls of her blond hair escape a white scarf. She looks sunburned and travel-worn, but her mouth is gaping in a smile I hardly ever saw in reality, as though she'd just received the best news of her life. "How do you have pho-tographs of both of my parents before they'd ever even met?"

He looks away, mouth chewing on all of the words he might say to me. "Your mother," he says, finally. "When she saw the photograph of Winston on my wall, she said she recognized him."

My eyes snap to his face. "They didn't meet until later, when he was in the hospital in Monterey." I'd heard the story a thou-sand times: his picture in the paper, her candy-striper dress. My heart begins shuddering, pounding so hard against my ribs I feel it reverberate inside each of my bones, all the way to the floor.

"I only know there are many reasons people keep secrets," he says, and he casts his eyes toward your sleeping form in your hospital bed. I hope you've heard all of this, Pepper, that you're really still in there. That I am not on this quest all by myself. "He does not look like he's sleeping," your dad says, his voice creaking. "He looks like a puppet with all the strings cut."

I cast my eyes down at you again. The last time you heard my voice, I was telling you we weren't friends.

And now you may never wake up.

"I'm afraid."

I hear him mumble something, and I think he's saying, "I am, too."

Something swells in my chest, a feeling of not wanting to sit in this room waiting anymore. Of wanting to go out and fix you, Pepper.

I can't fix you, though.

In fact, there's only one thing that I can think to do at all, and even that won't bring you back. "Can I ask you for something?" I say to your dad.

He nods. "Anything."

"Would it be all right if I borrowed your boat?"

Margaret picks me up from the hospital in Auntie Ro's Civic. I've had no sleep and my clothes are still damp in my waistband and the armpits of my shirt, but the sky is bright and I am going to solve this thing, for both of us. At your house, we hitch up your dad's small boat to the back of the car.

"Are you sure we can do this?" I ask, grunting.

"We are the girls of summer," Margaret says. "We can do anything we want."

Downtown, the streets are quiet. Margaret pulls into the pier parking lot and, across the street, something catches my eye. On the roof of a nearby cannery, a man stands, waving at us with his whole arm. His wiry beard catches on the morning light.

"Marty?" Margaret shouts, opening her door and craning her

neck to look across the street at him. "What are you doing?"

"Is he going to jump?" I ask, suddenly terrified.

But even from all the way down here, I can see that he's grinning. "I am giving my gift to the city!" Marty's voice calls down to us.

He's waving something at us, and I realize it's one of his blankets, the ones he's been knitting for the past several months. "It's his project," I said. "He's finally finishing it, whatever it is."

"Come back at dawn!" Marty calls. He waves once more, then goes back to working on whatever it is he's doing.

At the pier, I guide the boat into the water while Margaret backs the Civic down the ramp. Margaret does a flying leap off the dock into the boat, and after banging the prow into the pier supports, the two of us eventually get it pointed in the right direction. Margaret pulls the cord on the engine, and it rips to life, and the sound unzippers something inside of me. The hope that I will see my mother alive has got competition. Because, as much as I want to see her, the knowledge that you're back there in a hospital bed is tearing me up just as bad. Almost worse. We plow across the flat water, the boat bobbing across surf. When we arrive at the island, Werner's boat is parked at the dock. I wonder how often he comes here. I wonder who it is he's visiting.

"I want to do this by myself," I say.

"Why?"

"Because I think—I think my mother's in there."

Margaret looks away. She nods slowly. "I'm here if you need me."

I run up the stairs cut into the stone and climb up onto the island, across the black rock where tide pools dot the surface.

This is the place Ava and Lido first met.

This is where she taught him to light fires.

This is where my father became an arsonist.

The path to the Rake Island Asylum is overgrown with spidering plants, strung together by a net of white roots. Overhead, the canopy of trees smudges out the sun and everything is in shadows. I don't notice the crumbling brick buildings until I am right upon them. Some are so draped with vegetation, it's not obvious a structure is buried underneath all of that green. Occasionally, a white bird peeps from the trees, but there is no sign of Werner, or anyone.

A tall building rises up out of the gloom, and I have a feeling this might be the residence hall where Ava lived. I peer into a grimy, wired window and see what must have been the big recreation hall. The green felt of a pool table is saturated and peeling at the edges. The couches are sprouting small plants. When my father walked through that doorway the day he met Ava, she must have stood just beyond this window. A chill shoots through my body.

They were both alive, then. They were young and broken but at least alive.

At the end of the winding path, only one building remains before the vegetation becomes impenetrable, a small brick cottage. Unlike all of the other buildings, it hums with something like noise, barely audible. A hand-shape of smoke is reaching up from the chimney. Behind a curtained window, I make out the barest flicker of a fire.

I reach out to knock on the door. The sound it makes, meek though it is, shatters the silence of the island. My heart begins rolling around in my chest.

With a whine, the door opens. Werner's face fills the gap.

"You made it," he says simply. His mouth is flat, but his voice sounds strangely light, as though he's relieved to see me. "We hoped you would. Where's Pepper?"

My face betrays the answer to his question before I can get the words out.

"He couldn't—" My throat grows tight and I can't make myself say the rest, but Werner nods gravely, seeming to understand.

He stands out of the way and ushers me into the cottage. I enter a sitting room, a warm place with book-lined walls and couches and chairs with the stuffing coming loose, and too many pillows and blankets draped over every chair back. My eyes search, unconsciously, for my mother. Instead, I spot a squat old woman with shorn gray hair and a plaid shirt. She sits in an old upholstered chair with a cup of tea in her hands.

"Molly," she says in a thick accent. Her eyes trace my face, as though studying me. "You are most welcome."

A sick feeling is growing in my stomach. My mother would be embracing me right now. She'd be sitting me down and explaining everything. "Who are you?" I ask the old woman. "Where's—" I begin to ask, but I know. She's not here.

My hopes crash to the floor.

The woman shifts uncomfortably. "You mean you don't know?"

"No," I say, my eyes squirming because I am so tired of not knowing things.

Werner's bony hand finds my shoulder. He steers me toward a chair. "Allow me to introduce you to Mirka Dreyman."

The old woman's features and heavy accent configure into meaning. For just a moment, shock replaces my sadness. "You're Ava's mother?"

She entwines her fingers together and nods.

"What are you doing here?" I ask. "On this island. What— what are you doing here with *him*?" I stare at Werner, who is now reclining in an armchair beside her, legs crossed lazily at the knee.

"You don't need to worry about Heinrich," Mirka says. "He's mellowed a little in his old age." They share a glance, the look of two people who have known each other for a very long time. "As for why I'm living on this island, I suppose I wanted to be somewhere Ava lived." Mirka adjusts her feet. The floor is strewn with rugs and stacks of shoe boxes against the wall, storing tape and twine and plastic bags.

"By the time the Wall fell, I'd come to know Werner very well, after so many visits inside the prison," she says. "After I was released from that place, when East Germany was no more, I did not believe that Ava was dead. I traveled to all the old rendezvous points. Geneva, Dover, Sicily, Buenos Aires, Ahmadi. That's where she'd go. But I never found her. I wound up here and stayed."

"And how did you two find each other again?" I ask, nodding to where Werner is cupping a mug of tea.

"Quite by accident, just a few years ago. I asked him how he got so old, and he asked me the same thing. The years have dulled our edges, both of us. He's been helping me with this task. He wanted to tell you everything right from the start but I made him swear to let you discover the truth on your own."

"It was *you*?" I ask, shock coursing through my brain. "You sent Pepper and me on this quest?"

She nods.

"But—but why?" I ask.

"Why?" Mirka asks, shifting in her seat. "Why do you think?"

"I have no idea," I say. "My dad was in love with Ava when they were teenagers, but other than that, what do Pepper and I have to do with any of this?"

A shadow of disappointment crosses Mirka's features. "You

haven't figured it out yet? I thought you'd be a code breaker. Those things tend to skip generations."

"Haven't I figured what out? Who killed Ava Dreyman? Because I have no idea."

"No, no, no," she says, passing a wrinkled hand through the air. She leans forward, shaking her head seriously. "It was never about who killed her."

"I told you we should have made things clearer," Werner said. "You were the one who insisted on being dramatic and circling that line from the book."

I look from Werner straight into the old woman's eyes. There is something so eager and desperate there.

"Did Pepper ever find the answers?" she asks. "I hoped he would've, in time."

Slowly, I reach inside my vest. I let my fingers rest on the slim, black, card-covered notebook that you left by the pool. I pull it out.

"That's it," Werner says.

The old woman's eyes blaze.

"Have you read it yet?" Werner asks.

When I shake my head, Mirka says, "Now's the time. Go on, out loud."

I don't know what's going on, or why this old woman is looking between me and this slim notebook so ferociously, but I do as she says. I open the cover, turn aside the photograph of my mother in Kuwait. Her huge smile still shocks me. The next page is covered in familiar swirling handwriting.

*It feels so odd writing in a new diary. I've had that dirty, creased, bloody white leather book since I was fourteen. I hardly know what to do with this one Werner brought me.*

My palms have begun to sweat. "What is this?" I ask.

"I believe," the woman says, "that it's Ava's diary. Unless my sources have misled me." She shares a look with Werner, who smirks.

I feel the muscles in my face tighten. I open my mouth slowly. "Ava died."

The woman shakes her head. "Not in the way that you think."

# Ava

August 20, 1989

It feels odd writing in a new diary. I've had that dirty, creased white leather book since I was fourteen. I hardly know what to do with this one Werner brought me. This new diary will never see the light of day, not like my old one which, as I write, has been printed and distributed around East Berlin by a most surprising co-conspirator, Paedar Kiefer.

Though he doesn't know the truth of it. Nobody will, beyond Werner and me, and hopefully my mother.

Three days ago, Werner came into the torture chamber carrying a tray. On it was an electric kettle, two cups, and a clear plastic bottle. He plugged the kettle into a socket halfway up the wall and placed a cup in front of me, porcelain. Next to it, he set the bottle.

"This is peroxide," he said. I could smell the noxious fumes from where I sat in the corner of the room. I hadn't eaten for a day and the smell almost made my stomach turn inside out.

"Are you going to kill me?" I asked. "Make me drink it and watch me die?"

He smiled. "Can you imagine the kinds of things that have

gone on in this room? Dreadful things. You wouldn't want to know half of them. Though I suppose you're thinking about it anyway. What instruments I'll use, how slowly it'll take. If I'll get it over with quickly or drag it out. This room isn't fitted for listening devices. The men whose job it is don't like their activities recorded."

I swallowed. "Why are you telling me this?"

"Because I want to be very clear that nobody will ever know what happens to you, Ava Dreyman. Not tomorrow, not fifty years from now. There's a crematorium two floors above. Do you smell that chalky burned smell, like chicken that's gone for too long in the oven? It made me ill my first days here, but you grow accustomed to it."

My stomach was squirming. The water in the kettle began to boil loudly.

"The country is crumbling," I said. "It won't last the year, they say. What would killing me do?"

"There is always time for punishment, for people who deserve it," he said, pouring hot water over tea bags in porcelain cups. "That's the government's stance. You escaped. You threw egg on the faces of some very important men. Myself included. But your offense is worse than that. You abandoned our great mission. As a citizen, you are part owner of this country. Leaving goes against nature. Against decency. They want you dead."

"Then do it," I said, squaring my shoulders in the wooden chair. "I'm ready to die."

"Oh, I should hope not. That wouldn't make your mother very happy."

My eyes flew to his face. "My mother is alive?"

"At the moment," he said. "I've spoken with her, visited her in *Hohenschönhausen* these past years. And, well, you could say I've come around to her way of thinking."

He handed me one of the teacups, filled with brown steaming liquid that smelled like chamomile, and sat in the other wooden chair, across the table. I watched him drink first.

"You're not going to kill me?"

He pushed the peroxide toward me. "You're about to become a different person. I hope you feel all right about going blond."

I could only stare at him. Drinking tea, like we were friends. I thought he was so handsome once. Now, his face looked tired.

"What is it?" Werner asked.

"You've wanted to capture me for years. Maybe kill me. That's your job."

"It is my job," he said. "But I've decided to pursue other interests."

"Like what?"

He shrugged. "Maybe I'll take up sailing."

"I don't understand," I said. A man like Werner doesn't throw away everything they stand for, just like that.

He took a long sip of his tea. "The government, the party, the Stasi. None of it is what it once was," he said. "Or maybe it's not what it once dreamed of being. I had the privilege of speaking with our admirable Honecker not long ago. There was a demonstration brewing outside. You could hear it from the offices, the people shouting themselves hoarse. I asked Honecker what, if anything, he was ashamed of. It was a dangerous question, but I think he's always been a little afraid of me. He thought about it hard. I imagined all the people he's killed, every person shot on the Wall. He once ordered a girl to be infected with HIV as punishment for political activism. And believe me, he's tortured down here in the drainage rooms, don't let that face fool you.

"And do you know what Honecker said?" Werner smiled darkly. " 'You know, I'm not sure I have anything to be ashamed of. I'm a family man. I've been good to my wife, and my children have respect for others. But there is one thing I regret. At one of Mielke's football tournaments, I couldn't find a trash can, so I threw my hamburger wrapper on the ground. I thought about that for days afterward.' "

Werner's face broke into a massive smile, the grin cutting the meat of his cheeks in a way I had never seen. He laughed hard, a jerky kind of laugh that shook his entire skeleton.

"Do you understand now, Ava?" he gasped. "These men, *family* men, *diligent* men, *loyal* men—these are the types of men who once stuffed Jews into ovens. And his biggest regret? Littering. Pah, it would be funnier if it wasn't killing the country."

"I thought you were just like them," I said.

"Perhaps I was."

"What changed?"

His eyes shifted down, then back to meet mine. "I started listening to the prisoners. Your mother . . . I started to see the world the way those rioters see it. We tell them they should sacrifice some liberties for security. That they should thank the Stasi for protecting them, but who's protecting them from their own government? We have bankrupted the people of dreams. They don't want to bring children into this cold, gray world. And it takes a fucking decade to get a car!" He started laughing again, that strange laugh. "Sometimes all I want is to go somewhere warm by the sea, too."

"Where is my mother now?"

His smile fell away. He shook his head. He didn't want to say.

"Tell me."

"Your mother was placed on a kill list."

I stared. My limbs were fast going numb.

"They can feel it coming, the Turn, and when it does, there's nothing that will keep that Wall up. The country is in its death throes, but it's in moments like this when an administration tries to clean house. They will start shredding documents soon. To protect themselves. And they'll do the same to the political prisoners. Shred them. *Burn* them."

"Why?"

"If the country folds, there will be trials. War crimes. Honecker and the others might spend the rest of their lives in prison, if they're not torn apart in the streets." He took a gulp of tea. "They will erase the evidence."

"You have to save her," I implored, leaning across the table.

"Don't you think I've tried?" he asked. "She's been transferred to deep segregation in Leipzig. To travel there—even the Stasi cannot do so without permission." He clicked his teeth.

"What can we do?" I asked.

"There's nothing *to* do," he said. "If you want to save your mother's life, you'll have to take this entire country down."

"That's what she would say," I said. A spark was fizzing to life in my mind. "My mother told me fire is the cleanest way. I know what she meant now. You have to fight terror with terror. An eye for an eye. Unless someone's bleeding by the end, you haven't done your job. But a country like this has countless eyes." I leaned forward, leveling my eyes at Werner. "Someone out there has to stand up and unite the people."

He nodded, smiling.

"It'll be you, Ava. You will end the country." Werner pulled something from within his jacket. He placed it on the table before us.

My diary.

My eyes darted from its bent cream cover to Werner's face. "You've read my diary?" I sputtered.

"I did," he said. "And I think it can work."

"Work?" I demanded. "What are you talking about?"

He raked his hand over his stubbled face. "We could publish

your diary as a tragic account of one girl's life, overshadowed by the Wall, and spread it to the masses. Incite an uprising. But we'd need to alter some things. The ending, for instance."

"Ending?" I asked. The word struck me as odd, as though Werner was plotting out a story.

"It can't end with you escaping into hiding with the help of a Stasi officer. That will run contrary to the message. Would Anne Frank's diary have had the impact it did if she'd survived?"

"You're talking about faking my death?" I asked. "What— writing some fabricated entry where I get stabbed or poisoned, and publishing my diary and convincing everyone I've *died*?" I asked. "You're talking about propaganda. You're talking about my life."

"What I'm talking about is ending the war," he said. "And saving your mother. Do you think the history they write about this country will be truthful, anyway? Half of what's gone on here has occurred in complete secrecy. History is just myth that the public believes. So, Ava Dreyman will become a myth. She will become something bigger than the person sitting in front of me." Werner taps his fingers on the diary. "You have no idea what stories are capable of doing. Just you watch."

My mind was buzzing, my pulse beating like a heart in my throat. Could it work, really, what he was describing? Could I bring down the Wall? Could I actually save my mother's life this way?

"We will need to hire a stand-in, take some photos," he said. "If you're to live, nobody can know your face. You must consider what that would mean. Ava Dreyman dies, you must not hold on to any part of your old life."

I pictured a world with Ava Dreyman dead. I imagined stepping out of that name like taking off a dress after a long day. I thought it might not be such a bad thing, choosing a new person to become, cultivating a new identity like someone might a garden.

How will I grow? How will I bloom, given the chance to finally be free?

"Before we left Berlin, my father told me that I should do a burial for the name Ava Dreyman," I said. "It's taken me this long. There's almost nothing I'd even miss."

"There are things," he said. "Things you might not be aware of yet. If Ava Dreyman dies, you can't hold on to any part of that old life."

"My mother."

"If you wanted to see her again, it couldn't be on German soil."

"God, Werner, you can be a real pain in the ass," I said. It is only now, days later, in this tidy hotel room that Werner booked for me after he smuggled me out of the Stasi headquarters, that I realize what might actually happen. If anyone traces me to her, and they discover I'm alive, the entire enterprise will crumble. The Wall will never fall.

"Your mother will not be like the rest of the world," Werner said. "She won't believe you are dead."

"She won't," I agreed. "I will make sure of it, in fact. We will find each other again, somehow."

He didn't have to say it. I knew from his face that he wasn't so sure.

"Could we really stop the war?"

"The Wall is only dust right now. All it needs is the right person to push on it hard enough."

September 17, 1989

The air is growing chillier, and the window I gaze out of is gradually obscuring itself with tiny forked hands of frost. Werner tells me the people are talking about the diary, and me, but the government is making promises about change. Perhaps they will tamp down the stirrings. Perhaps none of this will amount to anything.

I pass the time by reading books that Werner brought me, four or five times each, and standing before the mirror, arranging my new blond hair, crispy and stiff from the peroxide. I admire my new passport, which Werner provided through one of his many back channels, the new identity that I will carry with me for the rest of my life. "What nationality do you prefer?" he had asked. "American?"

"Why not?" I said. "I speak English perfectly now."

"And how about a name?"

I hadn't considered this. Ava Dreyman, as much as it felt like mine, had still been chosen for me. Sally Bailey, too. I flipped open the book I've read the most, *Fahrenheit 451*, remembering how Lido snuck me a copy on Rake Island. I chose the first female name I saw. "It'll do you well," Werner said, but I wonder if I will ever get to use it. Perhaps the Wall will stay up. Perhaps I will never get out of here.

It's been weeks since my mother was placed on the kill list. Perhaps she is dead, even as I write.

November 9, 1989

Tonight, while I slept, I heard a loud noise from the street. I opened the curtain and saw people crowding the square below, with heavy coats and flashlights. I thought it was a demonstration, but I noticed something odd about their faces. They were smiling hard enough to strain muscles, celebrating. They streamed in the direction of the Wall.

I opened my hotel room door and saw a man running past, shoving his arm into a Windbreaker.

"What's going on?" I asked.

"The borders are open." He turned his beaming face to me. "The Wall—they say it's coming down tonight."

I put on my coat, covering my lower face with a scarf, and ran into the crowd.

"Ava Dreyman!" someone shouted.

I whipped around, my blood spasming in fear. I know Werner hired a girl to pose for my picture and there's little chance of my being recognized. Still, my heart shuddered when I heard it.

But when I turned, I saw a man I didn't know holding a printed copy of my diary above his head. "For Ava!" he shouted again, and a few others chorused along with them.

The crowd grew as we streamed through the streets, filling in with young people and old people, punks beside housewives, until I could stand on my toes and look out across entire city blocks and witness an unbroken sea of heads and Windbreakers and little children perched on top of shoulders.

When we arrived at the Wall, we poured through the checkpoint where my father had been killed, the brown-suited border guards standing around with their caps in their hands, looking lost. The Wall was covered with people running and jumping to climb it. Someone had lit a flare which screeched above our heads, burnished orange against black.

A punk girl with heavy, dark-rimmed eyes placed a metal pick in my hand. I went to the Wall and started hacking away. I remembered the story about the daughter of a construction worker, her body entombed inside the concrete somewhere. I picked at it harder and watched the Wall fall.


November 12, 1989

Werner and I arrived at the prison in Leipzig as it was being liberated, and I looked into every face that poured from the prison doors, the loved ones hanging on to each other by the necks, searching for my mother. She wasn't among them. I asked people if they knew Mirka Dreyman, but they all shook their heads. My chest is so full of sadness, I fear it will burst.

Werner doesn't need to tell me that she may already be dead.

He supposes she's out there, right now, looking for me. She will not believe that I am dead, not when we planted the clues about the bone-handled knife. She's the only person left alive, practically, who will know that it means the diary is a fake, that I did not really die.

I am certain, in a burning place inside my soul, that if my mother is alive, she is out there, looking for me. I leave in the morning for Geneva, the first rendezvous point on the map from all those years ago.

I will find her.

We will start over together.

December 16, 1989

Geneva. Weeks searching. I started knitting, clumsily at first, like Lido taught me. I made several knitted flames and tied them to lampposts, my signal to her. I thought they'd survive better in the weather than paper, and graffiti will only get painted over. I left them in tree branches and up telephone poles. Small, the size of my hand. It gives me something to do when I'm sitting at night in a hostel with nothing to think of but the ache in my heart.

December 26, 1989

Christmas in Sicily. The tiny cherub voices of the children singing, the lanterns marching over the hills and city toward the big basilica—it was too much. Time to move on.

- - - - -

December 2, 1990

I once recorded every important event, but now perhaps I have outgrown the impulse to see my life on paper. That happens when your words are printed for the world to see. It has been nearly a year since I last wrote. I feel like a shell of Ava Dreyman.

In Nice, I walked the promenade each day, searching for my mother, looking into the faces of strangers.

In Melbourne, I discovered an English translation of my diary at a bookshop on a tree-lined street. I stared for a long time at the face of the girl Werner found to stand in for my photo, the face everyone will think of when they picture Ava Dreyman.

Poor girl.

In Buenos Aires, I became ill and stayed in my hostel for weeks. It is the worst time I've had, the feeling of my body rebelling, knowing there was nobody nearby who would look after me, beyond the hostel owner who was happy to continue removing payment from my traveling bag for every night spent in one of her flimsy, buggy beds. Another traveler bought me medicine, a thick, vaguely sweet paste that coated my insides and made my warm body, at last, begin to cool.

A month later, I had made it to Britain, and took a ferry from Liverpool to Dover where I am currently residing. On the ferry ride, a talkative man beside me on the orange plastic bench in full-blast of the raging sea winds asked, "Have you read this?" He held out a copy of *The Arsonist*.

I shrugged.

"It's all fake," he announced. "Nobody could have all of those things happen to them in only seventeen years of life."

For the first time in months, I laughed.

April 5, 1991

Today, I arrived in Ahmadi, my last stop but for Monterey. Could my mother be here? Somehow, it feels as though she's not anywhere in the world. But I will search Ahmadi, if only to go through the motions, to spend more of Werner's money, to hang more knitted flames in trees where she'd probably never look anyway. And what will I do after I've exhausted all of the rendezvous points? Start over from the beginning? I've been traveling for a year and I'm tired and sore and still have a deep cough in my lungs from Buenos Aires, but I know the answer.

What else have I got? Who am I anymore? Not Ava Drey-man, certainly. Not Sally Bailey. If I keep running, I never have to answer that question.

April 7, 1991

There has been no sign of my mother in Ahmadi. My fingers are chapped and bleeding from making flames. Maybe it's the atmosphere here. All around, the earth is charred and the air smells constantly of smoke.

I think my parents and Georg and Margarita chose Kuwait because it's friendly to foreigners, but things have changed since they planned our rendezvous points. How like me to step right out of one war and straight into another.

I was tying a flame around a lamppost when a voice spoke from behind me.

"What are you doing?" I turned and saw a man. He spoke in English, and must have assumed I was an American or Brit, one of the aid workers or journalists or soldiers who have descended on the region since the war kicked off here.

"Looking for my mother," I told the man. He was stocky, and his face was fanned with wrinkles, though he was perhaps not much older than me. He held a tiny bundle in his arms and a miniature face poked through.

"Funny way to find someone," he said. "You look hungry. Come, I am making dinner."

If Georg and Margarita taught me anything, it's to trust no one, no matter how kind they appear. I cast my eyes down the dusty road, but there were only a few people about, a couple shopping in the market, a woman out for a walk. "Why should I?"

"Because I was helped by a stranger, not long ago, and since then I repay that favor when I am able."

I narrowed my eyes at him suspiciously.

"What's your name?" I asked.

"Ishaq. And this is Ibrahim," he said.

I stepped down, looking at the bundle in his arms. The little sleeping thing looked small and soft and perfect, and it had been a long time since I'd been around anything like that.

"Could I hold him?" I asked. I'd never held a baby, hadn't ever wanted to before.

The man smiled. "If you like." He passed the baby into my arms. He was heavier than I would have thought, and warm. In his sleep, his mouth formed a small smile.

"So, will you come to dinner?" the man asked.

"I suppose," I said. "I am fairly starving."

We walked the straight, planned streets built by the oil company to his house. In the smoky distance, the gleaming city peeked out of the fog and glinted in the sun.

While Ishaq cooked a dinner of rice and lamb, I held the baby, only a couple months old, eyes as deep and dark as the ocean. The baby squirmed around in my arms, flailing his tiny legs.

"He will be something great one day, with that energy," Ishaq said. "He was like that even inside his mother's belly."

"Where is his mother?"

"She is dead." He said it like he couldn't stand the taste of the words in his mouth. But the baby's face was pleasantly unaware, a gurgle escaping his lips. I wondered if it would be better for him to have lost his mother so young, rather than have her taken away later, like mine had been.

"*Un petit chou*," I whispered to Ibrahim. He flailed his little arms and legs in reply. "You know that expression in French? Little cabbage. But you're not a cabbage at all. You're too boisterous to be a cabbage. You're a—a *petit* chili pepper."

Ishaq smiled. "Are you American?"

I nodded, thinking of the papers that Werner had secured for me.

"An American soldier was here," Ishaq told me. "When my wife was close to giving birth, she ran into the oil field. She told me she wanted to find a public phone to call her cousins in the city. She said she couldn't stand the idea of having our baby in this miserable place. It was I who insisted we stay here. I didn't listen to her, and now she is dead."

I looked into his face, creased with pain.

"I can't imagine telling Ibrahim when he gets older," he said. "What does it tell him that his mother was so sad in the last moments of her life? To know your own father caused your mother's death, in a way?"

The silence tolled like a bell. I looked into the baby's face again, so peaceful. I thought, what kind of father would he be if he gave that heaviness to his son, just to make his own load lighter?

"You shouldn't tell Ibrahim," I said. "Children shouldn't know the dark parts of their parents' lives. It's better that way." As I said this, I noticed how oddly it sat in my mouth. This is the opposite of what I would have said when I was only a few years younger.

"I won't," Ishaq said, and he seemed grateful in being given permission to keep this secret.

"This American soldier," he said, continuing his story. "He found Ibrahim after . . . afterward, and he came back here and told me about a place—" Ishaq took a photograph off of the wall and handed it to me. "About a place called Monterey. He said it was the most beautiful place he had ever seen."

Ishaq trailed off because he'd just noticed the expression on my face. The photograph showed two men, one of them Ishaq, holding the baby in his hands. The other man—the other man was someone I recognized immediately.

"His name is Winston Mavity," Ishaq said.

The ground tilted beneath me. "I know him," I said. "I thought—I thought I would never see his face again."

In the photo, his red hair was shorter and his face had lost weight so his features protruded at angles. He looked so odd as a soldier. I couldn't imagine what would possess him to join up.

"Where is he now?" I asked, looking back at Ishaq.

He shrugged. "It's been months. He might have returned to America. He might be anywhere."

I realized something then. I could spend the rest of my life searching the globe for my mother, and I might never find her. I might grow old looking for her. I might even die.

But I could find Lido.

May 2, 1991

I saw his face in a newsstand.

I was making my way across from Fisherman's Wharf, where we always said we'd meet one day, when I saw his picture, gazing up from the local free weekly. WINSTON MAVITY, LOCAL HERO, RETURNS HOME.

I stared at it for entire minutes before I stretched my hand out to pick up a copy. I read the article about how he'd been injured, how he'd survived, how he was recovering at the Presidio hospital.

I tried to get into the hospital as a visitor, but when the woman at the front desk told me visiting hours were for family only, I stole a uniform and walked straight through the front door and into the convalescent ward. Nobody messes with a blond in a candy-striper dress.

I found him alone at the end of a long room filled with empty, white-sheeted beds. He lay beneath a thin blanket, gauze wrapped over his eyes and around his head. Even so, I recognized him, his hair brazen against the crisp, bleached hospital pillowcase.

My footsteps clicked against the floor.

"Who's there?" he demanded, neck straining off of the pillow.

I stopped walking. It was the first time I'd ever heard his speaking voice. It was high and thin and frightened.

I walked a few steps closer until I stood near his bed.

"Whoever's there, say something," he demanded. He lifted a hand to grope the air before him.

"Lido, it's me."

His lips parted, chapped and raw. "You?" he asked, extending his hand again. The skin there was dappled with burns, small dots of pink skin.

I took his hand in mine. In that moment, what we'd been through separately became too much to bridge. Where does one begin? Even "Hello" would be like trying to let only a little helium out of a hot-air balloon.

So I said nothing. And he said nothing. For a long time.

I finally spoke. "You went away to war."

"I waited," he said. "I waited for you. And I read your book. *The Arsonist*. Everybody—everybody thinks you died."

"I know," I said. I held a hand out to touch his cheek, rippled with sunburn beneath his bandages. "What happened to your eyes?"

"Sand burn. The doctors say it'll wear off in time."

I laughed. "Will I ever meet you with all of your senses?"

His smile showed for a moment and slowly disappeared. "Sometimes I think I'm never going to be completely whole."

There was something very different about him. The set of his jaw was sharper, his cheekbones hollowed. And something else, a darkness hidden beneath every syllable he spoke that hadn't been there when his voice was made of pencil and paper.

"I—I will make you whole," I said.

"You can do that?" he asked, unsure. And if I'm honest, I was uncertain, too.

I touched the pitted skin on his hands. "The name you went by, before you were Lido."

"Winston," he said. "Lido was just a name I had on Rake Island. But I've never been Winston to you."

"What if you were?"

His forehead furrowed.

"What if we could start over?" I continued. "What if we could be the people we were meant to be all along?"

He nodded slowly. "Who will you be—Ava or Sally?"

"Neither," I said. "I will be someone completely new."

The spark of a smile swept over his face, growing and growing until I saw all of his pale teeth, even the slightly crooked ones on the bottom row.

"Miss, I don't believe we've met. My name's Winston. I'm a brave war hero, and I'm looking to settle down. To whom do I owe the pleasure?"

"The name's Clarisse," I said.

"It's terribly nice to meet you, Clarisse."

I reached out to take his hand. "The feeling's mutual, Winston."

We were playing grown-ups with our grown-up names, but sooner or later we really will be grown. We'll have kids and a house and all we've been through will recede into the background. We will inhabit new skins, and never be disappointed by the old.

We only need to outrun our past, and we're both terribly good runners.

# Molly

Pepper,

The way we know things, deep down in our bones, is strange and unreasoning. I have known since Nice that my mother is not dead.

What I didn't know is that we can die over and over again within a lifespan.

We put new skin over old skeletons all the time.

I finish reading the final passage of my mother's diary aloud, and feel myself fade, the room disappearing at the edges so all I can see is the round, wrinkled face of Mirka Dreyman. *My grandmother.* A knot like a fist forms in my throat.

The old woman stares at the final page of the diary, eyes tracing the words, and tears are falling down her cheeks, plastering the cracks and wrinkles so her face looks younger, almost like my mother's. I wonder if this diary answered the questions she's spent all these years searching for. Not entirely, I think.

I open my mouth a few times to speak, but the silence eats my words, the silence stretching like an impassable barrier between us. I don't want to venture into a new universe where this woman is my grandmother.

Where my mother is Ava Dreyman.

"Why did she never tell me?" I ask at last.

Mirka draws in a deep breath. "I don't know if I will ever be able to answer that," she says, wiping tears from her face with an open hand. "Why does any person keep the truth from the people that they love?"

"Then it's true?" I demand. "She was—my mother was—"

"You know the answer to that."

I lean forward, feeling sick. My mind has turned gelatinous in my skull. I gather my hands inside my hair and sit like that a while, the old woman and Werner watching me. "Why didn't *you* tell me?" I say in a whisper.

"I—I—" The woman's voice comes out like a shaky violin string. "I traveled to every city on our map. All of the rendez- vous points. I never knew—never knew that Ava was searching for me, too. Those times were the worst of my life. Worse than *Hohenschönhausen*. In those cities, everything seemed so wrong. The grocery stores were stocked with food, the movie cine- mas were running, people laughed. I could hardly bear to see a world buzzing along with so much life when in my mind the world was a bombed-out place."

Her voice shakes as she says this.

Grief is a kind of war, I think now. Loss is like a bullet. A person can only take so much.

"The first time I saw you, Molly, you were twelve years old, and you were in Nice." My mouth widens in surprise. "The two of you walked right past me, down the promenade, a tall blond lady and her daughter. I saw you first, and I knew your face. You looked nothing like Ava when she was a child, but there was something so familiar about you."

"I met you," I say, in a breath, the reality of her words stretching in my mind. "You spoke to me on the boardwalk. You told me—you told me to never grow used to beauty."

She smiles in a pained way. "I had been living in Nice for many years by then. Ava must have heard that I'd been living there, or she took a lucky guess. It had been ages since I'd heard a scrap of news about her, so I set up a permanent residence inside a white stucco house, in view of the ocean. I thought I would die there."

As she talks, I follow the sunken lips of her, the high steely cheekbones. She looks like me, I realize, grown old and weathered.

"I was so stunned, I nearly lost you in the crowd. I saw you, just once again, your bright head bobbing in and out of the mass of tourists. You were climbing up to the Château de Nice."

My stomach goes hollow, the feeling of dread that comes with thinking about that day. Unconsciously, my skin remembers the warmth of that jewel-bright sky, the wind ruffling my hair.

"She wore a silk blouse and a skirt," Mirka continues. "She left you on a bench by the ruins, eating cookies from a cellophane package, and at the chain barrier, she slipped off her shoes, and stood on the edge of the cliff. I recognized what she was doing, staring at the ocean, picturing her death, like she'd described in her diary. I decided I would watch her a bit longer, let her have this moment of peace, because that's really what it looked like, something peaceful. And then I would touch my hand to her shoulder. And we would know each other again. But then—"

My throat is closing, the feeling in the room like an ocean current, dragging us down. I place my hands over my ears, but I still hear my grandmother say, "But then I saw my daughter jump."

Mirka's voice comes out choked. "I did not believe what I had seen, not for even a second, not at first. That night, I broke into the morgue, and I saw her. She really was there, blue-touched and all."

"You're wrong!" I say, jumping up. "She's not. She's not . . . You're lying!"

"She was my daughter," Mirka says, forehead cinched up like a curtain, pain flowing from her eyes. "I spent fifteen years searching for her. I would know her anywhere. I would—I would know her anywhere." She is breathing hard as though she's carried these words for a long time.

"And then—and then I walked to the promenade and I saw a girl with hair the color of flames sitting before the sea, surrounded by all of those cackling tourists, looking like she would never laugh again. I talked to you, and afterward I found the hotel room where you had been staying, and I wrote you a note. I placed a key inside the envelope, the one to the post office box I kept in Monterey, the one I left copies of with all of my contacts around the world. Ava was gone now and my contacts are dead or disappeared. It was my turn to leave something. Something for you."

I'm not sure if it's right for me to be angry at her, but that's what I feel, vibrating in my limbs. "But you waited for *years*," I say. "Not so much as a 'Hello.' I checked that box every week for five years."

"What could I tell you?" the woman demands, her voice raised. "I am your German grandmother who you never knew existed? And on top of that your mother was actually Ava Dreyman, who had faked her own death and had been living a secret life? You would believe I was a lunatic."

Grudgingly, I admit to myself that she's right. I lower myself to my chair again. "But why now?" I ask. "What changed?"

"I have been gathering evidence," Mirka says. "I have been putting together the pieces so when I told you the truth, you would believe me. For one, I met Werner again. My old enemy. My old friend." She hitches her eyebrow at him, and his mouth rises in a smile. "He told me the name of the woman whose face is pretending to be Ava's on the cover of *The Arsonist*. Thanks to Muriel Weisz, your mother had the chance at a normal life. One of Werner's more ingenious ideas."

"I take all the credit," Werner says drily. "It's almost worth the money I have to pay her every year to keep quiet."

"I cannot go back to Germany, not ever," Mirka says. "Not

when I am still wanted for the fire in the Stasi office building—
no, they did not forgive that. I needed you to find Muriel Weisz
for yourself. And then there was Paedar."

"You knew he had the diary," I say.

"He should have destroyed it, but I had some feelings that he
would not. He always struck me as too sentimental. I needed
you to find it."

I ball my fists, incredulous. "I could've died a dozen times,
you know. You'd really send two kids into a situation like that
knowing how dangerous it would be?"

Werner clears his throat. "Mirka always was a little ruthless
in order to get what she wants. And she's hardest on the people
she cares about the most."

"You are descended from a long line of fearless women,"
Mirka says. "I thought you could handle it. And I was right,
was I not?"

I cross my arms. "And what about Pepper? Why did you
bring him into this?"

"He had his part to play," she says simply. "The period after
the diary was published, when Ava traveled the world and
found Winston again, was a gap in both Werner's and my
knowledge. I had a suspicion that Pepper's father knew what
happened, though I had no idea Ishaq would have that diary.
She must have mailed it to him when she cast off Ava Dreyman
for good. We tried to meet Ishaq a few times, but he refused to
revisit the past. Too many secrets, he said, and what good would

it do to unearth them now? The three of them—Ishaq, Ava, and Winston—were cut from the exact same cloth. Stubborn cloth," she says like she's spitting. "But I knew he had a son."

My fingers are shaking, my mind racing with cold ideas, freezing and immovable. In finding the answers, you nearly died, Pepper. A feeling, dull and poisonous, loosens itself into my veins. You can't die, Pepper. You have so much more to do. I have so much to tell you.

Mirka pushes up from the sofa with her wiry arms and says, "Here, dear." She pulls a box of cookies from a cupboard. "Ava used to eat cartons of these as a child. She liked them best with yogurt."

She places a few cookies in my hand. Vanilla-colored, shaped like scallop shells.

Madeleines.

I bite into the cookie and swallow it in chunks. The sugar spurs the blood in my veins. I feel like I am waking up after a long sleep.

"The truth—the truth is hard," Mirka says, and I see that her eyes are glazed, and I think she may be saying this to herself more than to anyone else. "The truth is that my husband has been dead for something like decades. The Wall fell in 1989. And some time later, my daughter jumped into the sea."

I place a hand to my mouth. And then I speak, unable to stop myself.

"I know."

Pepper, I had been trying for a very long time not to speak those words. But when I let my mouth form them at last, relief falls on me like a cloudburst.

"She—she would stand on the edge of the lookout tower. She always got too close," I say, scrabbling up a mountain of something inside myself, finding it harder and harder to pull in full breaths.

"She saw her father killed before her own eyes," Mirka says. "She was betrayed by people important to her. She was imprisoned during her formative years. She lost your father, to his fires. The fires she taught him about. She lost her name, her identity. And when she went looking for it again"—Mirka's words are choked inside her throat. —"when she went looking for me, she couldn't find it."

Werner reaches out a hand and places it lightly on Mirka's. She weeps and I close my eyes, limbs trembling. Maybe this is the first time she's ever said this out loud. She is walking me through five years of grief in the span of a moment. She is walking herself through it.

Mirka's face creases. "I—I wanted there to be a reason, for what she did." She raises a palm to her eye to wipe away some cascading tears. "I was hoping you would find something that would explain it all. Make sense of it. I wanted that for you, but I also wanted that for me."

Mirka reaches out a hand, and I grasp it in mine. I have been looking, too, without realizing. I used to believe there are always answers, if only you keep waiting for them. Maybe for my mother, there were a million reasons, and maybe there were none. I don't need to know the reason, I tell myself.

Maybe someday, if I repeat it enough, I will believe it.

"In February, I broke my foot," I tell them. "I was standing on top of a bridge, and I knew I shouldn't have, but I looked down, and . . . and I thought about what it would be like to fall." I grip my eyes closed, imagining what I never wanted to, my mother's body a straight edge slicing the aquamarine sky, fluttering like a seedpod from a maple tree.

I run my eyes over my foot, and even inside my Croc, the scars crossing the surface are visible in puckered fault lines.

I think of you then, Pepper. Of the trip we took into the bay, when you poured those fish into the ocean. How you decided things would be different for your father, and for yourself.

"I don't want to be like my mother," I say. "Or my father."

"You don't have to be," Mirka says. She grasps her fingers together and looks at my face.

I meet her gaze. "How?"

"Do not hold on to the things that pin you down," she says. "Become an arsonist."

I shake my head, a noise like a scoff escaping my throat. "That—that's the worst thing you could say."

"It has never been about destruction," she says. "It's about clearing the world of what doesn't belong. Righting wrongs.

Your arson—it doesn't even need to involve fire. You can burn an idea just as easily as you can burn a building."

She stands and is gripping my hand now, the first time we've touched. Her rough skin abrades mine, and she feels more solid than my mother's soft hand ever did.

"Can you really burn an idea?"

She nods.

"I don't—I don't know how," I say.

Mirka drops my hand suddenly and moves toward a dresser against the far wall. She rummages in a drawer, then finds a metal gas can from beside the cabin's back door. It sloshes as she places it before my knees. She folds a book of matches into my loose fingers.

"I taught Ava how to light fires," she says. "It made her a fighter. Now, Molly, I'm going to teach you. Do you know how to hold a match?"

Pepper, my letter to you is almost over. I will print it out and leave it on your bedside table, and that will be the end of it. It will be there when you wake up. It will be there even if you decide not to.

Just one more thing to say now.

When Margaret and I arrive back at the dock, it is dark outside, and the only light comes from the stars piercing the sky, and the tiny beacon on Rake Island flashing every few seconds, warding away ships. I watch it for a moment, knowing it's there that I have left my family. Something about the light on the horizon, pulsing like a heartbeat, makes me feel weightier than I'd been before. The wind whistles in from the ocean making my eyes stream with something like tears.

Margaret drives your dad's boat back to your house for me. If she wonders what I'm planning on doing with a half-full can of gasoline, she doesn't ask.

I walk to the beach and climb the stairs of the lookout tower. Slowly, I do as my grandmother taught me, tip out the gasoline so it soaks evenly across the salt-pitted wood, the last place my family was together. I can almost see an afterimage of us in the air, standing like ghosts. My father is holding his face in his hands. My mother is looking at the ocean, like she always did, and now I know—she was searching for her death. I want to grab her face, turn it away, toward me. My throat grows tight.

I never could've done that. I never could have saved her.

When the fumes grow thick, I step onto the balcony where the night wind blasts, and for one moment, I look out on the sea, black and barely distinguishable from the dark sky.

I take a breath.

My mother is never coming back.

I return to the beach and roll a match between my fingertips. I strike it onto the flint paper, hold it to the wood, and step back when the flame drives up the tower. When it reaches the room at the top, there is a sound like a *whoosh*, the oxygen being sucked from the space, and soon the entire structure is burning.

For a moment, the air leaves the whole world.

There's nothing now but this flaming pyre. The final pieces of my parents burning. There goes Ava Dreyman and Sally Bailey and Clarisse Mavity. There goes Winston and Lido, nothing but wisps of black against a black sky. There go the lies I told myself about my family, the lies they told me, the pain they caused each other glowing orange in the night, streams of smoke coming away like clothes being shed. Lifting into the air, far above. Moving on to somewhere new.

I don't have to be like my parents, made of stories and smoke.

I can be made of something real.

I close my eyes, hearing the structure thunder as it pulls apart, molecule by molecule.

The fire whispers, *Who will you be now, Molly Mavity?*

At once, the tower leans to the side with a groan and collapses, flinging a cloud of sparks and embers into the air. I watch each cinder until it blinks out in the air. I stay until it burns down to embers the size of scattered seeds, and then nothing but soot which will be taken out to sea when the tide gets high. I'll wait for it to slough into the water, every speck, and then I will turn for home, relief lifting off of me in waves.

All these years, I held on to my mother like a balloon. She was trying to pull away, all this time. Now, she can fly.

And I am so much lighter.

# Pepper

Dear Ms. Eldridge,

It's been a month since I wrote to you last and, since then, it seems I have become something of a celebrity. Did you see all the times I was the subject of articles in the *Monterey Free Press*? I even made it on the local news! They described me as "Local disabled boy who was the victim of a tragic accident." They did not even get vexed with me for breaking into the Hacienda Street pool. And Bertrand was the subject of a five-minute human-interest story on *NBC Nightly News* where they called him a hero pug. He seems fully aware of his fame because now he will only eat hot dogs from ceramic plates.

Anyway, in case the news had not yet greeted you, I am alive! I am thrilled to hear of it. Not that I was remotely aware that I might be dead, but learning about it later, I am impressed with how close I got. The doctors are thoroughly in awe of my brainpower and vocabulary, and they require me to do basic math equations and respond to simple sentences, and they high-five me when I get them right. For the first time in my life, I am a genius. Who would have ever thought my brain cells would be such sturdy little guys?

But I suppose you are wanting me to go back to the beginning and present the facts as they occurred, since that is what you taught me to do in formal essays and letters. First, when I woke up—which, fun fact, doesn't feel so much like waking up as swimming up out of a deep well—my eyes did not work properly. Everything was blurry and unreal, like every surface was a TV screen all tuned to slightly different frequencies. For a long time, I just lay there as, gradually, my eyes worked out the meanings of several things on my bedside table, gifts that people left me since I arrived at the hospital including:

A vase of drying tulips from the Horsemen,

A get-well card from Petra, still unread,

Shawn's favorite replica Obi-Wan lightsaber pen that really lights up.

And a note from you, which informed me that you were still grading my final essay, and also that you had received your scar when your brother crashed a toy helicopter into the side of your head when you were eleven.

I did not open any of these things right away. My vision was apprehended by the view of Monterey outside of the window. Something about it was different.

My brain was still a foggy mess, and it took me a ridiculous amount of time to piece together what I was looking at: The faces of the buildings had changed. They were not brick and concrete anymore, but braided mixture of neon green and marigold and fuchsia.

My nurse came in a moment later and her face did a spasm when she saw me. I think she was mostly surprised to see me sitting up. It's true that my muscles felt like a puddle of goo, but everyone knows that I'm a powerful athlete. "You're awake," she said, examining my eyes, which were still clouding over. "You should lie down while I get the doctor."

"Wh-what happened to the city?"

She paused. "Someone covered all the buildings with blankets one night a few weeks ago. Knitted blankets. Bolted them to the surfaces so they won't come off."

I turned to look out the window again. My head was pounding and every few seconds my vision crossed and the room became doubled and milky, but I could not stop watching the face of the city. On one of the buildings, stitched into the yellow-yarned surface, I spotted a word. *Was.*

"That one spells something," I said, pointing with a finger made of Jell-O.

"Yes, it does," said the doctor, entering the room. She looked serious with wire glasses and lines around her mouth. She took her thumbs and pressed them over my eyebrows. "Can you tell me what two times three is?"

I'd woken up from a coma not five minutes previous and this doctor wanted me to answer a math problem? Typical.

"Six," I said. "What's it mean, *Was?*"

"In what city were you born?"

"Al Ahmadi, Kuwait. Can you tell me what that blanket means?"

"Ibrahim," the serious doctor said. "Do you remember anything about your accident?"

"Accident?"

"The reason you are in the hospital," she said. "You nearly
drowned."

I could hardly even care what she was saying, because
I was sitting up again, having just spotted another word,
stitched across a building in pink.

"*Pleasure*," I read aloud. "There's another word."

"You need to lie down, Ibrahim," the doctor said.

"I think the knitting spells a sentence," I said. "What's it spell?"

The doctor smiled at me in a way that I could tell meant my
good looks and charm were softening her professional exterior.
"Why don't you tell me?"

She cupped a hand beneath my elbow and helped shuffle me
to the window. I stared out over the city, picking out the words
which stood out on buildings of different heights, within blankets
every color of the visual spectrum stretching several stories high.
The words began parceling themselves into a sentence.

IT

WAS

A

PLEASURE

TO

LIVE

"They say it's from a book."

My heart was growing wings and flapping frantically against my chest. The doctor convinced me to lie back down on the bed and rest, even though apparently I've spent a month resting. She injected something into my IV to make my head feel soft and dreamy.

It was then that I noticed a stack of printer paper held together with binder clips on the side table. At first, I thought it was another school assignment and my heart nearly stopped and this was a very dangerous situation to be in because my heart had only recently stopped for real. I lifted it up and saw the words, "Dear Pepper."

It has taken me almost the entire day, sleeping on and off, but I read every word.

It is now the nighttime and my dad has visited and dropped off Bertrand, who is staring at me strangely from his shiny eyes, and I am gripping much too hard on the lightsaber pen that I am using to transcribe these thoughts.

Ms. Eldridge, I want to tell Molly many things at this moment. I want to tell her that she astonished me with her friendship. That she changed me. That I'm never going back to the old Pepper, the one who didn't know how badass he actually was. I want to tell her that I think she's the pearl her mother was looking for, all along. She's the pearl.

All of this almost dying has made me think about life, namely the portion I have still in front of me. Yes, I am thinking again on my future, Ms. Eldridge. Where it once looked like the black backdrop of an empty universe, now it looks like stars. Look at all the bright, shiny things I get to choose from. *Take your pick, Pepper*, they seem to say. *You can't choose wrong.* Perhaps I will continue writing like I have done so much this summer, or perhaps I will become a teacher, like you, or perhaps one day I might truly become president. Germany changed—who says America will not one day allow people like me to be in charge? Or perhaps I will not know for a very long time what I wish for my life. But, I know several things right now: I know that I will keep looking, and I will take steps—one in front of the next—until I get where I want to go, and also that I will feed Bertrand turkey hot dogs because they are healthier.

I know that, whatever I decide, I will decide for myself. I will only ever be what I want to be.

Is that silly, Ms. Eldridge?

No, I don't think so, either.

The nurses are coming back to slip some sleepytime drugs into my drip bag, so I suppose it is time to close this letter now. I just wanted to say one last thing: as a personal safety expert, remote-control helicopters are a hazard to your health and I hope you avoid them in the future.

Also, thank you. Thank you for believing in me.

Best wishes, signed, your academic friend,

Pepper Al-Yusef

# Acknowledgments

I am hugely grateful for the love and support that has come my way during the journey of writing *The Arsonist*. Huge thanks to my incomparable agent, Jennifer Laughran, and my incredible editor, Stacey Friedberg, without whose passion and guidance this book would not be what it is. The entire team at Dial Books for Young Readers is so dedicated, talented, and fierce in their advocacy for children's and young adult literature. Thanks especially to Lauri Hornik, Namrata Tripathi, Dana Chidiac, Rachel Wease, Alexis Watts, Carmela Iaria and the entire school and library team, Bridget Hartzler, the entire Penguin Young Readers sales team, Nancy Leo, amazing cover designer Kristin Smith, cover artist Antonio Mora for your brilliant art, and copyeditor extraordinaire Rosanne Lauer.

Thank you also to Fatema Akasha, Patrick Cornwall, and Traci Sele.

High fives and much gratitude to the staff and students of Libby Center in Spokane, Washington. Thanks for sharing a little piece of your world with me.

Thank you to all of the readers. It's been one of the greatest experiences of my life meeting and connecting with you. Thank you also to the hardworking staff of all of the bookstores, libraries, conferences, and festivals I've been lucky enough to visit as an author. You've welcomed me into the book community with open arms, and I'm so lucky to have met you all.

From preschool to grad school, I've been lucky to have had so many wonderful teachers. The impact you've had on my life is impossible to calculate, and I'm forever grateful to have had the opportunity to learn from you.

The Spokane writing community is so wonderful, supportive, generous, talented, good-looking (the list goes on...). Special shout-out to Kris Dinnison and Trent Reedy. I'd road-trip with you guys anywhere.

Thank you to Fran Bahr, Barb Jones, and Linda and Andrew Corbett. Finally, I am hugely grateful to my entire family for your ceaseless support, especially my brother, sister-in-law, and nieces, Adair and Meredith, the two brightest stars in my sky; my dad, whose enthusiasm is limitless (and who I think purchased all the copies of *The Sacred Lies of Minnow Bly* in eastern Florida and had a *Minnow Bly* T-shirt made to boot); and my mom, who is too wonderful for words. You have championed me at every turn and I couldn't be prouder to be your daughter.